FOR PAM —

CHILDHOOD FRIENDS ARE
NEVER FORGOTTEN.
WISHING YOU LOVE, LAUGHTER,
AND ALWAYS LIGHT.

MOST SINCERELY,

Lynn E. Lisiewell

Prairie Storm

Prairie Storm

Lynn E. Lisarelli

VANTAGE PRESS
New York

Color Illustration by Ken Landgraf

FIRST EDITION

Published by Vantage Press, Inc.
419 Park Ave. South, New York, NY 10016

Manufactured in the United States of America
ISBN: 0-533-14954-1

Library of Congress Catalog Card No.: 2004093555

0 9 8 7 6 5 4 3 2 1

To C. D.

Acknowledgment

With special thanks and gratitude to Logan, without whom this book would have had only a beginning and an ending.

Undaunted by condemnation we stand,
You and I, empowered by grace within
To love, and from that love to become one
In spirit, in flesh, in all that is decreed
By one God to be holy and sanctified.
We stand apart from the world and yet
We are not alone, for those who've gone before
Have paved the way, and more will follow still.
Thus offered upon the altar of God,
This be the wine we drink and the bread we break.

                                        —Poem by the author

Prairie Storm

One

The green forest was closed in upon itself, keeping all life tightly enveloped within its boundaries. It rose up on the very edge of a wide, flat prairie in Kansas and marked the end of the advancement of man. The trees had been left largely undisturbed and only a few narrow trails wound through the heavy undergrowth. It was dark and dense within the forest. Not many shafts of sunlight managed to penetrate through the covering to the ground, which was softly carpeted with old needles and dry, dead leaves from years past. Through the woodland scampered small animals and graceful deer, secure in the knowledge of a safe place in which to live and raise their young. The air was warm with the sweet breath of spring, dogwood trees were in full bloom, and numerous flowers had poked their way through the rich soil. It was May and the year was 1890.

The silence of the forest was suddenly disturbed by cries and shouts from men and the relentless pounding of the horses' hooves. A figure was running down one of the trails, breathless, stumbling, with six armed riders in hot pursuit. The runner was a young girl in her early twenties, with short brown hair and a slim figure which she concealed in a man's shirt, pants, and boots. Ann was impelled by sheer terror and desperation, a sinking feeling that she had to get away to hide. She knew the men would kill her if they cornered her. There would be no benefit of a fair trial. On she ran, unmindful of the sharp thorns that scratched her face and hands. She stumbled over exposed tree roots and fell headlong, but rose up and continued blindly on, her wild eyes searching the underbrush for a place to hide and rest. The men were close behind her now, their shouts and laughter echoing in her brain.

"Here!" said one.

"This way!" cried another.

"We've almost got 'er now!"

Ann tripped again and fell against a tree, a thin young sapling that bent under her weight as she crashed into it, frantically groping

1

for a handhold that would break her fall. One knee hit the hard ground as both her hands grabbed the rough bark and she pulled herself slowly upright, gasping and panting and longing for rest. She turned her body and looked back through the forest, back where the men were slowly but surely pushing aside the low-hanging branches and urging their horses forward. For one brief instant, Ann's eyes met and held those of the leader of the posse. He quickly swept his rifle up to his shoulder and fired. She tried to duck away, but due to her extreme exhaustion, wasn't fast enough and she dimly felt the hot flash of pain as the bullet entered her right shoulder just below the collarbone. The impact propelled her backward and she tumbled over the edge of a deep ravine, rolling down into a thick carpet of leaves which cushioned her fall. As she skidded to a grasping halt at the bottom, she felt her left foot slide into a small depression in the earth. There was a gentle whisper of sound as a spring was released and two steel jaws rose up through the leaves and met together in a firm lock around her ankle. Searing agony traveled up her leg as the cold metal bit through the leather of her boot into the flesh, but she knew if she screamed she would give away her location. She could hear the hoofbeats of the horses as the men drew closer to the edge of the ravine. Ignoring the pain, she scooped the leaves toward her and around her, making a covering for her body. There she lay with her back against a fallen tree. Then she passed out.

The leader of the posse, Ace he was called, reined in his horse on the flat area just above where Ann had fallen and peered down into the tortuous gully. His followers gathered impatiently around him, searching for a sign, a trace, a movement.

"Now where the hell did she go?" said Ace. "I'm purty sure I hit 'er."

"Y'think mebbe she's down there?" asked Tim, next to him.

"Don't see nothin'," Ace replied. "If I hit 'er, there should be some blood." He made a show of scanning the ground around the horses' hooves, but found nothing.

"Y'prob'ly missed 'er an' she's gone on down the trail," said John. "C'm on, we're wastin' time."

"When I think o' what she did t'that li'l gal," said Pete, "I could . . ."

"Shaddup!" Ace shouted. "She's mine when we find 'er an' don't none o' ya fergit it." He turned his horse and started off along the trail again. The others grimly followed.

2

Ann had no idea how long she had been lying under the blanket of leaves. She was brought back to consciousness by an increasingly insistent throbbing pain that seemed to begin at opposite ends of her body and meet somewhere in the center. She brushed the leaves away from her face with her one good arm, then slowly raised herself to a sitting position. She could hear nothing in the forest, no human sound. She felt grateful for the reprieve. She dug down through the leaves until she reached the foot that was caught by the trap. The leather of her boot had been torn by the sharp metal and she was now aware of a warm, sticky wetness that was trickling down inside the boot. Disregarding the ache in her shoulder, she reached out with both hands and grabbed the ends of the jaws, trying to pull the trap apart. It was old and rusted and did not want to give. She pried her fingers in between the metal teeth and pulled harder, exerting strength she didn't even know she possessed. Finally, the trap began to yield to her pressure and the jaws slowly, creakingly, came apart. Gritting her teeth, she raised up the injured leg and swung it outward, away from the trap. She let go of the jaws at the same moment she wrenched her body aside to escape the snap of the teeth coming back together again. The metal clanged harmlessly and jumped away from her.

Ann lay on her stomach now in the carpet of leaves on the forest floor. The pain had increased with the sudden wrenching of her body and she lay quietly, hardly daring to move. Her breath was still coming in short, sobbing gasps and she found she could not stop the flow of tears down her face. *So that's what it's like to be caught in a trap*, she thought. *Lord pity the poor animal.* Shortly, she was able to catch her breath and calm herself. She slowly turned over and sat up again. With trembling fingers, she carefully examined the rip in her shirt where the bullet had entered. The right side of her upper chest was covered with blood and when she reached over her shoulder to touch her back, she realized that the bullet had passed clean through because the back of her shirt was also wet and sticky. *Well, I think the ankle's worse,* she thought. She glanced around in search of a long stick that could be used as a supportive crutch. She selected one, discarded it, and chose another. She managed to get herself upright by grabbing onto the trunk of another small tree with her good arm and pushing up off the ground with her good leg. She tried to put some of her weight on the ankle but almost collapsed from

3

the pain, so kept the leg bent at the knee. She was a little unsteady at first, but then took a few tentative hops. *Where do I go from here,* she wondered. *Which way?*

After an agonizingly long time, Ann came to a clearing which was in itself the edge of the forest. As she leaned against a tree to rest, she was aware that both her ankle and her shoulder were aflame with pain. She had tripped and fallen many times, and the blood had now begun to cake on her clothes. Her hands and face were dirty and covered with scratches. A fever had caused the sweat to bead on her brow. She felt hot and in need of water. Beyond her stretched an unbroken line of prairie, and off to the far side lay farmland that had been recently tilled and planted. In the midst of this she saw a trim, neat-looking house. She took a deep breath and started across the field.

As she drew nearer to the house, she could not tell if it was presently occupied. She got to the middle of the yard and then her crutch snapped in two, causing her to fall again, twisting the bad ankle as she did so. With this fresh injury came more blood, oozing through the ragged tears in the boot. She began to crawl toward the front of the house, digging her broken nails into the hard dirt and leaving a trail of blood behind her. The two steps up to the porch seemed almost insurmountable to her broken spirit, but she dragged herself onward. She reached out for the wooden railing, heaved herself up into a half-standing position, and pounded on the heavy door.

When the door swung open, Ann looked into the clear blue eyes of a young woman with long blonde hair. All she could think of was her pain, exhaustion, and thirst.

"Who are . . . what happened?" exclaimed the woman, reaching down to steady her swaying figure.

"Please help me," Ann panted. "They're after me, they'll kill me."

She was conscious of a strong arm going around her waist as her good arm slipped up and over the woman's shoulder. She was half-carried, half-dragged over to a wooden chair by a long table at the side of the room and there the woman set her gently down.

"Where have you come from? Who's after you?"

"I ran through the forest. Six men on horses were chasing me. They shot at me and then I got my foot caught in a trap. I saw your house and I came here."

4

"But why are they after you?"

"They want to kill me."

"But *why*? What have you done?"

Ann did not have time to answer, for both of them heard the sound of approaching horses. The woman went over to the window and drew back the curtain.

"Six riders," she said.

"Oh, dear God, it's them!" Ann moaned, and attempted to rise from her chair.

"Stay there," the woman whispered harshly. "I will see what they want."

She grabbed the rifle that was propped by the door frame and stepped outside, firmly closing the door behind her. The men were obviously interested in the trail of fresh blood that led along the ground up to the steps. One of the men had dismounted and was down on one knee, rifle cradled in his arm, examining the dirt. At a glance, she saw that the blood was smeared on the railing and on part of the door as well.

"What do you want?" she said sternly. She kept her rifle pointed at the chest of the one older man who appeared to be the group's leader. She noted that he had a jagged scar on his cheek.

"Sorry t'trouble ya, ma'am," said Ace. "We're lookin' fer a fugitive."

"We couldn't help but notice alla blood here," said Joe. "Ace thinks 'e mighta shot 'er."

"Shaddup, I said!" roared Ace. "I'll do the damn talkin'." He turned back to the woman with a simpering smile on his face. "Like I said, ma'am, don't mean t'be no trouble, but we're lookin' fer a gal. She killed a child back up in the town. I mighta winged 'er, an' all this here blood's a mite suspicious, so if y'don't mind we'll jist c'm inside an' look around."

He made a move as if to dismount. Quick as a flash, the woman had her rifle cocked and aimed at a point right between his eyes.

"No, you will not!" she said coldly. "This is my land and my property, and *I* call the shots. There is no one here. You've said your piece and now you'd best be off. If you don't, so help me God, I will blow your head off."

"But . . . but what 'bout alla blood?" sputtered Lou.

"I slaughtered a hog this morning and dragged it into the house myself," the woman said. "Now go!"

"Blasted wimmen," Ace muttered. "C'm on, boys, let's go."

They moved away, occasionally glancing backward to see if the woman was still standing on the porch. She was, and the rifle was still aimed at them. When they were too far away to be distinguished clearly she went back into the house and set the rifle down. She moved over to the table where Ann was still sitting. Ann's gaze anxiously followed her.

"What did they say?"

"Enough. But they're gone now. Let's get you into bed, where you can stretch out."

The arms went around Ann's waist again and the woman helped her limp slowly into the bedroom. The quilt was pulled back, but Ann resisted being lowered onto the clean white sheets.

"I can't," she protested. "I'll get 'em all bloody."

"Never mind. They'll wash. Now lie down, girl. You're a mess."

Ann let her muscles relax and sank down onto the soft mattress. *Rest at last,* she thought. Out of the corner of her eye she saw a flaxen-haired child, a little girl no more than four years old, come into the room and stand by the open door. The woman noticed the direction of her gaze and turned around to face the child.

"Lissa! Don't just stand there. Get some rags and some water," she ordered. When the child hesitated, trying to look beyond her mother at the person on the bed, she said more loudly, "Did you hear me?"

The child was gone. The woman turned her attention back to Ann and began to rip the material of her shirt away from the injured shoulder. She lifted Ann's head up from the pillow and examined her back.

"Well, it's clean through, and it's stopped bleeding. Shouldn't be a problem there."

Then she moved down to the foot of the bed to have a look at Ann's ankle, which was already beginning to swell inside the boot. Her slightest attempt to touch it sent new waves of pain through the leg and Ann cried out once and fainted. Just then, the child came back into the room, bearing a basin of water and a few rags draped over her arm.

"Lissa, run down the lane and get the doctor. This is more than I can handle. Go quickly now." The child ran.

Dr. James McClintock was fifty-two, a kindly old soul with a shock of white hair and a gold watch chain hanging from the side pocket of his vest. The sleeves of his white shirt were rolled up, and he was just putting the finishing touches on the thick bandage around Ann's ankle. She was still unconscious and had offered no resistance. He had to use a knife to cut away the remnants of her boot and was appalled at the damage he found to the ankle. The shoulder wound was clean and already taped up, but the ankle might give rise to some infection later on. If the girl ever walked again, she should count herself lucky.

The doctor completed his job and put on his jacket. He motioned to the woman to follow him, and he stepped out of the bedroom, closing the door softly behind them.

"She'll be out for some time now," he said. "That was a bad accident. Devorah, do you have any idea how this happened?"

"She's my niece. She's been staying with us. She was out hunting in the woods this afternoon when it happened. She fell into the trap and then the gun discharged. Will she be all right?"

"Oh, her shoulder will be fine, but I don't know about that ankle. That will take time to heal. Keep it clean and change the bandage often. Keep her well-fed and quiet and don't let her go running around too much when she starts to feel better. And teach her a healthy respect for guns. She's too young to be out hunting—a girl at that."

"Yes, Doc, thank you." She saw him out the door.

Devorah went over to the brick fireplace where she built a small fire. Even though the days were warm, the nights could still get quite chilly on the prairie. It was twilight now and the sun had set some time ago. When it became too dark to see well, she lit the kerosene lamp. She also started a fire in the iron stove and made the child and herself some supper, after which she sent Melissa to bed. She boiled water for some tea for the young girl in case she should wake, but Ann slept through the night.

With the coming of the dawn, Devorah woke with a start. She rose and dressed quickly, made Melissa some breakfast, and sent her

7

outside to play. She went to the barn and milked the two cows, slopped the pigs, fed the chickens, and gathered the eggs. Then she turned the cows and the two horses out to graze. Just as Devorah returned to the house, she heard a loud crash from behind the closed bedroom door. Concerned for the girl, she entered the room and found her struggling to rise out of the bed. A picture frame had fallen from the bedside table onto the floor and the glass was broken. Devorah rushed over to the girl and pushed her good shoulder back onto the bed.

"Don't you dare get out of this bed!" she said sternly.

"But I can't . . . I want . . ."

"I don't care. You cannot be walking." Then, more gently, as Ann acquiesced, she asked, "What is your name?"

"Ann Johnson," she softly replied. "Who are you?"

"I'm Devorah Lee. My little girl's name is Melissa."

"Did those men come back?"

"No, only a doctor. You're safe." A pause. "Could you tell me why they were after you?"

"Didn't they tell you yesterday?"

"A man named Ace said that you killed a child. Is that true? I must know the truth." No answer. "Ann, did you?"

"No," Ann sighed, wincing at the pain. "No, I didn't, and I don't know who did." She frowned as she searched for some forgotten memory. "I don't think I know."

"But then why would they have thought that you did?"

"Well, because . . ."

"Yes? Because what?"

"It's a long story."

"Then start at the beginning. I have all day."

"It was a little girl," said Ann, groping for words. "Someone did unspeakable things to her and then she was found strangled. They thought I did it because nobody knew where I was that night. So they came after me, and I ran."

"I see. And where *were* you that night?"

"Out."

"With a man?"

"No . . ."

"By yourself?"

"No . . ."

8

"Well, *who* then?"

"Another woman."

"Oh! Uh . . . oh my!" Devorah blushed deeply. She tried to ask another question, but failed. Finally she collected herself. "That's enough talk for now. I want you to get some more rest. I will fix you something to eat now." With her long skirts rustling, she swept out the door.

After a week had passed, Dr. McClintock returned to check on Ann's progress. Her shoulder was healing nicely, and the arm was now in a sling. He frowned deeply when he examined her ankle. There was some evidence of healing, but there was also quite a bit of suppuration, especially around the edges of the wound where the rusted steel teeth of the trap had penetrated the flesh. *Infection,* he thought. *I'm not surprised.* He realized he would have to do something to prevent complete loss of the foot.

"Ann," he said to her gently. "This ankle is very bad. Gangrene could set in, and I'm going to have to burn this infection out."

"Hey, wait, Doc! That's my foot we're talking about."

"That's right, girl. You don't want to lose it, do you?" He turned aside to Devorah. "Go heat up a knife in the fire and bring her something to drink. Whiskey, if you have it."

When Devorah came back into the bedroom, she closed the door to keep Melissa out. She offered a cup with amber liquid to Ann and the girl reached out for it with shaking fingers. She sipped slowly, coughing as the bitter, burning stuff went down her throat. Devorah and the doctor stood aside making small talk and urging Ann to drink more whiskey. They waited until it seemed to be taking effect on the girl, and then the doctor said, "It's time." He left the room to get the knife, now made red-hot by the fire. Devorah sat down on the side of the bed, close to Ann's pillow.

"I'm scared," Ann whispered.

"Then hold my hand and squeeze hard," said Devorah.

"No," Ann countered, more strongly. "I have to be brave like a man. I can take it."

With the first touch of the hot knife to her skin, Ann let out a sobbing gasp and flung her hand out to meet Devorah's, grasping it tightly. *How young she is,* Devorah thought. *Poor thing.* She clasped her hand around Ann's, entwining their fingers, and gently smoothed

9

the hair back from Ann's forehead with her other hand. *Such pressure,* she thought. *This girl is so strong.* She brushed the tears away from Ann's face.

Dr. McClintock scraped the knife against bone, cutting away all the oozing pus and dead flesh. He had to also hold Ann's leg down because she was beginning to thrash and move around in response to this new pain. When he finished, he gently wrapped another bandage around the ankle. Ann was semi-conscious by now, drifting in and out, but she was quiet. He quickly cleaned up, rolled his sleeves back down, and then he and Devorah exited the room.

"I'm sure she will be all right now," he said, getting ready to leave. "Where does she come from? Does she have any family?"

"She's from New York State," Devorah answered. "Her father is my brother. My sister-in-law sent her here to spend the summer. She's never lived on a farm before."

"Doesn't know much about guns or hunting, either," he replied gruffly.

Three days later, Ann was beginning to feel much better. She was able to stay awake for longer periods of time, and her appetite had definitely improved. One afternoon after Ann had just finished a small lunch, Devorah pulled a chair up next to the bed.

"This tea is awful," Ann grimaced. "What do you put into it?"

"It's good for you," Devorah insisted. "I'm glad you're getting better. Would you like to tell me more about yourself?"

"What do you want to know?"

"Well, where you come from would be a start. Do you have parents, brothers, sisters?"

"My parents live down south in Texas. I have one older brother and two younger sisters. My father is rich. He owns a lot of land. He's a cattle farmer."

"What are you doing up here all alone?"

"Well, I *was* a schoolmarm down there, but then my father ordered me out. We don't get along any more, and I haven't seen my parents since I left two years ago."

"Why not? What happened?"

"Oh, they caught me once fooling around with some girl, one of my older pupils. We had this thing together. Daddy said nobody could teach school and be like that, so he threw me out. My mother was pretty broken up about it, and she didn't want me to go, but I couldn't stay."

"Where have you been all this time? What have you done?" Devorah was genuinely curious as to how a young girl could survive on her own since all she'd known was the hard work of a farm.

"I kept moving. Took odd jobs here and there, helped out with plantings and harvests. I cut my hair short so I could pass for a boy. This town was just one of the places I wound up at."

"I see. Where will you go from here?"

"Who knows? Just keep moving, I guess, until I can find some place to settle down."

After another week had passed, Dr. McClintock returned once again to see his patient. He was pleased to find new skin beginning to grow over Ann's ankle, and he assured her that the healing process was well underway, although he warned her that it would still be some time before she could attempt to walk. Ann was delighted when he presented her with a wheelchair since she had been mildly irritated at having to remain confined to bed all day. He assisted her in slowly easing her body down onto the chair and gave her some simple instructions on how to maneuver the wheels. During their conversation, Ann happened to mention to him that she was from Texas and still had family down there. The doctor was puzzled at the discrepancy between Ann's present statement and Devorah's earlier one, but he gave no sign and asked no further questions. He left Ann in the bedroom and went to speak with Devorah, who was sitting by the fireplace.

"Devorah," he began sternly. "Just *who* is that girl in there?"

"But, Doc," she said, not understanding, "I told you that she was my niece from New York and . . ."

"No, she's not. She just told me she was from Texas. *What* is going on here?"

Devorah looked down into the dancing flames. She had told him a lie, and now she could think of no easy way out of it.

"Devorah, I've heard rumors in town that they're chasing after some girl who killed Bonnie Anders. Is *that* the girl in there? Is it Ann?"

"Ann told me she didn't do it."

"You don't even know this girl, yet you believe her?"

11

"Yes," she said simply, looking up into his eyes. "I believe her. Doc, didn't you examine that little girl's body yourself?"

"I did," he answered, sitting down next to her and pausing to remember. "It was most unfortunate. The parents were greatly upset. Her genitals were ripped; there was much tearing of tissue. She was strangled by powerful hands. There were marks on her throat."

"The girl . . . this damage . . . couldn't it have been done by a man?" Devorah suggested the first thing that came to mind.

"Well, maybe," he mused. "Actually, the more I think about it, the more I think it *was* done by a man. I will reserve my judgment of Ann until later."

"Doc, please, you mustn't tell anybody that she's here. She said they would kill her if they found her." Devorah was anxious.

"Very well, then," he said slowly, "I won't. You haven't lied to me yet." He winked at her and smiled.

The next day, Ann insisted on being wheeled out to the front porch so she could enjoy some fresh air and sunshine after having been cooped up for so long. Devorah had already done her chores that morning and she dragged her favorite rocking chair onto the porch so she could be company for Ann. Melissa was playing near the barn.

"It's so good to be outside again," Ann said. "I can't wait until I can get out of this chair and run."

"Doc told you it would be a while yet. You have to be patient."

"But I want to be on a horse again. I want to run, I want to fly. I can't stand not doing anything."

"Ann, how old are you?" Devorah asked, changing the subject.

"I'm twenty-two. How about you? You don't look much older."

"Oh, but I feel older. I'm twenty-six."

"Have you always lived here?"

"No, I lived with my parents in Iowa. But five years ago in 1885, when I married Billy Lee, we moved here and bought this farm. Melissa was born a year later."

"Where is your husband now?"

"He's dead," she answered quietly. "He died two long years ago in '88. It was spring, and he was out plowing up the fields. The mule kicked him in the head. I was sitting right here on this porch when I saw it happen. By the time I got to him, he was already gone."

"How have you managed since then?"

"Well, it was hard at first. I've had to hire men to come and help with the plowing and planting and then again in the fall to take it all in. I've learned to do many things for myself, but it's still hard. This farm keeps me busy, but it wears me out." Devorah was silent a moment, and then she stopped rocking and turned to Ann. "When you get better, will you stay here with me? I could use your help, and it would give you something to do." She was hesitant to continue, not knowing what else to say.

"I might," Ann said thoughtfully. "I'll have to think on it."

Two

Devorah took Melissa with her in the carriage to Sutter's Ford for Sunday Meeting. The small town had only one main street, but boasted of several large shops including a bank, a general store, livery stables, a blacksmith, a saloon, and a hotel. The church was at the far end of town, along with the little schoolhouse. The normally bustling street was rather quiet now, and Devorah realized that most everyone must be already at the church. The bell high up in the steeple rang out, signaling the beginning of services.

She had hoped to be able to slip quietly into one of the pews at the back without being observed as a latecomer. Upon first glancing around, she was dismayed to find that she would have to walk down almost to the middle of the rows, thereby calling unwanted attention to herself. After she and the child had found a spot, Devorah tried to focus her mind on the preacher's sermon, but then she became aware of a muted whispering directly behind her.

"That's the widow, Devorah Lee," said one woman.

"I hear Doc's been spending a lot of time out at her place," said another woman.

"Wonder if we'll be seeing a wedding soon? His wife's been gone for fifteen years."

"Well, Heaven knows, it's about time she got herself another man. Can you imagine a *woman* doing all that work by herself?"

"Disgraceful!"

"Shocking!"

Devorah skillfully tuned them out. When the service was over she took the child's hand and attempted to exit through the milling people, giving the required nods and proper greetings. In the front foyer she was accosted by Ace Fairlane, who was all decked out in his Sunday best. He had shaved, his graying hair was slicked down and parted in the middle, and he reeked of cheap cologne. The long scar on his cheek did not make him appear handsome, and his nose looked as if it had been broken and badly set. He was forty-four.

"Ah, Miz Lee. Ah, howdy, ma'am," he said, twisting his hat in his hands.

Devorah looked up into his cold eyes and felt an immediate dislike for this man. She was uncomfortable in his presence and moved to sidestep him and continue on, but he followed her outside like an unwelcome cur.

"Ah, Miz Lee," he persisted. "Won't'cha be needin' some help fer the summer balin'?"

"I might," she replied, trying to be noncommittal.

"Wal, d'y's'pose I could c'm out an' help ya with it? I kin also fix fences real good."

"We'll see."

He lifted Melissa up and swung her onto the carriage seat. Then he turned and extended his big hand to Devorah, intending to be gentlemanly, but she ignored him, grabbed the side of the carriage, and assisted herself.

"Ah, Miz Lee, ma'am, mebbe we could git t'know each other better. We could have us some real good times, if y'know what I mean."

"I know what you mean," she glared at him. "The answer is *no*." She flicked the reins and went off down the street.

Ace stood there in the settling dust and watched her go. *Boy, she's one cold bitch,* he thought. *Mebbe I could make 'er warm up t'me.* He scratched the crotch of his pants and went into the saloon.

Despite the fact that Ace had not had a definite invitation, he turned up at Devorah's farm anyway for the baling. He was only one of five other men, all surrounding neighbors of Devorah, and he quickly established himself as the undisputed leader of the group, issuing orders and setting priorities. It was roughly a week's job, and Devorah dutifully, out of gratitude, prepared a hot meal for them every evening at day's end. When it was all over, the barn loft was piled high and crammed full of neat bales of wheat, which would provide fodder for the cows and horses through the coming winter.

During the times that the men were at the farm, Ann remained cloistered behind the bedroom door because she could not risk being seen by Ace. However, she did not lack for things to keep herself occupied, for she began to instruct Melissa in the basics of the alphabet and counting numbers. She found that she had a very apt pupil, for the child was bright and quick to grasp new ideas and concepts. By the time they emerged from their temporary retreat, Melissa had absorbed nearly all of the alphabet and was able to count up to twenty. She showed Devorah the small slips of paper that Ann had cut out for her with the symbols of the letters and numbers drawn in charcoal.

"Look, Mommy," she bubbled. "This is a 'c', an' this is an 'o', an' this is a 'w', an' you put them all together an' spell . . . uh . . ."

"Cow," Ann prompted.

"Cow," Melissa repeated. Devorah smiled.

It was the end of June. The strawberries were plump and ripe. Melissa gathered a bucketful one afternoon. That evening Ann cleaned them while Devorah whipped up a cream topping made with fresh milk. This was the dessert for their simple supper of fried chicken, potatoes, and early peas. Afterward, when the dishes were all cleaned away and washed, Ann and Devorah went into the living room, which adjoined the kitchen area, and drank their coffee by the fire. Melissa always went to bed soon after dinner, thereby leaving the rest of the evening open for Ann to read a book or for Devorah to catch up on her sewing.

"Ann," Devorah began, and hesitated. "Have you . . . have you thought about staying?"

"I've thought."

"And . . . ?" Devorah almost trembled.

"I'll stay. For a while, at least. I expect the child needs teaching."

Indeed, Devorah was relieved. With all the work she had to do each day, she was unable to spend as much time with Melissa as she would have liked, but she did not want the child to be neglected.

"I appreciate what you've done for Lissa," she said. Their eyes met and held. Devorah resumed her stitching.

July rolled in on waves of heat. It was now no longer necessary to keep the wood burning in the fireplace. Even the daily cooking was becoming an uncomfortable task. After Devorah finished her morning chores, she came in for a quick lunch and then spent the rest of the afternoon weeding and hoeing the large garden plot, which was laid out away from the plowed fields and close to the house. Many different kinds of vegetables had been planted there, including beans, peas, cabbage, turnips, potatoes, rhubarb, asparagus, cucumbers, onions, squash, beets, carrots, peppers, lettuce and tomatoes. Devorah knew from past experience which plants gave the best production. But keeping a garden involved a great deal of time and care and attention, and all these long days under the hot sun were beginning to make her short-tempered. The bandanna tied around her forehead did not do much to soak up the sweat that constantly trickled down her face. Her hands grew calloused and sun-weathered; the nails became caked with dirt and often broke. At the end of the day, she felt wrung out, exhausted, and very, very dirty. A relaxing bath was the high point of the day, something to which to look forward along with the anticipation of a good night's sleep.

One evening as Devorah dragged herself up the steps of the front porch, she heard Melissa's laughter coming from within the house. She opened the door to find Ann and Melissa working in the kitchen. Ann had permitted the child to assist her in making cornbread, and there was a disheartening mess all over the kitchen table and on the floor as well. Neither one seemed to care, and they giggled on. Devorah was in no mood to clean up the kitchen just then, and she felt her nerves being stretched to a breaking point. A moment, two moments, the point was achieved and passed. She stormed over to the table.

"Look at this mess!" she cried. "An absolute mess! I come in from sweating out there all day, and what do I find? Look at yourselves! You need a bath more than I do." Melissa quietly climbed down from her chair and sneaked out of the room, but Devorah took no notice, for her attention was still upon Ann. "Is *this* how you make cornbread? Can't you do any better than this?"

Ann was crestfallen. "I was just trying to show her. . . . We were just . . ."

"Just what?" she raved on. "A Texas cowgirl in the kitchen. If you don't know how to cook, then stay out!"

"How am I supposed to learn how to cook things unless you teach me?" Ann yelled back, becoming angry now. "You're so damned busy being outside that you don't watch what's going on inside. As long as I'm stuck in this stupid wheelchair, I can't do much of anything, but I can at least *try* to do some things. If you don't like it, that's just too bad! You're not the only one who's frustrated around here, and I mean that in more than one way!"

"Ann!" Devorah was shocked into abrupt silence. She left the room to see to Melissa, and she apologized to the child, but not to Ann. Devorah had much to think about and they ate in stony silence, eyes glued to their plates.

Ace Fairlane was on his horse, slowly plodding around the outer perimeter which marked the boundaries of Devorah's land. He was methodically inspecting the fence posts and barbed wire for any openings or breaks. He scrutinized one area, approved it, and cantered on. During his secret tour he came across several spots which were in obvious need of repair, the wire having torn away from the posts and giving rise to open gaps in the fencing. *Could stand a bit o' fixin',* he reflected. *An' t'day'd be a perfect day t'do it, bein' the Fourth o' July. Mebbe I could even squeeze a bite t'eat out o' the ol' gal. An' have us some celebratin' later on.* He chuckled softly, fingering the deep scar on his cheek.

He went back to Sutter's Ford and purchased the required supplies, picking up new rolls of barbed wire and a few more posts for good measure. Then he stopped at his own farm, hitched up the horse to the old rickety buckboard, tossed a spade in the back, and was off again. He returned to Devorah's place, crying out, "Ho! Anybody here?" as he pulled the horse to a stop in the front yard. Devorah had been inside when she heard the noise. She motioned to Ann to be quiet and stepped out onto the porch.

Ace hopped down to the ground and doffed his hat. "Ah, howdy, Miz Lee, ma'am," he said jovially. "Thought I might drop by an' see if any o' yer fences needed mendin'." He waved his arm toward the buckboard. "Brought all m'own s'plies, too. Whaddya say?" He stood there waiting for encouragement.

Devorah nodded brusquely. "I suppose you could. As long as you're already here."

Ace fell to his task with an ardor he had not been able to work up in ages. He didn't mind the labor under the hot sun. He toiled long into the afternoon, often passing his huge arms across his damp brow, and he finally finished the last stretch of fencing just as the daylight was beginning to fade. He tramped back to the house, pausing at the water pump set in the yard to douse his head with a cold, refreshing stream.

Devorah intercepted him as he was coming up the porch steps. "I do appreciate your help," she said grudgingly. "Would you care to stay for dinner?"

Ace grinned expansively. "Why, that's right nice o' ya, Miz Lee. Jist lemme secure m'tools an' I'll be back in a minnit."

Devorah hurried into the bedroom where Ann was playing with Melissa. "You must be quiet in here," she whispered. "He's staying."

"What?" Ann groaned. "He's been here all day. Why can't he leave now?"

"Because I'm obligated to fix him something to eat."

"Well, hurry it up," she grumbled. "I'm hungry, too."

Devorah did not waste much time in placing a meal in front of Ace, conscious all the while of Ann hiding just a few steps away. She reluctantly joined him at the table only when he insisted that she also eat something, but her appetite was not great and she picked at her food. She felt nervous and could only think of how best to get rid of him quickly. When she went around to his side of the table to pour out more coffee for him, he snaked his arm around her waist and roughly pulled her closer to his body.

"Why don't we git t'be on a first name callin' b'tween us, eh? Y'kin call me Ace an' I'll call ya Devorah." His hand slid up her back, and his eyes traveled lustily from her chin to her toes.

"I don't think that will be necessary," she said, politely twisting away from him. She tried to be cold and aloof.

It didn't seem to faze him. He grinned wider, more evilly, as he reached down into his pockets and extracted several small objects of various size, scattering them on the table.

"Lookee here. Fireworks. Picked 'em up in town. This bein' the Fourth o' July, we gotta have us a celebration. Go git yer li'l gal an' we'll go outside an' set 'em off."

He collected the objects and went out the door. Devorah opened the bedroom door and called for Melissa.

"Isn't he gone yet?" Ann whispered stridently. "What's he doing now?"

"He wants to light fireworks for Melissa. Come on, honey," she said, taking the child's hand.

"Oh Lord!" Ann cast her eyes upward and shook her head.

When Melissa saw the array of fireworks, she clapped her hands delightedly. Warning her not to step off the porch, Ace went to the middle of the yard and proceeded to set them off one by one. The child's eyes were dazzled by the bright display of colors, but she covered her ears tightly with her hands when the explosions came.

"Ooo, Mommy! Look at that one! Look at that!"

When the show was all over, she lost interest quickly, as a child will, and began to pester her mother to be fed and put to bed.

"Mommy, I'm hungry. I'm hungry *now*," she whined, pulling on Devorah's skirts.

"As you can see, my child is tired," she said to Ace. "I think it would be best for you to go."

Devorah stepped inside to get his hat. Without warning he was there, close behind her. Strong arms held hers pinned at her sides, and he turned her around to face him. He bent his head forward and covered her neck and cheek with kisses. He found her mouth and roughly pressed his lips to hers, ramming his tongue inside, forcing open her clenched teeth as he crushed her to his chest, taking her breath away. She was keenly aware of the stink of his sweat, of the stubble on his chin, of his relentless pressure. She felt a wave of disgust, total, utter, complete. She managed to slightly loosen one arm from his grasp and fumbled blindly behind her to where the rifle lay propped against the door. Her fingers closed around the barrel, and she slowly, carefully maneuvered the gun between their bodies. He was too carried away with his kissing to be aware of what she was doing, and he only stopped when he felt something cold jabbing into his chin. She had the tip of the rifle pointed directly at his throat.

"I would advise you to back off," she said in a cold, even voice.

Ace slowly released her and stepped back, wiping his mouth. His own rifle was out in the buckboard, so far away. Hers was leveled at him and cocked.

"Whassa matter with ya, woman?" he sputtered. "I thought'cha *liked* it."

"If you take one step toward me, I will pull this trigger. Now you will please go, and I do not *ever* expect to see you here again."

He swept his hat up off the floor, jammed it down onto his head, and rushed out. When Ann heard the noise of his wagon rumbling off, she quickly wheeled herself out of the bedroom and sought Devorah, who had lowered herself limply down onto a chair.

"My God!" exclaimed Ann, reaching Devorah's side. "Are you all right?" Her gentle hands touched Devorah's face, and she pushed

20

back a few trailing strands of hair. Her seeking fingers clasped Devorah's own, which were lying still on her lap. "That bastard!" Ann continued. "I couldn't stand not knowing what was happening so I opened the door a crack and saw it all. I felt so helpless. I wanted to kill him. If he ever tries that again, I *will* kill him!"

"Why?" asked Devorah, smiling shyly. "Are you jealous?"

In the weeks that followed, Ann was impatient and eager to be freed from the confinement of her wheelchair. The ankle had healed nicely, but the scar was still jagged, pink, and tender to the touch. Twice a day, Devorah would give Ann's legs a brisk rubdown to keep the muscles pliant and flexible. Then came the day when Ann tried to cajole Devorah into helping her walk again.

"But do you really think you should?" Devorah asked, most concerned. "Right this very minute?"

"Well, why not? I gotta start some time. Come over here." Ann held out her arms, but Devorah still hesitated, positive that this was too early an attempt. "Well, come on!"

As Devorah leaned over her, Ann put her arms around Devorah's shoulders and pushed herself out of the wheelchair with her good leg. She turned her body sideways so that she could keep one arm thrown around Devorah's neck while she used the other arm to support herself against the long kitchen table. She took her first tentative steps, slowly, haltingly, but when she put too much weight on the bad ankle she cringed with pain. She slumped against Devorah's breast as she fell and was caught and held by strong arms. Determined to try again, she straightened up. Just then there came a knock at the front door, and they both froze.

"Who is it?" Devorah cried out.

"Just Doc," came the answer, and he let himself in.

"Hi, Doc!" Ann said happily. "I'm trying to walk."

"So you are, young lady," he beamed. "It appears I've come just in time. I've got something for you. Figured you might be wanting it pretty soon."

He held out a new crutch for her, and she took it from him, running her fingers along the smooth wood. He showed her how to position it properly under her arm so as to cause the least strain, and he assisted her in taking a few more steps. Ann was exceedingly pleased, but he cautioned her not to overexert herself.

21

"Remember, there's always tomorrow," he said.

"Aw, come on, Doc," she protested. "I gotta get out today! I gotta move!"

"Well, don't go too far. Stay close to the house. And look, I brought you something else."

Ann took the package he was holding up, opened it eagerly, and found that it contained a bottle of black hair dye. She held it in her open hand, puzzled.

"What's this for?"

"Well," Doc said, "I thought if you really wanted to get out and go places, you could color your hair up a bit. It's already starting to get longer now, and you could just let it grow out. Put a skirt on you, and nobody'd know who you were. Then you really *could* be Devorah's niece from New York."

Ann blushed. Devorah had told her about the lie.

"Ann," he added, taking her small hand into his, "I want you to know I don't think you're the one who killed that little girl. It had to be a man. I promise you we'll find him."

Devorah had made the time for several days in a row to try to teach Ann how to do some basic cooking. Now that Ann was beginning to hobble around on her own, she was able to stand at Devorah's side and observe her as she fried eggs and bacon and made simple soups and breads. Ann, like Melissa, was also a fast learner, and she developed a great interest in trying new things. The child assisted at their projects in the kitchen and these activities served to keep her occupied. During the afternoons when Devorah was busy in the garden or out in the fields Ann continued Melissa's tutoring, and in the evenings when Devorah came home, the child would run to her mother with some new thing that she had just learned. Devorah was proud of her.

One morning Devorah rose two hours past her usual time. She was irritated with herself because she had expected to have the bread loaves already made before she went out to do her chores. *Well, no time for that now,* she thought. *It'll just have to wait.* She bolted a hurried breakfast, tied the bandanna around her forehead to keep the hair out of her eyes, and went out to the barn. The cows seemed to be a bit skittish, and one of them trod testily on her foot as she

22

was reaching down to grab the milk pails. *Oh mercy,* she thought as some of the milk spilled. *This is going to be one of those days.*

Melissa observed her mother out of the corner of the window, waiting until she had occupied herself with the garden. When she felt the coast was clear, she signaled to Ann, and Ann went about the task of making the bread. Melissa seized a bucket that had been hanging on the wall and scampered out the back door, calling to Ann that she was going to hunt for blueberries. She returned shortly with enough berries to make two pies. Ann winked at her and she giggled.

Devorah did not feel hungry enough to pause for lunch, so she decided to go on into the fields and check her crops. The corn was growing tall and strong, but the surrounding dirt was parched and cracked. *God, we need rain,* she thought, looking up at the cloudless blue sky. As she reached the end of the corn rows, she came upon the beginning of the grassy plain where the horses and cows were grazing. Suddenly she heard a mournful lowing from one of the cows, and she ran to where it lay on its side, struggling to rise. *Well, this old girl is finally going to drop that calf,* she realized. She crouched down and patted the taut belly, ran her hands along the heaving flanks, and made soothing noises to the agitated animal. Devorah could tell that this was going to be a difficult birth, and she could wind up out in this field for hours.

Time passed, and the cow appeared to commence the birth, but then stopped and lay back down as the calf was drawn back up into the body. This went on for an interminably long time and Devorah felt a cool rush of wind at her back. She glanced up to notice that the sun was gone, and she saw a low dark line of storm clouds sweeping in on the horizon. Bright bolts of lightning flashed down out of the rolling clouds, and then there came the distant sound of thunder. *Oh no,* she thought. *Not now!* The cow became frightened by the swift change in the air. It heaved itself upward, giving one last grunting push, and out slipped the little calf. Devorah was happy; she laughed aloud. She watched as the mother cow gave her attention to the calf, licking its face and standing near as it took its first tottering steps.

Then came the rain, gentle at first, but becoming harder. Devorah felt pellets of hail striking her body, and they bounced around her on the ground. *My crops,* she thought. *Oh dear!* She quickly

23

ripped off a wide piece of her skirt and wrapped it around the calf for protection. She gathered the bleating, newborn thing up into her arms and began to run back to the barn with the mother cow loping along behind her.

Devorah settled the calf down onto some dry hay, next to the mother. She slammed the barn door shut against the buffeting wind and trudged through the mud to the house. The hail had stopped, but the rain was still blowing in sheets. She slipped once and fell headlong in the slimy mire. By the time she reached the shelter of the porch she was cold, wet, and covered with mud. Her hair was plastered to her face, and she was thoroughly chilled to the bone. *What a rotten day,* she told herself, feeling angry and on the point of tears.

Wind and rain pounded at the door as she wrested it open with mud-slickened fingers. She stood there dripping, ready to snap at the first person who dared to say a word to her. She slowly became aware of the delicious odor of baking, and she looked around to see bread on the kitchen table. Ann was taking pies out of the oven. Devorah was overwhelmed.

"Did you have a bad day?" Ann quipped lightly.

"Oh, Ann . . .," she began. They laughed, they roared.

This truly broke the ice between them and made them comfortable with each other. The first thing they had to do was get Devorah out of her wet clothes. Ann assisted her down the narrow hallway to the bathroom, being careful not to get too close to her because of all the mud. A small but deep tub stood in one corner, and against the opposite wall there was a stove. Ann quickly got the wood fired up, ran kettles of water from the pump by the tub, and set the pots on top of the stove to heat.

Melissa helped her mother undress. "Ooo, Mommy," she squealed, scrunching up her nose. "You're all icky. Did you fall?"

"I sure did, honey. Flat on my face."

"You are such a mess," Ann said, and they broke into fresh laughter.

When the water was hot and poured, Ann helped her into the tub. Devorah slowly eased her body backward into the steaming water. *Ahh, this is so good,* she thought. Ann took a washcloth and the bar of lye soap and began to scrub her back, then her front, then her arms and legs, and finally Ann washed and rinsed out her hair. Devorah was so relaxed that she permitted herself to enjoy Ann's attentions and she didn't give a single fig what she looked like lying there naked. *We're both women anyway,* she thought. *What does it matter?*

"I sure wish I had some of that fancy hand-milled soap from France," she said to Ann. "These lye bars are so harsh on my skin."

Ann did not reply, but stored the comment in her memory. She got Devorah out of the tub and dried off, and Melissa brought in a change of clothes. They sat down to a good dinner of chicken with potatoes and carrots and the fresh bread. The blueberry pie made an excellent dessert, and Devorah complimented Ann on her improving skills.

"It was really Lissa's idea," Ann said. "She's the one who went out for the berries."

"But didn't she have on a pink dress this morning? Why is it blue now?"

"Well, you weren't the only one who had to get changed. She ate enough berries for almost another whole pie, and she got the juice all over herself."

All three of them washed the dishes together that night with Devorah soaping, Ann rinsing from the pump by the sink, and Melissa wiping. *It's just like we're a family,* Ann thought, *like we're really close. I wonder if this could be where I'm supposed to settle down.*

After the child had gone off to bed, Devorah offered to make a fresh pot of coffee.

"I've got an idea," Ann brightened. "Why don't we have it out on the front porch? The rain's stopped, and it's not as hot." Devorah agreed.

The summer night was peaceful. The whole prairie was wet, soaking up the welcome moisture. The crops rustled in the soft night breeze. One could almost hear the corn growing. The rain had cooled the air, and a white moon was attempting to shine through a wispy cloud covering. Crickets sang in the tall grasses, and somewhere near the barn an owl hooted. Ann was absorbed in the sounds of the night, and Devorah moved in her rocking chair.

"By the way, we have a new calf. I was out in the fields when Old Bess dropped it. That's how I got caught in the rain."

"You know, we ought to get us a steer. I'm getting awful sick of chicken."

"Well, maybe in the fall after I get some money from the harvest."

"Or we could butcher a hog early and have some pork."

"Possibly." A pause. "Ann, don't you think Lissa's doing rather nicely with her learning?"

"Oh, she's come a long way. Her speech is improving, and she loves to make things out of wrapping paper. If she helps me cook, I can keep her busy for hours."

"I don't know what I'd do without you, Ann. I just don't have the time to spend with her. I can see she's quite stuck on you."

"Well, after I can throw this crutch away for good, I can get out there and help you with everything. That way, we'll get it done faster and you'll have more time."

"I know. I get so tired lately. I can't even get up early any more. Ann, you haven't used that hair dye yet?"

"No, but I expect to pretty soon. That was sure nice of Doc."

"He's a good man to have around when you need him."

"Well, at least he believes me. Believes I didn't . . . do it."

"I think he cares enough to find out who did."

"It wouldn't surprise me if it was Ace. I hate that man. I keep seeing him with his hands all over you."

"You seem to be more afraid of him than you hate him."

"No, I'm not afraid of him. I'll kill him first before he kills me. It's just that there's something wrong . . ." Ann tried to jog her memory; some truth lay buried there.

"What do you mean, 'wrong'?"

"That night when the little girl was killed, when I was out. I was passing by one of the alleys in town, and I saw this . . . this person bending down over her body. It was a man, definitely a man because he was wearing pants. And he looked up at me before he ran. I saw him."

Devorah sat up straighter in the rocker. "Who?" she asked anxiously. "Who was it?"

"I don't know," Ann said, slumping back into her chair. "His face was in shadow. But that's what's wrong. I know I saw the outline."

26

"Well, don't worry about it too much. One of these days it'll come back to you."

"That time when Ace was here . . . you didn't . . . *like* it, did you?"

"Heavens, no! A man can be gentle. He doesn't have to grab." Devorah thought a moment and then glanced over at Ann. "Tell me, were you *really* jealous?" Ann kept her gaze outward to where the prairie lay. Devorah willed her to turn. *If I could just look into your eyes,* she thought, *I would know.*

"No . . . I was only concerned for you," Ann finally answered.

"Then why . . . ?" Devorah stumbled.

"Why what?" Ann's brown eyes looked deeply into her own, penetrated through them and went beyond. Devorah searched and could read nothing in those eyes.

She tried desperately to shift the focus away from herself. "Uh . . . don't you ever want to get married? Have children?"

"No, never," Ann replied firmly.

"Don't you like men at all?" Devorah instantly regretted her words.

"I got along with my brother. We had some good times together. I was his little tomboy sister, and he taught me a lot of things. How to ride, how to shoot. He was good, he was kind to me." She trailed off lamely.

"But what do you *want?*" Devorah persisted. To her, life's fulfillment came with bearing one's husband a child. That was the way of women, the way it was supposed to be. Ann's beliefs flew in the face of everything she had learned, and she was confused.

"A woman can be gentle, too," Ann said softly.

Just then Devorah peered up at the moon. The hazy clouds had drifted away, and the light was now shining brightly down, illuminating their faces. She spied a dim twinkling on the horizon.

"Oh, look!" she cried, pointing heavenward. "A star. Quick, let's make a wish." She shut her eyes tightly. After a moment, she turned to Ann.

"What did you wish for?" Ann questioned.

"I wished for happiness. And you?"

"I wished for love."

"Oh, Ann, I wish love for you, too."

27

"Come on, Devvie, speak your mind," Ann said earnestly. "Tell me how you feel."

Devorah was inwardly torn by mixed emotions. *She just used my name,* she thought, amazed. *No one's ever called me that before.* All the feelings that she had previously considered neatly categorized and labeled were now flying away from her, tumbling over and over. She was painfully aware of her heartbeat; she felt her throat constrict. This silence required an answer, and she had none to give.

It had grown exceedingly late. Devorah was sitting on the edge of the bed in her nightgown. She looked lovingly at the sleeping child and reached out to smooth her hair, adjusting the quilt around her face. Ever since Ann had arrived, Devorah had been sleeping with Melissa, thereby giving Ann the use of her own bedroom. She hadn't minded. Both beds were extra-large, and there was more than enough room for her here with the child. She turned the kerosene lamp down low, but did not completely extinguish the flame because she was not yet ready for sleep. She had too many thoughts to think, too many feelings to feel.

She cast her memory back to the days when Billy Lee was still alive. She recalled his tall gangling form, his young handsome face, his strong suntanned arms. She had been swept up and immersed in the intensity of his love. *Dear Lord, I miss him so,* she grieved. *I lie in this bed at night, and I ache for him. He was so eager, so full of life. Everything he did was for me, to please me, to make me happy. He built this house with his own strong hands. How much sweat, how many tears! He stayed up all night to finish my rocking chair. He worked so hard in the fields. He took me to the harvest dance. I gave him a child. Out of my own body, my flesh, for him. He adored her, bounced her on his knee, cradled her by the fire. Oh, my sweetheart, my heart's flame, my beloved!* Devorah felt the tears come, warm, rushing, unstoppable. A choking sob escaped her, and she covered her face with one hand.

She stared into the soft glow of the lamp on the bedside table. *And Ann, oh, Ann! Never to want the love of a good man, never to feel another life stirring within her. Never to be complete, always running, seeking, and never finding. Who are you to come to me and make me feel again? With your bright eyes and your gentle hands, your smile in which I take delight. Oh, I want to protect you, to keep you safe, to help you grow tall and strong. I want to lead you by the hand and show you so many things. I've been alone for two long years, and I'm tired. I want to be touched, to be loved, to be wanted and I don't understand this, what you make me feel. I loved Billy so much, but there are different kinds of love. Doesn't the Bible say that love is of God? Why should it matter as long as you love? Is it really so horrible for two lonely people to care for each other way out here on the prairie?*

Just on the other side of the wall, Ann lay awake in her bed, eyes darting across the dark rafters above her. She felt disturbed that their conversation had been left hanging, as if something more should have been said. She had wanted to open herself up and pour her heart out onto the ground, to be either trampled callously or lifted gently, sweetly, and put back inside. She had tried to step so softly, to be careful not to offend, but Devorah had closed up and withdrawn into herself.

Scenes flashed through her mind of how it used to be when she was still living in Texas. She saw herself growing up, laughing with her brother, fighting with her sisters. *Oh, Daddy, I miss you and Ma. I miss being with you. I haven't seen you for so long, I wonder if you still look the same. You don't even know where I am or don't care anymore. I can't ever come back, I hope you understand that. You tried to be so strict with me, Daddy. You tried to make me into what you wanted me to be, and because I couldn't fit your plan for me, you said I shamed you and Ma. You said I was a disgrace to your name. You said I was sick. How can it be sick if it feels so right? I can't help the way I am. I just have to go where my heart takes me. And something must have led me here, something must have showed me the way.*

Oh, Devvie, she agonized, twisting the quilt. *You've been so good to me, showed me such kindness that no one else has ever shown before. You teach me things, you make me laugh. And when you look at me the way you do, I feel so fluttery, as if I can't see straight. I want to do so many things for you, to make it so that you don't have to work so hard. I want to be with you. I want to share things with you. Was that a feeling I felt in you tonight? Can it be that I've finally found my mate?*

Three

Ace Fairlane was in the saloon, standing at the bar counter with one foot propped up on the low railing. His buddies, Tim and Lou, were positioned on either side of him, and they were drinking beer while Ace was belting down whiskey. He wasn't in a very good mood since he was still smarting from Devorah's rejection of his advances.

"Hey, Ace," said Tim, clapping him on the back, "whatever happened t'that gal we wuz chasin'?"

"Yeah, Ace," Lou added. "How's come we lost 'er?"

"I dunno," Ace mumbled. "I'm still keeping an eye out. Mebbe she'll turn up."

"Y'know, I been wonderin'," Tim said slowly. "We coulda been wrong."

Ace lifted his head. "Huh? Whaddya mean?"

"Wal, I been talkin' t'the doc . . .," he continued mysteriously.

Ace looked at him sharply, squinting. "Y'have? Whadde say?" There was a slight edge to his voice that neither one of his friends seemed to catch.

"He jist said there wuz somethin' funny 'bout the whole thing. Said there wuz stuff t'be found out."

"Hey, Ace, whyn't cha go down an' talk to 'im?" Lou suggested. "Mebbe y'kin git 'im t'spill."

"I might," he answered thoughtfully. He called for another whiskey.

"Mebbe ol' Ace has got 'er stashed away so 'e kin have 'er all t'imself," Lou said to Tim, winking as he spoke.

"Nah," Tim replied, winking back. "He's stuck on the Widow Lee. She really gave 'im what fer." He rolled his eyes and poked his elbow playfully into Ace's ribs.

"I tol'ja not t'say nothin'," Ace growled.

"Whassa matter?" Tim teased. "Can't'cha take a li'l fun?"

"Shaddup!"

"Ooo-hoo," Lou snickered, jumping into the game. "He can't wait 'til 'e gits 'is hands on 'er."

"I said shaddup!" Ace threatened, beginning to lose his temper.

The two men continued to chuckle among themselves. Ace grabbed Lou by the front of his shirt and drew back his fist. Behind him, Tim caught his arm before he could strike the other man.

"Hey, take it easy!"

"We didn't mean nothin'!"

"Aaah, hell with ya," Ace muttered, snatching his hat and stalking out.

He paused in the hot, dusty street. *Mebbe I oughtta go see the doc,* he thought. *Wonder if 'e knows somethin' 'e ain't tellin'.* He stumbled off, slightly dizzy from the liquor.

Doc McClintock was sitting quietly at his desk in the little office. Not many patients had been coming to see him during his office hours due to the stifling heat. *Well, plenty of time to think,* he mused, mopping his brow. He rose and went over to the cabinet where he kept all of his records, which was in the corner of the room next to the glass-enclosed dispensary. He located the file on Bonnie Anders and flipped through it, reexamining his own personal notes on the affair. He had also recently gone out to Devorah's farm and had a chance to privately talk with Ann. She had given him an honest confession of what had happened that night as she perceived it. *She could not have done it,* he thought, positive of his feelings. *I know that now. And yet who? Who could be that vicious to rip apart a helpless little girl?*

A loud noise commanded his attention, and he turned to find Ace entering his office. He was unsteady on his feet and had tripped against the step and fallen forward, grabbing onto a chair for support.

"Hey, Doc, how y'doin'? You 'n me's gotta have us a li'l talk." He slurred his words badly, and Doc could smell the whiskey on his breath. "I hear y'been sayin' things, Doc. 'Bout that li'l gal. Thought I'd come an' ask ya 'bout it, see what'cha know."

Doc raised his bushy eyebrows. "And what would I tell you, Fairlane?"

"Why, what'cha know, Doc, what'cha know."

"I know now more than what I knew before," he said, deliberately being evasive.

Ace tried to be properly concerned. "D'y'know who did it?"

"Where were *you* that night, Fairlane?" he countered, ignoring Ace's question.

"Me?!" Ace sounded shocked and offended. "Why, uh . . . I wuz uh . . . I wuz with them gals at the saloon. We went upstairs, y'know, Doc—have a li'l fun?" He leered and winked.

"Are you sure?"

"Wal, o' 'course," he insisted, trying to sound believable. "I like m'wimmen experienced, y'know?"

A few days later, Doc decided to stop by the saloon to enjoy a cold beer. A man was playing lively music on the old piano set in the far corner of the room. There were several drinkers standing at the bar, and a few scattered groups were seated at tables and quietly playing cards. The madam's girls, a half dozen of them, were attired in brightly colored outfits with revealing bodices, and they were circulating among the groups of men, giving out flattering attention and lavish praise. Doc ignored them; he considered himself too old for that sort of thing.

He glanced up from his drinking to observe the madam herself, Delilah Emerson, she was called, sweeping into the room. At forty-one, she was a large, commanding figure of a woman with flaming red hair, and she exuded a brisk air of authority over her girls, who rushed to do her bidding and obeyed implicitly. Delilah was followed by a slim young mulatto girl named Ruby, who, everyone knew, was her own personal favorite. Doc eyed the madam approvingly, as they were old friends of long standing. He had helped to keep her girls in the best of health.

"Hi, Doc!" she exclaimed, spying him at the bar. "Haven't seen ya 'round here fer a while."

"Lilah," he said, nodding affably to her. "A pleasure to see you." He also bowed politely to Ruby at her side. "Ah . . . Lilah," he added, suddenly remembering his earlier conversation with Ace. "Would you spare me the time for a private little chat?"

"Haven't done nothin' wrong, Doc," she said, throwing up her hands. "I run a tight ship here. M'gals're clean."

"No, no, nothing like that," he assured her, smiling. "An entirely different matter."

"Okay, Doc, whatever y'say. Ruby, you git along out there." She waved the girl away. "An' mind yer manners."

Delilah and Doc went up the staircase to the rooms above the saloon, which were used for additional entertaining of customers and which were also the girls' living quarters. The madam led the way down the narrow dimly lit hallway to her own room, which was larger and more grandly furnished than any of the others, in fit keeping with her station as the girls' employer and mistress.

Doc closed the door softly behind them. "Lilah," he began. "You remember that night when the little Anders girl was killed?"

Delilah's hand flew to her ample bosom. "Oh, mercy, yes! Such excitement—ever'body runnin' an' hollerin'. Don't expect t'fergit that in a long while."

"Ace Fairlane told me he was up here all the time. Is that true?"

"Nope," she replied, without hesitation. "Didn't see hide nor hair of 'im all night. Why? Y'think *he* did it?"

Doc rubbed his chin. "I don't know," he said slowly.

"Hmmph," she snorted. "Wouldn't s'prise me. Nope, didn't see 'im at all. An' I keep a sharp eye out on ever'body's comin's an' goin's. That's m' job. 'Sides, we wuz takin' care o' that other gal—the one who came in all dressed like a boy."

Doc looked up sharply and gave her his full attention. "What? Who was she?"

"Said 'er name wuz Ann somethin'-or-other. Said she wuz jist passin' through. Looked all wrung out, like she needed a good hot meal, so we fed 'er. An' then m'Ruby gave 'er a bath an' a good rubdown, y'know what I mean? Got 'er all perked up again. Ruby said she wuz quite a wild one." She threw back her head and laughed loudly.

"Where did she go?"

Delilah shrugged her massive shoulders. "Who knows? Said she couldn't stay, so she went out the back door."

Doc immediately went over to the jail to speak with the sheriff, a young man named Andy Hanks. Upon entering the little office, he found Hanks seated at the desk with his chair tipped backward and his boots propped up on the table top. Hanks was a soft-spoken, easy-going man and seemed to be in no rush to do anything, preferring instead to take his time and approach matters slowly. At the present moment, he was savoring a pungent cigar, drawing the smoke into his lungs and exhaling it in a gray cloud.

"Hanks, are you doing anything about that Anders girl?" Doc said brusquely.

"Hey, Doc, that's all over with," he responded, easing his feet down to the floor. "That wuz a long time ago."

"There is still a murderer out there," Doc insisted, pointing beyond the door.

"Aw, c'm on, Doc! Y'been jawin' at me fer months," he sighed. He sounded exasperated and tired of the whole affair. "Anyways, Anders tol' me he an' 'is wife wuz gonna have another kid. I don't think it'd be right t'dig up the whole mess fer 'em again. Can't 'cha jist let it rest?"

"Have you talked to Ace Fairlane about this yet? Seems to me you ought to. He told me he was up at Lilah's all night, and she told me he was never there at all. Now if that's not a lie, I don't know what is."

"Wal, Doc, I can't jist go haulin' 'im in here fer that," he said, spreading his hands, palms upward, across the desk. "Y'gotta have more proof."

Devorah's wagon rumbled into town, raising clouds of dust and scattering several barking dogs, who ran alongside and nipped playfully at the horse's hooves. She pulled to a stop in front of the general store, set the brake and jumped agilely to the ground. Entering the store, she handed the shopkeeper a long list of items that she needed. She always did her major purchasing either at the end or at the beginning of every month. She bought sacks of sugar, flour, coffee, cornmeal, salt, grain, and other minor foodstuffs, and then the apron-clad shopkeeper assisted her in transferring everything to the back of the wagon. She bid him a pleasant good day and continued on down the wooden sidewalks until she came to a small store that specialized in material, laces, and linens. *Ann definitely could use some more clothes,* she thought determinedly as she stepped into the shop, noting the shrill jangle of the little bell secured above the door. She browsed through the rows of material for quite some time, selecting this, discarding that, fingering another, until quite by accident she drew near to two other women who were standing apart and whispering among themselves. Giving them a quick glance, she recognized them as being the same two old biddies who had sat behind her in church.

"Did you see all that stuff she's buying?" said one woman.

"Wonder what she aims to use it for," said the other woman.

"Could be she wants to get all gussied out for Doc. I hear she's got him wrapped around her little finger now."

"Can you imagine a woman being so forward?"

"Unheard of!"

"Scandalous!"

Devorah was slightly irked, but she forced herself to put on a sweet smile as she turned toward the women.

"Sometimes I've a mind to get what I want," she said to them, spun on her heel, and moved off to seek out the store clerk. Their expressions became shocked and incredulous.

"Well, I never!"

"Maidie, quick, my smelling salts!"

Melissa dashed out into the front yard to greet Devorah when she returned home. She barely had a chance to step down off the wagon before the child was grasping at her hand and tugging her toward the house.

"Mommy, Mommy, come see! Come see what we did. We put color on Ann's hair."

"You must learn to wait, dear," she admonished. "I must put everything away first."

Devorah had only permitted the young shopkeeper of the general store to assist her because she had wanted to appear ladylike and deferential to him. Now she hefted the heavy sacks and swung them up to her shoulders. She made several trips back and forth from the wagon to the smokehouse, which doubled as a cooler and which stood in a shaded spot against the wood frame of the house. Massive blocks of ice were stacked on the floor of the smokehouse and helped to keep the inner temperature down during the hot and humid summers. The ice had to be ordered specially from an outfit in Kansas City, which lay ten miles to the east of Sutter's Ford.

Devorah was breathing hard by the time she finished her task. She unhitched the horse from the wagon and then finally allowed a fidgeting Melissa to drag her by the hand down the hallway to the bathroom, where Ann was just putting the final touches on her hair.

"Look, Mommy, see? She let me help."

"She's been changed again, too," Ann said laughing. "She got more on her than I did." She turned to face Devorah. "Well, what do you think?"

Devorah walked slowly around her so that she could observe from all angles. Ann's shoulder-length hair, which had once been a light ash-brown, was now colored a darker richer brown. Ann had added some henna to the black dye to prevent the overall effect from appearing too harsh.

"Hmmm, not bad," Devorah mused. "Not bad at all. I like it. Now we can use a ribbon to tie it back like this. Turn around." She swept the hair back from Ann's ears with both hands as she expertly tied on a pretty red ribbon. Then she let the hair fall into a short po-nytail.

"You really like it?" Ann asked, unsure.

"Of course I do," she insisted. "We'll make a woman out of you yet. Wait 'til you see what I brought home for you."

After dinner that evening, all three of them assembled in the living room by the fireplace to examine the assortment of materials that Devorah had gotten. Both Ann and Melissa expressed approval of her varied selections, and Melissa especially was quite taken with one particular bolt of bright green cloth. Ann favored the blue denim, for she also needed a new pair of pants.

"Oh, Mommy, will you make me another dress?"

"And I need new pants so I can get outside and help you."

"All right, all right, both of you," Devorah said, holding them off with upraised hands. "I promise. Now, young lady, to bed."

She got the child into her nightgown, tucked her under the quilt, kissed her gently on the forehead, and quietly shut the door. She saw Ann limping around the room with crutch tucked under one arm and a long piece of material draped over her shoulder, almost touching the floor.

Devorah reached for her sewing basket. "Might as well keep that on. I'm also going to make you a dress."

"Aw, Devvie," Ann protested. She used the name more frequently now, and Devorah was quite comfortable with it. "I hate to wear them. They don't feel right."

"Well, they look right. I want you to start coming into town with me, and you can't be wearing those pants. They're not fit. You're supposed to be my prim and proper niece from New York, and you'll have to be introduced."

"Do I have to go to Meeting, too?"

"Absolutely. You have to learn to act like a lady."

Ann grimaced and rolled her eyes heavenward. "But why can't I just stay here?"

"Because I want you to be seen. I want people to get used to you."

"What if Ace recognizes me?" she ventured timidly.

"Not like this, he won't. He'll never know you."

Ann helped her cut out the material according to pattern. Devorah basted portions of it together with even, practiced movements of the needle; other portions were held together with small pins. She worked quickly, having the nature of a person accustomed to long hours of tedious sewing. When she had a reasonable form of a dress completed, she told Ann to strip down and try it on for a first fitting. Ann stood there feeling very uncomfortable and self-conscious. This was the first time in years that she had ever put on a woman's clothes.

"Hold your head up," Devorah said smartly, lifting Ann's chin. "Don't look so sour."

"I don't know if I like it."

"*I* like it. It looks good on you, brings out your curves. You *are* a woman, you know. You *do* have curves."

Ann was embarrassed. "Not much."

"Nonsense. You have a fine figure."

"Honest? You really think so?"

"Of course. You'll make me proud to be with you."

Ann had never considered this. "I will? Really?"

"Yes. Now turn." Ann turned. "Now walk." Ann temporarily let go of the crutch and walked as if she were approaching a horse and getting ready to mount. Devorah clapped one hand to her head. "No, no! Stop! Watch me—like *this*." She minced across the room, the picture of daintiness and femininity. "You have to move your hips. Now try it again." Ann tried to follow her instructions, but did not show much improvement. "Never mind. We'll practice that later. Come here."

37

Ann stood above Devorah as she knelt on the wooden flooring. She ran her hands upward along the sides of Ann's hips and underneath her breasts, adjusting the material and pulling it tighter for a better fit. Ann was suddenly acutely aware of the pressure of Devorah's touch as she absent-mindedly moved her hands over her body. Ann closed her eyes and took a deep breath. *She doesn't even know what she's doing to me,* she thought. She clenched her fist, opened it, and looked downward to where Devorah was busily absorbed.

"Uh . . . Devvie . . ."

"Mmm?" she answered through a mouthful of pins. She did not glance up, but continued to work. "A tuck here," she mumbled, frowning, "and a little more there."

"Devvie . . ." Ann repeated. Her hands were beginning to sweat, and she felt as if she wanted to fold up and sink to the floor.

"What? I'm almost done. Hold still."

"If you don't stop . . ."

Devorah put both hands on her hips and finally met Ann's eyes. "What is the matter with you?"

"Uh . . . nothing," she sighed, leaning on the crutch for support. "Go on."

August came, and the days were still hot and long. After a week of patient and intensive instruction in the womanly arts of walking, talking, and bowing politely, Devorah felt that Ann was now ready to make her debut in Sutter's Ford. Ann was able to walk without the assistance of the crutch for short periods of time, although if she used the bad ankle excessively it gave rise to a dull aching pain. She still had a slight limp and favored the good leg, so she kept the crutch with her wherever she went. She could not yet go out into the fields, for that would have been too great a distance from the haven of the house, nor could she help Devorah with the care of the animals or the vegetable garden, but whatever chores she performed inside the house, she did well.

One bright Sunday morning, Devorah ushered them all out to the carriage in preparation for the ride into town. Ann was wearing her new dress and Devorah was quite pleased with her appearance. She hovered at Ann's side and grasped her arm firmly as she helped her up into the carriage. *She's getting stronger,* she thought. *I'm glad. Pretty soon she may run again.*

This time they arrived early for the worship services. Devorah had made sure there was plenty of time because she intended to present Ann to the townspeople in an unhurried and proper manner. As they passed up the steps and into the foyer of the church, Devorah spied many faces that she knew, nodding and smiling to them in greeting. Whenever anyone stopped to talk to her, she dutifully introduced Ann, who remained glued to her side, as her young niece from New York State, here to spend the summer. The reaction of the townsfolk was one of interest and smiling approval.

"Such a lovely child!"

"And only twenty-two!"

"Devorah, you must bring her out to our place for dinner sometime."

"I'm sure my son John would love to meet her."

Unnoticed to Ann and Devorah, Doc McClintock had insinuated himself next to them and was listening to the conversation and observing the people's reactions.

"Ah, Devorah, a pleasure to see you," he said, placing his hand on her arm. "And who is this young lady?" He nodded in Ann's direction.

Devorah played the game skillfully. "Doc, this is my niece Ann Johnson. She comes all the way from New York." Ann gave no sign of recognizing him.

"I am enchanted," he said, bowing deeply and kissing Ann's outstretched hand. "Have you ever been this far out west before?"

"No, sir, I haven't."

"I trust you will find farm life most interesting."

"Yes, sir, I do."

The bell in the steeple rang out, and everyone broke off conversation and assembled in an orderly fashion into the pews. Doc surreptitiously took Ann's arm and escorted her to a seat, conscious of the fact that she had been putting weight on the bad ankle and was at this moment without her crutch. She leaned against him, grateful for his support. Devorah followed with Melissa, and they all sat together. The service dragged on; the air was hot and still.

Afterward, upon leaving, Doc was approached by the Anders couple, who wanted to speak with him concerning the wife's new pregnancy. Ann and Devorah quietly slipped away toward the front door, and they were just about to descend the steps when they were again accosted by Ace Fairlane. Ace had spied Ann and he moved close to her, forcing her to back nervously up against the brick wall.

"Ah, howdy, Miz Lee. And who be this cute gal?" He grinned widely at Ann, eyeing her slowly up and down. Ann felt cornered.

"My niece," Devorah said abruptly.

"Quite a fine figger there. Young an' purty." He reached out to finger Ann's hair, and she cringed, turning her head away from him.

"She's of no concern to you," Devorah said coldly, taking Ann's hand and leading her down the steps.

Ace watched them go, staring hard at Ann all the while. *That gal looks mighty familiar,* he thought. *Know I've seen 'er b'fore.* He scratched his head thoughtfully and frowned, but then gave up the idea, put on his hat, and moved off to the saloon.

Ann and Devorah were riding home in the carriage and Melissa was snuggly esconced between them on the seat. The horse was kept to a slow and even pace, thus allowing them to enjoy the gently rolling beauty of the surrounding countryside.

"Now see, that wasn't so bad," Devorah said to Ann.

"I don't like being around a lot of people."

"You did all right. Wasn't Doc something, the way he talked to you?"

" 'I'm enchanted,' " Ann mimicked, making her voice low and reaching for Devorah's hand. They both laughed. "But Ace got me so upset." Ann shuddered at the memory of his fumbling caress.

"Yes, me, too," Devorah agreed soberly. "He's all eyes and hands."

"Devvie, you don't think . . . maybe he knew me?" she asked anxiously.

"No, I'm sure not," Devorah replied, trying to sound reassuring. She patted Ann's hand and clucked to the horse to trot faster.

After lunch, Melissa grabbed the pail and dashed out the back door, calling to them that she was going to hunt for raspberries. Ann smiled, knowing that the red and black berries would be used to make more pies. She enjoyed cooking for Devorah and the child, taking great delight in Devorah's smile when she came home from a long day's toil and found various surprises being taken out of the oven or a big dinner already on the table.

Devorah informed Ann that she was going to return to her work in the garden, and Ann moved out onto the front porch to be company for her as she labored a short distance away. *If I can't help her, I can at least be with her,* she thought, easing herself down onto the rocking chair. She watched the movements of Devorah's sun-darkened arms as she bent and stooped and systematically weeded the neat rows. *Your hands,* she thought, *how worn they are. I want to take them and hold them to my breast.*

"It'll soon be time for canning," Devorah called out to her. "I'll have to get some supplies from town."

"Will you teach me how, too?" Ann called back.

"Of course. It's so easy. We'll just . . ."

"Mommy, Mommy!" Melissa shouted, running into the yard. "Look what I found!" She was swinging the pail full of berries.

The child was so intent upon reaching her mother that she did not pay heed to where she was putting her scampering feet. She blundered into a small pile of stones which had been stacked at the edge of the dirt over by the beginning of the tall prairie grass. She tripped and fell, and the pail flew from her hand, scattering the berries on the ground. Melissa was undaunted and would have immediately picked herself up again had she not been frozen into rigidity by the sound of a menacing hiss which came from a spot close to her face. She had unintentionally disturbed a nesting rattler, and the snake slithered out of the grass and peered at this intruder. The long forked tongue darted in and out of its mouth, and the rattles on its upraised tail shook loudly. It coiled, getting ready to strike. The child fearfully looked at her mother.

"Oh, dear Lord!" Devorah choked, putting her hand to her mouth. "Oh, honey, lie still. Don't move!"

Devorah was also frozen into immobility by her own rushing fear. Ann had watched the scene unfold and as soon as she saw the coiled body of the snake, she surged upward from her chair and lunged behind the front door for the rifle. She crouched down at the railing and leveled the gun barrel, propping her elbows on the wood to steady her shaking fingers. The snake inched nearer to Melissa's face.

"Damn, she's too close!" Ann shouted. "Get her to move back!"

"Lissa, honey," Devorah said, trying to keep her voice even. "Don't jump. Pull yourself backward slowly. Very . . . very . . .

slowly." The child moved imperceptibly. The snake rattled louder and drew back its head, looming above her. "That's good, honey," Devorah continued soothingly. "A little more, just . . . a little . . . more."

Ann fired. The snake's head disintegrated in a spray of blood and bone, and its body sagged limply to the ground. Melissa jumped up and ran to her mother, burying her face in her skirts. Devorah was crying now as she hugged the child close. Ann breathed a sigh of relief and wiped the sweat from her brow.

Four

The days dragged on, endless, wind-blown, still-summer days. The wind came down out of the western skies and blew across the prairie grass, bending it, caressing it, before rushing on. The tall shocks of yellow corn rustled in the warm breeze, one stalk nuzzling against another, whispering a language that only it knew and understood. The rains came again, but gentle this time, and the life-giving water soaked the ground, running in little rivulets along the furrows between the corn rows. In Devorah's garden, the vegetables grew plump and firm. The whole farm lay languishing, growing, ripening toward the harvest.

During one such lazy afternoon, Devorah had busied herself out in the fields away from the house. Ann was restless, searching for some task to keep herself occupied. She had already passed the morning in tutoring Melissa, but the child's attention could be held for only so long, and now she was outside playing contentedly.

With her crutch tucked under her arm, Ann hobbled around the house, scanning the beams and flooring planks, scrutinizing the furniture, looking for some little thing that might be in need of adjustment or repair. She opened the back door and then closed it again a couple of times to make sure it was set securely in its frame. *Aha,* she thought, *there's something wrong here.* Upon closer examination, she could see that the two brass door hinges had only been nailed, not screwed, into the wooden door frame. One nail was missing, and two others were beginning to work loose, thereby causing the door to shut insecurely. *This thing could fall off one of these days,* she realized.

Ann went out to the small tool shed which stood just aside from the back door, gathered up a hammer and a handful of long screws, and returned to the house. It did not take her very long to extract all the old nails from the door and replace them with good solid screws. Soon she was looking around for something else to repair.

43

Melissa had come in to observe her while she worked and now the child passed judgment upon Ann's recently finished job.

"You do good work," Melissa approved. "What are you going to fix next?"

"I don't know, honey. Can you think of anything?"

"Mommy's always telling me to stay clear of the big pump outside. She says the boards are loose an' I could fall in."

"Well, let's go have a look at it, shall we?" Ann said, taking the child's hand and permitting her to lead the way.

At the water pump Ann carefully eased herself down to the ground so that she could thoroughly examine the wooden planking that had been laid across the hole in the ground. The nails had come loose from the boards, and some sections of the wood were rotting away. *This is really bad,* she thought. *Devvie should have had it fixed a long time ago.*

"You're right, Lissa. This'll be our next job. Where does Mommy keep some extra boards?"

"Back in the barn," she answered.

"All right, honey. You go in the house and bring me the hammer while I get the wood. And go into the shed and get me some long nails."

The child hastened to obey, filled with eagerness at the chance of being able to assist. Ann rummaged around inside the barn until she found the corner where the spare planking was stacked. She had to make several trips from the barn to the pump because she had only one free hand, the other one still grasping the crutch.

Warning Melissa not to come too close, Ann used the claw of the hammer to pry up the rotted boards surrounding the base of the pump. When she had all of the old wood cleared away and thrown aside, she began to lay out the new planks, making sure that each piece fit snugly against the other. Melissa handed her the nails as one by one she firmly hammered them into the wood. They were so engrossed in their task that neither one of them noticed Devorah as she came into the yard and moved to stand behind them.

"What is going on here?" Devorah asked sternly. "Lissa, you're all dirty—again."

"It's okay, Mommy. I had to help," she replied in self-defense. "But we're all done now, so I can go." She rose to her feet, brushed herself off, and scampered away.

Devorah turned her attention to Ann, who was still sitting on the ground and looking up into her face. Ann's forehead was smudged, and the ribbon had come untied from her hair. In spite of herself, Devorah had to smile.

"I didn't know you were so good at fixing things," she said.

"It had to be done. I also took care of the hinges on the back door. This place is falling down around your ears."

"I know," Devorah sighed, looking around at the house and the barn. "There's so much to do, so many things to think about. Billy always took care of everything so I wouldn't have to worry. And now he's gone," she ended sorrowfully.

"But Devvie—*I'm* here," Ann said. She reached up to grasp Devorah's hand and squeezed it tightly. Devorah pulled her into a standing position and handed her the crutch. Ann continued to clasp the hand, and her eyes traveled over Devorah's face—her hair, her nose, her chin, lingering on her lips. "I'll do it for you, Devvie. We can do it together." *And I want to give you the world,* she cried out silently. *I want to give and give until my heart is bursting and my soul is complete.*

Devorah steadily returned Ann's earnest gaze. *This girl is telling me something powerful,* she thought, *and I am afraid. Not for her, but for myself. Could I do this?* She felt her heart skip a beat.

Canning season arrived. They enjoyed many varieties of fresh vegetables with their meals, having large salads and even adding the ripening corn to their diet. They made daily inspections of the garden and carried in heaping baskets full of the produce. Doc McClintock continued to stop by at the farm for occasional visits, and they generously gave him some of the vegetables.

"This is just too much for us to handle," Devorah said to Ann one day.

"Then why don't we go into town for some supplies and start canning?" Ann suggested.

The next day, they made the short trip into Sutter's Ford, and after purchasing all the required items they spent the rest of the afternoon browsing around inside the little shops that lined the dusty street. They examined more material, ribbons, and laces, and Devorah tried on several hats. In one store, Ann lovingly ran her hands over the smooth leather of a pair of new boots. Up until now she had been wearing an old spare pair of Devorah's farm boots, but she wanted to have another good pair of her own.

"Devvie, look at this," she said excitedly, holding up one boot. "They're so well made. Oh, I do so need another pair!"

"After the harvest, girl. Then I'll give you some money and you can buy whatever you want."

They returned to the farm, spread their assortment of supplies out on the kitchen table, and surveyed the many baskets of vegetables on the floor, filled to the point of overflowing.

Devorah gave a small sigh. "This is going to be quite a job. Where do you want to begin?"

"Why don't we do some of these tomatoes first?"

And so they passed the remainder of the day and stayed up well into the night. They washed, peeled, sliced, and cooked until their movements became almost automatic. Ann pumped the water and boiled the numerous glass jars in a large pot on the stove while Devorah stirred the cooking tomatoes in another pot and then poured them into the jars. She showed Ann how to properly seal the lids. When the jars had cooled enough to be handled, they were stored in the smokehouse.

Over the following few weeks, they applied themselves diligently to this task of canning. They made pickles and spices, sauces and jellies, put up beets and beans. At some times, Melissa was permitted to assist them although she was more often a snitcher rather than a helper. At the end of the season, they were both exhausted but well pleased with the fact that they would have sufficient provisions to last through the coming winter.

"I declare," Ann said to Devorah one night as they were trudging wearily down the hallway to their bedrooms. "I've had about enough of this canning. If I never see another jar again . . ."

Devorah linked her arm through Ann's so they could support each other. "Ah, but we'll do it again next year, and you'll love it just the same."

"We?" Ann said, taken aback. "You expect me to still be here next year?"

"Why not? Good night." She reached her room and softly closed the door. Ann stood there for a moment, lost in thought.

Ace Fairlane had a rickety chair tilted back against one of the storefronts in town. He was sitting casually with his arms folded and his hat pulled down low over his eyes. The sun was an orange ball lowering itself through the purple clouds in the western sky, and the town streets were relatively quiet. He glanced up at the sound of footsteps to see a tall woman and her young daughter coming down the sidewalk toward him. The woman nodded to him politely; then she and the girl entered the shop right next to him. Ace readjusted his body on the chair and went back to his unhurried, absent-minded ruminating.

A few minutes later, he lifted his head again when he heard the light jangle of the bell as the door opened. He had expected to see the woman, but it was only the girl, and she was alone. Her mother was still inside the store. His eyes brightened and came alive as they darted over the girl's slim little body. She appeared to be about ten years old and she was standing in the street, pushing the dust around with the tip of her shoe.

"Hey, kid," he whispered. "C'm'ere."

The child looked up and eyed him suspiciously, unsure of what to do. Her mother had expressly warned her against talking to strangers, especially since her schoolmate Bonnie had been killed.

"C'm'ere, kid. I won't bite," Ace urged her soothingly. She took a couple of hesitant steps in his direction. "Atsa gal," he said, holding out his open arms to her. "C'm'ere. I got somethin' fer ya."

At the promise of a proffered treat, the child abandoned her feelings of inner caution and slowly sidled up to him. He reached into the pocket of his shirt and produced a piece of candy. Her eyes sparkled in the light from the storefront as he held the candy out to her with upraised palm.

"Lookee here. How 'bout that? Go ahead, take it." He thrust his hand toward her.

She reached out shyly and took the sweet, unwrapped it, and popped it into her mouth. As she stood there looking at him, he lifted his big hand to pat her head, then moved his fingers through her dark curls in a tentative caress.

"Yer a right purty li'l gal, y'know that?" His hand lingered on her cheek.

Just then the child's mother came out of the shop. She had not observed Ace fondling her little girl because at the noise of her arrival he had hastily withdrawn his hand.

"Sarah!" she called sharply. "Come along."

47

The child took her mother's hand, and they walked off down the street. She turned once to look over her shoulder and wave to the nice man who had given her a treat. Ace licked his lips and settled back in his chair.

On the opposite side of the street, Doc McClintock stood apart, concealed by the lengthening shadows of the fast-descending night. He had quietly watched the entire scene being played out from start to finish, and he had not liked what he had seen. *If ever there's a man not right in the head,* he thought, *it's him. If I only had some proof.* He shook his head sadly, remembering Bonnie Anders and the family's grief.

September's arrival provided some long-awaited relief from the summer's stifling heat. Ann was now able to leave her crutch unused for longer periods of time, although she still had a slight limp, and she expanded her limited boundaries to include the barn and the outer perimeter of the yard. She now assisted Devorah with her morning chores of feeding the horses and the cows, the pigs and the chickens. They set aside some of the milk and used it to churn fresh creamy butter.

Devorah's wearisome task of managing the farm was now made much easier with Ann's help. The chores were completed faster, and Devorah found more time to spend with Melissa at the day's end. She was amazed at the extent of the child's learning and knowledge, for Ann was a patient and competent teacher. Devorah felt as if the brunt of the labor had been lifted from her shoulders, for she was less tired and a new spring had come to her step.

"Ann, I can't thank you enough for all your help," she said late one evening as they were both drinking their coffee.

"Oh, it's nothing," Ann demurred. "I enjoy it. It gives me something to do."

"I'm so glad you can walk now and be outside with me."

"I am, too. I love the fresh air. I could spend all day outside doing things for you."

"Ann . . . ," she began hesitantly, lowering her cup. "I feel . . . I want you to know . . . that you and Lissa are the most important things in my life now." She wanted to say more, but the right words would not come. She was confused by this swirling of emotion.

Ann's clear eyes met and held her own, and the voice was low but firm. "Devvie, you are the most important thing in mine. You mean everything to me." Her gaze was too intense, and Devorah had to avert her eyes.

True to her word, Devorah had one of the hogs butchered early. It provided a welcome change from their monotonous diet of chicken. They had reached the end of their culinary imaginations for varying chicken recipes, and now they enjoyed tender pork chops, succulent roasts, and fresh bacon and eggs with their breakfast. While Devorah was toiling outside, Ann passed the afternoons in coming up with new ideas for dinner and in developing her skills in working with pork. She did almost all of the cooking now, and her greatest joy lay in Devorah's sweet smile of approval as she sat at the dinner table and exclaimed upon the delectability of the meals.

Late one afternoon, Devorah was just finishing up her day's work in the garden. She returned the rake and hoe to the tool shed and dumped out a basketful of collected weeds. She was just about to go into the house when she abruptly decided to walk out to the fields and check her crops. She passed slowly along the rows of corn, looking up at the tall stalks which now stood well over her head. *It's like a forest in here,* she thought, *so dense and close together.* She reached up and gently bent one of the stalks down closer to her face so that she could better examine the progress of the yellow ears. *This is good,* she thought, *almost ready. We'll have a good harvest this year.*

Devorah continued her inspection, unmindful of where she was placing her feet. She did not notice a large rock directly in her path; her foot came down upon it and slipped off, twisting her ankle and causing her to pitch forward in the dirt. *Oh fiddle!* she groaned inwardly, sitting up and clutching her ankle with both hands. *That hurts! How stupid of me. Well, nothing to do but get on home now.* She rose to her feet and cautiously tested the bad ankle, wincing once when she put too much weight on it. She was not far from the house.

Devorah limped slowly into the yard, hopped up the porch steps, and opened the door. Ann was stirring a large pot on the stove, and two loaves of freshly baked bread had been placed on the kitchen table. When Ann observed Devorah's disheveled appearance, she immediately set down the wooden spoon and hastened to her side.

49

"What happened?" she asked with concern. "Did the cow kick you again?"

Devorah replied with a quick shake of her head. "No, I tripped over a rock." There was an edge of irritation to her voice.

This time, Ann's strong arms went around her waist and Devorah permitted herself to be led into the living room and eased down onto a chair. Ann quickly unlaced the boot and drew it off along with the leggings, being careful not to move the foot unduly. Ann was kneeling on the floor in front of Devorah, the ankle cradled in both her hands, and she bent forward to examine it, tenderly running her fingers over the skin, which was now slightly reddened and beginning to swell.

"Yep, you turned it but good," Ann pronounced. "I'll have to get some ice."

"Oh fiddle!" Devorah repeated with more exasperation.

"Lissa, get a wash rag," she ordered the child as she went out the back door to the smokehouse for a small piece of ice.

Ann was only gone a moment, and she returned to Devorah's side, taking the wash cloth from Melissa's hand and wrapping it around the ice. She gently applied the pack to the ankle, which was now propped up on a small pillow. The coldness of the ice felt good to Devorah's hot skin.

"It's not bad," Ann assured her. "It'll be all right soon. We got to it in time, but you're going to have to stay off your feet for a couple of days."

"A couple of days?!" she protested. "But I can't! My work, my chores . . ."

"I'll take care of it. Devvie, you're just going to have to learn to rest," Ann said with finality. "Now, you must be starving. Wait right there, don't move. I'll get you something to eat."

Ann set up a small table in front of Devorah's chair and arranged upon it a tray of generous slices of the still-warm bread and a plate of butter. She went to the stove and ladled out three steaming bowls full of something that looked like a thick soup. Ann and Melissa each assumed a place on the floor, one on either side of Devorah.

Devorah took the hot bowl from Ann's outstretched hand and inhaled deeply of its aroma. "What *is* this?" she inquired curiously.

"Down in Texas, it's what we call trail stew. It's made with pork and kidney beans and onions and fresh tomatoes."

Devorah took a spoonful. "Mmm, super," she complimented. "I declare, you're getting to be a better cook than I am. You've almost thrown me out of my own kitchen."

Ann returned the compliment. "Only because you taught me, Devvie. I didn't know much before I came to you."

And I know still less, Devorah mused. *Or is it too much more?*

Ann had been correct in determining that Devorah had not twisted her ankle too badly. During the three days that she had been forced to remain in the house, Devorah had quite enjoyed Ann's attentiveness and caring concern. Ann helped her once again to take a bath, and she lay back in the relaxing water and closed her eyes as Ann shampooed her long hair. Suddenly her eyes flew open as she remembered something and she turned to Ann, unmindful of the soap bubbles running down her face.

"Ann, Lissa's birthday will be next week! On the seventeenth."

"Watch what you're doing," she warned. "You've got soap in your eyes."

"We must do something for her! A party, perhaps." Devorah's mind darted, full of ideas.

"Turn around and sit still."

"I am. Oh, we must get something for her, too! We could go into town and look."

"How about a new doll? Quit splashing."

"A doll! What a lovely thought! Do you think she'd like it?"

"Devvie," Ann said, losing her patience. "Shut up and duck your head."

A few days later, they all took the carriage into Sutter's Ford. Ann deliberately kept Melissa occupied in one shop while Devorah slipped alone into the general store. She spied a display counter of several brightly dressed dolls of assorted sizes, considered each one a moment, then selected one with a pretty blue and white checked smock and a yellow ribbon tied to the head. The clerk wrapped the doll up in untelling brown paper according to Devorah's instructions. When she stepped outside again, she found Ann and Melissa already waiting for her in the carriage. Ann smiled at her and took the reins while Devorah sat next to the child, giving Melissa a quick hug in her excitement.

The next day, after the morning chores were done, they sent the child off to play in the front yard with explicit admonitions not to leave its boundaries. Devorah brought out the flour, sugar, eggs, and spices, and the two of them secretly set about making a gingerbread cake. While the cake was baking in the oven, Ann rewrapped the doll in brightly colored fancier paper and added a bow to the front of the package. Devorah could hardly contain herself, for this was the first birthday she had truly desired to celebrate since Billy's death.

They stirred up a mixture of sugar, butter, and cream to make a thin icing for the cake. When it had cooled sufficiently they set the table, made some coffee for themselves, and poured a large glass of milk for Melissa. Ann went to the door to call the child inside while Devorah stood anxiously by her accustomed place at the table. Melissa came bounding in and when she beheld the cake in the center of the table with a gaily wrapped package next to it, her eyes grew round in wonder.

"Mommy, Mommy!" she exclaimed, running to her mother and hugging her skirts. "Are we having a party?"

"Yes, dear," Devorah replied, beaming down at her. "It's your birthday. Happy birthday, sweetheart." She embraced her tightly and kissed her cheek.

"Happy birthday, honey," Ann said, moving to stand beside them. She also held her close and bent to kiss her forehead. "How old are you now?" Melissa held up one hand with the five fingers splayed out. "Very good, honey," she said approvingly.

"Lissa, open your present," Devorah urged.

Melissa made short work of demolishing the wrapping paper, and with a squeal of delight she held up the new doll for all to see and admire.

"Oh, Mommy, she's just beautiful! I love her!" She clasped the doll tightly to her little chest.

Devorah was transported by the happiness of the moment. Her eyes misted over with tears, and in her choking emotion she reached out blindly for Ann's hand, seeking it, finding it, pressing it to her breast. *Dear Lord, I am happy,* she thought. *With these two people here that I love most, I am so happy.* She realized with a shock that she had not been thinking of Billy, and she wept.

One evening toward the end of the month, after the dinner dishes had been washed and put away and after Melissa had been sent to bed, Devorah brewed a pot of tea as a refreshing change from their usual consumption of coffee. Ann suggested that they drink it out on the front porch again, reminding her that not too many warm nights remained of the summer.

Devorah reclined with a sigh into her rocking chair, and Ann sat on the porch steps, propping her back against the wooden railing and stretching her feet out across one step to the opposite side. Together, they listened to the sounds of the night, which were quieter now, more hushed and gentle, since the season was fast drawing to a close. There was no moon this night and both their faces were softly illuminated by the glow of the kerosene lamp between them.

"How quiet the night is," Ann marveled, "and how dark. Even the air is still. It's almost as if everything out there knows that summer is over."

"Soon we will have our harvest," Devorah said almost in a whisper.

"And I get my new boots."

"And I buy us a steer."

They sipped their tea contentedly, each making her own plans. Devorah thought of the new clothes she would buy for Melissa and Ann thought of what she would buy for Devorah. Ann also remembered the one night several months ago when they had sat out here after a rainstorm and talked of things that concerned them. They had gone around in circles, she recalled, never probing into the heart of matters.

"Devvie," she said, looking up into her face, "do you remember that night when you saw a star and wished for happiness?" Devorah nodded. "Have you found that happiness yet?"

"Yes . . . I think . . . I have," Devorah answered slowly. She paused a moment to reflect and then continued. "It's different, though, from what I had with Billy. But it's still good," she added reassuringly.

Ann was curious. "How is it different?"

"Ohhh," she breathed. "Well, instead of watching and waiting for Billy, I have you to care for."

"You don't really have me yet, Devvie," Ann said softly.

Devorah was genuinely puzzled. "What? Why, whatever do you mean?" She peered down at Ann, frowning.

"You can't *have* me unless you *want* me."

53

There it was again, that penetrating gaze that held Devorah spellbound, probed beyond her eyes and caressed her mind with gentle fingers, impaled her soul to the back of her chair. Devorah trembled nervously; her hands fidgeted aimlessly in her lap. And oh, she knew, she *knew*.

October brought living fire to the trees. The leaves flared up in bright colors of red and yellow and orange. Bushy-tailed squirrels darted from one tree to another, collecting mounds of nuts and storing them in their dens. Flocks of birds darkened the skies as they winged their way southward. The nights had now begun to turn chilly again and Ann burned stacks of wood in the fireplace. Her slight limp was gone and she no longer needed the crutch at all, so it had been unceremoniously relegated to a corner of the bedroom wall. It had taken a long time, but now she was back on her own two feet again, and she reveled in her freedom of movement.

One morning, Ann hitched up one of the workhorses to the buckboard, took an axe, and went to the edge of the forest that formed a natural boundary for Devorah's land. She was searching for more firewood to add to their dwindling supply, and she gathered armloads of twigs and sticks, tossing them into the back of the wagon. She cut down several small trees, dragged them out to the clearing where the horse stood, and proceeded to cut and split the wood into log-sized sections. The hands holding the axe were strong, becoming calloused, the arm muscles were also strong and sinewy, and her aim with the sharp blade was swift and true. She chopped and split, heaved and threw for hours until the back of the wagon was piled high with wood. Only then did she pause for rest, easing herself down onto an old rotted log.

She passed one arm across her brow and looked around at the deep, dense forest which was alive with the brilliant colors of fall, yet dying surely as the close of the year approached. She felt exhilarated at this silent communion with nature, felt as one with its peace and beauty. *Devvie should see this, too,* she thought. She longed to have Devorah at her side.

The horse plodded slowly back to the house, straining under the heavy load of wood. Once in the front yard Ann jumped down from the wagon and neatly stacked all the sticks and logs on the woodpile. *That's good,* she thought approvingly. *A couple more trips like that and we'll be set for the winter.* She went into the house in search of Devorah, received no answer to her calls, went back outside, and strode to the barn. She spied Devorah walking toward her from the distant fields and ran to her side, seizing her arm in her excitement.

"Devvie," she said breathlessly. "You've got to see this!"

"What? See what?"

"The woods. Take a walk with me. Come on!" Ann tugged her along impatiently.

They stopped to get Melissa, and then the three of them set off for the forest with the child leading the way. They strolled leisurely along the narrow winding trails and penetrated deep into the heart of the woods. Ann pointed out many little secrets of nature to Melissa and helped her to identify the various species of trees. They saw a deer in a clearing far ahead of them and the child was silent with wonderment at observing its sleek wide-eyed grace. They turned over rotted logs and probed with sticks into hollows where insect life abounded and skittered away. Devorah was slightly squeamish at this, but she was impressed with Ann's knowledge of the forest. Then in their unhurried wanderings they came across a small but deep brook that ran alongside the trail, splashing noisily over the large rocks in its path. Melissa was delighted and Ann promised to take her fishing in the spring. Finally when the child grew tired, they turned their steps homeward.

"Ann, that was lovely," Devorah said. "Truly an experience."

"I thought you might be interested," she responded, smiling shyly. "It's a whole new world out there."

"Where did you learn so much about it?"

"From my brother. I told you he taught me a lot of things. You've got to take another walk with me in the spring. It's really different then, too, with everything coming back to life."

"You must really love the forest."

"Oh, I do!" she agreed emphatically. "It's a way to lift up your soul, to make you more aware, to give you release."

Devorah was aware that she also needed release, but at this point she didn't quite know from what.

The harvest was in full swing. The same five neighbor men who had performed the summer baling for Devorah now returned to take care of the corn crop. Ace Fairlane was thankfully not among them this time, so Ann assumed his place and made a sixth hand. At first, the men were deferential to her, almost condescending, but when they saw that she could pit her strength along with the best of them, they quickly welcomed her into their group, giving her a friendly acceptance and joking with her good-naturedly. The task took close to two weeks to complete, for each ear of corn had to be shucked before it could be stored in the tall silo next to the barn. Devorah again assumed the responsibility of preparing a hot meal for everyone at the day's end, and when it was all over, the silo stood filled to the top with the yellow ears.

Devorah's corn crop was more than twice the size of the wheat crop, and after setting aside enough corn to serve themselves and the animals for the winter months, she sold the large surplus to a buyer in Kansas City and received well over six hundred dollars in fair trade. One afternoon she and Ann and Melissa went into Sutter's Ford for the purpose of banking most of the money. Devorah generously gave Ann thirty dollars for her to do with as she pleased and after also giving herself a modest allowance, they all set off on a shopping spree. Ann went directly to the store where she had first seen the new boots and also bought a shirt and a heavy winter coat for herself. Devorah purchased a new hat and coat, but spent most of her money in getting Melissa another outfit of shoes, dresses, and a coat, for the child seemed to be growing like a weed. After an exhaustive day of shopping, they all wearily traveled home in the carriage. Melissa had fallen asleep and was snugly nestled against Ann's side.

"Devvie, I'm so happy," Ann grinned. "We've all got so many new things."

"And enough food and money to last us for a long time."

"We did all right, didn't we, with the harvest? We'll be all right, won't we?" Ann was anxious lest their good fortune somehow escape them.

Devorah reassuringly patted Ann's hand. "Of course we will. We did fine."

"Thank you for the money. I've still got a lot of it left. I can use it to buy Christmas presents."

Devorah rolled her eyes upward. "Oh, Christmas!" She hadn't realized that the holiday was just around the corner.

The following week they sported their new clothes at Sunday Meeting. Ann had insisted on wearing her boots, saying that since she had waited so long for them, she wasn't about to take them off and assuring Devorah that her full skirt covered them well enough that no one would notice. Devorah had to concede, realizing that Ann was just beginning to enjoy her newfound sense of security and belonging. *She's just like a child,* she thought, *all bright-eyed and excited.*

The townspeople milled about them, smiling genially and bestowing praise upon little Melissa. They expressed surprise at Ann's continued presence among them, but Devorah quickly explained that her sister-in-law had granted permission for Ann to remain through the winter. Even Doc McClintock came up to them and congratulated Devorah on a good harvest. His eyes twinkled as he looked at Ann.

"Young lady, I see you are not using your crutch," he said sternly, shaking one finger at her.

"Don't need it, Doc. Look!" She checked to make sure no one was watching, and then she danced a few steps in front of him.

Doc nodded and smiled approvingly. "Ah, the miracles of medical science."

"No, Doc," Ann disagreed. "You did that. I'm much obliged to you."

"Tut, tut," he said, dismissing it with a wave of his hand. "It's just the way of the body healing itself. I merely try to help it along." He bowed and held out an arm to each of them. "Bell's ringing. Shall we go inside?"

Upon the conclusion of the services, Ann and Devorah both invited Doc to come out to the farm for dinner within a few days. At the anticipation of a good home-cooked meal, he readily accepted, and after arranging for a date and time, they wished him a pleasant day. They passed into the front foyer, where Devorah readjusted her hat and Ann buttoned her coat. The air outside was brisk, and the wind gusted with a sharp chill.

Ann detected a movement out of the corner of her eye and turned to see Ace Fairlane edging up to them again with his familiar aura of threatening masculinity. He had been careless in his dress this morning, and the odor of cheap cologne had not been entirely successful in masking the underlying smell of sweat and booze.

He stood swaying unsteadily before them. "Ah, Miz Lee, might I be askin' ya t'the harvest dance?"

"No, you might not," Devorah replied determinedly.

He turned his attention, undaunted, to Ann, who shrank backward away from him. "Then how's 'bout this cute gal here?"

"She's already spoken for," Devorah said curtly, taking Ann's hand and brushing past him. They moved down the steps and mounted the carriage.

Ace peered through lowered brows at Ann. He racked his brain, trying to identify her familiar face. *It'll come t'me,* he vowed to himself. *One o' these days it'll come. An' I might even be s'prised.* He chucked softly.

As they were riding out of town, Ann looked curiously at Devorah, who was sitting ramrod stiff and staring straight ahead.

"Uh . . . Devvie . . . ," she began hesitantly, probing gently. "What did you mean when you said I was already spoken for?" Devorah did not avert her gaze from the horse's bobbing head and Ann was fearful that she would refuse to answer the question. "Devvie," she prompted, reaching out to touch her lightly on the arm, "what were you trying to say?"

Devorah turned so quickly that Ann was momentarily startled, and she withdrew her hand. "Well, what did you *think* I meant?" she hissed almost fiercely.

Ann had a slight glimmer of the truth, but she wasn't sure and she didn't dare ask.

The days passed swiftly by, and soon came the evening of Doc's dinner invitation. Ann had handled all the chores for the day, thereby leaving Devorah free to spend the afternoon in the kitchen. She made two apple pies, extra loaves of bread, peeled potatoes, and prepared a large pork roast for the oven. Melissa was excited at the prospect of company, and while the roast was cooking, she helped to set the table for four people. The heirloom clock on the fireplace mantel chimed the hour of six, and shortly thereafter Doc arrived, passing his hat and coat to Ann. Devorah escorted him to her seat at the table, which had now become the place of the guest of honor. Doc was her first formal dinner guest since Billy's death, and she slipped easily back into her role of solicitous hostess. The roast was sliced, the bread and potatoes and green beans were passed, and he dug in with a hearty relish.

"Ah, Devorah," he said after the first few bites, "I haven't eaten this well since my Martha passed on."

"Oh, pshaw, Doc," she demurred. "I'm sure you're a good cook yourself."

"That I am," he agreed. "You shall have to try my stew sometime." He grew sober and reached across the table to take Devorah's small hand in his own. "But seriously, Devorah, I'm most grateful for your kind invitation and I appreciate it sincerely."

"It's no trouble at all. We wanted to have you here. You've done so much for us and been so kind to Ann."

"Yes, Ann . . ." He looked at her and smiled in a fatherly manner. "How is the niece from New York?" Ann blushed. "Getting along all right on the farm?"

"Oh, yes, Doc," she answered. "I love every minute of it. Devvie always keeps me occupied."

He cocked his head at the familiar use of Devorah's name, but made no comment. Then Ann decided to broach a subject about which she still felt fear and confusion.

"Doc, have you found out anything more about Ace?" she asked.

"Mmm, as a matter of fact I have," he said, wiping his mouth with the napkin. He related to them the entire account of his secret observation of Ace and the child Sarah, and also added the fact that he had spoken with the madam, Delilah Emerson, who had sworn to him that Ace had not been at the saloon on the night Bonnie Anders was murdered. He discreetly omitted the disclosure of Ann's presence there that night, not wanting to cause her any embarrassment. "So that's where it stands now," he concluded. "A lot of suspicion and precious little proof."

Ann sighed. "I wish I could remember the face of the man I saw that night."

"Don't worry, my dear," he assuaged her. "Someday you will. The mind has a strange way of keeping secrets until the time is right."

They had the warm pie with freshly whipped cream for dessert and then Ann suggested that the two of them have their coffee in front of the fire while she remained behind to clean up the kitchen with Melissa's help. Devorah linked her arm through Doc's, and they settled themselves in the living room.

"Ah, Devorah," he said contentedly. "I can't thank you enough. That was truly generous of you both."

"Not to mention it, Doc. It was our pleasure."

Doc gazed into the dancing flames and remembered other such quiet evenings spent with his beloved wife in a time many long years ago. An idea popped into his head, one which he had briefly entertained once before, but had just as quickly dismissed as being impossible. *Just the dreams of a lonely old man,* he thought. *But then again, why not,* he reconsidered, pursing his lips. *Might as well test the ground, see if it'll hold up.*

"Devorah," he said, leaning forward in his chair, "you know it's been fifteen years now since Martha's been gone. Not that I haven't learned to cope with it, but it's just that . . . well, sometimes a man gets pretty lonely for someone to come home to, someone to share things with, someone to be with . . ." He trailed off lamely, not knowing quite how to put the words so that she would best understand and not misinterpret his intentions.

"Doc," Devorah said uneasily, knowing that Ann could hear their conversation, "what are you trying to ask me?" She knew full well, for her mind had leaped far ahead of his.

"Well, I know you haven't been widowed for as long as I have, but I'm sure you must get lonely, too. Do you . . . could I . . . oh, shoot!" He cleared his throat. "Devorah, will you marry me?"

A loud crash came from the kitchen as Ann dropped a cast-iron pot. Devorah instantly sensed that this was Ann's not-too-subtle way of letting her know she had heard Doc's fumbling proposal. She turned her head to meet Ann's eyes and was surprised at the thinly veiled expression of fear she found therein. Ann stood clutching the pot tightly with both arms, desperately waiting for Devorah's response. *She's afraid she's going to lose me,* Devorah realized smugly. *I've got them both hanging on my answer.* She turned her attention back to Doc, who was still sitting quietly in his chair. *Marriage,* she considered pensively. *A man. Acceptance in society. The right thing to do. And probably my only chance.*

"Doc," she said at last, trying to be gentle. "You are so sweet, truly you are. I don't deserve as good a man as you, and I love you for asking me, but I can't. I don't wish to marry just yet."

"Then will you do me the honor of letting me escort you to the harvest dance?" he said, accepting, understanding, taking it all in stride. "You'd make an old man feel right proud."

"Oh, yes!" she replied, laughing. "Oh, yes, I will!" She embraced him fondly and kissed his cheek. "I'd be honored to go with you."

Late that night after everyone had gone to bed, Ann tossed and turned under her quilt, seeking a comfortable position and not finding it. Her eyes would not stay closed, and sleep refused to come. This was only one of many nights of wakefulness that she had passed fitfully, and often the following morning Devorah would notice her red, tired-looking eyes and inquire after the cause of her sleeplessness, which Ann always dismissed as unremembered nightmares.

Oh, Devvie, Devvie! she cried out in longing as she stared up at the ceiling. *You don't know what you're doing to me, and you don't even care. Or maybe you do, and you're just doing it to torment me. I ache for you! My whole body melts when you look at me, when you touch me. I almost can't control myself. I want to sweep you into my arms and cover your sweet mouth with kisses. I want to touch you all over and make us as one. Oh, God, I almost thought I'd lose you tonight. I thought you'd marry him and then leave me. I'd have died if you had said yes. You don't know how scared I was. I don't know what I'd do without you because you mean everything to me. You are my world, my life, and my love. I keep feeling all these things from you. I know it's there, and yet you won't let it out. You keep giving me hints, hints all over the place, but you won't do anything about it. You won't come right out and tell me how you feel. And you lie sound asleep in that bed of yours, and you probably don't even think of me. Oh, I want to push open that closed door and carry you back in here with me. Can't you see how right it is? Why, why are you waiting?*

Unknown to Ann, Devorah also dealt with many nights of sleeplessness for the very same reason. Her feelings were a jumbled mass of confusion, sweeping over her, drowning her, threatening to disrupt her neatly ordered world and to dissolve her long-standing beliefs of a woman's place. Her mind was stretched to the very limits of its rationality, beyond which, if she made her choice, she would be either

61

saved or damned. She felt as if she just barely retained a tight grasp upon her heart, as if everything hung by a dangerously thin thread.

A marriage proposal, she thought somberly. *And I turned it down. The chance to be happy with a man. Not to have to go to bed alone any more. And I let it go. How could I have done such a thing? What could I have been thinking of? And yet, would I truly have been happy with him? Such a sweet, kind, gentle man! I do love him in a way, but I love Ann so much more. I love everything about her. I love her way with Lissa, her strong youthful body that's known so much pain, the way she moves, the way she looks at me. And oh, those eyes! How they hold me, how they look right through me. She said I couldn't have her unless I wanted her. I know what she means. I know what she wants. I'd be blind if I didn't and stupid as well. She is asking me, she is begging me. And what shall I do? What will my answer be? I love her, but am I* in *love with her? Could I do this thing which they say is forbidden? Is this what I really want? Why am I so afraid to let myself go? Why am I waiting?*

Five

The annual harvest dance came at the end of the month after everyone's crops had been taken in. The dance was always held at the spacious town meeting hall and for weeks prior to the event, all the wives of the local farmers freely donated their time and efforts to transform the normally austere hall into a glittering, sparkling fantasyland. Brightly colored paper streamers and ribbons were hung from the high wooden rafters; round paper globes hung down on varying lengths of twine and swayed gently in the draft from the door. A bandstand was set up in one corner of the room, and on the opposite side were arranged tables and chairs to accommodate the expected guests. The center of the room was dominated by a long, massive, wooden table which would serve to hold an enormous feast of food as each farmer's wife contributed her favorite dishes or most special recipes. The required attire of the evening was formal, with the men sporting their best suits and the women showing off their fanciest silks and laces. This was a momentous occasion that came only once a year, and it was something for which to be planned and eagerly anticipated as the one last fling before the winter's snows.

Ann was in the bedroom, helping Devorah to dress. Devorah had already taken her bath and washed her hair earlier in the afternoon, and now she was donning her corset and slip. Ann moved to the closet to get out the long floor-length gown. It was of a rich blue silk with lace adorning the edges of the short puffed sleeves and lacy ruffles down the front of the low-cut bodice. Ann held the gown up to herself and waltzed across the floor.

"Oh, Devvie," she said ecstatically. "This is just beautiful! Where did you get it?"

"Billy bought it for me when we went to our last harvest dance together," she reminisced, thinking of how the other couples on the dance floor had deferentially parted to make way for them as they waltzed on, lost in their love, eyes only for each other. "He died the following spring, and I haven't been to the dance since."

"Nobody's asked you?" Ann found it difficult to believe that an attractive widow such as Devorah would merit no further attention from interested swains.

"Actually, a decent man is hard to find in a small town," Devorah explained. "They're either too young or too old or too . . . whatever."

"Like Ace?" Ann suggested.

"Like Ace," she agreed. "Besides, I haven't really been interested in going out with anyone. I guess I just haven't found anybody worthy enough to take Billy's place."

"Then why are you going out with Doc?"

"Why not? I like him. He's a very sweet man."

"Are you thinking on marrying him?"

"No . . . I don't expect so."

"Then why are you going out with him?"

"Because I'm tired of working so hard on this farm, and I want to have some fun. I've been cooped up here for too long."

"So you get to go out and have all the fun while I have to stay here," Ann pouted, making a face.

"Now that's not the way it is at all, and you know it. I've done more than my share of work here while you were laid up. Before that, I ran this whole place all by myself for two years. Don't think it didn't knock me out half the time. Besides, I need someone to stay with Lissa and you're the only one I trust." She completed her grooming. "Now bring me my dress."

Ann helped her step into the long gown, pulling it up over her waist and around her shoulders and standing behind her to fasten the buttons. Then she stepped in front of Devorah to view the results.

"Your front is too low," she said disapprovingly. "You can't parade around like that."

Devorah dismissed her judgment. "Nonsense. It's supposed to be that way." She moved over to the bedside table to pick up a small bottle of expensive French perfume, carefully applying a few drops to her neck, the front of her bodice, and her wrists. "There, I'm all set. How do I look?" She stood before Ann, self-consciously smoothing her gown and primping her hair.

"You look lovely," Ann said admiringly. She inhaled deeply of the gently wafting perfume and found herself becoming lightheaded. "I wish *I* could be taking you to the dance."

64

"Now, now! Your jealousy is showing," Devorah chided, patting Ann smartly on the cheek. She lifted her skirts with one hand and glided out the door.

Doc McClintock arrived promptly at the hour of seven. The dance was scheduled to begin at seven-thirty, and they had plenty of time to make the twenty-minute trip into town. He assisted Devorah in putting on her knitted shawl, and then he chivalrously escorted her out to his carriage, which was large enough to have both a front and a back seat. She grasped his proffered hand as he helped her mount the one step up to the seat. They waved to Ann and Melissa standing in the open doorway. Doc called softly to the horse, and they started off down the drive.

"Devorah, you look positively ravishing tonight." He smiled at her tenderly.

"Thank you, Doc," she said coyly.

"Haven't been to the dance in ages. Nobody around to ask."

Devorah was surprised. "Is that so? A handsome man like you? I should think all the ladies would be swooning at your feet."

"Hmmph," he snorted. "I'm too old for all that."

"Bet you haven't forgotten how to waltz," she said teasingly.

"Ah . . . no. That and my famous stew are the two things I do best."

Devorah linked her arm through his. "And you also know how to treat a lady."

"Devorah," he frowned at her. "What has gotten into you tonight? You sound so . . . so happy and excited."

"Oh, I am, I am! This is the first chance I've had in a long time to get out and have some fun, to eat and drink, to dance all night."

"I fear you shall wear me out."

"Never! We will rest and then we will dance some more."

"Are you aware, young lady, that we shall cause quite a stir?" He tried to sound severe.

Her eyes grew round, and she was intrigued. "We will? Why on earth?"

"There are a few old gossips who say that you've set your sights on me."

"Well!" She considered this new development. "Then we'll really give them an eyeful." They both laughed. Devorah looked beyond the trees to where a full moon was rising. "Oh, look!" she exclaimed, pointing. "The moon!"

The harvest moon hung suspended in the night sky, a huge orange ball that seemed to caress the tops of the distant low-flung hills. The surrounding countryside was bathed in its shining light, the harvest was done, and the land was blessed.

Doc and Devorah entered the gaily decorated, brightly lit meeting hall. Most of the other couples had already arrived, and the men had established their own little smoking group while the women arranged the assortment of food upon the center table and enviously admired each other's flowing gowns. The band members assembled themselves on the platform in the corner of the room and tuned up their instruments, striving to attain the proper harmony. The men playing the banjos, guitars, and flutes broke into a lively reel. The couples stood around listening approvingly and applauding noisily. Someone called out, "One, two, grab your partner!" and everyone formed together into groups of four, and the square dancing began. Doc and Devorah were laughingly swept along with all the rest, and they bowed and curtsied, dipped and whirled, changed partners and started all over again.

After an hour's time of hectic dancing, the band ceased playing so that the couples could rest. Most of the people wandered up to the long table in search of refreshment, and Doc and Devorah joined the rapidly forming line. He piled his plate high with food, she more discreetly so, and they selected a table and sat down to eat.

"I'm famished," Doc said, attacking his plate. "That was quite a workout for these old bones."

"Oh, piffle," Devorah responded. "It just brings out the color in your cheeks."

She ate daintily, glancing around occasionally to see who else might be there that she knew. She saw all the familiar faces of those who had spoken to her in church. *My, the whole town's turned out,* she marveled. Some of Doc's old cronies stopped at their table to speak with him. Even the Anders couple came up to them, and Devorah noted with pleasure that the wife's new pregnancy was now beginning to be obvious, at least to her own eyes. Doc excused himself for a moment, saying that he was going to get them both some dessert and coffee. Devorah nodded politely and scanned the faces of the crowd again, suddenly becoming aware of an excited whispering directly behind her. She turned her head slightly as she recognized the voices of the same two old women who seemed to have nothing to do but gossip about her. *There they go again,* she sighed, shaking her head. *Can't they find anything else to talk about?*

"Did you see her flounce in here with him?" said one woman.

"And that dress! I happen to know her departed husband bought that for her," said the other woman.

"And she's still wearing it! What a disgrace to his memory!"

"Did you see how she carries on with the good doctor? As if she doesn't care what people think."

"What nerve!"

"Appalling!"

Doc returned to the table and sat down next to Devorah. *I'm going to have some fun,* she thought impishly. When he leaned toward her to place a piece of pie and a coffee cup in front of her, she threw both arms around his neck, pulled him close to her, and planted a big kiss directly on his lips.

"Whose benefit was that for?" he whispered conspiratorially.

"Two old biddies right behind us," she whispered back, winking at him. "Unless I miss my guess, one of them should have fainted dead away."

Devorah sneaked a quick glance over her shoulder at the occupants of the table behind them. She noted with supreme satisfaction that one of the women had indeed slumped in her chair, and the other was frantically patting her cheeks and rubbing her hands. Devorah giggled like a schoolgirl.

After a while the band resumed its playing, but this time the music was a slow waltz, and the quartet of violins and bass viola sang forth sweetly, beautifully, in good tempo. All the brightly lit kerosene lamps were now turned down very low, sending a softly muted light throughout the great hall.

"Ahh," Doc said, rubbing his hands together, "at last, something more my style." He rose from his chair and held out his hand to Devorah. "May I have the honor of this dance?"

"You surely may." She rose with him, and they joined the other couples moving out to the dance floor.

Devorah draped one arm casually around Doc's shoulders, and he held her gently but firmly. The music swirled about them, enveloping them on all sides as they glided across the floor. Doc's step was practiced and sure, and they meshed well together. Devorah let herself flow with the music, closing her eyes and smiling with its easy rhythm. Pretty soon she began to wonder why they were not colliding with any of the other couples since Doc seemed to be whirling her in ever-widening circles. She opened her eyes and found to her astonishment that they were alone on the floor. Everyone else had moved back, thus causing them to become the center of attention, just as it had been with Billy on that one night so long ago. *Oh, let them look,* she thought, *let them see. I don't care, I don't care.* She pulled Doc closer to her breast, and they danced on.

Ace Fairlane was also present at the meeting hall that night. Unseen by Doc and Devorah, he had managed to slip in and lose himself among the crowd. When the square dancing began earlier in the evening, he had dragged his date, a mere strumpet from Delilah's place above the saloon, to a lone table in the far corner of the room. The girl, Lizzie, very cheaply attired in both dress and makeup, had wanted to join in the dancing, but Ace had stubbornly refused her pleas and had insisted that they sit it out. Later on, he had allowed her to go over to the center table and get herself something to eat, although he had not wanted anything for himself, preferring instead to gulp secret swallows from a bottle of whiskey which he kept in the pocket of his rumpled suit.

As the harvest dance continued he became progressively drunker, but he doggedly watched Devorah's every movement through narrowed eyes. When Devorah had kissed the doctor, he felt a rushing surge of hatred. He had almost gone over to their table, but Lizzie had pulled him back down into his chair. When the slow waltzing began, his eyes hungrily followed Devorah as she swept across the floor in Doc's arms, and he jealously observed the way she touched him, the way she pulled him closer. He scowled darkly, and his mood grew uglier by the moment.

"Ace, honey," Lizzie said. "Why can't we dance? Don't'cha wanna hold me?" She put her arm around his shoulders and trailed her finger along his cheek.

He roughly pushed her hands away. "No. Git offa me."

"Aw, c'm on," she urged. "Let's have a good time. Or mebbe we kin leave, an' then I kin show ya an even better time." She lightly touched her finger to his lips and ran her other hand through his hair.

68

He seized her wrist, twisting it painfully. "I said lemme alone!"

"Whozzat woman over there?" she asked, noting the direction of his constant gaze.

"Nobody you'd know. She's too *fine* fer *you*."

"Why d'y'keep starin' at 'er? Is she better lookin' than me, izzat it? She don't know half the things I know," she said seductively.

He was fast becoming exasperated with this cheap tart. "Lizzie, whyn't'cha jist shaddup or I'll belt'cha one."

Ace took another guzzling swallow from the bottle, wiped his mouth on his sleeve, and pushed his chair back from the table. He stood up, swaying unsteadily, and staggered onto the dance floor. He went straight up to Doc and Devorah and tapped Doc's shoulder.

"Mind if I cut in?"

At the sound of his voice, Devorah's face lost its look of rapture, and her eyes flew open in fear. They abruptly stopped dancing, and Doc turned around to deal with this intruder. The crowd of onlookers buzzed with excitement, sensing that a fight was about to begin.

"Fairlane," Doc said, annoyed. "Why don't you go on home? You look as if you're going to fall flat on your face."

Ace roughly grabbed Devorah around the waist. "Not 'til after I've danced with m'gal here."

"*Your* girl?!" Devorah was shocked, incredulous. "I have never been, am not now, and never will be as long as I live, so help me God, *your* girl." She wrenched herself away from his groping hands. "You thoroughly disgust me!"

"Ah, thassa way! I like m'gals wi' some spirit." He reached out to caress her hair.

Devorah drew back her open palm and slapped him across the mouth, throwing all of her weight forward into the blow. Ace was caught off balance and reeled backward, striking the edge of a table, upsetting it, and crashing down to the floor. The crowd was suddenly hushed into disbelieving silence. Devorah stood over him, glaring at him with undisguised hatred and loathing.

"If I had my rifle here with me right now," she said in a shaking voice, "you'd be missing what you prize most."

Doc motioned to the men who stood closest to him. Three of them detached themselves from the crowd and stepped forward, grasping Ace under his arms and hauling him roughly to his feet.

"Hey!" he sputtered, shaking his head to clear his vision. "I ain't done yet."

"You most certainly are," Doc said. He took Devorah gently by the arm and led her to a chair. Another woman brought over a cup of water for her to drink.

Ace found himself being propelled unceremoniously out the door. He tripped on the step, landing on his stomach in the dirt. His date quietly slipped out to join him, and she bent over him as he lay mumbling incoherently.

Devorah slowly sipped her cup of water as Doc solicitously patted her hand. He was the epitome of concern, politely inquiring if she felt better. Her body had finally ceased its tremulous quaking. Her breathing was becoming steadier and more relaxed.

"The nerve of that man!" she shuddered. "How *dare* he speak to me that way!"

"There, there, my dear," Doc calmed her. "It's all over now."

"How could you have let him stand there and insult me like that? Why didn't you step in for me?"

"Devorah, I would not have allowed him to hurt you. But this was something between the two of you that only you could have handled. I had to let you do it in your own way."

She recalled the bitter words that she had spoken to Ace and was amazed at her courage. "I don't believe I said what I did."

"I don't either," he said, laughing easily.

"You don't suppose everybody heard me, do you?" she asked anxiously.

"Ah . . . I'm afraid they did. You were quite loud."

"Oh, mercy!" she groaned, shading her brow with one hand. "I'll never live it down."

"Nonsense," he placated her. "You mustn't feel embarrassed. Actually, I was quite proud of your gumption. A woman with spirit, indeed."

"Oh, Doc, you're too kind."

The music had switched back to a lilting reel again, and the couples were breaking up into small groups. Doc stood up and held out both his arms to Devorah, smiling down at her. His eyes twinkled in the light.

"Come, my dear," he said to her. "The night is still young. Shall we dance?"

After Ace got his wind back and his face finally stopped smarting, he slowly picked himself up off the ground. He stood there for a moment, gingerly rubbing his jaw, and was undecided as to whether or not he should go back into the meeting hall. He weighed the disadvantages carefully and then gave up the idea, conceding temporary defeat. He stumbled down the dark street toward the haven of the saloon with the girl, Lizzie, trailing along behind him.

Once inside, he staggered up to the bar and demanded another bottle of whiskey. Lizzie stood next to him as he drank and she tried her best to console him and cheer him up. His other two buddies, Pete and Joe, entered the saloon, and when they spied him they poked each other interestedly and sidled up to him.

"Hey, Ace," said Pete, clapping him soundly on the back and causing him to spill a little of the whiskey. "Where y'been?"

"Hoo-eee," ogled Joe. "Lookit them fancy duds." He fingered the coat of Ace's suit.

"Where y'been, all decked out like this?" Pete repeated.

"Bet'cha been t'the dance, huh?" suggested Joe.

Ace turned to them with a smirking grin on his face. He realized if he snapped at them in his usual gruff manner, they might start asking too many questions.

"Yep, I been there. I took m'gal here t'the dance." He grabbed Lizzie around the waist and pulled her closer to his side. She obediently snuggled up to him, eagerly seeking his favor. "An' now if ya'll be 'scusin' us, we got some unfinished biznizz t'take care of."

Ace took the girl by the arm and began to lead her toward the stairs leading to the rooms above the saloon. He got no farther than the first step, for he found himself looking up into the stern face of the madam. Delilah Emerson had overheard his conversation with the two men as she quietly descended the stairs, and now her massive girth steadfastly blocked his intended path.

"What'cha want, Ace?" she said sternly.

"Hey, Lilah," he began affably. "Me 'n Lizzie's jist gonna have us a li'l talk."

"No way."

"Aw, c'm on, Lilah," he begged. "Won't take long." He moved to bypass her; she countered his movement.

"I said no, Ace."

"Huh?" he said, not understanding. "Whaddya mean, 'no'? I already paid fer it."

"Y'paid t'take 'er t'the dance," she answered imperiously. "Y'want more, y'pay more."

He fumbled in his pocket for the money, eager to be done with her. "Wal, here, here then."

Delilah waved away the proffered bills with one heavily bejeweled hand. "Save it, Ace. Y'git no more t'night anyways. Yer drunker'n a skunk an' stink like one, too. I don't give m'gals t'the likes o' you. Now g'wan home."

Ace scowled thunderously but backed down from Delilah and quickly left the saloon, cursing all the while in a low voice. He paused in the street and looked from left to right, uncertain of where to go next. *Damn 'er*, he thought. *Damn 'em all. If I can't git it there, I know where I kin go. If Miz Hoity-Toity's gonna prance aroun' with Doc all night, I'll just go out t'the farm an' git me that other one.* He climbed on his horse and struck out for Devorah's place.

After Doc and Devorah had left the farm, Ann had taken Melissa into the bedroom and played a few games with her. They had made paper cut-outs of human and animal figures, and Ann had encouraged the child to think up little stories involving each one. When her eyes grew heavy, she had reclined against the pillow, clasping her new doll, and Ann had told her a bedtime tale about a family of birds in the forest. After she had finally drifted off to sleep, Ann tucked the quilt gently around her small body, kissed her on the forehead, and left the room, taking the lamp with her. She had then sat reading a book in front of the warm fire for the remainder of the evening. She would not go to bed until Devorah returned.

The clock on the mantel chimed the hour of ten. Ann glanced up to note the time and cast the book aside, unable to concentrate any longer on her reading. She rose from her chair and anxiously paced the floor, pausing every now and then to pull back the window curtain and peer out into the still, dark night. *Where are they?* she wondered. *They should have been back by now. What on earth is keeping them? Doesn't she realize I'm standing here waiting for her?*

The sound of a horse's hooves suddenly penetrated the silence and Ann rushed back to the window and looked out. She perceived a lone figure slowly ambling up the drive toward the house. When it came closer she recognized the person on the horse as being Ace. *Oh no!* she thought frantically, sucking in her breath. *It's him!*

She ran to the table and quickly extinguished the lamp. By the flickering light of the fire, she made her way to where the rifle lay propped against the front door. She opened the breech to make sure the gun was loaded, snapped it back together, and returned to her chair by the fireplace. She sat facing the door with the rifle cocked and balanced on her lap, ready to fire if Ace should attempt to break in. She would not even give him a chance to explain his presence.

Out in the yard, Ace drew his horse to a halt and dismounted. He was so drunk that he could barely stand. When his feet first hit the ground, his knees buckled under him and he collapsed. His bleary eyes would not focus properly; he saw everything as if through a misty haze. He pulled himself back up into a standing position, using the horse's saddle as a steadying prop. He hung grimly onto the pommel, refusing to relinquish his hold lest he fall again, and he bellowed loudly in the direction of the house.

"Hey! Hey, you in there!" A pause. "Answer me! I know y'kin hear me." Another pause. "Y'wanna have some fun? C'm on out here an' meet a *real* man!" He threw back his head and laughed. "C'm on, li'l gal! Bet'cha ain't never had one b'fore." Still no answer from the silent house. "Wal, if y'ain't gonna c'm out here, I'm gonna c'm in an' git'cha!"

Ace shoved the horse away from him and began to stagger toward the darkened house. He managed to attain the porch steps, but before he could reach out to grasp the railing, his boot struck the bottom stair at an awkward angle and he pitched forward. He lay there panting, sprawled half on the porch and half on the steps. Before he could muster the strength to rise, his senses failed him, having been pushed to their very limits, and his eyes closed in sleep. After a few minutes had passed, he began to snore.

Inside the house, Ace's drunken shouting had awakened Melissa. She tottered out of the bedroom and sought out Ann, rubbing her sleepy eyes.

"What's all the noise?" she mumbled. "Is Mommy home yet?"

73

"Shh!" whispered Ann, putting a finger to her lips. "There's someone out there."

"Why's it so dark in here? Why've you got the gun?"

Ann clapped her hand over the child's mouth. "Lissa, hush! I told you to be quiet!"

They waited, the minutes dragging endlessly by. Finally, Ann could stand it no longer and she sneaked up to the window, still grasping the rifle, drawing back the curtain slightly. She spied Ace's unmoving form on the porch. She wasn't sure whether he had knocked himself out or simply passed out, but she was grateful for this small salvation. She made sure the heavy iron bolt was securely fastened across the door and then she sat down again by the fire, drawing Melissa close to her. *Oh, Devvie, where are you?* she groaned.

Doc and Devorah were on their way home from the harvest dance and the horse was moving along at an even pace. Devorah was in a laughing, exhilarated state, having thoroughly enjoyed the evening. She snuggled up close to Doc's side and laid her head upon his shoulder. "Oh, Doc," she sighed happily. "I don't know when I've had such a good time."

"Well, my dear," he replied, "I'm pleased that you enjoyed it."

"Oh, I did! It was lovely."

"You were lovely, too. The most beautiful woman there." He smiled at her.

"Such flattery," she joshed. "There were other women just as beautiful."

"But none with your grace and carriage. Or temper, for that matter."

"How they shall talk!" she said in mock horror, placing her hand at her throat. They both laughed easily. "But you know, I'm so happy right now that I don't even care."

Doc turned the horse into the narrow lane leading to Devorah's farm. They were almost there.

"That's good," he said, patting her arm. "I want you to be happy, Devorah. I want only the best for you. It's been too long since I've seen you smile or heard you laugh like this."

"Yes, it has," she agreed. "Billy's death seems so far from me now. It's like it happened years ago. I have to get on with my life and make myself a new happiness."

"Of course. And you deserve . . ." At that moment, Doc spied Ace's horse standing in the middle of the yard. "What's this?" he frowned, becoming concerned. "Why, that looks like . . ."

"Ace's horse!" Devorah's heart leaped into her throat. "Oh no! Oh my goodness!"

In her mindless terror, she could not bring herself to wait until Doc had halted the slowly moving carriage. She leaped over the side and began running toward the house, noting that there seemed to be neither light nor movement from within. In her frantic haste to gain the porch steps, she stumbled over Ace's sleeping form and grabbed the railing to break her fall. He did not wake, and when Doc caught up with her, they both stood looking down at him. Doc could smell the reek of alcoholic fumes in the surrounding air.

"He's drunk," Doc said. "Passed out cold."

Devorah's fear was intense. "Oh, if he's hurt my child or Ann . . ."

"I don't think he even made it inside. I'm sure the door is still bolted."

Doc tugged on Ace's arms, attempting to clear a pathway for Devorah. She dashed up the steps, turned the doorknob, and found that the door would not open. She leaned against it, pounding on the heavy wood with her fist and rattling the knob.

"Ann, Ann!" she cried. "Are you in there? Open the door! Oh, dear God, please open the door!"

Devorah heard the sharp sound of approaching footsteps across the wooden flooring. The iron bolt was drawn back, the door swung open on its hinges, and Ann stood before her with an impatient look on her face.

"Well, it's about ti—" Ann never had a chance to finish. Devorah stepped over the threshold and flung herself into Ann's arms, clasping her tightly to her breast in a fierce embrace, covering her cheeks with kisses.

"Oh Ann! Oh my soul! Thank the Lord you're all right! He didn't lay a hand on you?"

Ann was flustered at Devorah's display of emotion. "Uh . . . no. No, he never got in."

"Where's Lissa?" She looked around anxiously for the child.

"In bed, sleeping."

Doc now moved to stand in the open doorway. "Are you sure you're all right, my dear?"

"Uh . . . yes. Uh . . . quite sure," Ann answered distractedly. She tried to remember the feel of Devorah's body, the soft breasts pressed against her own.

"Then I think I shall bid you both good night," he continued. "I'll take care of Ace."

Devorah followed him outside and watched as he bent down and hauled Ace to his feet. He swung Ace's flopping arm up over his shoulders, gripped him firmly about the waist, and dragged him to the carriage where he was bundled, still in a drunken stupor, into the back seat. Doc also retrieved Ace's horse and tied the reins to the rear of the carriage so that it could be led along with them. Then he turned to Devorah, taking both her hands into his own.

"I'm so sorry this happened," he said with deep concern in his voice. "I hope you will not let it ruin an otherwise lovely evening."

"I did have a good time, Doc, and I thank you again for taking me."

Doc leaned forward to tenderly kiss her cheek and she threw her arms around his neck to give him a warm embrace.

"Don't worry about Ace," he added. "I'll take him back to his place, and when I get done giving him a good talking to, he won't bother you again."

"Thank you, Doc. Good night."

Devorah waved to him as he left. She returned to the house, bolted the door behind her, and then turned to look at Ann, her body sagging with relief against the frame.

Ann eyed her curiously. "Devvie," she said, "were you really that worried?" Devorah nodded silently, biting her lower lip. "Do you care that much?"

"Why, of course I do." She put her arm around Ann's shoulders and they walked down the hallway to the bedrooms.

"How much, Devvie? How much do you care?"

"Why, a lot. Very much. Do you have to ask? Can't you tell? Of course I care."

"Enough to . . ." Ann allowed the question to hang suspended. She willed Devorah to feel her desire.

76

Devorah halted abruptly and dropped her arm. She briefly looked into Ann's searching eyes and just as quickly glanced down. "I don't know," she whispered, and she turned away.

Six

November gusted in under leaden skies. The clouds hung low and dark over the prairie and the chill of an early winter permeated the air. The wind whipped the bare branches of the trees and the last few remaining leaves clung fast with a tenacious hold. Several forgotten cornstalks withered under the touch of the first frost. The land lay shivering, stark, and bleak.

Devorah executed arrangements with a slaughterhouse in Kansas City to purchase a whole steer. The meat was cut up for her and delivered packed in ice to the farm, where it was stored in the smokehouse. They still had plenty of pork and bacon and a few hardy chickens, but now with this fresh supply of beef to complement all of their canned goods, they were secure in the knowledge that they would have enough food for the winter months.

During the course of the first week, Ann made six more trips to the edge of the forest with the horse and wagon for firewood. She had wanted to rest assured in her own mind that they would also have plenty of wood to burn. Devorah had tried to persuade her to cease her arduous task, saying that enough was enough, but Ann only stopped when the dimensions of their wood pile suited her.

Late one afternoon when Ann had finished stacking up the results of her sixth trip to the forest, she unhitched the horse, returned the axe to the tool shed, and entered the house through the back door, stamping her feet and rubbing her arms in order to get warm. She took off her heavy coat and moved to stand in front of the blazing fire. Her cheeks were red from the brisk outside air and her hands, although they had been covered with mittens, were fast becoming chapped and raw.

"Well, that's done," said Ann. "We've got enough wood for a while."

"I should think so," Devorah responded firmly. "You've been at it all week."

"Well, I had to make sure. I don't want us to want for anything."

"But it's so cold out there! You shouldn't be working so hard."

"Why not? It's a man's job, and I have to be the man around here. I have to fix everything like a man, don't I?"

Devorah smiled at her. "Only because I let you."

Ann was confused. "Don't you . . . don't you want me to be the man? Don't you want me to take care of you?"

"No, Ann. We take care of each other."

"But don't you want me to be strong for you? I can do most anything."

"I don't want your strength, Ann. I want your gentleness," Devorah said, attempting to explain. "I don't want you to change for me, I don't want you to be anything more than what you already are. I want your kindness, your softness, your . . ."

"My softness? Where, in bed?"

"You misunderstood," Devorah said quickly. "That's not what I meant."

"But that's what you *said*."

"Well, that's not what I meant." Devorah felt her cheeks turning crimson.

"You're blushing!" Ann exclaimed with satisfaction. "If that wasn't what you meant, then why did you say it?" No answer. Devorah stood tight-lipped, uneasily aware that she had slipped and Ann had caught her. "Devvie," Ann said, with her hands on her hips. "Do you want me to tell you what you meant?"

"No!" she answered, too quickly.

"Do you want me to tell you what you really want?"

Devorah refused to listen and she ran from the room. Ann stood looking after her and the glow of the firelight was reflected in her dark brown eyes.

One sunless morning, Ann and Devorah were both out in the barn milking the cows and feeding the horses, pigs, and chickens. The cows gave off an enormous amount of body heat and the two women pulled their three-legged stools closer to the animals' flanks to feel some of this radiated heat. They continued milking as the cows passively chewed their hay. Suddenly, they both became aware at the same instant of a plaintive cry, a piteous calling, and they glanced behind to see a large black tomcat with shining yellow eyes

79

enter the slightly open barn door. The cat appeared to be approximately two to three years old and his face was covered with old battle scars, but he sauntered in proudly, holding his ragged tail erect. As soon as he smelled the fresh milk, he went over to Devorah's side and lovingly rubbed his body along her skirts.

Ann reached down to stroke his head. "Well, Puss, are you looking for a new home?"

"I've never had a cat before," said Devorah. "I don't know about this one; he looks so beat up."

"He's probably traveled a long way. I'll bet he could use some milk and food and a warm place to sleep, eh, Puss?" Ann bent to scratch behind his ears; the cat purred loudly. "What do you say, Devvie? Shall we keep him?"

"I really don't think . . . ," Devorah started to protest.

"Aw, come on, Devvie," Ann urged her. "He'll take care of all the mice and rats. And Lissa will like him, I'm sure. I promise he won't be any trouble."

"Well . . . ," she hedged, still unsure.

"Good!" Ann pronounced, settling the matter. "Let's take him inside, feed him, and show him his new home."

They carried the full milk pails toward the house and the cat willingly ambled after them, stepping inside when they opened the door. Ann poured out a small saucer of fresh milk and set it on the floor. The cat eagerly lapped it all up and then moved to sit in front of the fireplace, where he began to lick his paws and wash his face. Melissa was delighted with him and petted his soft fur as he climbed into her lap, curled up tightly, and went to sleep, purring contentedly all the while.

"Look, Mommy," she said happily. "He likes me! Can we keep him, please, please?"

"All right, sweetheart," Devorah agreed, smiling. "I guess so."

"They say it's good luck if a black cat comes to you," Ann said. "He must have picked us out special."

"But what shall we call him? He must have a name."

"How about Tom?" Ann suggested.

"No, no," Devorah disagreed. "That's too common."

"How about Puss or just Kitty?" she ventured again.

"No, uh-uh. Don't like that, either."

It was Melissa who finally won out in the end with the name of Jody. Ann and Devorah looked at each other and smiled in deference to the child's wishes. It was a good name. Perhaps the cat would indeed bring them good luck.

Devorah took the wagon into Sutter's Ford for the purpose of picking up a couple of buckets of black pitch. Ann had requested this so that she could make sure all the openings and cracks in the wood around the outside windows were properly sealed. She had detected several drafts within the house, and she had gone from window to window, pointing out and defining all the potential problems to Devorah.

This was to be just a quick little excursion into town, and Devorah had assured Ann that she would not be long. However, she did have one nagging thing on her mind, and after she had purchased the pitch from the general store, she continued on down the street to Doc McClintock's office. She rapped smartly on the door, opened it, and stepped inside, where she beheld Doc seated at his desk directly in front of her. As soon as he recognized her, he set aside the large folder of papers on which he had been meticulously working and rose from his chair to greet her.

"Ah, Devorah, what a pleasure to see you," he said, beaming at her. She extended her hand to him, and he raised it to his lips. "What brings you into town on such a cold day as this?"

"Just a little errand for Ann. But to tell you the truth, Doc, I did want to speak to you privately, if I may."

"Of course, of course, my dear, anything. Sit right here." Doc pulled up another chair and held it for her. Devorah took off her hat and mittens and made herself comfortable. "Are you ready for winter?" he asked conversationally. "Do you think we'll be having an early one?"

"Oh, I'm just about ready. I'm waiting for the first snow any day now. It's been so cold lately," she shivered.

"That it has," he agreed, "but not as cold as it's going to get, you know. We can have some real blizzards way out here in the middle of nowhere."

"At least all the major chores are done. I plan to spend most of my time in front of the fire, catching up on all my sewing and knitting. Oh, I must knit a scarf and a new pair of mittens for Ann," she reminded herself.

"Devorah, you did say you wanted to talk to me. What's on your mind?" he asked kindly.

Devorah took a deep breath. "Doc," she began. "Did you . . . have that talk with Ace?"

Doc leaned backward in his chair and clasped his hands behind his head. "Ah, so that's what this is all about. Yes, I did talk with him. Most sternly, as a matter of fact. I assure you that he will not trouble you again."

"But why is he like this? Why is he always after me?"

"Well, possibly . . ."

"Has he always been like this?"

"Well, I imagine . . ."

"You've known him longer than I have, haven't you? Who was he? What did he use to be like?"

"Devorah," Doc chuckled, raising his hands to stop her torrent of words, "if you'll just hold on a minute, I could get a word in edgewise." He sat forward in his chair and thoughtfully rubbed his chin. "Perhaps the time has come for the story to be told," he said quietly.

Devorah was intrigued. He had captured her attention. "A story? What story?"

"Yes, there's much more here than meets the eye. At one time, Ace was actually married."

"Married?!" she echoed, disbelieving. "Oh, my goodness!"

"Ah, let's see now. . . . First, we shall have to go back long before that when Ace was only a boy. His mother had been the local madam—the one before Delilah. He never knew who his father was. It could have been any one of a number of men. When his mother discovered that she was pregnant, she didn't even want the child. She feared it would interfere with her business, so she tried to arrange for an abortion with the doctor who practiced here before me. He, of course, refused. She had the child after all, but she was never loving toward him. In fact, she often beat him severely.

"When he grew older, he immersed himself in his schooling and became quite a brilliant young man. He hired himself out for plantings and harvests and saved all of his money so that he could one day go to college in St. Louis. During his time there he met a lovely young lady named Victoria Harcourt, who came from a very socially prominent family of excellent background.

"After he graduated, they were married and moved back here to Kansas City. With part of her dowry, they bought a large farm just outside of the city and they enjoyed one prosperous year. The following year, Victoria became pregnant, but both she and the baby died in childbirth. Soon after, he learned from a friend that the child had not even been his. At first he had been devastated by Victoria's untimely death and he claimed that the child was responsible. But then when he found out about her secret infidelity, he grew to despise her memory.

"He sold their house and farm, not wanting to have anything more to do with either one and he bought a smaller place here in his old hometown. All of this happened . . . ohhh, some twenty years ago. He's about forty-five now. Since he began drinking steadily, he's gone straight downhill, and he is a far cry from the man he used to be. Believe it or not, Devorah, he was once tall and proud."

Devorah was stunned. She shook her head slowly, not knowing what to say.

"I might add," Doc continued, "that you very much resemble his wife Victoria, which could easily explain his interest in you. As for their child who died, I have a sneaking suspicion that his resentment of it could have in some way altered or warped his present feelings for children. He may have killed Bonnie Anders, but there is no way of knowing, and there is as yet not a shred of proof. This is why whatever memory of that night that Ann has locked up in her head is so important. One of these days, she may remember whom she saw, but by then it may be too late."

"God help us," Devorah whispered.

Ann passed most of the following afternoon in sealing all the wood around the outside windows with the black pitch. Using a flat narrow stick, she pushed the pitch deep into the visible cracks, spreading it smoothly and evenly over the wood. The air was cold, and the pitch dried quickly, forming a hard, impenetrable seal. She wiped her hands off on an old rag and then went into the tool shed to bring forth the wooden storm shutters. Working quickly, for her fingers were now becoming stiff with the cold, she attached the shutters securely to the window frames.

Her task completed, Ann went back into the house, shedding her coat and standing in front of the fireplace to get warm. After a short while, she walked down the hallway to the bathroom, where she scrubbed her hands and washed her face. As she reached to the side of the basin for a towel, she tripped over a small projection underneath the rug on the floor. Curious, she knelt and rolled back the rug, partially exposing a trap door that had been set into the wooden flooring. She had tripped over the handle of this door.

"Devvie!" she called, wiping her hands with the towel. "Devvie, come in here!" Presently Devorah came and stood in the open doorway. Ann pointed to the trap door. "What is this?"

"Oh that?" Devorah answered. "Didn't you know that was there?"

"No. Where does it go?"

"Down under the house. It's a storm cellar."

"Is anything down there?"

"Some crates and barrels. I keep a few things stored."

Ann's face brightened at the prospect of exploring. "Could I see?"

"Well . . . all right."

Together they rolled the rug all the way back, fully exposing the long narrow door. Devorah grasped the handle and tugged upward. The hinges moved slowly, creakingly. When the door was open, Ann could see a flight of stairs leading downward into darkness. Devorah held the lamp in front of her and descended the steps first, motioning to Ann to follow. When they reached the bottom, Ann found herself standing on a hard-packed dirt floor.

The shelter was of small but adequate size and the surrounding space was crammed with several waist-high barrels which were cloth-lined with tightly fitting lids. Inside the barrels were extra supplies of sugar, flour, salt, coffee, and various grains. Upon a low dirt shelf covered with burlap were arranged a few canned goods and several sacks of onions and potatoes. Slabs of bacon, assorted sausages, and beef jerky hung suspended on lengths of twine from the low ceiling rafters.

Ann looked around in amazement. "What are you going to do with all this stuff?"

"Nothing at the moment. These are all emergency supplies in case anything happens."

Ann spied two large wooden crates set next to each other on the floor. The tops of the crates were covered with burlap, and the word France had been stamped in large block letters on the front and sides. She moved over to one of the crates and gently removed the burlap covering.

"What's in these?" Ann asked, intensely curious.

"Just some things. Some very special things."

"Oh, could I see? Please?"

Devorah lifted the lid of the first crate, removed the cloth wrappings, and showed Ann a complete place setting for eight people of genuine Haviland china. The china was white and pure, unchipped, unmarked. She opened the second crate and brought out twelve exquisitely perfect hand-blown glass goblets. Also in the second crate were several bowls and other assorted glassware. Ann was in awe as she held one of the goblets up to the light of the lamp.

"Devvie, these are just beautiful," she said in a hushed whisper. "Is all this really from France?" Devorah nodded. "But why do you keep it down here where no one can see? Why don't you use it?"

"I keep it here because I know it'll be safe. When Billy and I were first married, this was our wedding gift from my parents. If we ever had a fire here or a twister, I wouldn't want anything to happen to them. I can always make them mine again even if I lose everything else."

"And this," Ann said, touching two small drawstring leather pouches which lay in the crate next to the goblets, almost at the bottom. "What's this?"

"Gold dust and nuggets—almost two pounds. It's my emergency fund. I've only had to use it once since Billy's death. It's still worth quite a bit."

"What did you have to use it for?"

"His funeral. I hope to God I shall never have to do that again for anyone else."

Devorah was silent as she rearranged the contents of the crates and closed the lids. Together, they ascended the stairs into the fading light of day.

On Thanksgiving Day, Ann took the rifle and went out to hunt for a wild turkey, insisting to Devorah that the holiday would not be truly complete without a bird on the table. While she was gone, Devorah passed the afternoon by baking bread loaves and two fresh pumpkin pies. Melissa assisted her as she worked, and later on she gave the child the job of setting the table.

"Is this a special day, Mommy?" Melissa asked eagerly, laying out the silverware.

"Yes, it is, honey," said Devorah.

"Why's that?" she questioned seriously.

"Well, it's just a time to be thankful for all the good things you have."

"Like my dolly an' my kitty?"

Devorah smiled. "Yes, sweetheart." She moved to stand beside the child, reaching over her shoulder to pick up a fork and move it to the opposite side of the plate. "The fork goes here, Lissa, not there, and the spoon goes over here."

The back door opened, and Ann strode triumphantly into the kitchen, holding up by the legs a large dead turkey. The bird hung upside down in her grasp, and its huge feathered wings fell outward away from its plump body.

"Well, how's this?" Ann said, grinning widely.

Devorah was impressed with Ann's effort. "Oh my! It's so big."

"I expect it's mostly feathers, but it'll do fine. I'll take it outside and clean it for you." She set down the rifle, picked up a small hatchet, and was gone again.

Later, while the bird was roasting in the oven, Ann and Devorah stood together at the kitchen sink, peeling onions and potatoes. Melissa was now reading her story book by the fire and the cat was contentedly curled up on her lap.

"This is our first Thanksgiving together," Ann said to Devorah. "Are you happy?"

"Yes, very," she replied. "The year has gone well. But Ann, surely you must miss being with your family."

"Oh, not so much any more. I guess they're all right, whatever they're doing. They don't need to worry about me," she ended firmly.

"But don't you ever want to go back? To see them again?"

"No. I can't, Devvie," she said softly. "It's not possible. Besides, I've made a new life for myself here with you."

"Well, you've come a long way since spring. You've learned a lot of things. But maybe some day you'll want to . . . to move on." Devorah was secretly anxious. She bit her lip and almost forgot to breathe, waiting for a response. *Please don't say you'll leave,* she thought. *I couldn't bear it.*

"Devvie, I don't want to leave. I'll stay here as long as you want me to. We've come a long way together, but we've still got a lot farther to go."

"What do you mean?"

"Well, you have to be taught, too, just like Lissa."

Devorah looked at her, frowning. "Taught what?"

"Ohh . . . things," Ann said vaguely with a slight shrug. "How to smile, how to share, how to love."

"But I do know how to love. What are you talking about?"

"No, you only think you know. You haven't even begun to feel all the love it's possible to feel. You keep yourself so tightly locked up inside, and you won't let me reach you." Ann gently placed her hands on Devorah's shoulders and turned her around so that they were face to face. "Devvie, don't you feel? Don't you ever want? Can you honestly tell me that you lie in that bed at night and you don't *want?*"

"I . . ." Devorah trembled under the intensity of Ann's penetrating gaze. It was too much for her, and she had to look away. "Yes . . . it's true. I *do* want. Oh, sometimes *how much* I want!" She felt the hot tears come unbidden, and she tightly shut her eyes.

"It's been too long for you, hasn't it?" Ann said tenderly. She reached out a hand to touch Devorah's soft cheek, caressed it hesitantly, fearfully. "Then please let me—"

"No. Oh, no." Devorah shook her head blindly and backed away from those comforting arms.

December swirled in one night on dancing flakes of granular snow. The ground was dusted with a light powdery covering and when the wind blew, the snow skittered before it in sweeping waves. Most of the small animals that had abounded during the summer months were now nowhere to be seen, hibernating safely in their underground burrows. Only a few hardy birds remained to peck at the fast-freezing ground.

Ann, Devorah, and Melissa all bundled into the wagon for their main monthly supply trip into Sutter's Ford, huddling as close as they could to each other for warmth during the windy ride. Ann had brought along the remaining money that she still had from Devorah's gift to her after the harvest. Both women were thinking of buying each other Christmas presents, although neither one gave voice to her anticipation. When they arrived in town, Devorah took Melissa's hand and went in one direction while Ann slipped off by herself.

Ann moved slowly down the sidewalks, peering into the front windows of each store and trying to decide which one would be most likely to have what she was seeking. She stopped in front of one window display that featured various imported goods, considered this a moment, and then entered the store. She walked up to the clerk at the counter and waited patiently until he had finished jotting down some figures in a large black record book.

"May I help you, ma'am?" he said, looking up at her.

"Uh . . . yes. Do you have any fancy hand-milled soap?" she asked timidly.

"Why, yes we do. One moment." He turned to the tall shelves behind him, selected a small box, and set it on top of the counter. He opened it and held out a bar of soap for Ann to inspect. "These come from France—the finest available."

Ann held the soap to her nose and breathed deeply of its delicately perfumed scent. *From France,* she thought. *Devvie loves things from France. I'll bet it's expensive, but I don't care. She should have something good and fine.*

"Yes, this is perfect," she told the clerk. "I want two bars."

Ann exited the store with the package tucked securely under her arm, feeling excited and pleased with herself. *Wait 'til Devvie sees this,* she thought, smiling. *I didn't forget what she said about wanting it. But she should have something else, too. What else? What else could I get her?* She resumed her close scrutiny of the store windows and then she found herself standing in front of the same store where she had purchased her new boots. On display in the window was a shiny new pair of women's high-button black shoes. Ann drew a sharp breath and stared. *Oh, how fine they are,* she thought, *how fancy-fine! Devvie should have them. She could wear them to Meeting.* She entered the store, bolder this time, and sought out the clerk.

"I want to see that pair of black shoes you have in the window. I want to try them on."

A moment later, she stood looking down at her feet, which were clad in the new shiny shoes. She turned this way and that, walked up the aisle, walked down. The shoes were well made, and they felt good on her feet. She knew Devorah wore the same size that she did, for she had once borrowed an old pair of Devorah's farm boots until she had been able to purchase a pair of her own. She took off the shoes and ran her hand over the soft leather, inwardly admiring the intricate stitching.

"These shoes are just right," she told the clerk. "I'll take them."

There was a new spring to her step as she walked along the sidewalk. She was elated and looked forward to giving her gifts. Not wanting to forget Melissa, she stopped at another place and bought the child a picture story book, a small stuffed animal, and a pound of penny candies with the last of her money.

In the meantime, Devorah and Melissa were having just as much fun and enjoyment on their shopping tour. Devorah found it hard to contain the child, for she was always darting ahead of her to examine different displays of merchandise, and her little high-pitched voice chattered incessantly.

"Look, Mommy! Look at this."

"Lissa, honey, stay close to me." Devorah tried to be stern.

"An' look at this. Isn't it pretty?"

"Lissa, don't touch!" The child was off again. "Don't go too far. Come back here!" Devorah shook her head and had to smile.

They entered one shop which specialized in women's wear and underclothes. Devorah searched for a suitable petticoat for Ann, knowing that she herself would prefer something with frills and laces, but also realizing that Ann would want something more tailored and simple. *I've only just gotten her back into a dress,* she thought. *I can't push her too far or she'll balk just like a mule. I know I'll never get her out of those boots and yet she should have something good and decent to wear under that dress I made her, something of her own. Hmmm . . . ah, here, this looks good.* She selected a slim white petticoat and held it up against her waist to judge the size. It looked right; it was becoming. Devorah bought it.

Next they went into another store in search of more material. Devorah intended to make both a new dress and a long warm nightgown for Melissa for Christmas. *I can never buy her enough clothes,* she thought. *I want her to have everything.* She was most content when she spent her leisure time in sewing or knitting for someone she loved. A brief pain flashed into her mind as she recalled all the things she had made for Billy. His handsome laughing face seemed to be growing ever more distant now, fading farther away.

Devorah carefully chose the materials for Melissa's new clothes and then together they went over to the racks of brightly colored yarn. She explained to the child that she was going to knit a new scarf and mittens for Ann and she wanted to know if there was any particular color that the child liked best.

"How about this one, Mommy?" she said, pointing to a deep rich brown.

Devorah nodded approvingly. "Very good, Lissa. That's a lovely color. I'll give her the scarf and when I make the mittens, that will be your present to her, all right? How does that sound?"

"Fine, Mommy. I need to give her something, too," she said solemnly.

Devorah paid for all her purchases and allowed Melissa to carry the bag of yarn. They left the shop, and as they were standing out on the sidewalk Devorah saw Ann striding toward them. She waited until Ann stood beside her before she spoke.

"What did you get?" she asked Ann.

"Oh, nothing," Ann said lightly. She feigned disinterest in the packages she was carrying. "What did *you* get?"

"Not much." Devorah's armload belied her words. They both stood eyeing each other's purchases and then they burst into giggles. "Christmas is coming," said Devorah, winking at Ann.

"I know. I can tell. You've got that gleam in your eyes. Probably means you're up to no good."

"Heaven forbid!" she exclaimed in mock horror.

"Come on, let's go get the rest of the supplies, and then let's go home." Ann took her by the elbow and steered her toward the wagon.

Over the ensuing days, the wind blew harder still out of the northern skies, but there had been as yet no actual accumulation of snow on the ground. The animals in the barn huddled close to each other, seeking warmth and spending most of their time in quiet sleep. On days when the air wasn't too nippy, Ann turned the horses and the cows loose in the barren fields for some exercise, but she always brought them back before the afternoons grew too late and gave way to falling temperatures. She now performed the majority of the outside chores, enjoying the crisp air, and she urged Devorah to stay inside so as not to fall ill.

"Oh, piffle!" Devorah chided her. "What do you think I did all last winter? Stay inside and toast my toes? I was out there every day, just like you are."

"But things are different now, Devvie. I'm doing it for you. There's not a whole lot to be done out there anyway, so you might as well stay in."

Devorah sighed and rolled her eyes upward. "I'm not exactly a weak woman. I don't need to be pampered. You treat me as if I were about to give birth."

"Well, it's about time somebody pampered you. Lord knows, you won't do it for yourself." Ann put on her heavy coat.

"Where are you going now?" Devorah inquired. "I thought you were all through."

"I found some rope in the barn this morning. I've got to go set it up between the porch steps and the barn door."

"What for?"

"It's a lifeline. You've got to have it up before the first snowfall. If we have a really bad blizzard, you could go out there and not find your way back except for the rope."

"I never thought of that before."

"Well, I have. I've seen too many bad ones—snow so thick you can't see, can't hear, can't breathe. It doesn't take much to fall in a drift and die out there. I wouldn't want anything to happen to any of us, especially to you."

"Well, what about you? Don't you think I worry about you, too?"

"Sure, Devvie," she agreed easily, "but you don't feel as much for me as I do for you. I got enough worrying to do for both of us."

"Oh . . . go, then." Devorah waved her away. *But you're wrong,* she said to herself intensely. *I do feel for you, more than you ever realize, but I can't seem to bring myself to tell you just yet. I don't know how to tell you because I don't even know myself.*

One week flew by and was swiftly followed by another. The holiday was approaching quickly, and in the evenings after dinner was over and the dishes were done, Devorah sat in front of the fire, busily stitching the finishing touches onto Melissa's nightgown. She had already completed working on the child's new dress, which now hung in the bedroom closet, waiting to be wrapped. She sat in a comfortable position in the rocking chair with her legs crossed and the material draped over her lap. The needle moved quietly in and out, catching the glinting firelight.

On the round hearth rug in front of her sat Ann and Melissa. Ann was engaged in telling the child stories of Christmas past, of how it used to be when she was just Melissa's age. The child listened enrapt, her upturned face a mask of delight, occasionally reaching out to stroke the soft fur of the cat, who stretched and purred, basking by the fire.

". . . and then we'd all have to go to bed early, otherwise Santa Claus wouldn't come. But first, we'd be sure to hang up a stocking over the fireplace. Then in the morning when we woke up, we'd all run down the stairs and open our presents. All kinds of good things—oranges and candy and clothes and lots and lots of toys."

"Did you always get everything you asked for?" Melissa wanted to know.

"Oh, most everything. Sometimes things I didn't expect."

"Mommy, did Santa bring you things, too?" she asked, turning to face Devorah.

"Yes, honey, lots of things." Her needle continued to move.

"But you have to be a good girl," Ann admonished. "You have to eat all your carrots even if you don't like them, and you have to say your prayers every night."

"I am so a good girl," she defended herself. "Aren't I, Mommy?" She looked up at Devorah for support.

"Of course you are, sweetheart, but it wouldn't hurt to eat your carrots."

"I think it's time for bed now, Lissa," Ann reminded her. "Come on, I'll tuck you in."

The child kissed her mother good night and trotted off down the hallway. Ann helped her unbutton her dress and then stood by while she slipped into her nightgown, noting that the old gown was worn and had been patched at the elbows. Melissa knelt on the hard wooden flooring, clasped her small fingers together, and began to mumble her prayers. Ann listened silently. Suddenly she became aware of the light, subtle fragrance of Devorah's perfume lingering in the surrounding air. She inhaled deeply of the aroma and closed her eyes. *Oh, Devvie,* she sighed. *You always smell so good. I want to burrow my head in between your breasts and stay there forever, not moving, just holding you and touching you. I wonder if you feel as soft as the breath of this perfume on the air. I want to caress you, to slide my fingers up . . .*

"Hey! Aren't you going to come kiss me good night?" Melissa had climbed into the bed and lay with the quilt pulled up around her face.

Ann was jolted out of her blissful reverie. "Huh? Oh!" She quickly leaned to kiss the child on the forehead, extinguished the bedside lamp, and left the room, closing the door quietly behind her. She slumped unsteadily against the doorframe, breathing deeply, willing control. *Oh Lord, Devvie, what you do to me,* she groaned. *You make it hard to . . . hard not to . . .* She shook her head and pressed her lips tightly together.

The first snowfall stole silently in on the wings of night. The wet heavy flakes descended steadily without letup. By dawn, the ground was buried inches deep under a solid blanket of white. The sun peeked hazily out from a scudding gray mantle, then shone brighter as the clouds lifted and parted and the blue sky appeared.

After a hurried breakfast that morning Ann and Melissa donned their woolen underthings and their coats and boots, scarves and mittens, and went outside to play. The child was enchanted by the pure white fairyland and she wanted Ann to help her build a snowman.

"Why don't you come with us, Devvie?" Ann urged her as she stood by the front door, one hand on the knob. "It'll be fun. Come on, you need to get out."

"No, no," she demurred. "You go on. I have some things I have to do."

"They'll wait. Come on," she beckoned, insistent.

"No, they won't. Now go." Devorah began to clear the dishes off the table.

"I could pick you up and carry you out there and throw you in a drift," Ann threatened.

"Don't even consider it," she warned. "Will you please go?"

Melissa grabbed Ann's hand and dragged her out the door. Devorah quickly rinsed the dishes and set them up to dry. Then she went into her bedroom and retrieved the bag of brown yarn that she had kept hidden in a drawer. She selected two knitting needles from her sewing basket, seated herself by the fire, and began to make Ann's scarf. The needles clicked together as she hummed softly to herself.

In the front yard, Ann and Melissa rolled through the deep snow, laughing and shrieking and tossing snowballs at each other. They set up forts and battle lines and lobbed ammunition back and forth. When they tired of this sport, they started to make a snowman, grunting and pushing and shoving to get the wet snow rolled up into firmly packed balls. The snowman turned out to be three-tiered and slightly lopsided, but they were highly pleased with their efforts. Ann shoved two thin sticks into the sides for the arms and Melissa held out a handful of coal which Ann proceeded to use for the eyes and mouth and buttons down the front. A carrot formed the nose and completed their work of art.

"That wore me out, Lissa," Ann said, wiping her brow. "Let's go inside for a bit and rest up. These mittens are wet and my hands are getting cold."

Melissa burst into the house ahead of Ann and ran up to her mother, chattering excitedly. At the noise of their arrival, Devorah had jumped quickly up from her chair, anxious lest Ann should see what she was knitting. She tried frantically to hide the evidence, stuffing yarn and needles back into the bag. She had just time enough to whip the bag behind her back, and she stood there smiling crookedly with both hands out of sight.

"Devvie, what are you doing?"

"Notheeeng."

"What've you got there?" Ann reached behind her, but Devorah expertly evaded her grasp.

"Christ-mas is com-ing, the goose is get-ting fat," she sang in a lilting sing-song voice.

"Whaaat? What's the matter with you?"

"Notheeeng."

"You're daft!" Ann took Melissa by the hand and led her off down the hall to change into dry clothes.

Only a few days remained before Christmas. One afternoon, Ann decided it was time to decorate the tree, and she took from the tool shed the axe and a coiled length of rope.

"Come on, Lissa, let's go get ourselves a tree," she called to the child, putting on her coat and scarf.

"Oh goody!" Melissa cried, jumping up. "Mommy, can I go?"

"Yes dear, but be careful," Devorah said.

After they left, Devorah tried to do some additional work on knitting Ann's new mittens. The brown scarf had already been finished several days ago, and in just another few more days' time the mittens would also be completed. She had tried to work on these projects during the times when Ann was out of the house, and so far she had been able to keep her secret well hidden.

Ann and Melissa tramped off through the snow toward the edge of the forest. It took quite a while to get there, for the snow was still pretty deep, and the going was tiring to the leg muscles. The child didn't seem to mind this at all since she was greatly keyed up. Ann enjoyed doing things with her and making her feel that she was being helpful.

They walked along the outer perimeter of the forest, looking for a suitable evergreen. Most of the trees they saw were either too tall or too short, but finally they found one that was just right, appearing to be roughly six feet in height. Ann motioned to the child to stay well back so that she would be clear of the swing of the axe. With long, practiced strokes she made short work of cutting down the tree. Melissa handed her the rope, and it was tied securely around the trunk. Ann threw the rope over her shoulder, wrapped it twice around her wrist, and grasping the axe in the other hand, headed homeward, dragging the tree along behind her through the snow.

Ann stood the tree upright on the front porch, vigorously shaking all the snow off of the branches. She let it lean up against the side of the house while she went out to the barn in search of two small flat pieces of wood. She gave the wood to the child to carry and then she opened the door and dragged in the tree.

"Here we are," she called to Devorah. "One tree, made to order."

"Oh, that looks good. It's just perfect."

"Come over here and hold it while I set it up."

Devorah held the tree steady while Ann took a hammer and nails and fastened the two pieces of wood to the base, one on either side of the trunk, forming an X-shaped stand. They placed it in one corner of the living room, away from the fireplace, and stood back, admiring its shape and form.

"Do we get to put the decorations on now?" asked Melissa.

"Not just yet, honey," Ann said. "Wait 'til after dinner. We have to let the tree dry off a bit first."

Later on that evening, Devorah rummaged deep in her bedroom closet and brought forth several small crates of ornaments. An old red woolen blanket was draped around the base of the tree, thus hiding the crude stand. Ann and Melissa sat on the floor, cutting out colored pieces of paper and pasting them together to form a circular linked chain. Devorah made batches of popcorn in a big pot over the open fire. Needles and thread were taken out of the sewing box, and they all sat huddled together making long strings of popcorn and bright red cranberries, which were draped over the branches of the tree along with the colorful paper chain. Devorah opened the crates of ornaments and handed out bunches of red and green ribbons which were tied onto the ends of the branches.

Ann stood back to admire their work. "This tree is really looking good," she commented.

"Yes, but we're not quite done yet," said Devorah. "I've got some special things here." She reached into another crate and withdrew four shining hand-blown glass ornaments. "Look at this," she said, holding two of them up so that they reflected the firelight.

Ann reached out to take one and held it gently. "Gosh, Devvie, they're beautiful. Where did you get them?"

"Billy gave them to me for our very first Christmas." Devorah had a sweet, sad smile on her face as she lovingly hung each glass ball on the tree. "Look, there's more," she added, reaching down into another crate. She showed Ann half a dozen assorted wooden ornaments in the shapes of stars, bells, and wreaths. "He made these; he carved them for me."

"He did good work," Ann complimented. "I wish I could do half as good a job as he did."

"He was always making things. His hands were never still. Oftentimes he'd be out here late at night, working on something, and he'd keep on working until he got it right."

The wooden ornaments were also hung on the tree, and then Devorah opened the last crate and lifted out a shiny tinfoil star that

96

had been hand-folded and had five tapering points. She stood on tiptoe to place the star at the very top of the tree. With this last addition the decoration was complete.

"How do you like our tree, Lissa?" Ann said. No answer came. "Lissa?" she questioned, turning around in search of the child. Melissa lay fast asleep on the rug in front of the fire.

"I guess I'd better put her to bed," Devorah stated. "All this excitement knocked her out." She bent over and gently scooped the sleeping child up into her arms and left the room.

She returned shortly, bearing yet another crate which she set on the floor in front of Ann. *More?* Ann thought, puzzled. *That tree can't hold much more.*

"What's this, Devvie?" she asked.

Devorah was silent, her face expressionless as she pulled back the lid of the crate and carefully unwrapped a dozen small bundles. They were delicately carved wooden figurines of animals, shepherds with staffs, kneeling Wise Men, a hooded Mary, a somber Joseph, and the little Baby Jesus complete with tiny cradle. A three-sided, slant-roofed, handmade wooden stable completed the entire set. Devorah arranged all the pieces on the blanket around one corner of the tree and sat back on her heels, staring blankly, lost in thought. Ann had watched all of her motions and now moved to sit beside her on the floor.

"He made that for you, too, didn't he?" she said quietly. Devorah nodded and bit her lip, not wanting to turn her head lest Ann should see the tears welling up in her eyes. "It really is beautiful. I wish I had known him, too."

"Sometimes I go for weeks without thinking about him, and then all of a sudden it just hits me." She swallowed, sniffling once. "All I can see is his face, and I hear his voice, how he used to talk to me, how he used to laugh." She sniffed again; the tears ran freely down her cheeks. "And how he used to . . . to hold me . . . and touch me . . . and I think . . . that I'll never see him again . . . and I just . . . I can't . . ." She half-lifted one arm and then let it flop helplessly back into her lap.

Ann leaned closer and tenderly put one arm around Devorah's shaking shoulders. "I know, Devvie, I know," she murmured comfortingly.

"Oh, God help me, I want him . . . I want him . . . I *want him!*" she moaned in anguish, stabbing her clenched fist again and again into her thigh. Sobbing, she let herself lean sideways and lay with her head resting upon Ann's shoulder.

Oh Devvie, Ann grieved with her. *Don't . . . don't . . . it hurts me, too. How can I make you forget? How can I make you see that I'm here to take his place? How can I make you take all that I've got to give?*

Seven

Ann was just finishing up her morning chores when she heard the jingling sound of approaching harness bells. She came out of the barn to find Doc McClintock easing his horse to a stop in the front yard. In back of his carriage, tied by heavy ropes to the carriage frame, was a rickety old buckboard wagon.

"Hi, Doc. How've you been?" Ann said, stroking the horse's velvety nose.

"Fine, my dear," he answered, stepping down to the ground. "Busy, too. Seems like everyone's catching a bug these days. I've been paying a lot of calls and drowning in paperwork." He shook his head in mock exasperation.

Ann pointed to the old wagon. "What have you got there?" she asked curiously.

Doc smiled. "Ah, that's a little surprise for you. Let's go take a look at it, shall we?"

They walked to the rear of the carriage and stood looking at the wagon. It was in quite a state of disrepair, with spokes missing from the wheels and open gaps in the sides where rotted wood had broken off and fallen away. It appeared forlorn and in need of someone's loving care.

"I bought it cheap, but you can have it if you want to fix it up," Doc gestured freely.

Ann's eyes shone with fervor as she gazed at the old wreck. "Honest? You really mean it?"

"Well, sure. You replace those spokes there, add some good wood to the sides, give it a fresh coat of paint, and it'll be as good as new. And it'll be all yours, too."

"I don't know how to thank you, Doc." Ann could hardly believe her good fortune. She finally had something that she could call her own.

"Oh, posh, it was nothing," he said, dismissing the gift with a wave of his hand. "I thought you might like something to work on, something to do with your hands. Now, why don't we haul it into the barn where it'll be out of the weather?"

They detached the ropes from the underside of the carriage and tugged and pulled until the wagon was safely inside a far corner of the barn. The barn was large and roomy, and there was plenty of space for Ann to maneuver around the wagon while she worked on it. Doc left her standing there, wondering where to begin, and he went into the house to see Devorah.

"Doc! What a pleasure to see you!" she exclaimed as he stepped through the door. She strode up to him and kissed his cheek, then smiled fondly at him. "It's been too long."

"That it has, Devorah," he agreed, patting her hand. "My duties at the office have made me neglectful of you."

"What brings you out here . . . besides me?"

"I came to give Ann an old buckboard that I picked up cheaply. I told her she could have it if she were willing to fix it up. We put it in the barn, and she's out there now."

"How nice of you, Doc! Thank you!" she said sincerely.

"I also came to request the pleasure of your company on my trip into Kansas City tomorrow morning. I thought perhaps you'd like to get out, see the city, maybe do some shopping."

Devorah's eyes lit up with anticipation. "Oh, I'd love to! I truly would. It'd be so much fun."

"Very well, then I shall pick you up at nine o'clock. Good day, my dear."

Devorah did not want him to leave. "Can't you stay for a little while? Have some coffee?"

"I wish I could, but I have appointments to keep. I'll be back soon enough, and we'll have all day together tomorrow." Doc bowed to her, lifting her hand to his lips, and then he left.

That evening as they sat at the dinner table, Ann could hardly contain her excitement. She described to Devorah in glowing terms how she intended to repair the old wagon, saying that she had already pulled off some of the rotted wood. Devorah listened patiently as Ann rambled on, smiling and nodding her head politely at intervals.

"And I could work on it every day, at least until it gets too cold to be out there," she bubbled. "And then surely by spring I'll have it done, and it'll look just great."

"Ann, your meat is getting cold. Eat."

"But, Devvie, I'm so excited!" she went on eagerly. "Don't you see what this means to me? It's something that'll be mine, something I've done with my own two hands."

"All right, Ann. I'm happy for you. Now please eat," Devorah urged her.

Ann took a few small bites of food and chewed thoughtfully, then looked up across the table again. "That sure was nice of Doc, you know. Devvie, do you think I should give him something, too? Maybe make something for him?"

"Well . . . if you want."

"How about . . . um . . ." Ann racked her brain, frowning deeply. "Ah, I've got it! How about a new sign for his office? I could take a piece of wood and carve his name on it. Do you think he'd like that?"

Devorah nodded, considering it. "Yes, I think that's a nice idea."

"Good. That's what I'll do then. I could start on it tomorrow and have it finished in a day or so. It wouldn't take long—just a simple sign. And I could . . ."

"Ann," interrupted Devorah. "Ann, listen to me. There's something I must tell you."

"Huh? What?" Ann looked at her, expectant. "What is it?"

"Um . . . Doc and I . . ." She didn't quite know how to say it, stopped, began again. "He asked me . . . we're going to Kansas City tomorrow." She toyed with her fork.

"To Kansas City?" Ann repeated blankly. "What for?"

Devorah shrugged. "Ohhh, to do some shopping. To have some fun."

"How long will you be gone?" Ann asked, her voice hardening.

"Probably the whole day. I expect we'll have dinner there. It could be quite late before we get back." She had detected the tenseness in Ann's words. *Please don't get angry*, she worried. *Don't make a scene.*

"I see." Ann said slowly. "It was just a bribe, wasn't it? He gave me that wagon so he could get you in return. 'Let's keep Ann busy so we can go off together,' huh?" Her eyes were cold, flinty.

"Oh, Ann, no," Devorah replied, her heart sinking. She placed her hand gently upon Ann's clenched fist. "That's not the way it was at all. He only wanted to . . ."

"Why don't you go ahead and marry him, Devvie, if that's what you really want." Ann dropped her fork with a loud clatter onto her plate, abruptly pushed back her chair, and stormed angrily away from the table.

The sun was out, bright and shining in a cloudless blue sky. The snow was packed down firmly on the well-traveled road to Kansas City, and Doc's carriage clipped along at an even pace. Devorah sat next to him, wrapped snugly in her long black woolen cape.

"Oh, Doc," she said happily. "What a lovely morning!"

"Yes, it is, my dear," he agreed.

"I'm so glad you asked me to come with you. We'll have such a good time. All the stores, all the people! Oh, I can hardly wait!"

Doc chuckled. "Well, Devorah, I'm pleased that you accepted. I certainly didn't want to go alone." He smiled affectionately at her, his eyes twinkling, his white hair ruffling in the passing breeze. "Are you ready for Christmas?" he asked her.

Devorah nodded vigorously. "Oh, yes! We put up a tree the other day. Ann and Lissa worked so hard on it, making strings of popcorn and cranberries. I made a new dress and nightgown for Lissa. And I finally finished the scarf and mittens for Ann—she doesn't even know about it," she ended with a giggle, pleased with herself.

"I see she's quite taken with the wagon."

With a slight pang of guilt, Devorah suddenly remembered Ann's resentment. "Oh . . . yes."

"That's good. Devorah, I want this to be one of the happiest Christmases you've ever had," he told her sincerely, with deep feeling. "I want everything to be just right for you."

"I hope it will be, too, Doc. I so desperately want us all to be happy."

"Are you warm enough, my dear?" he questioned solicitously. "There's another blanket on the back seat if you need it."

"No, I'm fine, Doc." She snuggled closer to him and linked her arm through his, resting her head upon his strong shoulder. She breathed in the scent of his cologne; she was happy, content. "Listen to the harness bells—how merry they sound."

They rode on, arriving in the city before noon. They stopped at a little café for a quick lunch and then passed the rest of the afternoon in walking up and down the city blocks, pressing through the crowds of milling people, listening to groups of carolers, examining all the artful window displays. They took their time, not wanting to miss anything, and the hours rolled swiftly by.

Doc pulled Devorah off the sidewalk into a fancy millinery shop. Devorah's eyes went wide as she viewed the many different varieties of women's hats, all displayed on little pedestals both in the front window and all around the store. She reached out to touch one hat and then drew back her hand with a sharp intake of breath as she noted the price tag that dangled from the lacy brim. Doc urged her to select something she liked, telling her that cost was of no consequence.

"Oh, but, Doc, I just couldn't," she protested weakly. "They're all too expensive."

"Nonsense," he dismissed her. "This is a fancy store. Go on, Devorah, I insist. It's my gift to you." She stood there, hesitant still. "Come on, now. How about this one?" he suggested, pointing to the hat nearest him. "Or maybe this one?" he said, choosing another.

Devorah finally gave in to his wishes and picked out a hat of lovely soft blue. It was her favorite color, and it matched her eyes. The clerk offered to wrap it for her, but she declined, saying that she preferred to wear it right then.

"Doc, you're too good to me," she said, kissing his cheek.

"Tut, tut, my dear. It looks perfect on you. Come, one more stop we must make, and then we shall go to dinner."

They walked farther on down the street. Then they turned a corner, and Doc led her into a large apothecary store. He explained that he did most of his business here, often stopping in to pick up additional drug supplies or to order them sent to his office. While he was occupied with the clerk in a discussion of the advantages of the latest surgical implements, Devorah moved quietly along the rows of display counters, searching for something suitable that she could give him. *I don't know anything about this stuff*, she thought. *I couldn't even begin to guess what he might need or what he might already have.* She paused in front of a shelf that held several brand new black medical bags, and a sly smile came to her face. *Oh, he could use this!* she realized excitedly. *His other one is so old and worn. I'll bet he's never given thought to replacing it.* She surreptitiously caught the attention of a second clerk, glancing over her shoulder to make sure that Doc had not seen her, and quickly paid for the bag, tucking the package out of sight under her arm. As they left the store, Doc seemed to not even notice. They walked back up the street, arm in arm.

"Are you ready to eat yet, Devorah?" he asked her. "I'm getting pretty famished."

"Oh, yes, we've done so much walking. I need to get off my feet and rest."

"What?!" he exclaimed in amazement. "The fast pace of the city wearing you out?"

Doc steered her into a corner restaurant that didn't appear to be much from the outside, but as soon as they stepped through the door Devorah could immediately tell that it was an elegant place. Rich brocades and tapestries hung from the walls, and thick rugs carpeted the floor. The tables were small, set widely apart, and flickering candles burned at each one. Doc seated her in an out-of-the-way corner; he took her cape and hat and placed them upon the chair next to him.

Devorah looked around. "My, this is impressive."

"Do you think so? I dine here often when I come into the city. It's a nice quiet place, away from all the crowds."

Doc ordered a thick steak, and Devorah opted for the seafood. Doc also had a bottle of the house's finest wine delivered to their table. They ate slowly, savoring the excellent food and enjoying each other's company. After dessert, Devorah decided that the time was right to give Doc her surprise gift and she shyly held the package out to him.

Doc raised his bushy eyebrows. "What's this, my dear? For me?" He unwrapped the paper and revealed the shiny black leather medical bag. "Oh, Devorah, you shouldn't have!"

"Of course I should have. You needed another one. I wanted to give you something, too."

Doc smiled at her. "Thank you, Devorah. I love you for it." He leaned to kiss her cheek.

Later on as they were riding homeward in the carriage, Devorah reached into the back seat and unfolded the blanket, spreading it across both their laps. She nestled close to Doc's side, and they chattered happily about the day's events. Devorah had never felt happier, and she told him so in glowing words. Presently she felt herself growing sleepy, and she leaned against his arm and closed her eyes, her words trailing off into silence. She drifted into a light slumber, awaking much later with a start as Doc pulled the horse over to the side of the road and stopped.

Her eyes flew open. "What is it? What's wrong?"

"Nothing," he asssured her. "Don't be afraid. I can't wait any longer." He turned to her, taking her forcefully into his arms and pressing his lips to hers.

Devorah was swept up into the intensity of his kiss. Her arms slipped around his neck, and she pulled him tightly to her breast. All the long months and years of denial of her desire fell away in an instant, and she felt herself giving, yielding, responding. She was aware of her pounding heart; she was soaring, flying. Doc broke off the kiss, and they looked at each other in newfound wonderment. Devorah's breathing was ragged. Her whole body felt weak and drained.

"Devorah, we've got to talk," Doc said quietly. She nodded mutely, still stunned at her reaction. "I can't seem to think straight any more. When I'm not with you, I keep seeing your face and hearing your voice and when I'm with you, I can hardly stop myself from coming right out and telling you that I love you." He seemed surprised at himself now that the words were finally out. "There, I've said it. Does it surprise you? Oh, it's true, Devorah, my dearest. I do love you, so much, *so much.*" He kissed her hands, her face, her neck, returned to sear her mouth. She pushed him gently away; she had to have air.

Devorah's hand went to her throat and fluttered there nervously. "Oh, Doc! Oh my goodness!" she gasped, totally flustered.

"Is it possible that you could learn to feel the same about me?" he asked her kindly.

"I . . . I . . . uh . . . "

"Have you reconsidered what you said before about not wanting to marry just yet?"

"Oh, Doc . . . this is all so sudden," she said, stalling him. "I don't know . . . I truly, truly don't know. I need more time to think."

"Quite all right, my dear," he said with infinite understanding. He pulled her close to him so that her head rested once again on his shoulder. He lightly caressed her face and ran his fingers gently through her hair.

After a while, he started the carriage moving again, and they rode the rest of the way in silence. Doc fantasized about a possible church wedding, picturing in his mind Devorah slowly coming down the aisle toward him to the accompaniment of sweet strains of music. He saw them living together, loving together, saw his own tender smile as she handed him the son he never had.

Ann glanced at the clock on the mantel and saw that the hour was growing late. Dinner had long since come and gone, and she had prepared a small meal for both Melissa and herself, but she had eaten sparingly, not feeling very hungry. They had done the few dishes together, and then afterward they had sat in front of the fire, playing games. The child had been somewhat cranky, not having seen her mother all day, and when she had finally started to nod off, Ann put her to bed with a sigh of relief.

Ann returned now to the kitchen table where she had been diligently working on the new sign for Doc's office. Earlier that morning, she had found a good piece of wood out in the barn and had spent most of the day carefully carving out the letters of his name into the fibers of the wood. The job had gone smoothly, and she was almost done. The sign would read: J. MCCLINTOCK, M.D.

She pulled the chair up to the table, picked up the knife, and began to carve another letter, hunching closely over the block of wood. *Well,* she reflected, *I didn't think I could do it this fast, but it's almost done. If they stay out just a little bit longer, I'll be able to give it to him tonight. I really shouldn't begrudge Devvie for wanting to go to the city. I can see how she might get tired of being stuck here all the time. And I'm not mad at Doc, really. It's just the way she sprung it on me that she was going with him. I wish I hadn't said what I did to her, thrown it in her face like that. I'll make it up to her somehow. I'll be extra-special nice to her when she gets home. I'll ask her if she had a good time. I'll bet she'll be awful tired. I could sit her down by the fire, pull off her shoes, prop her feet up on a pillow. I could make her some fresh coffee and then apologize for the way I carried on. She's got to understand, she's got to forgive me. I didn't mean any harm. I do want her to be happy.*

Ann finished carving the last letter, and she set down the knife. She leaned back, looking over her work and nodding approvingly. She rose from the chair, taking the lamp, and went out into the tool shed in search of a small length of chain that she thought she had seen there earlier. She found the chain off in one corner and also rummaged around for two sturdy metal eyelets that could be used as holders for the chain. She returned to the house and sat down at the table again, using a small pointed awl to make holes in the top of the sign. She inserted the eyelets, hammered them in securely, and then attached the chain, looping it through the metal. The sign was finished. Smiling, she held it out at arm's length.

She stood and stretched, twisting her back from side to side. *Boy, I'm tired,* she realized. *It's going on nine o'clock. I've got to go sit in a comfortable chair.* She moved to the fire and eased herself down into Devorah's rocking chair. She rocked slowly back and forth for a while, gazing steadily into the dancing flames, and then her eyelids grew heavy. She stopped rocking, laid her head back, and closed her eyes. Not too much later, she was jolted awake by the sound of laughter as Doc and Devorah came through the front door. She stood up groggily, rubbing her eyes.

Devorah was laughing at something Doc had just said. "Oh Doc, you're too much!" She took off her cape and new hat and reached to take his coat. "You must come in and warm up first before you go home. I'll make a fresh pot of coffee for you." She linked her arm through his and started to lead him toward the fireplace, stopping abruptly when she saw Ann. "Oh . . . Ann!" she said. "How long have you been sleeping there?"

"Not long," Ann mumbled.

"Why didn't you just go on to bed?"

"Because I was waiting up for you. Did you have a good time?"

"Oh, a lovely time! An absolutely marvelous time!" Devorah went into the kitchen and put the coffee pot on the stove.

Doc sat down in front of the fire and rubbed his hands together to warm them. "You look tired, my dear," he observed to Ann.

"I am," she admitted. "I've been working all day." She walked over to the table, picked up the sign, and held it out to him with a satisfied smile. "I made this for you. I'd be much obliged if you could use it."

Doc reached out to take the sign and ran his fingers along the carved letters. "Well, Ann, I'm impressed. This is truly a handsome piece of work. You didn't have to do this, but I thank you for your consideration. I shall most certainly use it."

"Ann, did you finish that sign already?" Devorah called out to her.

"Um, yes, I spent the day on it."

Devorah poured the hot coffee into cups and passed them out from a tray. They all sat around the fire, and Ann listened somewhat sleepily as Devorah bubbled on and on about their trip to the city, detailing the fancy dinner at the restaurant. After close to another hour had passed with Devorah showing no signs of slowing down, Doc set down his empty cup and rose from his seat.

"Devorah, I must get these old bones home and get to bed. I'm not as young as you are any more, you know."

"All right, Doc. I'll see you to the door," she offered.

"Good night, Ann." He bowed to her.

Ann stood up. "Night, Doc."

Devorah held his coat for him while he shrugged into the sleeves. Then she turned him around to face her, tying his scarf snugly around his neck.

"Doc, I had a wonderful time. Thank you so much," she said happily, beaming at him.

"Of course, my dear. Good night."

Devorah impulsively raised herself up on tiptoe and gave Doc a light but lingering kiss on the lips. He embraced her and she allowed herself to be taken into his arms again. Ann scowled darkly and averted her eyes. When he was gone, Devorah picked up her new hat and put it on her head, prancing around the room in a state of ecstasy and humming softly to herself. Ann followed her with her eyes, rapidly working herself into another temper.

"Did you waste your money on that hat or did he get it for you?" she demanded.

"Why, he got it for me, of course. And why not? It *is* Christmas, you know."

"Take that blasted hat off, Devvie." Her voice was frigid.

Devorah was defiant and refused to back down. "Why? What have you got against it? Just because he gave it to me?"

"It looks awful expensive."

"It is. What's wrong with that? Don't you want me to have anything fine?" Her good humor was quickly evaporating. She removed the hat and stood there, glaring at Ann.

"Well, sure, but . . ."

"But what? But what?" Devorah pounced on her, relentless. "I have just spent a lovely day with a wonderful man and I don't need to come home and listen to this."

"Oh, a wonderful man, huh?" Ann sneered. "And you stand there with your hands all over him . . ."

"My hands were *not* all over him!" Devorah denied hotly.

"And you kiss him like you really meant it . . ."

"Well, maybe I did mean it! Maybe I liked it!"

"You want to go to bed with him, don't you?" Ann accused bitterly.

"Ann! You're jealous!" she whispered vehemently.

"Damn right, I am."

"You've no right to be."

"Why not?" Ann insisted. "You're throwing yourself at him. You're begging for it."

Devorah had had enough. She stepped up to Ann, raised her open hand, and would have slapped her smartly had not Ann caught her wrist as the blow descended.

"Don't, Devvie," she said softly. "I'm jealous because I love you too. I feel like I'm in competition with him."

Devorah slowly lowered her arm as Ann released her hold. "What? But there *is* no competition. You don't know . . ."

"Oh yes, there is. You can't see it or feel it, but I can. And I'm scared he's going to win and I'm going to lose."

"But he's won nothing yet. You've lost nothing yet."

"But the game is still being played. You're the ball that's bouncing back and forth."

"Ann, I'm just so confused," she moaned miserably. "I need more time to think, to sort my feelings out. I couldn't bear to have to choose between you both."

"You have to, Devvie, you have to," Ann said solemnly. "We can't go on this way much longer. It's tearing us both apart inside."

Eight

It was Christmas Eve. The night was hushed and still. After dinner Ann read quietly by the fire, her fingers absent-mindedly stroking the fur of the cat as it lay curled up on her lap. They had intended Jody to be a barn cat, and indeed he spent most of the day outside, but more often than not they allowed him to come inside for the night. Devorah had gotten used to his presence and didn't seem to mind as long as Melissa treated him with respect and didn't pull his tail or yank at his fur.

Devorah and Melissa were both in the kitchen, baking sugar cookies. The child had insisted on leaving out a special treat for Santa, and Devorah was certainly not of a mind to disagree with her. Melissa crammed most of the cookies into her mouth, but she dutifully set aside half a dozen on a small plate and placed it along with a glass of milk on the table in front of the fire. Her task completed, she permitted herself to be led off to bed. Devorah helped her change into her nightgown and then stood leaning against the doorframe while she quickly recited her prayers.

"An' God bless Mommy an' Ann an' kitty an' everybody else. An' I'm sorry I didn't eat my turnips tonight, but I don't like them either." She hopped into the bed, and Devorah tucked the quilt around her small frame.

"Mommy, do you think God really hears me?" she wondered.

"Of course He does, sweetheart, if you really mean what you say."

"Do you think He loves me, too?"

"Why, of course He does," Devorah assured her. "He loves all little children."

"Do you think He'll be mad at me because I spilled my milk today?"

"Noooo," Devorah said with a smile, shaking her head. She bent over to give Melissa a firm hug and then kissed her on the forehead. "Now go to sleep. I love you, honey." She kissed her again and smoothed the hair back from her face. *Oh yes, I love you, sweetheart,* she thought tenderly. *More than you'll ever know. Sleep sweet and dream of only good things.* She rose and extinguished the lamp.

"Mommy?" the child mumbled in the darkness.

"Yes, Lissa?"

"You won't forget to hang up my stocking, will you?"

"Of course not, honey. I'll do it right now."

"Promise?" she persisted.

"Promise." Devorah shut the door.

She went straight to the fireplace and attached the tiny stocking to the mantel. Then she poured herself another cup of coffee and sat down in her rocking chair, intending to relax. Ann glanced up from her reading and eyed her intently.

"Devvie," she began hesitantly. "I've been thinking . . ."

"Yes?"

"I'm awful sorry . . . about what I said the other day."

"It's all right. It's forgotten," Devorah answered softly. She leaned back and closed her eyes, visualizing the hostile scene and hearing again the angry words that she would never quite forget.

"No, it's not all right. I feel really bad."

"You should."

"I do," Ann said guiltily. "Please say you forgive me. I can't sleep right until you forgive me." No answer. Devorah still kept her eyes closed. "Devvie? Are you falling asleep on me?"

"No, I hear you." *I want you to squirm,* she thought. *I want you to beg.*

"Then please say you forgive me." Ann waited, hopeful, expectant. Still no answer. "Do you want me to beg?"

"Yes," Devorah said, quite simply.

"All right, then, I will." She rose from her chair and knelt in front of Devorah, moving close to her skirts and reaching out to take her folded hands into her own. Devorah opened her eyes and looked down into her pleading face. "Please forgive me. I'm really sorry."

"And what will you do if I don't?" she asked, now beginning to smile.

"Oh, don't say that! I couldn't bear it!"

"All right, then. I do forgive you. But oh, Ann, what a mouth you've got!"

111

Ann breathed a sigh of relief and leaned forward, resting her head upon Devorah's lap. Devorah hesitantly lifted one hand and then lowered it, gently touching Ann's hair and running her fingers through the softness. They both remained in this position for a few minutes, neither one of them wanting to move away, and then Ann spoke first to break the spell.

"Devvie?"

"Mmm?" Her fingers still traveled through Ann's hair.

"Why don't we bring out the presents and put them under the tree now?" she said, looking up at Devorah.

"Well . . . if you want."

Ann went into her bedroom and retrieved her gifts, which had already been wrapped, from their hiding place under the bed. Devorah also slipped quietly into her room, being careful not to wake the sleeping child, and brought forth her gifts from their place in the closet. They met again in the living room, and first one, then the other arranged her packages on the blanket under the tree. Ann devoured the cookies and drank the milk while Devorah filled Melissa's stocking with an orange, an apple, and some of Ann's penny candies.

Ann admired the full tree. "It looks good, doesn't it?"

Devorah nodded. "Yes, it does. And tomorrow Lissa will really tear into it. Don't expect to sleep too late because she'll be wanting to drag us both out here before we're dressed."

"Well, we might not have a lot of presents, but at least we have each other."

"Uh . . . yes, I suppose we do." *And I* will *have you, Ann,* she vowed to herself. *One way or the other. But I will not come to you until I am very, very sure.*

When the first faint streaks of dawn began to lighten the sky, Melissa stealthily eased herself from the bed and padded out into the deserted living room to inspect the tree. Her eyes lit up when she saw all the presents, and she turned and ran excitedly back down the hallway, rushing up to Devorah's still-sleeping form.

"Mommy, Mommy!" she chattered, shaking her mother's shoulder. "Wake up, wake up now!"

"Huh? What?" Devorah was in a fog.

"Come see all the presents! Can we open them now?"

"Oh, Lissa," she moaned. "The sun isn't even up yet."

112

The child would not be deterred, and she pulled back the covers and attempted to drag her mother out of bed. Devorah sat on the edge of the mattress, sleepily groped for her warm heavy robe, and pushed her feet into the slippers on the floor. She stood up and stumbled off to the bathroom, where she brushed her teeth and washed her face. Awake now, she went into the living room, started the fire going, and moved into the kitchen, where she put a pot of coffee on the stove. Melissa hovered anxiously at her side.

"Can I go wake up Ann now? Can I?" she asked eagerly.

"Might as well," said Devorah. "Just don't jump all over her. She's liable to be grumpy."

The child dashed back down the hall and entered Ann's bedroom, cautiously observing her as she slept with one arm thrown backward over the pillow. She quietly tiptoed up to Ann's face and planted a light kiss upon her cheek.

"Devvie," Ann mumbled, with her eyes still closed and her mouth drawing back into a smile.

"Mommy's already up. Come on, you gotta get up, too."

"Oh, Lissa, it's you," she groaned, disappointed. She rolled over, facing the opposite wall. "Go 'way."

"There's lots of presents out there. Don't you want to come see?"

"No. Leave me be," she grumbled.

"Come on! You have to get up!"

Ann finally yielded to the child's persistence and rose, throwing on her robe and feeling for her slippers. After a short trip to the bathroom she shuffled into the kitchen, where Devorah set before her a steaming cup of coffee.

"Good morning!" Devorah said cheerily.

"Oh, coffee," she muttered gratefully. "I've got to have my coffee."

"Did Lissa wake you up, the dear girl?"

Ann nodded, yawning hugely. "What would we do without her? I'm glad this only comes once a year."

"Now remember how it was when you were a child," Devorah chided. "I'm sure you were up bright and early, too."

They took their coffee cups and moved to sit by the fire. Melissa interpreted this as her signal, and she immediately pounced upon her presents, ripping off the wrapping paper and tearing open the

113

packages. She hugged her mother tightly when she found the new dress and nightgown, but she was puzzled when she discovered the story book, the stuffed animal, and the bag of candies.

"Who are these from?" she wanted to know.

"Probably from Santa," Ann said, winking at Devorah. "Did you check your stocking?"

Melissa detached her bulging stocking from the mantel and emptied out its contents on the rug. She was delighted to find the orange and the apple and more candies. She unwrapped one of the candies and popped it into her mouth.

"Now don't eat them all at once, Lissa," warned Devorah. "I don't want you getting sick before the day is over. Go give Ann her presents."

The child selected two packages from underneath the tree and handed them both to Ann. Ann carefully tore off the paper, wanting to prolong the moment, and she was greatly surprised to find the new scarf and matching mittens and the white petticoat.

"Merry Christmas, Ann," said Devorah. "The scarf and petticoat are from me, and the mittens are from Lissa."

"Gosh, Devvie, they're nice," Ann said, holding up the mittens. "So this is what you've been sneaking around about. Thought I didn't know, huh?"

"Well, you didn't know what it was."

"No, but I knew you were up to something. Thanks, Devvie," she said sincerely, smiling at her. "I sure can use them. And the petticoat, too, I guess," she conceded, making a slight face. She bent down in front of the tree, retrieved the last two presents, and shyly handed them to Devorah. "This is from me to you. Merry Christmas, Devvie."

Devorah opened the smaller package first and with a cry of delight held up a bar of fragrant soap in each hand.

"Oh, Ann!" she exclaimed. "How did you know I wanted these?"

"You mentioned it a long time ago back in the summer. You said you liked this special soap from France. I always intended to get it for you."

"You shall have to use it too," she insisted. "You'll like it—it's very creamy and fine on your skin."

"All right, all right. Now open up the other one."

Devorah tore off the paper on the larger package and withdrew the high-button black shoes. She gasped and stared at them, disbelieving.

"Oh, Ann! Oh, my goodness! You shouldn't have."

"Why not? They'll fit. I tried them on myself."

"But they must have been expensive. I don't want you spending all your money on me," she protested.

"Devvie, cost doesn't matter to me where you're concerned. I know you like fancy things, and if it's at all possible, I want to get some of these things for you. I want you to have everything good and fine. I don't want you to want for anything."

Devorah was supremely touched and at a loss for words. Her eyes filled with tears as she scrutinized Ann's face, but she blinked them back quickly and rose from her chair, moving to stand in front of Ann. She leaned forward, her hands clasping Ann's upper arms, and she kissed her softly, lingeringly, on the cheek, then took Ann into her embrace, holding her tightly, closely, rocking gently from side to side.

The kitchen was redolent with the luscious odors of baking. Ann and Devorah had been making fresh bread loaves and another pumpkin pie, and now they started on a mince pie, a special treat for a special occasion. As Ann rolled out the pie dough, Devorah went out into the smokehouse and returned shortly, bearing a small jar of mince filling.

"I didn't even know you had that," Ann said, pointing to the jar. "Where did you get it? I don't remember putting it up this fall."

"We didn't. Doc gave this to me a long time ago, and I've just been saving it for the right time. He's always getting things from all the little old ladies he treats for rheumatism or lumbago. Sometimes they can't pay him, so they give him some of what they've put up. He says his pantry is too full, so once in a while he brings a few jars over to me."

"Well, that's nice of him."

"Yes, he really is a generous man."

They had a tender ham for dinner along with a dish of baked apples and sweet yams and, not to be omitted, some homemade cranberry sauce. After eating the pie for dessert, they were quite stuffed and leaned back against their chairs, sipping their coffee.

When the dishes were all washed and put away, Devorah ushered Ann and Melissa into the living room, saying that it was time to have a quiet Bible reading. Oftentimes due to the winter's snows they would not be able to make the trip into town for Sunday Meeting, so at-home Bible studies would become an important part of their weekly routine.

Devorah brought out the heavy leather-bound Bible that she had also received as a wedding gift from her parents. She sat in her rocking chair, opened the book to the second chapter of Luke, and began to relate the story of the birth of Jesus and the shepherds in the fields tending watch over their flocks. Ann and Melissa sat on the hearth rug in front of Devorah, listening intently to her sweet, soft voice. When she finished the story, the child was full of questions.

"Mommy, do you think Jesus was cold, lying there in the manger?"

"I don't think so, honey," Devorah replied. "He had all those animals around Him to keep Him warm."

"How did the Wise Men know where to go?"

"They just looked up and followed the star."

"You mean the star moved?" Devorah nodded. "But you told me stars can't move."

"This one did. It was a very special star."

"But why did they go to see Jesus?"

"They went to worship Him, honey, because they knew He was going to be a very special little boy."

"Did He grow up to love God, too?"

"Of course He did. He did many good things, too, for people who were sick or had problems."

"Are we all supposed to love God, too?" Devorah nodded again. "But how can we love Him if we can't see Him? What's love, Mommy?"

"Uh . . . well . . ."

"Let me tell her, Devvie," Ann interrupted. She turned Melissa around to face her, cupping her little chin in her hand. "Lissa, love is a very special feeling that you have for someone who's close to you, someone who helps you and does good things for you."

"Like Mommy?" she brightened.

"Uh-huh. When you feel this love for someone, you're also loving God at the same time because the Bible tells us that God is love."

"Did God make love?"

"He made everything, Lissa. Wait, let me read you something." Ann took the Bible from Devorah's lap, set it on the floor, and flipped through the back pages. She stopped at the fourth chapter of the first letter of John, and her finger traveled down the page in search of the right verse. "Here it is. Listen: 'Beloved, let us love one another; for love is of God, and he who loves is born of God and knows God. He who does not love does not know God; for God is love.' "

"Is love just one big feeling, then?"

"No, Lissa. There are many different kinds of love."

"Are they all good?"

"Yes, they're all good." Ann met Devorah's eyes, tried to drill through them with her gaze. "All love is good," she repeated firmly. *Did you hear that, Devvie?* she wondered. *Do you understand what I'm trying to say? Do you believe it too?*

Late that evening, Devorah sat alone and wakeful in front of the fire. Ann had long since retired to bed. Devorah had assured her that she would soon follow, but still she sat, rocking slowly, her mind a tumbled confusion of emotions.

I have to think this out, she considered. *I have to come to terms with it. I have to know . . . It's been so long since Billy died. I almost can't see him anymore, can't feel him. I couldn't help myself the other night when I thought about him though. It just came, just swept over me. But if he could be here tonight, he'd be telling me that I have to go on without him. I have to realize that he's gone, I have to accept it and let him rest. I loved him, and he'll always be a part of me, but that part of my life is over now. I have to look elsewhere for love. To whom do I turn? To Doc? Oh, dear Doc! Such a sweet man—so kind, so gentle, so giving. He loves me, he really loves me. He wants me to marry him. He'll be asking me again, he won't let it rest until I've given him an answer. I told him I would think about it, and I must reach a decision.*

I've learned to be on my own since Billy died. It's taken a long time, but I've come this far without a man. I don't want to have more children—Lissa's enough of a handful. I don't want to give up my freedom, either, to be married again. I'm content with my life the way it is right now. I'm content to have Ann here as a companion. Oh, Ann! I do love you, I truly do. You'll never know just how much. With your endearing ways, you've worked yourself into my life and into my heart. Do you think I enjoy lying in that bed alone at night? How many times I've wanted to come to your room and tap softly on the door and come in and lie with you. Yes, I want, yes, I have desire. The more I'm with you, the more I'm losing my fear. What you said tonight about God being love—yes, I understood what you were trying to say, yes, I believe it too. I think . . . maybe . . . possibly . . . yes, I know . . . I'm in love with you now. May God forgive me for saying this, but I am.

Devorah shut her eyes and shaded her brow with one hand, then slowly lifted her head and stared into the dancing flames. *Doc, I love you as a dear true friend, but I'm not in love with you. I cannot marry you, it wouldn't be fair to you. It would be a cruel deception, a denial of what I really want. How can I tell you this so that you'll understand? I'm afraid to tell you because I don't want to hurt you. I don't want to lose your friendship, I don't want you to hate me. Ann's right—we can't go on this way much longer. It is tearing us all apart. It's time for me to make my decision. All right, then, I choose . . . and I just pray that this is right.*

For the remainder of the week, Devorah was mostly silent, performing her daily chores and duties with an air of detached, almost automatic functioning. She scrubbed out clothes in the bathtub, she dusted the furniture again and again, she dropped to her hands and knees to scour the floor, she baked herself into a frenzy. The Christmas tree was stripped and chopped up for firewood. All the ornaments were carefully returned to their crates and stored away for next year.

Ann tried to keep out of Devorah's way, busying herself in caring for the animals, working on the old wagon, and playing with Melissa. She was keenly aware that Devorah was intently preoccupied. She desperately wanted to talk to her and find out what the problem was, but her nagging feelings of insecurity forced her to remain quiet and aloof. *I wish she'd talk to me,* Ann fretted. *I wish I'd be brave enough to sit her down and demand that she talk to me. I know something's bothering her. I can see her mind going when she stares off into space like that. What could she be thinking about? Doc? Is she thinking on marrying him? Am I going to lose*

118

her after all? What did they talk about that day when they went into the city? What is she hiding from me?

Ann's anxious feelings culminated on the night of New Year's Eve. She had been looking forward to spending a quiet evening at home with Devorah, perhaps opening an old dusty bottle of wine and drinking a toast to each other at the hour of midnight. However, shortly past ten o'clock, there came a subdued knocking at the front door and Devorah opened it wide to reveal Doc McClintock standing on the porch. She invited him to step inside, offering to take his hat and coat.

"Hello, Doc," Devorah said quietly. "What brings you out here tonight?"

Doc leaned to kiss her cheek. He apparently had not noticed her changed mood. "Ah, Devorah, my dear, I came to tell you that the church is having a special watch night service tonight at midnight. I thought perhaps if you weren't too tired, you could come along with me. And Ann and Melissa, too, of course," he added, almost as an afterthought.

Devorah was hesitant. "Well . . . I don't know. It'd be awfully late."

"But New Year's comes only once a year," said Doc. "Please come with me. I can assure you it will be a lovely service."

"Well . . . what do you think, Ann? Should we all go?"

"Hah!" Ann exhaled sharply. "You go if you want, but not me! I'm not getting all dressed up to go to some midnight service. There's no way you'll ever drag Lissa out of a nice warm bed to go traipsing off at this hour. She won't stand for it. If she stays here, then I do, too!" She folded her arms across her chest and stood there, un-moving.

"Oh . . . uh . . . if you'd really rather not . . ." Doc lapsed into an embarrassed silence.

"I guess that settles it, then," said Devorah, turning back to face Doc. "*I'll* be happy to go with you. Just give me a few minutes to change my dress."

He smiled. "Splendid, my dear."

Ann watched dejectedly as Devorah left the room, ignoring her pleading eyes. *You've made your choice, haven't you, Devvie?* she thought miserably. *I guess I never should have hoped that you would*

119

pick me. She bit her lip and turned away in agony, hot tears springing to her eyes and blurring her vision.

The watch night service was quiet and dignified. Tall candles burned like little beacons in each of the stained glass windows of the church. Additional candles were arranged upon the low front altar, which was covered with a white cloth symbolizing the purity and goodness of the coming new year. The pews were sparsely populated that night, not many of the townspeople having wanted to venture out so late. Devorah permitted Doc to hold her hand as they sat together, and she had to fight to keep herself from nodding off several times.

At the conclusion of the service, Doc escorted her back outside into the cold crisp air. Their boots made crunching noises as they walked across the tightly packed snow cover, and their breath swirled in visible clouds around their faces. Doc assisted her in stepping up into the carriage, and then he climbed in beside her, reaching down to grasp the reins.

"Lovely service, wasn't it?" Doc inquired.

"Yes, it was," she responded. "The hymns were well done, and the candlelight was very beautiful."

"Devorah," he said as the carriage began to move, "why don't we stop over at my place on the way home? We could have ourselves a little toast to the new year. I've got some fine dandelion wine—made it myself, so I know it's good."

"All right, Doc," she acquiesced with a little laugh. "That sounds nice." She tried to seem agreeable, but inwardly she was becoming nervous. *Please help me say it right,* she prayed silently. *I know we'll have to talk tonight. Just don't let him hate me for what I'm going to say.*

They arrived shortly at Doc's small farm, and he ushered her into the darkened house. He lit the lamp and took her cape and hat, draping them over a nearby chair. He invited her to make herself comfortable on the small love seat in the living room while he proceeded to start a cheery fire in the grate. Then he left the room for a moment and returned bearing a wicker basket that contained four old medicine bottles full of what appeared to be his own home brew.

"I have a little surprise for you, Devorah," he said, handing her the basket. "I've got a little still out back, and I made this myself. I want you to take this home for yourself and Ann. It's my New Year's present to both of you."

Devorah looked at the bottles and then glanced up at him. "Oh, thank you, Doc. If you made this, I'm sure it will be good." She set the basket on the floor beside her.

Doc left the room again and came back with a bottle of the promised dandelion wine. He poured the wine evenly into two glasses, handed Devorah a glass, and sat down on the love seat next to her.

"Now, my dear, I have two toasts to propose. First of all, here's to 1891. May this year be full of happiness and prosperity."

"Yes, to 1891," Devorah echoed. They raised their glasses and clinked them together; they drank.

"Secondly here's to you, Devorah," Doc continued. "To one of the loveliest women I have ever known. May this new year bring you love and peace and everything that you desire."

"Oh . . . thank you, Doc." She blushed modestly. They clinked glasses and drank again.

They each related their hopes and plans for the coming year. Devorah talked of her farm, of Ann and Melissa. Doc talked of his flourishing medical practice and also told her several humorous stories of his early school days. The hour grew later, the wine passed more freely, and they both began to loosen up. Doc sat closer to Devorah, and she allowed him to run his fingers lightly through her hair, lovingly pat and hold her hands, and kiss her tenderly on her cheeks and forehead from time to time. Finally the talking ceased, and they sat with arms entwined in front of the fire, quietly aware of each other's presence.

"Devorah, I love you very much," he whispered to her. "You know that, don't you?"

"Yes, Doc . . . I do." Devorah was slightly light-headed. Doc's home brew was powerful stuff.

"Then you must also know that there's nothing I wouldn't do for you. I'd give you the world if I could." He sat up and placed their glasses upon the low coffee table, then turned to her and took her into his arms. His lips sought and found her mouth, and he held her, not forcefully this time, but gently, tenderly. Devorah felt a small stirring within her, but it was not the intense rush of passion that she had experienced the first time he had kissed her. Doc broke off the kiss, but still kept his arms around her and caressed her cheek with his strong fingers. "Oh, Devorah, my dearest," he breathed huskily. "Please say you'll marry me. You'll make me the happiest man on earth."

Her eyes traveled over his face. "Oh, Doc . . ."

"We don't need to make any fuss about it. We could go back into town tonight and find the preacher and get married right away. Please say yes, Devorah," he urged her. "I want you to stay here with me tonight."

"Doc . . ." She wondered how to begin, what to say.

"Yes, my love? I'm not giving you a chance to speak, am I?"

"Oh, Doc . . . I can't . . ."

"Can't what? Can't do it tonight? Very well, then, we could wait until tomorrow. Whatever you want, my dear." He was so eager to please her.

"No, I mean I can't . . . marry you." She watched his smiling face crumple in an instant.

"You can't . . . marry me . . . " he repeated dully, in total confusion. "But . . . but why not? I thought . . ."

"Dear Doc, I'm sorry," she whispered sadly, "but it wouldn't be fair to you." She felt his pain, saw the twinkling light go out of his eyes. *Oh, I've hurt you,* she thought. *I didn't want it to be this way.*

Ace Fairlane was celebrating his New Year's evening at the saloon in Sutter's Ford. His five best buddies were with him, and they had all sat huddled around a table, playing poker for hours on end. The surrounding air was thick with dense blue cigar smoke, and the beer flowed freely among the men. The madam's girls hovered solicitously about them, draping themselves across the men's laps, kissing them, teasing them, trying to capture their attentions.

Ace had already won quite a bit of money in the card game and he was feeling pretty well. The one bottle of whiskey that he had nearly consumed lent considerably to his cheerful spirits. His girl Lizzie sat on his lap and toyed playfully with his hair. Ace studied the cards in his hand with thoughtful concentration, and when the final bidding was completed, the ante upped, and additional cards passed out, he spread his hand on the table with a slowly widening grin.

"Hah!' he crowed. "Four aces. Got'cha again." He reached to the center of the table and raked in another pile of money. The other men groaned resoundingly.

"Ace, honey, can't'cha quit fer a while?" Lizzie begged. "It's after midnight."

"Yeah, so it is. So what?"

"Wal, it's a new year now. I thought we might g'wan upstairs an' have us a li'l celebratin' of our own," she purred, tickling him under his stubbly chin.

"Wal . . ." He paused to consider it.

"Aw, c'm on, honey," she insisted. "I'll make y'feel good."

"Awright, Lizzie, yer on!" He quickly guzzled the remaining whiskey and stood up, carelessly tossing the empty bottle to the floor. "You guys g'wan without me," he said to his buddies.

Ace grabbed Lizzie by the hand and towed her up the stairs. When they reached her room, he allowed her to enter first, then closed the door behind them and locked it securely. He turned to face her, his eyes lighting up with an evil gleam. She stepped up to him and wrapped her arms around his neck, drawing him into her soft embrace. He let her kiss him, his coarse dirty hands pawing roughly at her body. His fingers closed over her breast, and he squeezed it, twisting it painfully.

"Ouch!" she yelped, slapping his hand away. "That hurt!"

All of a sudden Lizzie's face was gone, and he saw instead Devorah standing before him. The old anger and resentment surged within him, and he wanted to strike out, to inflict pain, to punish her for her rejection of him. His eyes blazed with a cold fire.

"Ya bitch!" he seethed. "I'll learn ya t'lay a hand on me. I'm gonna git'cha good!"

He backhanded Lizzie cruelly and she fell sprawling across the bed. Ace leaped on her, straddling her with his legs, pinning her arms over her head. She panted and thrashed, jerking her body from side to side, seeking to be free of his crushing weight. He released one arm and began to violently rip the clothes from her body, exposing her breasts. He pounced upon one greedily, taking the nipple into his mouth and biting down upon it. When she shrieked in pain he became incensed and drove his fist into her face in an attempt to silence her.

123

Still seeing Devorah, he continued to beat the girl relentlessly, feeling his hardness increase with each blow until the front of his pants was stretched taut and bulging. The sight of the blood flowing from Lizzie's battered face made him wild, and he was unaware of the spittle drooling from his own mouth. When at last she lay whimpering helplessly, he tore the rest of the clothes away from her body, his eyes glinting feverishly at her nakedness, and he fumbled at the buttons of his pants, reaching for himself. Just then, a loud pounding came at the door, interrupting his thoughts.

"Ace! Are y'in there?" Delilah shouted. "Y'haven't paid me yet!"

"Aw, Lilah!" he yelled back. "I'll pay ya later. Scram!"

"What's goin' on in there?"

"Nothin'! We're just havin' a li'l fun. G'wan, go 'way!"

"Don't sound like fun t'me! I hear an awful lotta hollerin'!" She rattled the doorknob. "Y'open this door right now, y'hear me? Otherwise I'll git the barkeep, an' we'll blast it open with a shotgun. Y'hear me, Ace? I'm gonna count t'five. One . . . two . . ."

"Awright, awright, Lilah! I'm comin'."

Ace reluctantly fastened his buttons and tucked his rumpled shirt back into his pants. He stumbled to the door, unlocking it, and Delilah Emerson burst into the room. She took in the gruesome scene with one quick sweep of her eyes, then turned furiously upon Ace.

"What the *hell* is goin' on here?" she demanded. "Y'beat up gals fer kicks?"

"Aw, Lilah, c'm on, now, that's not what happened. She jist fell an' I wuz jist tryin' t'help 'er, that's all," he said, attemtping to smooth things over.

"Fell?" she snorted, not believing a single word. "Then why's she buck-assed nekkid? Looks t'me like she wuz beat!" She cuffed Ace about the head, and he ducked, throwing up his hands to ward off the blows. "Y'scoundrel! Yer lower'n a pig sty!" She shoved him out into the hallway and, grasping his collar, propelled him toward the stairs. She landed a solid kick on his buttocks that sent him tumbling head over heels all the way down the stairs, and he landed sprawling, bruised and winded, at the bottom. "Beat it, y'bastard, afore I fill y'with buckshot!" she screamed furiously, shaking her fist at him. Ace gingerly picked himself up and lumbered away without another word.

Delilah returned to Lizzie's room, trembling with anger. She lowered herself gently onto the bed where the girl still lay, moaning and sobbing softly. She reached out to comfort Lizzie but quickly withdrew her hand with a sharp intake of breath when she saw the girl's ruined face. Delilah covered her up with the sheet and then called out for Ruby, anxiously pacing the floor until Ruby arrived.

"Git in here, gal," Delilah ordered her sternly. "I want'cha t'go wake up yer boy Jesse an' send 'im after the doc. Do it right now! An' then y'come back in here an' help me clean this poor kid up."

Doc sat stunned beyond belief on the edge of the love seat. All his dreams and fantasies of remarriage and a son to call his own had suddenly vanished, had been shattered in a moment. He lifted his aging, bowed head and looked at Devorah, the hurt and pain showing clearly in his eyes.

"I want to know your answer once and for all," he said. He still could not believe that Devorah had done this to him.

"I'm sorry, Doc," Devorah replied. "As I said before, it just wouldn't be fair to you."

"But why?" he pleaded, not understanding. "I thought . . . I thought you loved me the way I loved you."

She desperately tried to explain. "I do love you, Doc," she insisted. "But only as a friend. I'm not in love with you. Can't you see?"

"But surely you could learn to love me in time. Surely . . ." He was grasping now.

"No, Doc, no," she said softly. "It wouldn't work. It just wouldn't be right. If some day you could find the right person for yourself, I'd be happy, oh, I'd be so happy for you. But I can't let you go on deceiving yourself about me and thinking that maybe there'll be something there, something to hope for, when there really isn't. I just feel so . . ." She trailed off, shaking her head, at a loss to comfort him.

"Devorah," he said gazing at her earnestly. "Are you sure? Are you absolutely sure?"

"Yes, I'm sure. Oh, I've been so afraid to tell you this for fear of losing your friendship."

"My friendship," he muttered tonelessly.

"Yes, your friendship. It means everything to me. You've done so much for me, been so kind to me. I don't want to lose all that just because of this one thing. I don't want you to hate me."

125

Doc was about to respond again when they were both startled by a knocking at the front door. He motioned to Devorah to remain where she was. He rose from his place, walking over to the door and opening it to reveal Ruby's son Jesse standing there.

"Mistah Doc!" the boy exclaimed breathlessly. "Miz Lilah sent me t'git'cha. She sez ya've got t'come quick! It's Miz Lizzie—she been hurt real bad."

"All right, son," said Doc. "You go back and tell her I'll be there as fast as I can." He watched while the boy climbed back onto his mule, and then he shut the door, reaching quickly for his coat and his medical bag. "Devorah, we must go. Come, I'll take you home," he said brusquely. "We'll discuss this later when we're both sober."

"No, Doc," she corrected him. "There's nothing more to discuss."

They traveled the short distance to Devorah's farm in total silence broken only by the muted jangling of the horse's harness bells. On the way, Devorah dug into the wicker basket for one of the bottles of Doc's home brew, uncorked it, and began to sneak a few more drinks, occasionally casting sidelong glances at Doc, who sat stiffly upright with his jaw firmly set. *Oh dear, it's just as I expected,* she thought. *He's upset, he's angry, he hates me for what I've done.* She took another drink and returned the bottle to the basket at her feet.

When Doc finally drew the horse to a halt, he stepped down to the ground and went around to the opposite side of the carriage, intending to assist Devorah. He lifted her out, placing his hands upon her waist, and they both stood there for a moment looking at each other.

"I'm sorry you felt it had to be this way between us," he said quietly, "but I'll always be your friend. Just send for me if you ever need me."

Devorah touched him gently upon the cheek. "Oh, *dear* Doc . . . I'm sorry, too."

"I won't be back for a while. Have to sort out my feelings, think about things, you understand. I'll see you in the spring."

Doc led her toward the house, carrying the wicker basket in one hand. Ann had been watching them through the window curtain, and when she opened the front door, Devorah stepped inside without a single word of greeting. Doc offered the basket to Ann, and she accepted it from him, puzzled.

"Here," he said to her gruffly. "This is your New Year's present. Happy New Year."

"Why, thank you, Doc. Uh . . ." He had already turned and was striding swiftly away.

Devorah slowly, deliberately, took off her hat and cape and put them away. She had a soft faraway look in her eyes, and when she passed by Ann, Ann could smell the alcoholic fumes in the air around her.

"I thought you went to church, not to the saloon," Ann admonished her. "You reek of booze."

Devorah did not immediately respond, but stumbled her way over to the rocking chair in front of the fire, taking the wicker basket along with her. She plopped herself uncertainly down, almost upsetting the rocker. She uncorked another bottle and continued drinking.

"Devvie, you're drunk!" Ann blurted out. She went up to Devorah and attempted to take the bottle away from her.

Devorah clasped the bottle to her breast and gave Ann a gentle shove. "Oh no, you don't! I need this, believe me, I need this."

"Why?" Ann shot back, becoming exasperated.

"Well, it's 1891, isn't it? Aren't we supposed to be ringing in the new year?"

Ann glanced up at the clock on the mantel. "Devvie, do you have any idea what time it is?"

"Nope, and I don't wanna know. Come on, drink up. You should have some, too. It's good stuff, cleans you out." She uncorked one of the bottles and handed it to Ann. "Drink it, I said," she urged her. "We're having a party."

Ann took a tentative swallow, coughed, grimaced, shook her head to clear it. "Hoo-eee! That's strong stuff."

"Tol'ja it was good," Devorah confirmed.

"Devvie," she said kindly. "Why don't you tell me what happened?"

Devorah raised her eyebrows and smiled crookedly at Ann. "Why, nothing happened. What makes you think anything happened?"

"Come on, Devvie, don't deny it. I've never seen you like this before."

"That's 'cause I've never been drunk before," she admitted, wagging her finger in the air.

"Don't you want to talk about it? Maybe it'll help if you do."

"Talk about what?" Devorah still pretended not to know.

"About whatever's got you in such a state. Come on, Devvie, you can tell me. I'm here for you, and I've got some pretty big shoulders to cry on."

As if this had been the cue that Devorah had been waiting for, her face suddenly crumpled, and she dissolved into tears. Ann quickly knelt in front of her and produced a handkerchief. Devorah snatched it up and loudly blew her nose into it.

"Oh, Ann!" she wailed. "I've almost lost a friend tonight."

"You mean Doc?" Devorah nodded, sniffling. "Well, what happened? What did you say to him?"

"He'd asked me to marry him again, that day when we went into the city. And I told him then I'd have to think about it. I told him I wasn't sure. And so I thought and thought, and finally I came up with an answer. And that's why I went with him tonight because I knew he'd keep asking me until I gave him an answer. I wanted to be ready. I wanted to give him that answer."

"What did you tell him?" Ann held her breath.

"I said no. I told him I . . . I couldn't."

Ann exhaled in a rush, disbelieving. "You *what*?"

"I turned him down. Now he's all upset, and I think he's angry, and he doesn't want to see me again, and I think he hates me, and . . ." She wailed anew, burying her face in the handkerchief.

Ann comforted her soothingly, patting her gently on the back. "There, there, Devvie."

"It's just that I . . . I couldn't possibly be with him every day like I am with you. He can't give me what I really want, only I didn't tell him that."

"What do you really want, Devvie?" Ann inquired softly.

"Oh, I didn't want to hurt him! I truly didn't mean to!" she rushed on, ignoring Ann's question. She reached out for the bottle again and took another long swallow.

Ann gently disengaged her fingers from the bottle and set it aside. "Come on, Devvie, I think you've had enough. I think you'd best get to bed."

Ann helped her to rise from the chair and supported her carefully as they walked down the hallway to Devorah's bedroom. Ann stripped her of her dress and slip and leggings, unlaced her shoes and pulled them off, then slipped the nightgown over her head, helping her to locate the armholes. She led Devorah over to the bed, sat her down, and then eased her slowly backward until her head touched the pillow. Ann began to pull the quilt up over her body, glancing to the other side of the bed to make sure that Melissa had not awakened. The child was still sound asleep.

"Good night, Ann," Devorah mumbled groggily. "Thank you for being there."

She impulsively lifted both her arms and wrapped them around Ann's neck, pulling her down closer to her face. Devorah kissed her then, full upon the mouth, long and passionately, sweetly and tenderly, her lips touching gently, pushing harder, probing deeper. Her hand snaked down the front of Ann's shirt, unfastening the buttons, slipping inside to fondle a breast.

Ann's breath was suddenly taken away. All her senses were acutely feeling, reeling, overwhelmed. Her midsection contracted sharply, her stomach sending forth waves of delicious pain. Her knees turned to rubber, and she feared she would faint. She leaned into the kiss, taking, giving, yielding herself totally, completely. She felt the crotch of her pants becoming uncomfortably soaked.

Devorah gradually broke off the kiss and opened her eyes to find Ann bending over her, breathing raggedly as if she had just surfaced from deep water. In an instant, Devorah was hit by a flash of recognition of what she had just done, and all the old fear surged anew and forced her to withdraw.

"Oh! No . . . no . . . What am I doing?" She tried to push Ann away.

"Devvie . . . oh, Devvie!" Ann said ardently, tenderly caressing her face. "Oh my Lord!"

"No . . . no . . ." Devorah turned on her side, instantly passing out, and she lay with her hair fanned across the pillow.

Ann stood looking down at her as she slept, and she reached out a hand to brush back a few trailing strands from Devorah's face.

"I always knew you would, Devvie," she whispered lovingly. "I always knew this would come." *Perhaps now we can truly start,* she thought, *and we can go where we've never been before.*

Later on that morning, Ann bounded out of bed bright and early. She had been unable to sleep well, still being highly keyed up, and she had tossed and turned restlessly underneath the quilt. When the first rays of the sun began to stream into her window she had decided it was time to rise, throwing back the covers and tiptoeing quietly to the bathroom.

Ann washed and dressed herself quickly, shivering at the chill in the air, and then she went out into the living room to build up the fire. When the wood was crackling brightly, spreading its welcome warmth, she went into the kitchen, lit another fire in the stove, and set a pot of coffee on to brew. Melissa had awakened at the sound of the early morning noises, and she tottered sleepily toward Ann, yawning widely and rubbing her eyes.

"Morning, honey," Ann said to her.

"Why're you up so early?"

"Because there's a great big beautiful day out there just waiting for us," she answered cheerily.

"How come Mommy's not up yet?"

"Your mother had a very long night last night. She's tired."

"Should I go wake her up now?" the child volunteered.

"No, Lissa, let her be. She'll get up when she's ready. We'll let her sleep in for this one day."

Ann fixed the child and herself some breakfast and then shepherded Melissa out to the barn to do the chores, the cat following them with its tail held high. They did the work together, feeding the animals and milking the cows. Ann showed Melissa the old wagon sitting in a corner of the barn, and she patiently explained to the child the restorative work she was doing on it.

A couple of hours later, Ann quietly opened Devorah's bedroom door and looked in on her, checking to make sure that she was all right. Devorah was just beginning to stir, and Ann went back to the kitchen to prepare a late breakfast for her. She arranged bacon and eggs on a plate, put the plate on a small serving tray, poured out a fresh cup of coffee, and then brought everything in to Devorah, tapping softly upon the door before she entered.

"Morning, Devvie," said Ann. "Rise and shine."

"Huh? Oh . . . I must have overslept." Devorah attempted to sit up in the bed, but then a wave of dizziness passed over her, and she leaned forward, clasping both temples in her hands. "Ohhh, my head! It hurts. It's pounding!" she groaned.

"Well, it's no wonder. You drank enough last night to float a schooner." Ann placed the tray of food on the beside table and offered her the coffee. "Here, drink this. It'll help you wake up."

"I guess I did have a bit too much," Devorah admitted ruefully, taking small sips of the strong coffee.

"Do you feel better now about what you told Doc?"

Devorah frowned. "What? Oh . . . oh, that. Poor man. Well, it had to be done. There was just no sense . . ."

Ann reached out to take her hand and held it firmly. "Now we can go on together, right, Devvie? Now we can finally start." She smiled tenderly.

"Start what?" Devorah asked blankly. Her head was still throbbing.

"Why, us, of course."

"Ann, *what* are you talking about?" she said, quickly becoming irritated.

"But, Devvie, I thought you . . . Don't you remember? Last night you . . ." Ann was confused now; her face rapidly fell, the smile vanishing.

"I remember being upset about Doc," Devorah told her. "And drinking too much. And you had to help me to bed."

Ann couldn't believe what she was hearing. "And that's all?"

"Why, yes, that's all," Devorah insisted. "What else is there to remember?" She looked up at Ann, thoroughly puzzled.

"But you . . . you kissed me."

Devorah dismissed her with a wave of her hand. "Well, I've done that before."

"No, no. On the mouth."

Devorah stared at Ann, her eyes widening. "I *what?*"

"Yes, you did. You . . . you grabbed me, pulled me down . . ."

"Oh, Ann, no!" she protested. "I could never have done such a thing. I might have been drunk, but I wasn't that drunk."

"But, Devvie, you did! I swear you did!"

"I most certainly did not," Devorah ended conclusively. "I know I would have remembered something like that."

"But, Devvie!"

"No, Ann! That's enough!" Devorah reached for the plate of food and Ann hung her head in dismay.

Nine

Doc McClintock and Delilah Emerson stood talking in subdued tones by Lizzie's bedside. Doc had spent a good part of the night before in attending to the girl's injuries, and she had finally drifted off to sleep with the aid of liberal doses of strong whiskey. Doc had returned now in the morning to look in on Lizzie and to satisfy himself that he had done all he could for the girl.

"Oh, Doc, I'm so glad y'came last night," said Delilah, placing her bejeweled hand upon his sleeve. "I dunno what I woulda done without'cha." Now that all the excitement was over, she felt an immense relief and was deeply grateful for Doc's presence and assistance.

"That's quite all right, Lilah," he replied, patting her hand. "I'm just glad Ruby's boy found me."

Delilah glanced over at the still sleeping girl. "D'you . . . d'y' think she'll be all right?" she asked anxiously.

Doc sighed and ran his fingers through his hair. "Well, she's been beaten pretty badly, but in time, she'll start to mend. The only thing I can't heal, though, is the hurt to her spirit. No telling how much damage there is there." He shook his head sadly.

"Oh, m'poor gal," Delilah whispered. She dabbed a perfumed handkerchief to the corners of her eyes and then turned to face Doc. "Somethin's gotta be done," she stated firmly, anger lending a hardness to her voice. "We jist can't g'wan like this. That Ace is gittin' t'be worse an' worse alla time. He's gotta be stopped *now* afore 'e kills somebody."

Doc rubbed his chin. "You're right, Lilah," he agreed. "I've had about enough of him myself. What he did last night was just too much."

"D'y'think the sheriff'll lissen t'us now? We got proof that Ace did this." She stretched out her arm, palm upward, in Lizzie's direction.

Doc nodded slowly. "Yes, I think he'll have to hear us out. It's time for both of us to pay him another visit."

"Wal, 'e'd better!" she asserted. "Land sakes, I'll tell 'im so m'self. I 'spect t'go with ya!"

Later on that same afternoon, Doc and Delilah entered the jail with an air of commanding authority about their movements. They also had the local preacher, Amos Todd, in tow. Reverend Todd was a thin, timid man who appeared forceful enough when dealing with the members of his congregation, but who shrank within himself when he was not behind the safety of his sturdy pulpit. He seemed in awe of Delilah, who stood massively planted next to Doc, and he felt himself quickly becoming nervous and uneasy in her presence. Delilah was impresively garbed in a long flowing dress of deep red silk which set off her flaming red hair to its best advantage. Over her shoulders, she had draped one of her fine silky furs, and on her head was perched a huge plumed hat.

Sheriff Andy Hanks had been reclining in his usual position with his chair tilted back, hands behind his head, and feet propped up on his desk. When the trio of townspeople arrived he quickly rose from his seat, removed the cigar from his mouth, and tried to appear dignified. He eyed the group warily and assumed that Doc was the spokesperson.

"Wal, Doc, uh . . . ," he sputtered genially. "What . . . uh . . . what kin I do fer y'all?"

"Hanks, we've come to talk to you about Ace Fairlane," Doc spoke first.

"Why? What's 'e done?"

Delilah rolled her eyes upward. "What *hasn't* 'e done!" she snorted.

"Hanks, this man is becoming a danger to the community," Doc continued. "His acts of violence are getting to be beyond control."

"Wal, what's 'e done this time?" the sheriff sighed, resigning himself to hearing yet another complaint.

"He beat up one o' m'gals, that's what 'e's done!" exclaimed Delilah. "Smashed 'er face in, got 'er all bloody. I 'spect a li'l rowdiness once in a while, but not an outright maulin'. This time 'e's gone too far!"

"How bad is she, Doc?" the sheriff asked, truly concerned.

"Well, she'll live, but she's a sad sight," Doc answered. "Her nose is broken, her upper lip is split, one eye is black, and she's lost two front teeth. Not to mention other cuts and bruises all over her face."

"He can't go aroun' treatin' m'gals like that," said Delilah with a toss of her red curls. "An' not only that, but 'e's destructive, too. He breaks chairs, smashes bottles, causes fights, an' 'e's hard on m'property. He costs me money cuz I have t'fix all this stuff. An' 'e owes me money, too, cuz 'e don't pay 'is bills. He wants t'come in an' have a good time an' 'e don't pay fer services. He's even disrupted m'biznizz so much that some o' m'best customers've gone home early."

Reverend Todd had been quietly listening to Delilah's bitter denunciation. He had been standing slightly aside from her wildly gesturing hands, breathing in the heady scent of her perfume, and he was now becoming uncomfortably aware of a strong physical attraction to her. *My, what a fine figure of a woman,* he thought to himself. *What a bosom. Uh . . . oh my . . . oh dear! Satan, get thee hence from me!* He shook his head tightly and prayed silently. Suddenly, he realized that the conversation had halted, and all attention was directed toward him.

He shifted his position and cleared his throat. "Uh . . . excuse me," he apologized. "Uh . . . what?"

"I wuz jist askin' ya, Rev'rund," said the sheriff, "what'cha had t'say 'bout all this."

"Yeah, c'm on, Parson," urged Delilah. "Tell 'im a thing or two."

"Uh . . . well, yes, I quite agree with Miss uh . . ."

"The name's Lilah, Parson," she prompted him.

"Uh . . . yes, Miss Lilah. Uh . . ." He cleared his throat once again. "It's quite true. Mr. Fairlane has caused a lot of grief to the members of my congregation. They resent his hanging around after the church services, and they deplore his unkempt appearance. He stumbles into the church, reeking of alcohol, and he causes some of my parishoners to have to move away from him. They have also complained to me about his rather strange actions toward children. He is quite an undesirable character."

"Hanks, I've warned you before about the way he acts around children," Doc said. "I'm telling you, he's not right in the head, and we have no way of treating this kind of mental disorder."

"An' look what 'e did t'my Lizzie!" Delilah fumed. "She may never be able t'work again. I tell ya, the streets ain't safe t'walk on with 'im around!" She brought her clenched fist down hard upon the sheriff's desk, jarring an empty tin cup.

"Sinners must be dealt with under the full letter of God and the law," the preacher solemnly intoned, shaking his finger at the sheriff.

"Awright, awright, simmer down, ever'body!" Hanks shouted, attempting to be heard over the angry insistence of their voices. "I promise ya I'll do somethin' 'bout it. Now Miz Lilah, what's the charges gonna be? Does assault 'n battery suit'cha?"

"Yes, an' it oughtta be highway robbery, too!" she huffed, drawing herself up to her full height.

"Awright, I'll go find 'im an' haul 'im in." Hanks buckled his gun belt around his hips and reached for his hat and coat.

Hanks first walked over to the saloon, fully expecting to find Ace there, and was greatly surprised when the bartender told him that Ace had not been seen in town at all that day. Hanks then mounted his horse and rode out in the direction of Ace's farm. When he arrived there, he saw Ace's horse standing forlornly in the front yard. Hanks led the animal into the barn, stripped off the bridle and saddle, forked out some hay, and stood for a moment gently stroking the horse's flanks. He strode back to the house and pounded loudly on the door. When no answer came, he raised his fist and pounded again.

"Ace! Open up!" he shouted. "It's the law."

Hanks heard the shuffling sound of footsteps approaching from beyond the door. He waited while the bolt was drawn back, and then the door was pulled slightly ajar, and Ace peered questioningly out at him. He looked disheveled and appeared to have just awakened from another alcoholic stupor.

"Whaddya want?" Ace said suspiciously.

"Fairlane, yer gonna have t'come with me," Hanks stated firmly.

"Hey, what fer?" he protested. "I ain't done nothin' wrong."

"Doc 'n Lilah sez y'have. Sez y'beat up one o' her gals last night. Now c'm on, Ace, ain't that true?"

"Wal . . . ," he hedged, shrugging his shoulders. "Have y'seen the gal? Last time I looked, she wuz all right."

Hanks shook his head. "Sorry, Ace. They gave me proof enough. Yer jist gonna have t'come with me."

"You arrestin' me? Izzat what'cher sayin'?"

"Yep," he affirmed. "I ain't got no choice this time. Mebbe if y'cool yer heels fer a coupla weeks b'hind bars, ya'll learn t'control that temper o'yers. Now c'm on."

"Aw, hell," Ace muttered.

Hanks allowed him to retrieve his hat and coat, and then when he had shut the door, Hanks brought out a pair of metal handcuffs and slapped them onto Ace's wrists. With both his hands thus secured behind his back, Ace was led out to the waiting horse.

"Hey, wait a minnit," Ace said, stepping backward. "Where's m'horse?"

"I put 'im in the barn," Hanks replied. "Y'don't take much care o' him, do ya? 'Sides, y'won't be needin' 'im anyways since y'won't be comin' back here fer a while."

Ace was still reluctant to leave. "But . . . but what 'bout m'place? I can't jist go off an' leave it."

"Wal, I'll have t'send somebody out here t'keep it up, then. Now quit stallin' an' let's move!" He shoved Ace roughly toward the horse.

Hanks mounted first and then reached down to haul Ace up by the arm so that Ace was sitting behind him, propped up unsteadily on the horse's rump. Ace gripped his legs tightly around the horse's belly for added support, and they moved slowly back down the road to town. When they finally arrived at the jail, Hanks dismounted, helped Ace reach the ground, and dragged him inside. Ace was led to a small cell in the far corner of the jail, the handcuffs were removed from his wrists, and he was unceremoniously pushed forward, the cell door clanging shut and locking behind him.

Ace massaged his sore wrists. "Hey, how long I gotta stay here?"

"I tol'ja two weeks," Hanks answered. "Longer if y'don't keep yer mouth shut an' b'have." He walked away as Ace lowered himself dejectedly onto the small cot that served as a bed.

A week passed. The weather was bright and clear, and the sun's warming rays melted much of the deep snow. On the second Sunday of the month, Devorah decided that it was time for them all to make

137

another appearance at the church, and she assisted Melissa in donning the new dress that she had made her for Christmas. Ann stood in the doorway of Devorah's bedroom, uncomfortable in her own dress. She felt more at ease when she was wearing shirts and pants.

"Devvie, do we have to go?" Ann whined. "You know how I hate this dress. It binds me; I still don't feel right in it. Can't we just stay at home and have our own Bible reading?"

"Yes, we have to go," Devorah insisted. "We've missed Meeting long enough, and there's no excuse for not going as long as the roads are open. Besides, you really ought to get used to acting like a lady. You've been a spoiled brat ever since just before Christmas."

"I have not!"

"Oh yes, you have! Why, even Lissa acts better than you. I've never known anyone to pout as much as you do."

"Well, that's because—"

"No, Ann. No reason is good enough. Now I want to have an end to your long face, and I don't want to hear another word about it. Glue a smile on if you have to, but I want you to be nice." Devorah finished dressing. "Are you ready?" she asked, turning to Ann.

As they were riding along in the carriage, Ann sat quietly with her arm around Melissa, wondering what would happen if they should run into Doc at the church. He was sure to be there, and Ann was trying to think of the best way to avoid him. She wasn't overly worried about her own feelings toward him since she no longer considered him to be a threat to her developing relationship with Devorah, but rather she was more concerned about Devorah's possible reaction if she should see Doc. Considering that Devorah had terminated their brief romantic involvement, Ann wondered how they would act toward each other. She didn't want Devorah to become upset again.

"Devvie, what if . . . what if we should see Doc?" Ann inquired, voicing her fears.

"Well, so what?" Devorah said nonchalantly. "We'll smile and say hello and ask him how he is. He and I are still friends, you know. We're still speaking to each other." She glanced quickly over at Ann.

Ann's forehead was furrowed by a deep frown. "I hope so, Devvie, I hope so."

They rolled into town and halted in front of the church. They had arrived somewhat early, and only a few of the townspeople were already there. Ann, Devorah, and Melissa walked up the steep steps, passed through the vestibule, and entered into the main area of the church. They selected a pew close to the front on the left side of the aisle, and they quietly sat down, listening attentively to the soft organ music.

As they waited for the service to begin, Devorah allowed her thoughts to wander. *I feel so good sitting here,* she thought. *I'm glad we came. I need to be purified, to be cleansed. I feel so guilty about getting drunk that night. Dear Lord, please forgive me. I'm so sorry I lost control. Never again, I promise, never ever again. Give me the strength to resist . . . to resist what? Did I really kiss Ann the way she said I did? Why can't I remember? Well, if I did, I'm not sorry. I won't ask forgiveness for that. I pray to be fulfilled in it, to be happy. I deserve some happiness. I should take my chance before it slips away.* Devorah became aware of a form passing her on her right side, and she looked up to see who was moving into the empty pew in front of her. Her eyes widened as she recognized Doc's face, and she drew her breath in sharply.

Doc had come down the aisle in search of a seat closer to the front because most of the rear pews were already full. Just before he turned to slide into the seat, he saw Ann and Devorah and he stopped abruptly. His eyes met Devorah's and he held her gaze, unmoving, unspeaking, for an interminably long moment. Then he turned and walked back up the aisle, selecting a seat well at the rear on the right side.

Ann bit her bottom lip and tried her best to suppress a smile. *Hah,* she smirked in silent elation. *You lost her, Doc. She could have picked you, she could have said yes, but she didn't. And you can't even face her. But does this mean that I've won? How could I have won if she can't even remember she kissed me? Do I have to start all over again? Devvie, I wish I knew what was in that mind of yours, but you still won't talk to me. You won't tell me what you're really feeling.* Ann sneaked a sideways glance at Devorah, who continued to sit stiffly upright, her face betraying no emotion. Suddenly Ann became aware of a hushed and excited whispering coming from the occupants of the pew directly behind them, and she concentrated in order to pick up the sound.

"Did you see that?" said one woman.

"Oh, did you see the look on his face?" said the other woman.

"They've had a spat! And he's gone clear over to the other side."

"They're not even sitting together any more. Must be serious!"

"He's probably just finding out what a shameless woman she is."

"Oh mercy! Do you remember how she carried on at the harvest dance?"

"I'll never forget it. Such affrontery!"

"She'll never catch a man that way. Not unless she mends her ways and stops sinning."

Ann was amused and she glanced at Devorah again to see if she had also overheard the two old women. Devorah's cheeks had flamed a hot red color. She bowed her head briefly, shutting her eyes, but quickly opened them and lifted her head up proudly.

After the service had ended Ann, Devorah, and Melissa exited the church quickly, with Devorah pausing only briefly to speak a few words of greeting to some of the townspeople. Doc McClintock stood aside in one corner of the vestibule and sadly watched them leave. He had not been able to bring himself to say anything to Devorah as he was still feeling too much hurt, too much pain at the way she had so conclusively turned down his marriage proposal without any intimation of future hope that she would someday change her mind.

Presently Doc observed Reverend Todd enter into the vestibule, followed closely by the Anders couple, Joseph and Cora. Doc listened passively to their conversation as they had not yet taken notice of him. Cora Anders moved ponderously, ballooning in her seventh month of pregnancy, and Doc had determined that she was so far in excellent health. There was a distinct possibility that the woman might give birth to a set of twins since her stomach was already so large.

"I am so glad to see you here, Mrs. Anders," said the preacher with a deferential bow in her direction. "It truly lifts my heart to see you looking so well."

"Thank you, Reverend Todd," Cora smiled shyly.

Joseph reached out to take his wife's hand. "Yes, she does look well, doesn't she? Pretty soon we won't be able to come for a while because of her . . . ah . . . condition."

"Of course, of course," the preacher nodded. "Perfectly understandable. You must take care of yourself," he admonished her.

"We've come a long way since last May," said Joseph. "We're very happy now with another baby coming."

"If you're implying that I've forgotten about our Bonnie, no, I haven't, not for one moment," Cora disclaimed. "I keep thinking of her precious face and her bright eyes, and I will never be at peace until justice is done for her."

"My dear woman, you must realize that she is at peace," the preacher said kindly. "We must never question God's will. Remember, the good Book tells us that there is 'a time to be born, and a time to die; a time to weep, and a time to laugh.' "

"And it also tells us 'An eye for an eye, and a tooth for a tooth,' " Cora added firmly.

"Yes, but 'Vengeance is mine; I will repay, saith the Lord,' " the preacher continued. "Mrs. Anders, everything is in the hands of God. He will not forget."

"Come, dear, don't take on so," Joseph pleaded. "I'm sure they'll find the man who did it."

"Woman," she corrected him. "I've heard rumors that it was a woman. What do we really know about that girl who lives with the Widow Lee? I find it most odd that she just showed up one day out of nowhere—a perfect stranger to these parts. I'd say she needs to provide a better accounting for herself."

Doc decided it was time to step into the conversation, and he moved to stand beside Mrs. Anders. "Cora," he began, gently taking her elbow. "Cora, I want you to know that your suspicions of Ann Johnson are unfounded. It was indeed a man who killed Bonnie, and I will stake my professional reputation on it. I assure you that some day the whole truth will be known."

"Do you know who did it, then?" she questioned accusingly.

"No," he replied softly, "but have patience. The wheels of justice move slowly, but they do move."

One day in the middle of January, Ann took the rifle and went out to hunt for wild rabbits. Her step was jaunty as she approached the edge of the forest, and she breathed deeply of the crisp winter air. The sky was overcast, but the snow was still melting, and her boots sank deep into the slush. *Maybe we'll have an early thaw,* she thought. *And then comes spring and flowers. Oh, what a great time to be alive!*

She pushed deeper into the forest, following the narrow winding trails. A few rabbits scampered in front of her, but their movements were so quick that she didn't have time to draw a bead on them with the rifle. She was content to just wander along, taking in the hushed beauty of the quiet woodland.

Shortly, she became aware of a thrashing sound which seemed to be coming from somewhere in the glade that was coming into her line of sight. She stepped off of the snow-covered trail and cautiously approached the clearing, peering out from behind the safety of thick-trunked trees. She spied a deer, a young hart. It was not yet full grown, for the body was still small, and the antlers had not completely budded forth. Its front foreleg was caught securely in the jaws of a metal trap and the animal was frantically thrashing about, vainly attempting to escape from this unexpected pain. The deer's struggles gradually became more feeble, and its legs finally buckled. It pitched forward into the blood-flecked snow, its sides heaving, trembling with exhaustion.

Ann stealthily approached the wide-eyed frightened animal, keeping herself hidden behind the trees and remaining downwind so that the deer would not detect her scent. When she drew closer, she could see that the foreleg had been almost severed by the cruel teeth of the trap, and the animal was now dying, its beautiful eyes swiftly glazing over. Ann lifted the rifle to her shoulder and fired a single shot. The bullet entered the deer's brain, and it jerked once and lay still.

Ann trudged over to the body and stood silently looking down at it. Tears came to her eyes, and she was filled with an intense hatred for the nameless person who had set the trap. She remembered how she had once been caught by such a trap, and she felt a rushing empathy for the dead deer. She bent over and pried apart the teeth of the trap, gently extracting the animal's foreleg. Then she gave a mighty yank to the trap's chain. The chain was old and rusted, and the links that secured it to the base of a thin sapling parted easily. Ann held the trap in her hand, looked at it with an expression of disgust, and then threw it onto the ground beside her.

She uncoiled the length of rope that she carried at her belt and tied it around the hind legs of the deer. With the rope slung over her shoulder and grasping both the rifle and the trap's chain in the other hand, she headed toward home, dragging the animal along behind her. Although the deer had been a relatively young one, it still weighed quite a bit, and Ann found herself struggling mightily to keep her footing in the slushy snow.

When she reached the house, she continued on to the back, where she left the deer lying on the ground while she went inside to put away the rifle. Devorah glanced up from her sewing to see Ann enter the kitchen, stamping the snow from her boots and scowling furiously.

"Ann, what is it?" she asked, concerned. "Didn't you find any rabbits?"

"No, but I found a deer."

Devorah was surprised. "A deer!"

"Yes, and it was caught in this trap." Ann held up the clanking, ugly thing for Devorah to see. "It was half dead and I had to kill it."

"Oh, Ann, I'm so sorry," Devorah sympathized.

"It's the same type of trap that got me," she raved on.

"Really?" Devorah said curiously. She stepped forward to examine it more closely.

"There oughtta be a law against it. Damn traps," Ann grumbled.

"Oh well, we'll have venison. It'll be good."

"I suppose. But I don't like the way I got it." Ann picked up a long sharp knife and went back outside to gut the carcass.

Almost to the end of his second week of incarceration, Ace Fairlane lay supine on the cot in his cell, both arms behind his head, staring up reflectively at the ceiling rafters. He had been feeling exceptionally well lately, and his booze-tortured body was finally beginning to enjoy some semblance of health. He had not touched one drop of whiskey during his stay at the jail, and his mind was no longer clouded in an alcoholic fog. He had also benefited from eating three square meals a day and from passing his nights in sound, restful sleep. He was looking forward to being released soon and was pondering his next move.

The front door of the jailhouse opened and closed. Ace heard the voices of the sheriff and another man, but he did not turn his head to see who the visitor was until Andy Hanks called out to him.

"Hey, Ace!" Hanks yelled from across the room. "Y'got somebody here t'see ya."

Ace levered himself upright. "Huh? Whozzat?"

"It's the Rev'rund. Prob'ly here t'call down the wrath o' God on ya," Hanks chuckled.

Ace grimaced in disgust but stood passively aside while the sheriff selected the proper key from his heavy key ring and unlocked the door of the cell. Reverend Todd, smartly dressed in a conservative blue suit, stepped inside the cell and waited patiently until the sheriff had locked the door again and returned to his desk.

"Mr. Fairlane," the preacher began hesitantly. "I have come to pay you a visit." He looked around for a chair, found none, and remained standing.

Ace glared suspiciously up at Reverend Todd. "What fer? This ain't no social call. Last thing I need's a Bible spoutin' preacher."

"I have only come to find out how you are getting along. Are you eating well?" Ace nodded wordlessly. "Are you sleeping well?" Ace nodded again. "Is there anything you need?"

"I need t'git outta here," he said determindedly.

"I am told that you will be discharged in two more days."

"Good. It's 'bout time," he grunted.

"My son—"

"I ain't yer son!" Ace growled.

Reverend Todd spoke softly, trying to ignore Ace's surly mood. "Have you given any thought as to what you will do when you leave this place?"

Ace shrugged noncommittally. "Mebbe. A li'l."

"Have you thought of how you are going to repay certain . . . ah . . . debts that you owe?" The preacher recalled Delilah's ample form, colored slightly, and cleared his throat.

"I'll work it off."

"How?" he prodded. "You have no job, no steady income."

"I'll think o' somethin'."

"Mr. Fairlane, I want you to know that I have been personally responsible for maintaining your farm." Ace glanced quickly up in surprise. "I have enlisted the aid of some of my parishioners, and we have taken care of your animals and cleaned up your house."

"Why, uh . . . that's right nice o' ya, Rev'rund." For once Ace truly didn't know what to say. He was amazed that people could still show kindness toward him.

"You have a small farm, but the land is still good. I would like to see you apply your God-given talents to the land and plant a good crop and use it to pay off your debts. It is true that a man reaps what he sows, and if you could put yourself back into your land, you would be richly rewarded for the sweat of your labors."

Ace considered the preacher's words. "Ahhh . . . wal . . ."

"Think of it, Mr. Fairlane. Think of how well you feel right now, having been away from the demon rum for two weeks. Your head is clear, your eyes are focused, you're standing up straighter. It does my heart proud to see you like this. If you could remain off of the spirits, you could become a truly fine man of whom this community would be proud."

Ace scratched his head uncomfortably. "Aw, shucks, Rev'rund, I ain't nothin' like that."

"But you could be if you really desired to change your ways. There's nothing that a man can't do if he really wants to, if his heart is in the right place. 'I lift up mine eyes to the hills from whence cometh my help.'"

"Wal, now, I don't go thinkin' much o' all that God stuff, but mebbe y'really got somethin' there. Talkin' 'bout the land an' all that. I s'pose m'place could stand a li'l fixin' up. Proud, huh?" he mused thoughtfully, rubbing the stubble on his chin.

"May I suggest one more thing, Mr. Fairlane? It would be to your advantage to have a bath, a shave, a haircut, and possibly another change of clothes. You have a rather . . . uh . . . offensive odor, if you will pardon my saying so."

Ace grinned. "I jist might, Rev'rund. I jist might s'prise y'all."

Ace was never released as scheduled. During the night the weather changed drastically, and a bitter wind swooped down out of the northern skies, bending the bare branches of the trees and howling across the flat prairie land. The snow began to fall, lightly at first, but then the cloud cover intensified, and the flakes became wet and heavy, swiftly burying the land under a deep white layer. The blowing wind quickly turned the storm into one of blizzard proportions, swirling the snow into immense drifts against the trees, the barns, the houses. By morning, all roads and sidewalks were impassable, and the town of Sutter's Ford lay dead and deserted. Only the saloon and the jailhouse remained open. None of the other shopkeepers had dared to brave the elements and venture into town. Still the blizzard raged on with no signs of abating.

Devorah stood at the curtained window, anxiously looking out at the falling snow. They had risen that morning to gaze upon a world of white, and even then they could barely perceive the large barn through the fiercely blowing wind and snow. Melissa had wanted to go outside and play, but Devorah had expressly forbidden her to leave the house.

"Looks like it's going to be a bad one," Devorah observed with a hint of worry in her voice. "It'll probably last all day."

"Well, we've got plenty of supplies to sit it out," Ann told her. "It's just one of those good old-fashioned blizzards I was telling you about." She buttoned her heavy coat, wrapped her scarf around her head, and pulled on her mittens.

"Ann, must you go out?" Devorah asked, deeply concerned.

"Devvie, I have to. The animals have to be fed. I have to bring in more firewood. Don't worry," she said reassuringly. "It's just a little snow. I've been out in worse than this."

"Promise to be careful?"

"Devvie, I promise! The rope's out there. I'll be fine."

Devorah had to let her go. She stood at the window and watched Ann's slim form pushing forward against the buffeting wind, one hand clutching the guide rope. Devorah lingered in her place until Ann was swallowed up from her sight; then she let the curtain fall and turned to take care of the breakfast dishes.

Ann performed the chores quickly, not wanting to remain out in the cold any longer than was necessary. She fed the pigs, forked out hay for the horses and cows, and scattered feed on the floor of the barn for the chickens. She cleaned out the larger animals' stalls and carried in fresh water for them. Lastly, she milked the cows and brought the full milk pails, one by one, back to the house. She stayed inside by the fire for a little while in order to warm up a bit, and then she made her way out to the woodpile and carried in several armloads of wood. When she finally finished all of the morning chores, she stripped off her wet outer apparel, hung her things up in the bathroom to dry, and collapsed on a chair in front of the fire, cradling her stiff fingers around a hot coffee cup.

"Boy, it's cold out there!" Ann said, shivering. "You were right—it really is bad."

"You were gone for a long time. You must be frozen," Devorah answered her.

"I'll be all right. I'm warming up now," she said, sipping the coffee. "But I'm gonna have to keep going out there all afternoon."

"Why?"

"Have to keep the pump going. We don't want the water to freeze up on us. We'll have to keep using the inside pumps, too, maybe run some extra water into buckets."

Devorah sighed. "Oh dear, I'd forgotten about that."

Ann made hourly treks to the outside water pump while Devorah sat in front of the fire and sewed and Melissa played quietly at her feet. The almost constant exertion in the freezing temperatures, between operating the pump and bringing in additional loads of firewood, soon brought Ann to the point of exhaustion. By dinnertime, she could barely hold her head up at the table, and although she was hungry, she hardly had the strength to eat anything.

"Ann, you look really tired," Devorah said, frowning with concern. "Why don't you just go on to bed?"

"Can't, Devvie," she replied, shaking herself awake. "I have to feed the animals one more time, and then I want to check that pump again."

"But Ann . . ."

"Won't take long, Devvie. I'll be right back."

Ann shrugged wearily into her outer garments, which had never quite dried out completely, and opened the front door, bracing herself against the frigid blast of wind. She struggled to pull the door shut behind her and stood bent almost double on the porch, grasping the wooden railing for support. She slowly inched down the steps, groping for the assurance of the thick rope. When her mittened fingers found it, she held onto it tightly with both hands, stepping directly into the bitter wind and pulling herself along toward the barn.

Once there, she hurriedly took care of all the animals, pausing occasionally to pat a flank, rub a nose, scratch behind an ear. Then she prepared herself to make the return trip to the house, but halfway along the rope path, she suddenly stopped and stood there for a moment with her back against the driving wind. *Maybe I ought to bring in one last load of wood*, she thought. *Then we'd be sure to have enough for the night. Where is that woodpile? It's so white I can't see. Should be over there somewhere.*

The water pump momentarily forgotten due to her weariness, Ann squinted into the night, trying to determine the dark outlines of the woodpile. She let go of the safety of the rope and stumbled through the deepening snow, one arm outstretched, groping for the edge of the woodpile. When she reached it, she stepped behind it and paused to catch her breath. Then she stood up unsteadily and began to stack a few pieces of wood on the ground beside her.

The small space behind the woodpile, being in a sheltered spot from the wind and the drifting snow, was a relatively open area. Ann was standing in very little snow, but she was not attentive enough to notice a solid rock-hard patch of ice at her feet, made by the previous days' thaw and swiftly refrozen during the blizzard. Ann stepped backward, her boot hitting the slick ice, and she lost her balance, both feet sliding out from under her. She was airborne for a split second, and then she came crashing down to the ground, the back of her head solidly connecting with the hard ice. She grunted at the jolting pain in her head, and then everything became black, drawing her down into unconsciousness.

More than an hour had passed since Ann had left the house, and Devorah's fears for her safety were becoming almost overpowering. Together, she and Melissa had washed and dried the dinner dishes, and then Devorah had sat in her rocking chair by the fire, taking the child onto her lap and attempting to read her a story in order to keep her own thoughts off of Ann's whereabouts. Melissa had been quick to sense her mother's worried state of mind, knowing that she wasn't concentrating on what she was reading and picking up the slight tremor in her voice.

"Mommy, why is Ann taking so long?" she asked, looking up into Devorah's drawn face.

"I don't know, honey," Devorah answered truthfully. "I suppose she's very busy out there."

"Do you think maybe she could have gotten lost?"

"I don't think so. She knows where the rope is." Devorah quickly brought the story to an end and set the book down on the low table beside her. "All right, sweetheart, it's time for you to get to bed."

When Devorah returned from listening to Melissa's prayers, tucking her into bed, and kissing her good night, another half hour had gone by and still Ann had not come through the door. Devorah anxiously paced the floor, stopping briefly at the window to draw back the curtain and peer out into the white night. *Where could she be?* she wondered frantically. *Why isn't she back yet? She shouldn't have been out there this long. Oh, Heaven forbid, what if something happened to her? She could be lying out there hurt, frozen, dead! Oh my goodness, I've got to go look for her!*

Devorah grabbed her woolen cape and flung it over her shoulders. She tied her scarf around her head, tugged on her mittens, and snatched the lamp from its place on the table. She flung open the front door and was startled when the force of the wind tore the doorknob from her grasp. She held the lamp high in front of her, but its feeble light could not penetrate the swirling snow. Realizing that the lamp was useless, she put it back inside and then struggled mightily to pull the door shut behind her. She stood on the porch, buffeted by the chilling wind, not knowing which direction to take. "Ann! Ann!" she shouted, but the wind blew the words from her mouth, and she could hardly hear her own voice, much less that of another person calling to her.

Devorah seized the guide rope in a death-grip, fearful of losing her way, and she managed to attain the safety of the barn. Once inside, however, she saw that the barn was dark. She groped around for the kerosene lamp that was kept in a corner by the huge doors, found it, lit it, and held it before her to dispel the gloom. "Ann! Are you in here?" she cried, but only the sleepy stares of the horses and cows met her searching eyes. *Oh dear . . . oh dear,* she thought. *Where is she?*

Devorah extinguished the lamp and went back out into the shrieking storm. The wind ripped the scarf from her head and whipped the hair into her face. She felt wet icy flakes of snow falling into her collar and melting there, trickling down the back of her neck. She clung to the rope, slipping and falling in her abject panic. *Oh my dear sweet God!* she screamed silently. *Where could she be? If she's fallen in a drift somewhere, I'll never find her. The woodpile! What if she's gone to the woodpile? That's the only other place.*

Devorah was reluctant to release her hold on the guide rope, but her fear had made her strong. She set out in the general direction of the woodpile, lumbering through the drifts. She finally reached it, leaning against it and gasping for breath. The cold air seared her lungs and made her cough. She pressed on, unheeding, to the rear of the woodpile, where she stumbled over Ann's unconscious form. She dropped to her knees in the snow, the folds of her dress flying about her, and she reached out to touch Ann's cold face.

"Oh, Ann! Thank the Lord I've found you!" Ann did not stir. "Ann! Can you hear me?" Still there was no response.

Devorah ripped away the buttons of Ann's coat and placed a hand upon her breast, frantically feeling for a heartbeat. The beat was still there, still strong, and Devorah exhaled a sigh of relief. She grasped Ann underneath the arms and began to tug her body back to the house, the bitter wind angrily driving the snow into her face and making her eyes water uncontrollably. She tugged the heavy form on and on, calling upon reserves of strength that she didn't even know she possessed. After she had dragged Ann up the porch steps and into the house, she collapsed upon the floor.

Devorah lay there for a long time, winded, panting, trying desperately to calm herself and to catch her breath. When at last she felt strong enough to stand, she rose unsteadily to her feet and began to drag Ann down the hallway and into the bathroom. She quickly fired up the small stove, pumped out kettles full of water, and set them on top of the stove to heat. Then she divested herself of her wet outer clothing, throwing her cape and mittens and dress into a pile on the floor. She stooped down and rapidly stripped Ann of her frozen clothes, tossing them unmindfully into the same pile. She lifted Ann bodily, placing her into the tub. When the water was heated but not too hot, she slowly poured the contents of the kettles into the tub. She allowed the water to reach a level of several inches, and then she knelt by Ann's head, rubbing her hands and patting her cheeks.

Ann felt a gradual warmth returning to her body and spreading out along her stiff limbs. She moved her head, and her eyes fluttered open; then she groaned in sudden pain as she lifted her hand to gingerly touch the swollen lump at the back of her head.

"Ohhh, my head!" she moaned, tightly shutting her eyes. "What . . . where?"

"Let me see," Devorah said briskly. She leaned forward to examine Ann's head, passing her fingers lightly over the lump. "You gave yourself quite a crack. You're lucky your head's not split open."

"Feels like it," Ann mumbled.

"What happened out there?"

"I . . . uh . . . was coming back from the barn, and I . . . decided to get some more wood and . . . I fell . . . slipped on the ice . . . hit my head. Guess I must've blacked out. How long was I gone?"

"Long enough. I was worried sick! I had to come out looking for you, and if I hadn't found you . . ." Devorah shook her head, not wanting to consider the possible consequences.

"You mean you . . . dragged me back to the house . . . all the way in here?"

"I did. All by myself."

Ann's face broke into a sarcastic smile. "Well, Devvie, I didn't know you cared."

"Of course I care. I'm relieved that you're all right." She reached down in the water to clasp Ann's hand, holding it tightly to her own breast.

While Ann was soaking in the bathtub Devorah went into her bedroom, changed out of her damp underthings, and put on her nightgown. Then she returned to the bathroom, bearing Ann's own nightgown. She helped Ann stand up, slowly, carefully, for the girl was still slightly dizzy, and she got her out of the tub, briskly toweled her down, and slipped the nightgown over her head. With one arm grasping Ann firmly around the waist, Devorah led her down the hall and into her bedroom, where she eased her gently down onto the mattress. She propped a pillow behind Ann's head and pulled the quilt up close around her body.

"I'm still cold," Ann said, beginning to shiver.

"I'll make you some warm milk, then."

Ann reached out for Devorah's hand. "No, don't leave me," she said tremulously.

Devorah calmed her, patting her hand. "I won't be gone long."

A few minutes later, Devorah sat down on the edge of the mattress and held out a glass of warm milk. Ann took it from her and sipped the liquid slowly, feeling its welcome warmth spreading throughout her stomach.

"I'm *still* cold," she said, handing back the empty glass. "My stomach's warm, but the cold's deep down inside my bones."

"All right, then, I'll warm you. Move over."

Devorah lifted up the quilt and slipped into bed beside Ann, resting her back up against the wooden headboard and drawing Ann protectively into the crook of her arm. Ann rested her head upon Devorah's breast and draped one arm about her waist. She lay there quietly, unmoving, absorbing the heat of Devorah's body. *Oh, I love it, I love it,* Ann thought, closing her eyes. *I could stay here forever.*

"Devvie . . . ," she spoke softly.

"Mmm? Are you getting warm now?" Devorah rubbed Ann's shoulder, squeezing the muscle.

"Yes." Ann experienced a brief flashback to the night when they had exchanged their first kiss, and she drew her breath in sharply as another sweet pain coursed through her body. "Almost too warm," she whispered.

Devorah glanced down at her, frowning quizzically. "What? What do you mean?"

"I mean . . . I want . . ." She trailed her fingers across Devorah's midsection, caressing the flesh through the material of the nightgown, sliding tentatively upward in search of a breast. "Devvie, you're so soft . . . so warm . . ." Her breathing changed, becoming deeper, heavier.

Devorah caught her seeking hand before it could travel too far and held it tightly, firmly. "Ann . . ."

"But I love you, Devvie," she insisted ardently, rising up on one elbow. Her pleading eyes moved over Devorah's shadowed face, and she reached out a hand to touch her face, letting her fingers follow the angular jaw line. "I want you. With all my heart and soul, I want you. I want to make love to you."

"Ann, you're in no condition . . ."

"Please, Devvie. Stay here with me tonight." Her eyes were bright, full of love and tenderness and longing.

"Ann . . ." Devorah lay there, uncertain of what to do or say. *Oh, how she wants me,* she thought wonderingly. *Doc never looked at me like this. This girl is truly in love. This is my chance. But should I take it? Could I do this now? Somehow I don't feel . . . ready.* Devorah gently pushed Ann's hand away. "No, Ann. I can't," she whispered, sadly shaking her head.

152

"What? But why?" Ann said dejectedly. "I won't hurt you. I thought . . . with what you told Doc . . . that you . . . Don't you love me, too, Devvie? Don't you want the same thing?"

"I just don't feel ready yet. This is a big step for me."

"Well, how long is it gonna take you to get ready?" Ann exclaimed in exasperation. "I've been more than patient with you, and it's killing me, it's driving me up the wall!"

"Well, they say patience is a virtue," Devorah quipped lightly.

"Don't play games with me, Devvie," she said sternly. "I can't take it. I thought you made your choice."

"I did," Devorah answered, recalling the expression of hurt on Doc's face.

"Well, then, act upon it. Do something about it. Don't just leave me here all tied up in knots."

"I will . . ."

Ann tried to pin her down. "When? When the spring comes? After the crops are planted? By the next harvest dance?"

"Soon . . ."

"Devvie, you don't realize what you do to me!"

"I'm sorry . . . I don't mean to."

Ann reached out for Devorah's hand again. "I'm just so afraid I'll lose you. I couldn't bear it. I can't live without you." She pressed the hand to her lips.

Devorah smiled shyly. "No, Ann, I'm more afraid I'll lose *you*. That's why I'm so hesitant. I don't want to give myself to someone, to give all my love, my everything, only to have that person taken away from me. I've had enough of grief and tears in my life, and I do want this happiness between us, oh, believe me, I do!" she said earnestly, sincerely. "But I can't just leap right into this. I have to know, I have to be sure."

"But, Devvie, *I'm* sure. Isn't that enough for us?"

"No, Ann, I have to be sure, too. Please don't be angry with me."

Ann also smiled. "I'm not; just frustrated. I'll always be here for you, Devvie. I'll never leave you. But only if you swear . . . that some day . . . you'll come to me."

"I will . . . I swear it," Devorah said firmly. She leaned forward and tenderly kissed Ann upon the forehead, then gently pushed back the damp strands of hair from her face.

153

The following morning, Ann awoke with a splitting headache. She attempted to rise from the bed, but her legs would not support her weight, and the room spun dizzily around her. She fell back limply onto the pillow, clasping her temples and tightly shutting her eyes. After Devorah had gotten dressed, she came into Ann's bedroom and sat beside her on the edge of the mattress.

"How are you feeling today?" Devorah asked with concern.

"Ohhh, awful!" Ann groaned. "My head feels like it's out to here. It's pounding . . . I feel dizzy."

"You could have a mild concussion. You'd better stay in bed today."

"But the chores . . ."

"Well, I'll just have to do them, won't I?" Devorah stated with finality.

"Did it finally stop snowing?"

"Yes. It's deep out there, but it's not too bad."

Ann remained in bed for the next two days. Devorah brought her meals in to her, and Melissa curled herself up on the bed and read stories aloud from her storybook. On the third day, Ann's headache finally began to wane, and she felt strong enough to walk around and sit quietly by the fire. Devorah still refused to permit her to go outside, insisting that she should not overtax her gradually returning strength.

Devorah, however, was very tired. She had performed all of the chores as well as all of the cooking by herself for the past three days, and her muscles, unused to such labor, were aching and sore. That evening as she and Ann relaxed together in their chairs by the fire, Devorah realized that she was now beginning to get a sore throat. She swallowed painfully, gingerly rubbing her throat.

Ann glanced up from her reading. "What's the matter, Devvie?"

"Throat's sore," she whispered hoarsely. She felt a sneeze coming on and whipped out her handkerchief to blunt its force.

"Oh dear," Ann sighed. "You're coming down with something."

" 'Fraid I am," Devorah agreed, nodding. "Probably just a cold."

"Devvie, that night when you came out to find me . . . Your clothes were wet, too, and you didn't bother to take a bath, did you?"

"No, I didn't," she admitted ruefully. "I suppose I should have, but I was just too worried about you." She sneezed again, blew her nose, sniffed loudly.

Ann set the book down and rose from her chair. "Well, then, come on," she said, taking Devorah's elbow. "I'm going to give *you* a hot bath now."

The next day, Devorah was feeling no better. The cold had hit her with full force, and she was now confined to bed. Her nose was clogged up, her sinuses were inflamed, and her eyes were red and watery. She developed a fever, mild at first, but gradually soaring over the next few days, and her entire body ached and throbbed. Her cough became deep and hacking, irritating her already raw throat, and her form shook with wracking spasms. The cold became worse and she grew weaker still.

After yet another night that Devorah had passed tossing and turning feverishly and mumbling incoherently, Ann was frantic with worry. She sat beside Devorah now, gently mopping her sweating face with a cloth that had been dipped in cooling water.

"Devvie, you've got to let me go for Doc," Ann urged her.

"No . . . no . . ," she protested weakly with her eyes closed. Her body shook as another violent coughing spasm assailed her, and this time she brought up blood-tinged phlegm.

"But Devvie, you're sick! You're getting worse, not better!"

"I'll be all right . . ."

"No, you won't! You could catch pneumonia and die!"

"Oh, I won't die." Devorah attempted to smile, but the effort was almost too great.

"You haven't eaten for days. Your strength is going."

"Doc won't come. He doesn't even want to talk to me."

"Well, I've done all I can for you. You could at least let me go into town and see Lilah."

"Why Lilah?"

"Maybe she's got some home remedies. I don't know! I've got to do something!"

"Go . . . if you want." Devorah waved her hand feebly in dismissal and Ann was gone.

Ann trudged out to the barn and saddled up the horse, feeling that this would be faster than taking the wagon. She swung herself onto the horse's back and moved off, plodding quickly but cautiously through the deep snow. The surrounding countryside was beautiful in its stark whiteness, but Ann did not have time to consider this since her thoughts were preoccupied with Devorah's debilitating illness.

She soon reached the town of Sutter's Ford and noted as she passed down the center street that the shopkeepers were beginning to dig themselves out from under the drifts. The sidewalks were now clear, and the stores had reopened. Ann pulled her horse to a halt in front of the saloon, dismounted, and went inside in search of Delilah Emerson. It had been a long time since she had last seen the madam on that one fateful spring night, and she idly wondered if Delilah would recognize her. She found the madam lounging up against the piano in the far corner of the room, swirling a glass of liquor in her hand and listening to the soft music.

"Uh . . . Miss Lilah," Ann said bravely, stepping up to her side.

"Yeah, honey, what kin I do fer ya?" Delilah eyed Ann's slim form with approval, her gaze slowly traveling over her body. "Sayyy, ain't'cha . . ." Recognition began to dawn on her face, and she snapped her fingers in sudden remembrance. "Ain't'cha that gal that's been stayin' with Miz Lee? Yeah, y'are! Yer name's . . . Ann, ain't it?"

Ann shifted uncomfortably. "Uh . . . yes."

"What'cha doin' here? Need 'nother workout?" She threw back her head and laughed raucously.

Ann felt her face turning red, and she desperately wanted to sink into the floor. "Miss Lilah, I need your help."

"Yeah, I'll bet'cha could stand 'nother good time."

"No, no," she continued. "It's Devvie—she's sick. I need your help, *please.*"

"What? Sick, y'say? What's she got?"

"An awful cold . . ."

"C'm on, gal, come with me," Delilah said abruptly. She took Ann's arm and led her up the stairs, down the hall, and into her elegantly furnished room at the rear of the building. She motioned for Ann to sit on the edge of her huge bed, and then she plopped herself down beside her. "Now what's this yer tellin' me? She's sick?" Ann nodded. "How sick?"

"Awful bad," Ann told her. "She caught a cold a few days ago, and it's turning into something worse."

156

"Pneumonia?" Delilah questioned, arching her eyebrows. Ann shrugged her shoulders unknowingly. "Wal, why haven't'cha been t'Doc?"

"Devvie doesn't want me to get him," she attempted to explain. "They've . . . had a falling out. You're the only other person I thought to go to. Can't you help me, tell me what to do?" She leaned forward anxiously.

"Hmmm," Delilah mused, frowning. "Has she got a fever?" Ann nodded. "Is she coughin' bad?"

"She's bringing up mucus."

"Wal, that means 'er lungs're clogged up," she pronounced ominously. "We've got t'unclog 'em fast, otherwise she's had it. Lissen, gal, y'know what an onion poultice is?" Ann shook her head. "Y'cook up a mess o' onions an' wrap 'em in a cloth, an' y'put 'em direckly on 'er chest. If that don't work after a coupla hours, y'do it again."

"What's it supposed to do?"

"It'll make 'er heave 'er guts out, but she'll bring up all that mucus, an' 'er fever'll break." Ann flinched at the prospect of making Devorah temporarily sicker. "Do it, gal," Delilah insisted sternly. "It's the only thing." She rose, walked over to the heavy walnut dresser, and selected two bottles of dark liquid from among her store of medicines. "An' then when she's done upchuckin', y'make 'er swaller this," she added, holding out the bottles to Ann. "It'll make 'er feel better an' it'll kill the cold."

Ann smiled gratefully. "Thanks, Lilah. I'm much obliged."

"Not t'mention it, honey. Sometimes people come t'me fer more'n jist a good time."

Delilah stood in the open doorway of her room, watching Ann's disappearing form moving quickly toward the stairs. The door next to her opened softly and Ruby came to stand beside Delilah, pouting jealously.

"Who was she?" Ruby demanded.

"Why, she's one o' us," Delilah grinned broadly, throwing her massive arm around Ruby's shoulders. "Sure's I'm standin' here, she's one o' us. An' that Widow Lee's got quite a fine figger 'erself. Yep," she nodded knowingly, "she sure picked a good one!"

Ann hurried home and went straight into the kitchen, where she promptly fired up the stove. She set a large pot of water on to boil,

157

and inside the pot she placed a metal colander. She dumped a sack of onions on top of the kitchen table and sorted through it, setting aside a dozen extra large onions. With knife in hand she sat down and started peeling as Melissa stood by her side, watching her curiously.

"What are you doing?" Melissa asked. "Are we having these for supper?"

"No, honey," Ann replied, "These aren't for eating."

"Then what are you doing with them?"

"I'm going to make a poultice out of them to put on your mother's chest. It's for her cold."

"She's sick, isn't she?" the child said gravely. Ann nodded. "Is she bad sick?"

"Well, Lissa, she's got a very bad cold, but she'll be all right, don't worry. That's why I have to do this—so it'll help her feel better." *Oh, please God, I hope,* she prayed fervently. *Please let her be all right. Please let this stuff work.*

"Do I get to help?" the child volunteered eagerly.

"No, Lissa. When I go into that bedroom and shut that door, I don't want you coming in for any reason unless the house is on fire. I don't want you bothering your mother just yet, and I want you to promise to stay out of the way."

"Okay," she agreed easily. "Are you going to make Mommy well?"

Ann ruffled Melissa's hair. "I'm going to try, honey."

When the onions were steamed and soft, Ann lifted them out of the colander, broke them up into individual segments, and scattered them thickly on an old bath towel. She covered the steaming onions with another towel and rolled up the edges so that the pieces would not fall out. She slid her arm through the handle of the berry bucket, and then also carrying the onion poultice, she went down the hall to Devorah's bedroom. The door was slightly ajar, and she nudged it farther open with her elbow, stepped into the room, and closed the door with the toe of her boot. Devorah was only half asleep. She stirred and opened her eyes at the sound of Ann's approaching footsteps.

"Ohhh," Devorah mumbled sleepily. "Are you back?"

"I've been back for a while. I had to make something in the kitchen." Ann laid the folded towels on top of the bedside table and lowered the bucket to the floor. She sat on the edge of the mattress and began to unbutton Devorah's nightgown.

"What . . . what are you doing?" Devorah protested weakly. She attempted to brush Ann's hands away.

"Hush, Devvie, lie still," Ann soothed her. She grasped Devorah's shoulders, pulled her up into a sitting position, and stripped off the upper half of the nightgown so that Devorah was nude from the waist up. Ann gently lowered her head back down to the pillow, alarmed at how listlessly her body flopped about. *Oh Lord, she's half gone already,* Ann thought. *Please don't let me be too late.*

Ann spread the hot, wet, odorous poultice across Devorah's chest, tucking the towels in securely around her ribs in order to keep the onions in place on her skin. Devorah made no further attempt to stop her, but only lay there quietly with her eyes closed. Ann left the room then and returned to the kitchen to fix Melissa and herself a quick dinner. After they had both done the dishes, Ann went back to the bedroom to look in on Devorah. She still was lying in the same position. Ann sat in front of the fire and played a few games with Melissa, and then after a little more than an hour had passed, she put the child to bed in her own room.

Ann selected a book from the small shelf in the living room and went in to sit on the chair beside Devorah's bed. She turned up the lamp on the bedside table, but found that she could not concentrate on her reading. Her eyes kept leaving the printed page as she glanced from time to time at Devorah's haggard face. Devorah still had not moved, and the room reeked of onion fumes. *What's taking so long?* Ann agonized. *Did I do it right? Is there something I've missed? It's been two hours; it should have worked by now. She's lying there so still! Is she dying? Oh, Lord, if You let her live, I'll do anything, anything. Oh please!*

Devorah's eyes popped open in sudden fear and she looked around wildly. She struggled to rise, but Ann leaped out of her chair and put a restraining hand on her shoulder.

"Devvie, take it easy! What's the matter?"

"I . . . feel awful," Devorah whispered, one hand clutching her throat. "I think . . . I'm going to be sick." She swallowed hard, clapped a hand to her mouth.

Ann lunged for the bucket and held it under Devorah's chin as she leaned over the side of the bed. The towels fell forward, and the

159

pieces of onion cascaded to the floor. Devorah coughed and gagged, vomiting forth yellowish gobs of mucus that splattered noisily into the bucket. Again and again she heaved, her stomach muscles contracting almost continuously, and Ann stood over her, supporting her trembling form and brushing the hair back from her face. When at last she could bring up no more and the violent contractions had subsided, she sank back exhausted onto the pillow, the sweat beading on her forehead and running in little rivulets down her sunken cheeks. Her breath came in short gasps, and she passed a hand weakly across her brow.

Ann quickly wiped up the scattered onions and dumped them into the bucket. She sat on the edge of the bed, dipped a fresh cloth into a basin of cooling water, and gently sponged Devorah's face and chest with love and tenderness in her every movement. She pulled the nightgown up again and quietly patted Devorah's hand for a few minutes. When she attempted to rise, her own hand was gripped in a strong hold.

"Don't leave me," Devorah said timidly.

Ann smiled. The very thing that she herself had said to Devorah just the previous week. "Devvie, I'm going to make you some tea," she said. "I'll be right back."

Ann removed the soiled bucket from the room. A few minutes later, she returned and handed Devorah a cup of warm weak tea. She sipped the liquid slowly, and Ann was relieved to see the color finally beginning to come back into Devorah's worn features.

"How do you feel now?" Ann asked solicitously.

"Much better," Devorah nodded with a slight smile. "What on earth did you do to me?"

"Onion poultice. Lilah's home remedy. Sure worked, didn't it?" she grinned.

"My land, I don't think I've ever been so sick . . ."

"Hush, Devvie. Lie still."

Devorah reclined against the pillow and closed her eyes, although she did not drift off to sleep. Ann pulled the chair up close to the bed and sat holding Devorah's hand for a long while. After enough time had elapsed for Ann to be sure that Devorah's stomach would retain the tea, she uncorked one of the medicine bottles and poured a generous dose of the liquid into a glass.

"Drink this, Devvie," she said. Devorah took one small sip and grimaced at the taste. "Come on, drink it all down," Ann urged her. "That's it . . . a little bit more . . . good."

Devorah made a face as she handed back the glass. "What awful stuff! Where did you get it? I told you not to go to Doc."

"I didn't, honest. This is from Lilah. She told me what to do for you."

Devorah was amazed. "Lilah? Of all people!"

"She's a good woman, Devvie. Her heart's in the right place. Now go to sleep." Ann tucked the quilt about her face, kissed her softly upon the forehead, and extinguished the lamp.

By morning the fever had finally broken and Devorah's brow was cool to the touch.

Ten

Ace Fairlane was released from jail early in the first week of February. Due to the preceding month's unexpected blizzard, he had been forced to remain where he was and wait patiently for a break in the inclement weather. At first he had protested loudly, but then he soon came to realize that receiving three square meals a day wasn't such a bad deal after all. He had also been able to occupy himself by playing a few hands of cards with some of the other prisoners through the narrow bars of his cell.

On the morning of his release, the sheriff came up to the front of his cell with keys in hand and began unlocking the door. Ace was reclining on his cot and staring up at the ceiling.

"Awright, Fairlane, on yer feet," drawled Hanks. "Yer leavin'."

"Leavin'?" Ace repeated in disbelief. "Y'mean yer lettin' me go now?"

"'At's right," Hanks affirmed. "I'm gittin' mighty tired o' lookin' at yer ugly face." He held the cell door open wide. "G'wan, beat it 'fore I change m'mind."

Ace needed no further urging. He scrambled to his feet, grabbed his coat and hat, and headed toward the door. He was just about to turn the knob when he halted abruptly at a shout from behind him.

"Fairlane!" Hanks called after him. "Y'stay the hell outta trouble, y'hear me? I don't wanna see yer face back here again!"

Once out on the sidewalk, Ace went directly over to the barbershop, where he indulged himself in the luxury of a clean shave and a much-needed haircut. Afterward he briefly considered stopping in at the saloon, but then quickly shook his head, thinking better of the idea. He jammed his hat down tighter over his eyes, buttoned up the open neck of his coat, and began the long walk home with the even, measured steps of a man who had just been granted a new lease on life.

Less than an hour later, he turned into the lane leading to his farm. He strode up to the rundown house and let himself inside,

162

surveying his surroundings to determine just how much work had indeed been done by the preacher and his parishoners. Ace was amazed at the cleanliness and orderliness of the house and its furnishings. He entered the kitchen, noting that the stacks of pots and pans and dirty dishes had all been washed, dried, and put away. He went out to the barn to check on his animals and found that the floor of the barn had been recently swept. The animals' stalls had been cleaned out and strewn with fresh hay.

Ace lifted his hat, scratching the top of his head. *Wal, not bad, not bad at all,* he mused, taking it all in. *That Rev'rund wuz true t'his word.* He went back outside and stood looking up at the dilapidated roof of the barn; then his eyes moved to scan the outside of the house. *I s'pose I oughtta do some fixin' up aroun' here,* he conceded to himself. *Never realized the place wuz this bad b'fore. An' I think I'll plant me some crops this year, too. Wonder if the ol' plow's still any good. Wal, I'll show 'em, I'll show 'em all. Ol' Ace is gonna really s'prise 'em! Might's well start now, I s'pose. Need t'keep busy.*

He returned to the barn to check out his pile of spare lumber. It would take him a long time, probably several months, but he would do it all and become a stronger man for the effort.

Doc McClintock was a very harried man this winter. He had quite an influx of patients, and he had kept himself busy not only with his office appointments but also with paying various house calls, some routine, others emergency, to the sick, the infirm, the shut-ins. Doc found himself constantly on the move, and although he knew he wasn't getting any younger, there was as yet no other man to take his place, so he determinedly continued his frenetic pace.

One afternoon, he was leaving his office for yet another house call. He hastily donned his coat and hat and, without thinking, reached for his black medical bag. As soon as his hand touched the shiny new leather he paused, and a brief flash of pain entered his mind as he recalled the night that Devorah had given it to him, her eyes bright and sparkling, her mouth upturned in a dazzling smile. How deeply in love with her he had been, still was, always would be. How much he had wanted to share his life with her and make her a part of his world. He shook his head sadly in dismissal of his thoughts, opened the door, and stepped out onto the sidewalk, nearly colliding with Reverend Todd.

"Well, Dr. McClintock!" the preacher said in greeting.

"How are you, Reverend?" Doc responded politely, giving a slight nod.

"Quite well, thank you. And you? I must say, you seem rather in a rush."

"Ah, that I am," Doc told him. "This winter season has been very hard on everybody. They all seem to be sick with one thing or another, and I'm always on the go. No rest for the weary, they say."

"But, Doctor, you really should take some time for yourself, you know," the preacher suggested.

Doc shrugged, "Ah, well . . . can't be helped."

"Tell me frankly now, how are things going for you?"

Doc signed heavily, shaking his head. "Ohhh, professionally fine, but . . . not in any other way."

"Do I detect a troubled heart?" the preacher questioned kindly, arching his eyebrows.

"I suppose one could call it an affair of the heart that ended badly."

"But, Doctor, surely you must know from your profession that hope is something that springs eternal in the human breast."

"Yes, quite true," he agreed, "but there is no hope here."

"Do not despair, Doctor. The Bible tells us to look to the Lord for solace. He is our comfort in affliction."

"It also says 'Physician, heal thyself.' If you will excuse me, Reverend . . ." Doc smiled tightly, turned, and strode away.

On Valentine's Day, Ann and Melissa sat at the kitchen table, busily cutting out red paper hearts. Melissa had made one huge heart, and Ann was now helping her to carefully paste pieces of white paper lace around the edges. In the center of the heart the child had written I LOVE YOU, MOMMY in huge block letters. When the enormous thing was finished, it was a formidable work of art, and Melissa was quite proud of her efforts.

"That's really good, Lissa," Ann complimented her.

"Can I go give it to her now, please, please?" the child begged eagerly.

"Well, all right. I don't see why not."

164

Melissa snatched up the paper heart, jumped down from her chair, and trotted down the hallway to Devorah's bedroom. Ann followed behind her, knocked softly upon the door, and then turned the knob. Devorah was reading in bed, sitting upright with her back propped against the pillow. She glanced up as they entered and laughed when Melissa leaped onto the bed, throwing herself into her mother's arms.

"My goodness, child," Devorah exclaimed, "you're getting to be so big and heavy!"

"It's Valentine's Day, Mommy," Melissa bubbled excitedly.

"It is?" Devorah said wonderingly. She winked at Ann, who smiled back at her.

"Uh-huh. An' I made this for you because I love you." She thrust the heart forward, and Devorah took it, read the words.

"Oh, honey, it's just beautiful! And I love you, too, very, very much." Devorah kissed the child and hugged her tightly to her breast.

"When are you getting up, Mommy?" she asked.

"Soon, dear," Devorah assured her. "I'm feeling much better now, and I'm almost well."

"I sure hope so because Ann can't cook as good as you do."

"Lissa!" Ann said in mock horror. Devorah laughed.

The child gave her mother a quick peck on the cheek, clambered down from the bed, and scampered out the door.

Ann moved to sit on the edge of the mattress and reached out to take Devorah's hand. "Devvie, I'm so glad you're all right. I don't know what I would have done if that poultice hadn't worked."

"Well, it did, and I'll be fine, thanks to you."

"You were awfully sick."

"I know. Don't remind me."

"Well, maybe next time you'll take better care of yourself," Ann hinted.

"Only if you don't go getting lost in snowstorms," Devorah instantly shot back. They both laughed. "You know, Ann," she said seriously. "I think once I get on my feet again, I ought to pay Lilah a visit to thank her, maybe take her a freshly baked nut bread."

"Good idea, Devvie. She'll like that," Ann approved. "Want me to go with you?"

"No. I think this is something I should do alone." She paused thoughtfully, then glanced at Ann. "Hey cook, where's my dinner?" she said playfully.

Ann saluted, standing up. "Coming right up, ma'am! But are you sure you want to eat my cooking?"

"Why not? I taught you everything you know."

Ann nodded. "So you did. And some day, Devvie, it'll be my turn to teach you," she said softly.

Before Ann left the room, she handed Devorah a small red paper heart. It was devoid of any superfluous white lace, and it had been folded in half. Devorah opened it and read the printed words in the center of the heart. The statement was simple, straightforward, to-the-point. It read BE MINE. Their eyes met and held.

Ann was having a nightmare. She turned her head from side to side on the pillow, her hands fluttered aimlessly at the quilt, and her legs jerked spasmodically under the covers. Still held in the grip of sleep, she whimpered and mumbled incoherently.

She was at the saloon, upstairs in Ruby's room. She was lying naked on the bed, and the mulatto girl was giving her a relaxing rubdown. The fingers moved over her body, kneading the muscles, pushing, pulling. The pressure became softer now, more caressing, and the fingers lightly brushed her breasts, teased the nipples into pointed rigidity, moved slowly up the inner curve of her thighs, threaded through the dark curly hair. Ruby's body lowered itself upon Ann's, arms caressing, legs entwined, and breast on breast. Lips met lips in a lustful, passionate kiss; thigh moved against thigh in erotic sensuality. Ann felt herself rising, soaring higher and higher, approaching the breathlessness of climax . . .

She was outside now, walking through the deserted streets of town. It was dark, it was late at night, but the white moon was attempting to peek out from a concealing cloud cover. She passed through the shadowed alleys, heard the strident cries of cats, heard the muffled barks of dogs. She turned a corner and saw a form, an indistinct shape, bending over another smaller form that lay sprawled and still upon the hard dirt ground. The larger form moved, turned toward her, and she saw that it was a man, saw the evil glint in his eye, saw the hint of a deep scar upon his cheek. She could almost identify him; it was . . . it was . . . and then the revealing light of the moon suddenly winked out. The hulking shape of the man threateningly approached her. She stepped slowly backward, spun around,

166

began to run, her boots pounding the hard ground, her breath coming in choking gasps. The man was close behind her, reached out to seize her hair . . .

"No! No!" Ann heard herself scream. She sat bolt upright in bed, panting, her eyes wide and staring, and then she buried her face in her hands to blot out the memory, to thrust it far away.

The door to her bedroom flew open and Devorah rushed in, bearing the lamp. She quickly set the lamp down on the table and hurried to Ann's side, enveloping her in protective arms, holding her tightly, smoothing the hair back from her face, rocking her gently.

"There, there," Devorah soothed. "It's all right . . . it was just a dream . . . it's over now . . . relax . . . it's all right . . ."

"Oh, Devvie! Oh God!" Ann's panic gradually began to subside, although she still clung tremblingly to Devorah.

"Do you want to tell me about it?" she asked softly.

"It was . . . it was *him*. I saw him again. He was bending over her body . . . and then he came after me. The moon was out, and I saw him . . . I saw his face . . . and I almost . . . I almost knew him!"

"Hush, be still. Don't think about it."

Ann clenched her fists in frustration. "Devvie, *I know this man!* But my mind won't let me remember."

"It's all right, Ann," Devorah calmed her. "Doc said not to force it. He said you'd remember in time, when you're ready."

"But what if it's too late when I remember? What if he kills again?"

Devorah wordlessly tried to allay Ann's fears, but she couldn't help but recall her secret conversation with Doc when they had discussed Ace's past. Doc's words now echoed ominously in her brain; he had said, "One of these days she may remember whom she saw, but by then it may be too late . . . too late . . . too late . . ."

One afternoon toward the end of the month, Devorah took the wagon alone into Sutter's Ford. She purchased a few minor supplies at the general store, but her primary intent was to pay a social call to Delilah Emerson. She strode briskly down the sidewalk, carrying a basket that contained two wrapped loaves of cranberry nut bread that she had just baked earlier that morning. She went into the saloon and looked around for Delilah, but did not immediately see her.

Devorah was an impressive woman, standing tall, slim, and straight in her flowing skirts, her long blonde hair tied up in a tight bun, and she soon became aware of an uneasy silence as the men ceased their talking and riveted their attention upon her. Having thus made her presence known, she moved up to the bar with easy, self-confident steps.

"Excuse me," she said to the bartender. "Is Miss Lilah here?"

"Upstairs in 'er room," he motioned with his thumb. "Go alla way down t'the end o' the hall."

Devorah felt all eyes upon her as she quickly ascended the stairs. She passed to the rear of the building and rapped smartly upon the last door.

"C'm on in," Delilah called out. She had been adjusting her makeup in front of the mirror, and she turned to see who her visitor was. "Why, Miz Lee!" she said in genuine surprise. "C'm in, sid-down." She hastened to pull out a chair for Devorah. "What brings y'here? I heard y'wuz sick, but yer lookin' good."

"I am well now, thank you. I have come to express my deepest gratitude to you."

"T'me? Fer what?"

"When I was ill, Ann came to you and asked you for help. You told her what to do for me and it worked, although I must say, I wouldn't wish an onion poultice on anybody," Devorah smiled broadly.

"Wal, I'm glad t'hear that," she grinned back. "That wuz an ol' recipe o' m'gran'ma's. Comes in handy sometimes."

"Lilah, you saved my life."

"Aw shucks," she said, averting her eyes. " 'T'weren't nothin'. I woulda done the same fer anybody."

"But it wasn't just anybody; you did it for me."

"Naw, that gal o' yers did it. I jist tol' 'er what t'do."

Devorah shook her head. "No, Lilah," she insisted quietly. "If it weren't for you, Ann wouldn't have known what to do. I might not even be talking to you today."

"Aw, heck." Delilah was at a loss for words; she was unused to receiving such sincere praise.

Devorah held out the basket of nut loaves. "I would like for you to accept this small token of my esteem."

"Why, Miz Lee, that's right nice o' ya. I'll share this with m'gals."

"Please do. It is obvious to me that not all Christians go to church. There are other souls like you whose hearts are in the right places and who truly mean well. Thank you, Lilah." Devorah stepped up to her, embraced her quickly, and left her standing there with basket in hand, totally flustered and almost ready to weep.

March breezed in with a blustering wind. The days were warmer, and the sun finally melted the last remaining vestiges of snow from the ground. The earth was soggy, the trees still stark and bare of foliage, and deep within the forest, the level of the small brook rose slightly as it received the runoff from the melting snow.

Devorah now spent more of her time outside, slowly readjusting the muscles of her body to cope with the sometimes strenuous load of daily chores. She raked the front and back yards, cleaning up the fallen branches and twigs and other winter debris. She went into town and purchased numerous bags of seed in preparation for the coming planting, stacking the bags in a far corner of the barn.

Ann passed most of her afternoons working diligently on the restoration of the old wagon that Doc had given her. She had replaced the missing spokes on the wheels, even making a whole new wheel when she had determined that one of them could not be repaired. She had replaced the rotting side boards with new panels, nailing the wood securely into place with firm, practiced strokes of the hammer. All that remained now was for her to apply a solid coat of black paint to the wagon in order to seal the wood and protect it against further decay. She paused in her work, stepped back from the wagon, and stood with her hands on her hips, approving her progress. Devorah came into the barn, looking for her, and moved to stand beside her.

"Ann, that really looks good," she said, admiring the wagon.

Ann turned at the sound of her voice. "Doesn't it, Devvie? It's almost like new again."

"You've worked hard on it. I want you to know I'm proud of you." Devorah slipped one arm across Ann's shoulders and gave her a quick complimentary hug.

"Really?" Ann beamed.

"Of course. I wouldn't have had the patience to fix that thing up myself. Or the expertise. You've done well."

"Thanks, Devvie," she said, shyly accepting the praise. "It makes me feel good to know I've done something with my own hands."

"Well, you have many talents to be proud of. You should believe in your own capabilities."

Ann pushed around the scattered hay with the toe of her boot. "No one else has ever believed in me before," she stated quietly.

"I believe in you," Devorah told her simply, and meant every word. "I believe in the quality of your mind, in the sincerity of your heart, in the strength of your hands."

"You almost make me feel as if I could do anything."

"You can," she said firmly. "The world is yours."

"But are *you*, Devvie? What good would it do me to have the whole world if I could not also have the one I love?" Devorah was silent, and Ann placed a tentative hand upon her hair. "The world is only mine for me to lay at your feet." *Oh Devvie*, she yearned. *How much I would give you, how much I would worship you.*

The days passed swiftly. Ann finished the wagon, and then both she and Devorah butchered another hog. They cleaned out the intestinal casings and used them to make sausages, which were hung from the low rafters of the smokehouse along with ham shanks and bacon slabs. A compact fire was kept burning in the center of the smokehouse floor, and water was periodically sprinkled onto the flames to produce billowing quantities of acrid curing smoke.

They stripped the fat from the carcass of the hog and used it to make lye soap. The lye was obtained by pouring warm water through wood ashes, and it was boiled with the chunks of fat in a large iron kettle. Salt was added to the mixture, which allowed the creamy soap forming within it to rise to the top, thus separating itself from the unwanted residue beneath it. The soap was then placed in cloth-lined wooden molds and left to set for a couple of days, after which it was cut and shaped into crude bars.

Both of these tasks required a great deal of time and patience, and Ann's and Devorah's hands were rough and stained from the harshness of the chemicals. One night after dinner, they both sank wearily into their chairs in front of the fireplace. Devorah rocked slowly back and forth, coffee cup in hand, while Ann bent forward and eased her boots off of her aching feet.

"Boy, I'm glad that's all done," Ann said with relief.

"Yes, so am I," Devorah agreed. "We'll have enough soap to last us for a while."

"The stuff sure stinks," she proclaimed, wrinkling her nose.

"Well, we can't always have the fancy bars from France. We'll just have to do without."

"I'll get you some more sometime, Devvie. I'd rather you'd have soft hands."

"Quit worrying about me and start thinking of all the plowing you're going to be doing pretty soon," Devorah reminded her.

"Ohhh, the plowing!" Ann sighed and sank farther down into her chair, stretching her legs out in front of the fire.

"Winter is over; no more easy days. Planting time is almost here."

"Slaving from sunup to sundown again, huh?"

"Absolutely," Devorah confirmed. "You'll have earned every blister."

"Gosh, if I could just be one of Lilah's girls, I wouldn't have to lift a finger all day," Ann mused dreamily. "I could lie around on perfumed sheets and pop chocolates into my mouth."

"And what would you have to show for it—not a single ounce of muscle."

"But I'd be pampered," Ann simpered.

"Such talk! One thing I don't do around here is pamper. You get out there and you work for your keep."

"I'd rather be a kept woman."

"You are one. I'm keeping you. But I never said it would be easy living with me."

Ann shook her head sorrowfully. "No, it isn't, Devvie. It really isn't." Then she looked at Devorah, and they both burst out laughing.

Early one morning long past the hour of midnight, Doc McClintock was awakened out of a sound sleep by an insistent pounding at his front door. He swung his legs over the side of the bed, fumbled to light the lamp, and rubbed his eyes, squinting at the sudden glare from the bright flame. He hastily shrugged into his robe, stumbled toward the door, and slid back the bolt. Holding the lamp before him, he beheld the rumpled figure of Joseph Anders standing on the porch. The man's normally neat hair was tousled, his eyes blinked and darted frantically, and he was panting for breath.

"Doctor, you've got to come quickly!" he gasped, sucking in great lungfuls of air. "It's Cora—her labor's started!"

"Take it easy, man," Doc attempted to calm him. "Step inside and wait for me. I won't be but a minute."

Doc dressed quickly, threw on his coat, and snatched his medical bag. He did not have time to waste in harnessing his horse, so he went with Anders in his own carriage. They traveled at a swift pace back toward the town.

"What time did the labor begin?" Doc inquired, firmly holding onto his hat.

"Several hours ago," Joseph said nervously. "She said she felt funny, so I helped her to bed. She had a few contractions at first, but then they started coming faster and closer together, and she sent me after you. I'm sorry it's so late, but . . ."

"Quite all right," Doc assured him. "I'm used to this."

"But she's not due for another two weeks yet. You told us at the end of the month."

"Well, sometimes the Lord sees fit to speed things up a bit. Calm down, Joseph! It will be all right."

"She's in terrible pain."

"Joseph, I swear to you she will be just fine."

The Anders couple lived in the quarters directly above a small women's wear shop which they owned and operated. Cora managed the store while Joseph worked at his job at the bank. He was the nephew of the bank president, and he hoped to someday assume his uncle's prestigious position. He and his wife were both still young; he was thirty-five and she was thirty-two.

Joseph now drew the carriage to a careening halt at the rear of the building. He tethered the horse to the hitching post and both he and Doc quickly ascended the narrow wooden staircase leading to the upper apartment. As they burst through the door, Doc was immediately aware of high-pitched strangulated cries coming from the direction of the closed bedroom door. He stripped off his coat and outer jacket and began rolling up his shirt sleeves. After instructing Joseph to set some water on the stove to boil, Doc grabbed a handful of towels from the bathroom and entered the bedroom, shutting the door quietly behind him.

Cora lay flat on the bed, clutching her swollen stomach with both hands and grimacing in pain as another strong contraction swept over her, further draining her ebbing strength. The bedcovers were in total disarray, and she was sweating and straining and gasping for breath. Doc moved over to her side, leaning to smooth the hair back from her damp forehead.

"Well, Cora, it's time, isn't it?" he spoke softly. She could not answer him, but only looked up at him with frightened eyes. Another contraction gripped her and she opened her mouth in a soundless scream. "Here, take my hand," Doc offered. "Squeeze it hard. There, there, dear, it will soon be over."

Joseph knocked on the door and entered, bearing a basin of steaming water. He left the room and returned again, this time bearing another basin of cold water. He set them both on the bedside table, then stood there fidgeting, uncertain of what further action to take.

"Good, Joseph, thank you," Doc said. "Please wait outside now. There is nothing more that you can do here."

After Joseph had departed, Doc assisted Cora in levering herself up into a half-sitting position on the bed. He propped the pillows behind her back and then gently pulled up her nightgown so that she was nude from the waist down. He spread towels over the sheets underneath her buttocks, noting that the mattress had been soaked by the breaking of her waters. He pulled a chair up next to the bed and settled back to await the imminent birth.

The labor was long and tedious; the hours dragged on endlessly. Several times, the baby's head appeared between Cora's outspread legs, but as the contraction passed, the baby was drawn back up into the birth canal. Doc had already sterilized his instruments in the hot water, and he was prepared to use the forceps if necessary. Finally Cora gave one last straining push, and the baby's head popped out, followed by the rest of the body. Doc barely had time to cut and tie the umbilical cord, suction the baby's nose and mouth, and make sure that it was breathing before a second baby moved down and out through the birth canal. Two children—twins; a boy first and a girl second.

173

Doc cleaned up the babies, wrapped each one in a towel, and placed them in Cora's outstretched arms. He removed the soiled towels from the bed, noting with satisfaction that they contained both expelled placentas. He then turned his attention to Cora, dipping a clean cloth into the basin of cold water and tenderly sponging off her now relaxing body. He gently kneaded her uterus through the stomach muscles and wiped the dripping sweat from her brow.

Cora was sublimely happy. She couldn't help the tears coursing down her cheeks as she lovingly gazed at the angelic faces nestled in the crook of each arm. The past was erased, the pain of Bonnie's death was eased, and she was once again fulfilled. The babies began to cry lustily, and she unbuttoned the top of her nightgown to offer each one a milk-filled breast.

Doc smiled at her. "Well, Cora, you've done well. Didn't I tell you it might be twins?"

"Oh, Doc! I'm so happy . . . my children!" She laughed and cried at the same time. "Thank you, Doc, thank you, thank you," she murmured over and over.

Doc opened the door and went out into the living room where Joseph had been anxiously pacing the floor and running his fingers through his disheveled hair. As soon as Joseph saw Doc, he rushed up to his side.

"Doc! My wife, my child . . . how are . . .?" he stammered breathlessly.

"Fine, Joseph, fine," Doc beamed. "You have a son . . . *and* a daughter."

Joseph was overcome with emotion and he dashed into the bedroom, kneeling reverently at his wife's side.

Eleven

Ace Fairlane was perched on top of a wooden ladder that had been propped against the side of his frame house. He had already completed the task of repairing the inside of the barn, and he was now fixing up the broken and sagging storm window frames on the house itself. He glanced up at the sound of approaching hoofbeats and spied Reverend Todd's carriage entering the front yard. Ace clambered down from the ladder and went to greet the man, wiping his dirty hands on an old rag.

"Howdy, Rev'rund," he grinned congenially.

Reverend Todd stepped down from the carriage. "Mr. Fairlane," he nodded cordially.

"What brings ya alla way out t'these parts?"

"I have come to pay a social visit, Mr. Fairlane, to ascertain how you are getting along."

Ace winked at him. "Y'jist wanna check up on me, eh, Rev'-rund?"

"Quite the contrary," he said in denial. "I have merely been concerned about your . . . ah . . . state of health."

Ace spread his arms wide. "Why, I'm jist fine as y'kin see."

Reverend Todd inhaled deeply, concentrated, could not detect the slightest trace of alcohol on Ace's breath, and visibly relaxed. He scanned the surrounding grounds and saw the ladder.

"You are working, Mr. Fairlane?" he inquired curiously. "Have I interrupted you?"

"Nah," Ace replied with a wave of his hand. "I wuz jist gittin' ready t'take me a rest anyways. C'm on, I'll show y'what I done."

Ace led the preacher on a quick tour of the barn, pointing out the various repaired spots. They also walked around the outside of the house, and Ace rattled on talkatively about his immediate plans for the place.

"Now soon's I git done wi' these windows here, I'm gonna shore up that saggin' front porch. An' then when it gits a bit warmer, I'm gonna paint the whole house. Nice white paint with a li'l black aroun' the windows, huh? An' then I gotta git out there an' plow." He gestured expansively toward the distant fields. "Gonna plant me a good crop o' corn this year."

"Mr. Fairlane, I must say, I'm quite impressed," the preacher said in amazement.

"Aw, hell—'scuse me, Rev—a li'l hard work never hurt nobody."

"Well, I'm pleased to see that you're keeping yourself occupied. Good works profiteth a man well. You will lay up treasures for yourself in Heaven."

Ace shrugged. "I'm jist gittin' back t'the land is all. Got me 'nuff treasures right here on earth 'thout havin' t'worry 'bout what comes after."

Reverend Todd cleared his throat somewhat disapprovingly, but chose not to comment further.

Ann was out plowing up the fields. She had been toiling at it for days, eager to be done with the task and to have the land ready to receive new seed. She had hitched up one of the strong work horses to the plow, and she kept her gaze downward, eyeing the curved blade of the plow as it gouged out a trench through the dark fertile soil. Occasionally, she paused to stoop and pick up numerous rocks and stones, placing them into a canvas sack that she had tied around her neck and shoulders. She continued on, passing the back of her sleeve across her sweating face, and when she reached the end of the long row she dumped the contents of the sack into a small pile on the ground, turned the horse around, and started back the other way.

Devorah was standing in the middle of the garden plot. She had cleared away the dead scattered leaves and the litter of sticks and twigs, and she was now spading up the soil. She used a shovel to overturn the dirt, then raked it down smoothly. After a while, she paused in her labors and looked up across the fields, shading her brow with one hand against the warm spring sun. She spied Ann pressing on doggedly down the rows and watched her for a few minutes, leaning heavily upon the shaft of the shovel. *How hard she works*, Devorah thought admiringly. *How strong she is. I can't imagine how I ever used to do that all by myself. She must be getting tired. Perhaps I should bring her some water.*

Devorah let the shovel fall from her hands and walked over to the water pump that stood in the yard. After rinsing her hands and face in the cooling stream, she took the bucket that sat nearby, filled it with water, and set off toward the distant fields.

Ann saw her approaching from afar, reached the end of her row, and reined the horse to a halt. She eased the sack of rocks from her aching shoulders and sank wearily down onto the ground to catch her breath. She waved at Devorah and smiled.

"I thought you'd like a drink," Devorah called out to her. She reached Ann's side, set the bucket on the ground, and sat down next to her.

"Thanks, Devvie," Ann said gratefully. She dipped the ladle into the cold water and gulped a long refreshing drink. "That's sure some hard work. Haven't done this in a while, you know."

Devorah took the ladle and also drank. "Why don't you quit for now and call it a day?"

Ann shook her head. "Can't, Devvie. I have to finish this part here and then get the wagon and pick up all the rocks. I've only got a few hours of daylight left."

"It'll still be here tomorrow," Devorah suggested, gesturing at the land.

"I know, but once I get started, I like to keep right on going." Ann dropped her handkerchief into the bucket of water, wrung it out, and mopped her dirty face. "How are you doing with the garden?"

"Pretty well. I'm spading it."

"We should be able to plant the wheat by . . . oh . . . middle of April, don't you think? And then the corn by the beginning of May."

"If the weather holds," Devorah said uncertainly.

"It'll be all right, you'll see," Ann assured her. "We'll have another good crop this year."

"Well, I hope so."

"We've got good land, good seed, lots of rain and sun to make things grow. What could possibly go wrong?"

Devorah didn't know, but she suddenly experienced a nagging premonition of impending disaster.

Easter fell on the last Sunday of the month, and the day was obscured by a cool drizzling mist. Devorah donned her Easter finery,

177

selecting a pale yellow dress that she had not worn in two years but which was still relatively new. She buttoned up the fancy dress shoes that Ann had given her for Christmas, put on the hat that Doc had given her, and draped a white shawl over her shoulders.

Ann and Melissa were already dressed and waiting for her, and as they went out the door Ann took along the parasol. They all piled into the carriage with the child sitting in the middle of the seat. They set off through the misty patches of white fog and Ann held the open parasol over their heads in an attempt to stave off the falling rain.

Presently they arrived at the church and took their customary places at the front, close to the altar. Devorah kept her gaze riveted straight ahead as she listened to the soft organ music, but Ann turned in her seat and watched the incoming townspeople. She saw Doc McClintock enter and sit toward the center on the opposite side. Then her eyes widened in surprise as she caught sight of Delilah Emerson, who was followed by two of her youngest girls and Ruby, her personal favorite, and Ruby's little boy. Ann poked Devorah in the ribs, whispering excitedly to her and urging her to turn around.

Delilah was arrayed in an eggshell colored skirt with matching jacket and beautiful white ruffled blouse. She wore white kid leather high-button shoes and white gloves. Perched on top of her fat red clumps of sausage curls was an enormous plumed hat with lavender and cream colored ribbons trailing down the back and a thin netting covering the front. She also carried a lavender parasol and the numerous jewels on her fingers sparkled and shone as she moved down the aisle. Behind her came two of her girls—one blonde, dressed in sky blue; the other brunette, dressed in jade green. Ruby and her son Jesse brought up the rear of the train, and they were no less handsomely attired.

Delilah made a commanding entrance into the church, sweeping down the aisle as if she were a queen followed by her loyal attendants. At first, the townspeople were shocked into a stunned silence, but then they soon recovered and sent up an exciting whispering. Doc turned his head at all the commotion, and when he beheld Delilah, he rose deferentially from his seat and stepped out into the aisle.

"Why, Miss Lilah Emerson!" Doc declared with a wide smile. He took her extended hand, kissed it, and bowed deeply to her. "Will you do me the great honor of sitting with me?"

"My pleasure, Doc," she acceded, gliding into the pew and followed by her retinue. She sat immediately next to Doc and chuckled with undisguised pleasure as she heard the outraged voices of two old women sitting directly behind her.

"Oh! Did you see that?" said one woman.

"Why, I can't believe my eyes!" said the other woman.

"Such nerve! A woman like *her* coming into a holy place."

"The Widow Lee is a saint compared to her."

"And did you see the good doctor's disgraceful behavior?"

"Consorting with a woman of her kind! Oh, mercy!"

"Someone should speak to the Reverend about this."

"Maidie, hold my hand. I fear I shall faint!"

The townspeople quieted down when the service began. Reverend Todd stepped to the front of the pulpit and scanned the somber faces below him. His eyes fell upon Delilah and her entourage. His lower jaw dropped open in shock and he became aware of a hot flush spreading slowly over his face. *Oh dear. Oh my,* he thought in consternation. He swallowed hard, closed his eyes, and silently prayed to his God for guidance. It was all he could do to continue the service.

The time soon came for the long-handled collection baskets to be passed along the pews. Everything went smoothly until the basket bearer stopped at Delilah's row. She rose from her seat, took a deep breath that swelled out her magnificent bosom, and waited until she was sure she had everyone's undivided attention. Reverend Todd glanced up in panic.

"Parson," she said in a loud voice that carried well to the back of the rows, "this here's m'generous donation t'yer fine church." She waved a sealed white envelope in her bejeweled hand. "It comes outta the true spirit o' m'heart. An' there's enough money here fer ya t'give this place a good coat o' paint an' put in a new sidewalk an' git some new shrub'ry an' even git yerself 'nother bell cuz I heard the ol' one wuz cracked. I've been in this town fer twenny years now, an' it's high time I did somethin' fer alla its fine upstandin' citizens." She tossed the envelope with a flourish into the collection basket and sat down again.

At first there was a disbelieving silence and then pandemonium reigned as everyone began talking at once. Doc gave Delilah an affectionate hug and leaned to kiss her cheek. Ann started to laugh uproariously, and even Devorah bent over double in her merriment.

179

After the service had ended, Reverend Todd stood in the vestibule of the church and greeted his departing parishoners. They all expressed surprise and delight over Delilah's gift, and many of them were full of additional suggestions as to what to do with the money. When Delilah herself came up to him, he gripped her hand in a limp and timid handshake only because he felt compelled to do so.

"Uh . . . Miss uh . . . Miss Lilah," he stuttered nervously, totally in awe of her presence and that of her followers. "I must thank you for your generous gift to the church."

"Oh, pshaw, Parson," she replied with a wave of her hand. "Jist see that'cha use it right."

"I assure you that we most certainly will. We shall . . . uh . . ." His eyes roamed over her sparkling jewels, traveled up the front of her ruffled blouse, centered upon her full bosom. He cleared his throat uncomfortably.

"Good boy." Delilah smiled, winked at him, briefly patted his cheek, and swept out the door.

Doc stepped up beside the preacher and clapped him jovially on the back. "You'd better get ready for another christening, Reverend."

"What?" he asked blankly. He could still smell the lingering scent of Delilah's perfume. "Pardon me, I'm sorry. Who?"

"Cora Anders has had her babies. Twins!"

"Oh, really? Splendid!"

"Yes, I . . ." Doc broke off abruptly as he spied Devorah and Ann moving toward him in the crowd. Devorah had not seen him yet. "Excuse me, Reverend," he said and hastily pushed through the milling people until he was face to face with Devorah. This would be the first time that they had spoken to each other in almost three months.

Devorah looked up into his familiar face, stopped dead in her tracks, and absently reached down, fumbling for Melissa's hand. They stared at each other for an endless moment, neither moving nor speaking, and finally Doc was the first one to break the spell.

"Ah, Devorah . . . ," he attempted hesitantly.

"Hello, Doc," she smiled sadly.

He had to reluctantly tear his eyes away from her in order to give a polite greeting to both Ann and Melissa.

Melissa gazed up at him with wide dark eyes. "How come you don't come out an' see us any more?" she asked innocently.

"Well, I've uh . . . I've been very busy," Doc explained uneasily.

"Devvie, I'm going to take Lissa out to the carriage," Ann interrupted quickly. "It's stopped raining, and we'll wait for you there. Nice to see you, Doc."

"Yes, good day, Ann." He watched her leave and then turned back to Devorah. "Ah, Devorah . . . how are you doing?"

"Quite well, thank you. And you, Doc?"

"Oh, fine, fine. I've been busy."

Devorah nodded politely. Doc searched her face for some unknown sign, found none, and averted his gaze. A silence loomed between them, so thick that it could have been cut with a knife.

"Did you uh . . . finish all your plowing?" Doc blundered on.

"Yes. Ann's been doing it."

"Fields are ready for planting, then?"

"Almost."

They lapsed into another strained silence. Doc shifted his position uneasily, met her steady gaze, and glanced away again. He felt suffocated by the tenseness of the situation.

"Uh . . . Devorah . . . about that night. Have you . . . have you thought about it?"

"Yes," she admitted truthfully.

"And?" he prompted encouragingly.

"And what?"

"Have you . . . possibly changed your mind?"

"No, Doc," she sighed. How difficult he was making this on himself, how hard he was taking it. "I meant what I said," she added softly. She saw the pain in his eyes and ached for his despair. "I want you to be happy, but please, please let me go." She reached out her hand and gently touched his lined cheek. "I do love you, but not the way you want me to. I want us to be friends and I'm so afraid that you hate me now."

"No, Devorah. I could never hate you," he said earnestly.

"Then, please, let's just keep it this way, and I could still have your friendship to hold on to."

"But, Devorah, I love—"

"No, Doc," she interrupted him firmly. "Please don't speak of love. Please, no more, no more. Not when I cannot return it."

"We must talk about this again in a better place."

181

"Doc, for the last time, I beg you, I entreat you to *let me go.* There is nothing more to be said."

"Devorah, you have left me with a broken heart."

"I'm sorry, Doc, I truly am. Believe me, I didn't want it to be this way. Now please, I must go. They're waiting for me." Devorah blinked back her brimming tears and exited the church, leaving him standing with bowed head, dejectedly alone.

Melissa burst into the house on scampering feet. Ann and Devorah soon followed, roaring with uncontrollable laughter, tears streaming down their faces, trying to hold each other up. They both collapsed on the chairs at the kitchen table, wiping their eyes.

"Wasn't Lilah something today?" Devorah marveled.

Ann rolled her eyes upward. "Oh, she was dressed to the hilt! And she sure can strut!"

Devorah recalled Delilah's grand entrance into the church and shook her head in wonderment. "I never would have believed it if I hadn't been there."

"Well, I kept poking you to get you to turn around. And did you see the look on everybody's faces when she was walking down the aisle? Just like a parade!"

Devorah thought of all the old biddies who would be thoroughly scandalized. "She certainly caused quite a stir. A madam in a church!"

"Oh, but the money she gave them—it must have been quite a lot. She turns a good profit on her business. Owns the whole saloon, you know."

"Really? How do you know that?" Devorah asked curiously.

"I heard it once from somebody on the street one day when we were in town doing some shopping," Ann replied. "What did you think of the Reverend today when he saw Lilah sitting there on *his* bench in *his* church? Did you see his face turn red?"

"He was so nervous he could hardly conduct the service."

"I think he's got a hankering for her."

"Ann!" Devorah pretended to be properly shocked, but she laughed again.

"Well, why not? He fell all over himself, dropped his Bible. It was written all over his face. You could see it plain as day the way he stared at her."

"How about when Lilah stood up right in the middle of the collection?" Devorah knew that as long as she had been going to this particular church, no one had ever dared to stand up and speak during the services.

"Oh, she did it with such flair!" Ann howled anew, bending over to clasp her aching sides.

"She's really a good woman."

"Yes, that she is, Devvie. I admire her for her guts—a madam with a heart of gold."

Melissa came over to where they were sitting and tugged impatiently at her mother's skirts. "Mommy, can we color the eggs now?" she wanted to know.

Devorah reached out to tousle the child's hair. "All right, sweetheart. We're a little behind on that, but I suppose we could do it now."

"Good, Mommy. I get all the blue eggs."

"But, Lissa, what if I want one?" Ann said.

The child shrugged. "You'll just have to eat the others."

Devorah took the eggs that had been gathered earlier that morning and set them in a pot of water on the stove while Ann filled up half a dozen old coffee cups with cider vinegar and various dyes. Later on after the eggs had boiled and cooled, Ann helped Melissa to carefully dip them into the coloring agents. The eggs were placed upon a piece of cloth to dry, and then after everything had been cleaned up Devorah allowed the child to select two eggs and go off by herself to eat them. She and Ann still remained at the table. Ann chose an egg of her own, cracked it, peeled it, and began to sprinkle salt on it.

"Um, Devvie, what did you and Doc talk about?" she inquired nonchalantly, biting into the egg.

"Oh, things."

"Well, can't you be more specific? What things?"

"We talked about the plowing and the planting. He told me he'd been busy. Then he asked me . . . about that night . . . if I'd ever thought about it . . . if I'd changed my mind."

"And what did you tell him?"

"I told him no. I told him I wanted his friendship, and then he said he still loved me."

"I hope you haven't broken him, Devvie. He's a fine man." Ann detected her almost imperceptible wince. "Devvie?" she frowned.

"I begged him to let me go."

"Where?" Ann probed gently. "Where are you going?"

"To . . . to another," Devorah whispered softly and caught her breath at the enormity of her own boldness.

Reverend Amos Todd sat alone in his study, which was located in a small corner at the rear of the church. He had been counting out the collection money that had been received from the recent Easter services. He had set aside Delilah's fat white envelope, intending to make it the very last one he opened. He now glanced over to where the envelope reposed upon his desk. He reached out a tentative hand, picked it up, and turned it over, examining it nervously. He was afraid to break the seal.

He let his eyes travel about the cramped office, taking in the badly peeling paint on the walls, noting the cracked plaster, the worn wooden floors, the seedy condition of the surrounding furniture. *Would it truly be possible,* he wondered, *to finally be able to fix this place up after all these years of neglect? New plaster, new paint, new windows, new fixtures, even a new bell and landscaping outside?* He envisioned his beloved church surrounded by a brand new sidewalk, enhanced by bright flowers and tall evergreens.

At forty-three, Reverend Todd had never married, choosing instead a life of celibacy and quiet devotion to his God. His normally austere thoughts of personal purity and moral strictness instantly departed from him whenever he confronted the madam in all of her imperious splendor. He thought of Delilah now, his mind traveling unerringly back to her handsome face, her captivating smile, her glittering jewels, the tantalizing scent of her perfume, the undoubted softness of her expansive bosom. He rapidly blinked his eyes and shook his head, not understanding his inexplicable physical attraction to her. It was highly unsuitable for a man of his dignified calling. *Father, forgive me,* he prayed earnestly. *Please help me to deal with the temptations of Satan.*

He returned his attention to the bulging envelope in his hands. He took a deep breath, hastily tore it open, and withdrew the contents. He gasped involuntarily at the thick stack of bills in front of him. With a disbelieving look on his face, he quickly counted the money. It came to a total of five hundred dollars. The color drained from his features.

The arrival of April hinted delicately of nature's renewal, whispered gently of the promise of spring. The still bare branches of the trees sprouted forth tiny, tight green buds which would soon unfurl into replenished foliage. The warming rays of the sun caressed the land, slowly dried it out, encouraged the regrowth of the wide-bladed prairie grass.

On one such beautiful day, Ann stood on the front porch of the house with both hands on her hips, inhaling the fresh smell of the air and permitting the warm wind to ruffle her long tresses. Her hair had grown considerably over the past year, now hanging down well below her shoulders, although it was still not quite as long as Devorah's thick mane. Ann would soon have to ask Devorah to give her a haircut because during the hot summer months she preferred a shorter style, not wanting the hair to feel bothersome upon her neck.

Devorah came out onto the porch and stood beside Ann, wiping her hands on the apron tied around her waist. She had just finished baking fresh bread loaves for their evening meal, and she had decided to take a brief rest to see what Ann was up to.

"I thought I heard you go out, Ann," she said. "What are you doing?"

Ann smiled. "Oh, just standing here. This weather is so warm, so wonderful. It makes me feel . . . I don't know . . . renewed. After all those long months of being inside . . ."

Devorah smiled back at her. "I'd say you had a touch of spring fever."

"Probably. I feel like . . . I want to take a walk, Devvie," she said eagerly. "Please come with me, will you?"

"A walk? Where?"

"To the woods. Remember last fall when we took a walk there and I told you it was best to come back in the spring? We can take Lissa. Come on, Devvie, say yes!" Ann's eyes were bright.

"Well, all right," she assented, taking off her apron.

Ann opened the door and called out for Melissa, who immediately left her doll and came running. They walked briskly toward the edge of the forest with the child dashing ahead and leading the way. They found the beginning of one of the many trails and slowly

185

followed its winding path, pushing deeper into the woods. They strolled leisurely along, stopping occasionally to stoop and examine clumps of wild crocuses and daffodils that were stubbornly pushing their way through the covering of dead leaves above them. Melissa picked a handful of the pretty flowers and shyly held them out to her mother, who gave her an affectionate hug and kiss for her efforts.

"Look, Lissa! A rabbit!" Ann exclaimed, pointing farther down the trail. The child scampered after it.

"Don't go too far, honey," Devorah warned. "Wait for us!" They walked on.

Ann spread her arms in a wide embrace of the surrounding forest. "Oh, Devvie, isn't this just wonderful? Doesn't it just make you feel alive? It's finally spring!"

"My, but you're quite carried away with it all, aren't you?"

"I can't help it. I feel so happy."

Devorah was enjoying Ann's elation. "Well, I'm glad for you."

"I want you to be happy, too," Ann said earnestly. "I want us both to be happy." She reached out to hold Devorah's hand.

"Ann," Devorah said fearfully, glancing around.

"Why not? Who's to see? Come on!" Ann tugged her down the trail.

Delilah Emerson had realized a substantial profit from the operating of her lucrative business and she had deposited some of the money into her sizeable account at the bank, had given some to the church, and had decided to use the rest of it to pay for some much-needed repairs on the building that housed the saloon. She was planning to spruce up the storefront by giving the building a fresh coat of paint and by installing new front steps and a flat stone walkway all around the perimeter of the building. A new sign would be attached to the front of the saloon, and on the inside, the walls would also be freshly painted, a long mirror would be hung over the bar, new tables and chairs and another piano would be purchased.

Today Delilah was on a spring shopping spree in the town of Sutter's Ford. With Ruby and her two youngest girls in tow, she had struck like a whirlwind every single women's apparel shop in town. She lavished praise upon her charges as they tried on numerous dresses, shoes, and hats and even treated herself to the purchase of several new outfits. Delilah was free and generous with her money.

All of the store clerks fawned over her subserviently, hastening to please her and to obey her commands. She and her troupe walked back to the saloon now, their arms laden with packages, excited and pleased with their selections.

"Thank you, Miss Lilah, thank you," the two girls chorused in unison.

"Don't mention it, gals," she disclaimed. "We all needed us some new duds anyways. What'cha think, eh, Ruby?"

"I think yer blowin' too much o' the green stuff," Ruby answered her. "It don't grow on trees, y'know."

"Why, that's what it's fer, child, t'spend! 'Sides, it's spring. C'm on, suck in that air, lift them feet, git inta the swing o' things," Delilah urged cheerfully.

"Are y'really gonna fix up the place?" Ruby asked, referring to the saloon.

"Shore thing, I am! 'Bout time we give it a new look. Why, when I git done with it, y'won't even reckanize the place. Be good fer biznizz, too, y'watch 'n see. Purty soon ever'body'll be doin' the same thing, an' this town'll really start t'look right."

Ann and Devorah hastened to complete the planting of the spring wheat by the middle of the month. Ann had recently finished the arduous task of plowing the fields, and she and Devorah now walked up and down the long rows, scattering the viable seed from heavy canvas sacks slung over their shoulders. The job took the better part of the week to complete, for there were several acres of ground to be sown.

When the planting was finally done, they turned their attentions to the vegetable garden near the house. Devorah sowed various flower seeds all around the outer perimeter in order to produce a colorful border while Ann planted generally the same crops that they had had the previous year. Only the corn remained to be done, but that would come early in May.

Devorah rose wearily from her kneeling position in the dirt and bent her neck and spine backward to stretch her aching muscles. Ann was still moving along the rows, bending, stooping, spilling out the seed, gently patting down the soil. Devorah enjoyed sometimes watching Ann without her being aware of it. She delighted in seeing the graceful movements of her strong young form at work so busily,

187

so earnestly. *How far she's come from a year ago,* Devorah marveled with a slight shake of her head. *And to think she couldn't even walk, had to learn how all over again. She has truly healed in both body and mind. Dear Lord, let me be worthy of this girl.*

Ann reached the end of the row and paused to rest. She turned around and noticed Devorah's brazen stare. "What are you looking at?" she asked, her face breaking into a smile.

"Just you."

"Why? Is something wrong?" she wondered.

"No. I like to watch you move."

"Oh. Well . . ." Ann shrugged and resumed her work.

At the end of the day, they both collapsed on the steps on the porch. Ann bent her head forward upon her knees, and Devorah anxiously scanned the darkening sky for signs of approaching rain.

"Hope it rains soon," Devorah said, wiping the dirt and sweat from her brow.

"It will, Devvie," Ann assured her. "God's taking care of this land. We've done our part, and He's blessed it."

"How can you be so sure? This could be the calm before the storm."

"Well, they say God helps those who help themselves. Where's your faith, Devvie? You worry too much."

"I can't help it, Ann. I just feel, I don't know . . . strange. Almost afraid."

"Afraid of what?"

"I really don't know," Devorah said honestly. She was aware that a blessing could sometimes turn out to be a curse in disguise.

Doc McClintock was present at the church for a special afternoon christening ceremony. The Anders couple had requested him to stand in as a sponsor to the newborn children, and Doc had been quite pleased and deeply touched to accept this honor. He and Joseph and Cora were the only people at the church that day. They were all congregated in front of the altar, waiting for Reverend Todd to appear and for the ceremony to begin. The babies were quiet and half asleep. Joseph held the boy and Cora held the girl. Doc stood beside them, dressed in one of his best suits with a boutonniere gaily decorating the lapel of his jacket.

Presently, Reverend Todd, wearing his usual conservative blue suit, came out of the study and assumed a position beside the font. Doc and the parents moved to join him, forming a small semicircle in front of the preacher. Reverend Todd opened the black Bible that he held in his hands and began the opening prayers. The ritual was short and simple, and when it was time for the babies to be baptized, Joseph stepped closer to the font and held out his son.

"I christen thee Jeremiah Jason Anders," the preacher solemnly intoned. He dipped his fingers into the water and traced the sign of the cross on the child's forehead. "In the name of the Father and of the Son and of the Holy Spirit."

Joseph stepped backward and Cora moved to take his place, holding out her daughter. Again the preacher performed the same gesture for the second child.

"I christen thee Katherine Elaine Anders. In the name of the Father and of the Son and of the Holy Spirit."

The little girl began to wail. Doc experienced a brief vision of himself and Devorah standing there as man and wife in place of the Anders couple, holding out their own son to be baptized and blessed. *It might have been*, he thought sadly, and quickly thrust the vision from his mind.

Delilah Emerson stood with her hands on her wide hips in the street in front of the saloon. With evident pride she surveyed the new look of the building. She had hired half a dozen of her most reliable customers to do the work of repainting the storefront and laying the flagstone walkway, and the men had fallen to their labors with a cheerful will, having also been promised free rounds of drinks upon completion of their tasks.

Delilah watched them work now, chuckling as she overheard the friendly camaraderie of their shouted jokes and good-natured joshing. She hoped they would be finished with the outside jobs before the arrival of the spring rains. She looked around and observed the rest of the town, noting with satisfaction that many of the other shopkeepers were also performing repairs to their buildings. *Looks t'me like I mighta started somethin'*, she thought, pleased with herself. *Wal, good. 'Bout time we all took some pride in this town.* She lifted her skirts as she walked up the steps and entered the saloon.

She was passing by the bar on her way upstairs when she was stopped by the voice of the bartender as he called out to her.

"Hey, Miz Lilah!"

"Yeah, Sam?"

"C'm'ere a minnit. Got a coupla fellers here who wanna speak t'ya."

Delilah moved over to the bar and stood looking into the faces of two strangers that she had never before seen. Both men had several days' growth of whiskers on their faces, and they were dressed in dusty, rumpled clothes and battered old hats. Delilah sized them up with one quick glance and assumed that they were probably homeless drifters.

"You the owner o' this here place, ma'am?" the taller man asked politely.

"Yeah. What'cha want?" she replied briskly.

"Wal, me 'n m'buddy here—I'm Bob an' 'e's Ray—we wuz jist passin' through, an' seein' as how y'been doin' allat work out there, we wuz jist wonderin' if mebbe y'could use a coupla more hands fer a while."

"We're hard workers, ma'am," the shorter man said encouragingly.

"Nope. Ain't hirin'," Delilah stated firmly.

"Y'know any other place we kin find us a job?" said Bob. "We kin do most anythin'."

"We're dependable, too," added Ray. "Can't'cha help us out, ma'am?"

"Wal," she considered thoughtfully, "tell y'what. I heard tell somebody's been fixin' up 'is place, an' e' might be able t'put'cha t'work there. Name o' Ace Fairlane. Owns a farm a few miles outta town t'the south o' here. G'wan out there an' tell 'im I sent'cha."

"Thank ya, ma'am. Much obliged." Bob tipped his beer in a salute to her, drained the glass, and then both men left the saloon.

By the following day, Delilah's inner curiosity was almost to the point of being overpowering. During her moments of spare time, she had been thinking about Ace and had been seriously wondering what he was up to. She had not seen him since his New Year's Eve debacle when he had so viciously abused poor Lizzie. Delilah had heard various scattered rumors that Ace was now a changed man, that he had given up the hard drinking, that he was putting his efforts back into the land and was occupied with the restoration of his rundown farm. Knowing the complete scoundrel that he had become over the past few years, Delilah wasn't sure exactly how much credence to give to these new rumors of his sudden rehabilitation. She decided with a firm resolve to go out to his farm and see for herself.

"Ruby!" she commanded. "C'm on, gal. You 'n me's gonna take us a li'l ride."

They both climbed into Delilah's carriage, which was usually kept at the rear of the saloon, and started off toward the southern end of town. Ace's farm was not far, being the fifth one past the city limits, and when they turned into the long narrow lane and approached the house, they soon became aware of the busy sounds of hammering. They reached the front yard, and Delilah reined the horse to a halt and stepped out of the carriage, although Ruby remained seated.

Ace and the two drifters were busily engaged in shoring up the sagging porch. The rest of the house had already been given a fresh coat of paint, and even the barn itself was half done in a bright red color. After Ace had finished nailing a wooden post that the other two men had set into place for him, he let the hammer slide out of his hand onto the ground and walked toward Delilah, mopping his face and brow with an already soiled handkerchief.

"Wal, if it ain't Miz Lilah!" he said in greeting. "I'm shore pleased t'see ya."

"Don't'cha 'Miz Lilah' me, y'ol' coot!" she answered stentoriously. "I ain't fergot what'cha did t'my Lizzie."

"Aw, c'm on, Lilah. Can't'cha let bygones be bygones?" he pleaded. "How's she doin' anyways?"

"She's all right, no thanks t'you. Did'ja learn anythin' from bein' locked up?"

"Why, I shorely did! Parson taught me a lesson I'll never fergit."

"Hmmph," she snorted scornfully. "What could 'e possibly say that'cha wouldn't let go in one ear an' out the other?"

"Why, 'e showed me the error o' m'sinnin' ways. I'm a changed man, Miz Lilah, b'lieve it or not." He placed a hand over his heart to emphasize his sincerity.

"You ain't changed, Ace. No way!"

191

"Can't'cha give a man the benefit o' the doubt?" he said earnestly.

"I ain't givin' *you* nothin'! I've known ya fer too long," she scowled.

Ace gestured toward the house and the barn. "But looka what I been doin' here. I been doin' all this fixin' up—"

"Y'shoulda done it years ago 'stead o' lettin' yer place go t'pot."

"An' I been so busy wi'the plowin' an' the plantin' that I jist ain't had time t'take a drink. Now don't that sound t'ya like a *re-formed* man?"

"Hmmph," she snorted again. "I don't b'lieve a single word!"

"Aw, c'm on, Lilah. I swear t'ya!"

"I wouldn't care if y'swore on a stack o' Bibles. A leopard don't go changin' 'is spots."

"Aww, Lilah!"

"Time'll tell," she pronounced imperiously. "Time'll tell."

As Delilah and Ruby were riding back to town, Delilah sat frowning deeply, lost in intense concentration. Ruby glanced over at her and spoke softly to intrude upon her thoughts.

"Mebbe 'e really means it," Ruby suggested.

"Nah," Delilah refuted, shaking her head. "That wuz all a line a mile long. It won't last, y'watch 'n see."

Twelve

Ann was walking slowly, aimlessly, across the flat expanse of the fields that stretched endlessly for miles ahead of her. In the distance, she could see part of the barbed wire fencing that established the boundaries of Devorah's land, and beyond that the land merged into other fields and farms that did not belong to her. The warm afternoon sun shone through a cloudless blue sky. The birds had returned and swooped and called around Ann as she walked on unheeding, deep in pensive thought.

She was beginning to feel extremely frustrated again with Devorah's standoffish mood, and she was very quickly approaching the limits of her patient endurance. The highly erotic dreams involving herself and Devorah that Ann had been recently experiencing served only to heighten her frustration and to make her uncomfortably aware that a stalemate was swiftly looming for the two women. Ann had wanted to get away from the house and be alone with herself for a few hours in order to ponder the situation and possibly arrive at a definite determination of what to do.

Ann reached the fence boundary and stopped, then bent over to pick a wild crocus. She stood there with both arms folded across her chest, holding the delicate purple flower up to her nose and letting her eyes travel over the distant fields in front of her.

How much longer do we go on like this? she sighed. *It's been almost a year since I came here, and we've been through so much together. Good times, bad times, laughter, tears. I've shared my thoughts and feelings with her, I've let her know I care. Oh, Devvie! How can you not know I care? How can you continue to refuse me, how can you keep on holding yourself back? I know you care, too. I can see the want in your eyes, and it pains me to know it's there unfulfilled. Don't you know I'm here for you to take that want away? Can't you see that it's right? If I could just somehow break down those barriers you've put up, if I could just find the right key to open*

193

up your heart . . . I've got so much love to give you, so much of myself, and yet you still, still refuse to take it. You keep telling me you have to be sure, but of what, of what? I thought you made your choice months ago when you told Doc you couldn't marry him. And then that night when you kissed me . . . Ann closed her eyes, remembering the impulsive passion of that first kiss, and then she realized that she had better sit down because her knees were threatening to give way again. She lowered herself down onto the ground and sat clasping her bent knees to her chest.

Oh, Devvie, how happy you made me that night! I thought you really meant it, you really wanted to, and then when you . . . couldn't remember . . . Oh, dear Lord, I can't take this any more! I'm trying to be so polite and considerate and patient, and I just can't . . . I can't stand it! I've done everything; I've hinted and begged and pleaded, I've even come right out and told her I wanted to make love to her and . . . nothing. She hasn't even told me she loves me. She said she cares, but that's not the same as saying she loves. Maybe she doesn't really love me at all, maybe she's just leading me on, just keeping me here to help out and making me think . . . Well, I won't have it! I won't be wasting my time like this! I could just pack up and leave and go where she'd never have to worry about me again.

If I had left right when I got well last year, I could have been a hundred miles away from here by now. I could have been doing all this work for somebody else and gotten pay for it and made my own way. I might have even found somebody by now—somebody who really loved me and wanted me, too. Devvie, I love you so much, I'll always love you, but we're not getting anywhere with each other, and I'm tired of this love that's only giving me pain and hurt. Maybe it's time for me to move on. Maybe once I've gone, you can go back to Doc and tell him you've changed your mind.

Ann considered the idea that she might lose Devorah to Doc after all, and she suddenly felt a surge of anger. She stood up, threw the wildflower onto the ground, and with the heel of her boot she crushed the soft petals into the dirt, purposely obliterating its sweet, fragile existence.

By the time Ann finished mulling over her disjointed thoughts, the sun was already hanging low in the sky and evening would soon be descending. She had passed the entire afternoon wandering alone over the fields, and she now began the long hike homeward, stepping briskly because she knew that the evening chores still remained to be done. She resolved to speak to Devorah after dinner about her plans of leaving, although she felt uncertain as to the best way to broach the subject.

Ann arrived in the front yard and saw no sign of Devorah, so she went on into the barn and mechanically performed the chores. She was not remiss in her duties, for she truly cared about the animals' welfare, but she felt dispirited and no longer concerned about what might happen tomorrow. The cat sought her out for his nightly treat of fresh milk, and she bent to stroke his scarred head as he weaved, purring loudly, between her legs. After all of her tasks had been completed and the barn door shut and barred, she walked slowly toward the house, pausing for a moment on the porch, taking a deep breath before she opened the door and stepped inside.

Devorah was standing at the kitchen stove, busily preparing the evening meal and Melissa was setting the table. Devorah had been somewhat anxious at Ann's long disappearance that afternoon, and as soon as she heard the sound of the door opening, she spun around with a worried look upon her face.

"Ann! Where on earth have you been all day?" Devorah confronted her.

"Just out," she replied, shrugging her shoulders. "Just walking in the fields."

"Walking? All day?"

"I had to be alone to think."

"About what?"

"Things." Ann tried to keep her answers brief and unrevealing.

"Ann, you were gone so long I was beginning to be worried. I was afraid that something might have happened—"

"Oh, stop it, Devvie!" she snapped in sudden anger. "I don't want to hear it!"

Devorah was stunned at the harshness in her tone of voice. "Why, Ann! What's the matter? What's wrong?"

Ann kept her eyes averted from Devorah's face. "Nothing," she said sullenly.

"Can't I help?" Devorah reached out a hand, intending to smooth the hair back from Ann's forehead.

Ann rudely shoved the hand away and stepped backward. "No. Leave me alone. I'm going to wash up." She turned abruptly and left the room, heading toward the bathroom.

Oh dear, Devorah thought, gazing after her. *What have I done? She is most upset with me. Or is it what I haven't done? I fear we shall have a confrontation before this night is over.*

The meal was going very badly; there was an almost palpable tension in the air. Ann had taken a quick bath and changed into clean clothes, and she was now sitting at her customary place at the table with her eyes downcast upon her plate. Even though she was hungry, she did not have the desire to eat, and she half-heartedly took a few bites and pushed the rest of the food around with her fork. Devorah glanced over at her from time to time, still concerned as to what had caused her to become so upset and withdrawn, wondering whether or not she should say something to her. Melissa sat across from Ann, and even the child had become aware of the strained conversation passing between the two adults.

"Aren't you hungry, Ann?" asked Devorah.

"Yeah, I guess."

"Then why aren't you eating? Don't you like the food?"

"It's all right," Ann mumbled. "I'm eating."

"Would you like to go into town tomorrow?"

"What for?"

"Ohhh, maybe we could buy something," Devorah suggested hopefully. "A new dress for me, new pants for you."

"My pants are fine."

"Well, then, something else for you. Surely there must be something you need."

"There's only one thing I need, Devvie."

Aha, Devorah realized, lapsing into silence. *So that's it. I should have known.*

Melissa spoke up brightly. "Ann, will you play some games with me tonight?"

"No. I'm too tired."

"Pleeeze?" the child entreated.

"I said no. Don't whine."

"But you haven't played any good games with me lately. You keep saying you're too tired," she pouted.

Ann glared at her threateningly. "Shut up, Lissa!"

"Be quiet, dear," Devorah said gently to the child. "Finish your dinner."

The remainder of the meal passed in stony silence. Melissa quietly excused herself, hopped down from her chair, and went to play alone in front of the fire. Devorah drank the last of her coffee, then stood up and began to clear the plates from the table, stacking them neatly beside the sink.

"Ann, I want to go take an early bath. Would you please take care of the dishes?"

"Yeah, sure," she said, still in a surly mood.

"And after I give Lissa her bath and put her to bed, then we'll talk."

"In circles again, I suppose," Ann grumbled.

"We *will* talk," Devorah stated firmly, but Ann refused to meet her eyes.

After Devorah had bathed herself, she slipped into her long nightgown and put her robe on over it. She brushed out her hair and dabbed a little bit of perfume on her wrists, her neck, down the cleft between her breasts. Her grooming completed, she returned to the bathroom and poured out more hot water into the tub, calling to Melissa that it was time to start getting ready for bed. She helped the child get out of her clothes and watched passively as she hopped into the water and began to scrub her arms and legs with the washcloth. Melissa was quite proud of the fact that she could give herself a bath and she only required assistance in washing her hair.

Devorah escorted the child into the bedroom, listened attentively to her nighttime prayers, and then tucked her underneath the quilt, placing a loving kiss upon her cheek. She extinguished the bedside lamp, closed the door softly behind her, and went out into the living room in search of Ann. Not finding her immediately, Devorah looked around, frowning in puzzlement, then realized that Ann had probably stepped outside. She opened the front door and found Ann standing on the porch, leaning up against one of the tall wooden posts.

The night was hushed and still, and the air was cool but not overly chilly. A full white moon gleamed brightly in a cloudless sky; the stars twinkled and shimmered in the far off reaches of space. Ann was gazing up at the face of the moon, and its light was so

197

brilliant that there was no need of the kerosene lamp. Devorah moved to stand beside her, being careful not to touch her in any way and curbing her own surging insticts to embrace her and hold her close.

"Beautiful moon, isn't it?" Devorah began. Ann nodded in reply, but did not turn to face her. "It reminds me of that one night last summer when we both saw a star and wished on it. Do you remember that, Ann? I wished for happiness."

"And I wished for love."

"Well, I got my happiness."

"But I never got my love," Ann said sadly.

"Of course you did, Ann," she insisted. "You have me. You have my love."

"That's a nice thing to say, Devvie, but you haven't really given me anything yet—only promises and more promises. I've been more than patient with you. I've tried to be kind and gentle and understanding, and I've gotten nowhere fast." Her voice was cold, her features expressionless.

"That's not true," Devorah softly denied.

"Oh, it's true, all right. You're acting like some bashful school-girl—playing games with me, leading me around by the nose, teasing me, and then when I try to get serious about it, you throw up your little hands and back off all shocked and upset. Why, you can't even remember that you kissed me—*you* kissed *me*, mind you, not the other way around—and yet when I told you about that, what did you do? You denied it!" she hissed fiercely. "You denied your feelings, denied yourself . . ."

"If you say I kissed you, I won't deny it now," Devorah said quietly.

"Devvie, don't you know what I really want?"

She stared boldly at Ann. "Yes . . . I do."

"Don't you want the same thing, too?"

"I . . . ," she faltered. This was it; she had to do or die. She had chosen; why could she not declare her love? She dropped her gaze.

"That's what I mean, Devvie," Ann said in disgust. "You go just so far and no further. Well, I've had enough of it! You can't expect me to go on like this. I can't take it any more!" she cried in exasperation. She paused, inhaled a deep breath to calm herself, and continued on. "I've been thinking on leaving."

Devorah was appalled. "What?! *Why?*"

"Because I think it's best for both of us. I can pack my things tonight . . ."

"No, you can't!"

"And I can be gone by morning . . ."

"No, you mustn't!"

"You'll never have to see me again."

Devorah was frantic. "No! Don't do this!"

"You'll be all right, Devvie. You can go back to Doc like you always wanted to, except for me. You can marry him if he'll still have you," she said dispassionately.

"But I don't want him. I told him no. I did it all for you!"

"You did it all for me," Ann mocked her derisively. Her voice was scornful, her mounting anger just barely held in check. "I'm sorry, Devvie, but it wasn't good enough. It's over now, and there's nothing left. Your great choice has left you empty-handed and alone once again," she said cruelly.

"But . . . but what about the corn? It's not planted yet." Devorah was grasping now.

"Well, you'll have to find somebody else to do it or just do it yourself. I'm through." Ann stepped off the porch and began to walk away from the house, taking long, easy, striding steps.

"Where are you going?" Devorah called after her.

"For a walk!" Ann yelled back, not bothering to turn around.

"At this hour? Come back here!" Devorah received no response from the swiftly retreating figure, and she dashed down the steps to run after her. "Ann! Ann, wait!" Devorah gathered her long skirts and ran faster. She finally caught up with Ann, seized her roughly by the arm, and spun her around so that they were both face to face. "Please! You can't . . . you can't leave!" Devorah was panting and out of breath.

"Why not, damn it!" Ann shouted. "Give me one good reason!"

"All right, I will! Because . . . because I love you!" There, it was out, she had said it, she was at long last free.

"You *what?*" Ann stared at her incredulously. She could not believe what she had just heard, and her mouth hung open in unexpected shock.

"Oh, I love you, I love you, *I love you!*" Devorah flung her arms wide in supplication, laughing aloud to the night sky.

"Devvie?" Ann said questioningly. "Are you daft?"

"No . . . oh, no. I've just realized that I've waited too long." She was smiling now, and the white light of the moon illuminated her beautiful features, highlighted her golden hair.

Ann still hesitated to believe. "Are you sure?"

"More sure than I've ever been of anything else before," she said slowly and determinedly. She closed the distance between them and put her arms around Ann's neck, trailing the fingers of one hand through her hair, sensuously caressing the back of her head. "I do love you and I want you. I want you *now*," she whispered urgently.

"Oh, Devvie . . . Dev . . . how I dreamed you would say this," Ann said in complete adoration.

Devorah parted her lips and closed her eyes, and there in the revealing moonlight she bent her head forward to receive Ann's kiss. Their lips met tentatively at first; then the pressure increased as the surging waves of passion rolled in, crested, and broke over them. They clung to each other with a fierceness born of long-repressed desire. Their breasts were tightly crushed together, their hands roamed freely over each other's body, their senses were drowning in this all-consuming want and need. Ann was the first one to end the wild kiss, much as she didn't want to, but she found that she could no longer stand up.

"Dev . . . lie down . . . lie with me here," she gasped. She reached for Devorah's hand and began to tug her downward to the green blanket of prairie grass, but Devorah resisted her pull and remained standing.

"No, Ann, not here," she said with a shake of her head. "Come . . . come with me. Let's go to bed."

"Where you lead, I will follow." They walked back to the house.

Devorah first looked in on Melissa to make sure that the child was fast asleep, and then she led Ann by the hand down the hallway to the other bedroom—the one that used to belong to both herself and Billy. She lit the bedside lamp and turned around to face Ann with a soft light of love and longing in her eyes. She unbuckled Ann's belt and slowly undid the buttons of her shirt. In turn Ann reached out to untie the sash of her robe, and Devorah allowed it to slip from her body. Ann also unbuttoned the front of her nightgown and slid the material down over her shoulders, and Devorah unprotestingly let it fall to the floor. She was naked and unashamed now in front of Ann, and she pulled off Ann's open shirt and helped her push the pants down over her hips. When Ann was also naked, Devorah stepped up to her and held her in a close embrace, not wanting anything between them but the feel of soft warm skin. They stood kissing each other wantonly, allowing their passions to rise unchecked, and then Devorah reluctantly tore herself away from Ann long enough to pull the covers back from the bed with one swift tug.

Devorah lay supine on the bed and, still holding Ann's hand, pulled her into bed beside her. They let their eyes travel over each other's body, reveling in the breathtaking beauty of a woman's flesh. They let their hands roam freely, seeking, feeling, discovering new delights of the sensation of touch. Words did not need to be spoken, for desire was expressed in the burning eyes, in the groping hands, in the almost violent pressure of the lips. Their feverish explorations quickly brought them to the height of panting frenzy, and Devorah was no longer content to be patient.

"Ann . . . oh, Ann," she breathed huskily. "I want you. Take me . . . make me . . ."

Ann moved to lower herself on top of Devorah's body. She covered Devorah's face and mouth with hot kisses, nibbled gently at her earlobe, nuzzled deep into her neck. She trailed her lips and tongue wetly down the front of Devorah's chest, pausing to inhale the heady scent of perfume. She lovingly caressed each soft breast, closed her mouth over each firm, erect nipple, sucked gently at the swelling hardness. She moved farther down Devorah's trembling body, kneading the flat stomach, running her fingers teasingly along the sensitive flesh of the inner thighs, barely touching the curling golden hairs. Devorah spread her legs apart then, and Ann sought the opening, found it unerringly, and sank a finger deep into the wetness, stroking the soft inner flesh. Devorah moaned softly and arched upward to meet the thrusting finger, to envelop it, to clamp her muscles around it.

"Oh, Ann . . . no more . . . please, *now*," she urged.

Ann shifted her position so that her body was between Devorah's outspread legs. She brought her face down to the damp hairs and continued to plant kisses all over the padded mound, nuzzling her nose through its softness, breathing deeply of the musky smell

201

of arousal. Her tongue flicked out and touched the center, the very core of Devorah's sweeping desire, and her mouth moved slowly in a steady rhythmic caress. *This is my temple,* Ann thought to herself, *and this is the wine I drink.*

Devorah felt as if she were on fire. The rushing sensations consumed her in an avalanche of swiftly mounting passion, and she felt herself rising higher and higher, touching lightly such spiraling heights. In one breathtaking instant she had approached the point of climax, attained it, passed into it and beyond. Her neck was arched backward upon the pillow, her eyes were tightly shut, her hands were gripping Ann's head; then her mouth opened in a soundless scream, the lips pulled back over white teeth, and her breath came in short, panting gasps as her body lost all control. She released a guttural, half-strangled, whimpering cry as she bucked and lunged, and Ann heard her, burrowed her tongue deeper, seized her thrashing hips in a strong armlock.

"Oh . . . oh . . . my . . . dear . . . sweet . . . God!" she groaned.

After the contractions had subsided, Devorah let her body collapse back onto the bed. She lay with her mouth still open, her breath still coming in ragged gasps, drenched in sweat, fully aware of her wildly beating heart. She slowly opened her eyes and looked at Ann, who had propped herself up on her elbows and was regarding her with a wide grin of delight.

"What . . . what are you smiling at?" Devorah asked weakly. She felt completely drained.

"At you. You do carry on." Ann winked at her impishly.

"Oh, hush up. Come here." She held out her arms, and Ann moved into them.

For a while they lay quietly beside each other, touching gently, kissing lingeringly. When Devorah had regained her strength, she began kissing Ann with greater ardor, her lips pushing insistently, her hands seeking demandingly. With a firm shove, she rolled Ann over onto her back and instantly moved to cover her body with her own. Again the motions of love were followed, and Devorah found herself acting instinctively, knowing in her heart what would please her lover. She caressed Ann's small breasts, trailed her wet tongue around the pointed brown nipples, threaded her fingers through the dark curly hair at the juncture of the thighs. She inserted her finger into the hot, wet core, thrust it gently in and out, smeared the musky white fluid over the dark hairs. When at last she positioned herself between Ann's legs and lowered her face to worship at the same temple, she had to suppress a smile of triumph. *This is what I have been waiting for,* Devorah thought to herself. *This is where I belong, where my heart is, and my soul. I may be damned, but I have no regrets.*

Devorah began the motions, concentrating all of her attention upon maintaining the uninterrupted rhythm. She was amazed at the supreme pleasure that her movements gave, she was awed at the power that she held over Ann, and when Ann finally attained the same sweeping point of breathlessness and lost herself in the uncontrollable lunge of climax, her choking cry was sweet music to Devorah's ears.

"Dev . . . Devvie . . . don't stop . . . oh . . . Dev . . . .oh, *now!*"

Ann sank back weakly onto the bed, and Devorah did not wait until she had regained her breath, but moved instead to gather Ann into her protective arms, covering her mouth with soothing kisses. As Devorah held her in a tight embrace she suddenly became aware that Ann was crying softly, and she lifted her head to regard her with concern mirrored in her deep blue eyes.

"Darling, why . . . why are you crying?"

Ann smiled through her tears. "Oh, Devvie, I'm just so happy. If you only knew how much I dreamed of this and prayed for it to happen."

"Hush, my love." Devorah bent to kiss the tears away.

"Devvie, I love you so. I adore you."

"And I love you, too, Ann. Very, very much."

"Are you happy now?"

"As long as I can be with you, yes, I am. I feel . . . I am finally fulfilled."

Ann made her voice very small and quiet. "Do you remember the story of Ruth and Naomi?" she asked.

"Mmm-hmm," Devorah murmured, reaching out to brush the hair back from Ann's face.

" 'Entreat me not to leave thee, or to return from following after thee; for whither thou goest, I shall go, and whither thou lodgest, I shall lodge . . .' "

Devorah finished the quote. " 'Thy people shall be my people, and thy God my God.' " She gazed tenderly down at Ann, and her eyes were bright and moist from this moving declaration of enduring love.

"Devvie, you won't . . . leave me tonight, will you?"

"No, Ann. This is our bed now, and I will stay with you. I will never leave you, for you mean the world to me. You will always be mine, my first, my very own."

"I am lost in your love," Ann said wonderingly. She wrapped her arms around Devorah's neck, pulled her down, and sought her mouth once again. The pact had been made and sealed; they would go on together, side by side, joined as one under the all-embracing love of God.

Devorah pulled the quilt up over their bodies and leaned to extinguish the lamp. They nestled closely to each other; Ann rested her head in the crook of Devorah's arm, next to her breast, and Devorah laid her cheek upon Ann's hair. Just before Ann drifted off to sleep she placed one hand upon Devorah's soft breast, and Devorah immediately covered the hand with her own. And so they slept, holding each other tightly, never moving far away. And they were blessed.

Ann was already awake by the time the softness of dawn first began to lighten the sky. She lay there quietly, letting her eyes travel lovingly over the relaxed lines of Devorah's sleeping face. *How much I love you,* she thought in blissful contentment. *Oh, how much, how much!*

Devorah stirred, turned toward Ann, and slowly fluttered open her eyes. When she saw that Ann was awake and looking at her, she closed her eyes again and smiled.

Ann placed a warm hand upon Devorah's cheek. "Good morning, love," she said softly.

Devorah clasped the hand, held it to her lips, and kissed it. "Mmmm . . . morning. Is it time to get up already?" she mumbled sleepily.

"No, we don't have to. We could stay in bed and make love all day."

"Wouldn't be right. Too many things to do."

"They can wait." Ann leaned forward and began kissing Devorah's neck and shoulders.

"No, they can't, but you can." Devorah grabbed her, and they wrestled playfully. She was strong, but Ann was stronger, and Devorah soon found herself pinned to the mattress with both arms outstretched. "Stop!" she panted. "You win."

Ann released her hold. "I love you, Devvie," she said somberly.

"Oh, I love you," Devorah smiled. She wrapped her arms around Ann's neck, pulled her down, and kissed her tenderly.

"Dev, you are my world."

"And you are mine."

"I guess that was the key, then," Ann said half to herself.

Devorah frowned, not understanding. "What? What are you talking about?"

"The key," she repeated. "The way to your heart—to threaten to leave. I racked my brain trying to think of how best to finally win you, and I guess I just found the right way without even realizing it."

With both hands, Devorah firmly gripped Ann's face and regarded her sternly. "You had me in such a state! Don't you ever, ever do that again!"

"I won't, I promise. I will be with you always," Ann vowed.

"And I with you, I swear it." They kissed again. "Come on, let's eat. I'm starved!"

They dressed quickly in the chill morning air, and then Devorah went into the other bedroom to awaken Melissa while Ann went out to the living room to build a fire. Devorah prepared a hearty breakfast of bacon and eggs and fried potatoes, and as they all sat together around the kitchen table Melissa kept glancing curiously at her mother.

"Didn't you come to bed last night, Mommy?" she finally asked.

"Of course I did, honey," Devorah answered.

"But you didn't sleep with me. How come?"

"Well, sweetheart, I've decided you're a big girl now, and you need more space for yourself and for all your toys and clothes. So I'm going to let you have your own bedroom back again while we adults have a room to ourselves. All right?"

"Okay, Mommy," she agreed easily, taking it all in stride. "But you'd better watch out," she warned Ann in a serious tone of voice. "Sometimes she kicks!"

Ann and Devorah both laughed; then Ann nodded and winked in approval of Devorah's smooth, unruffled handling of the situation. *Good, Devvie,* she thought, *very good.*

May blossomed forth under a gentle sun. Bright purple violets and white lilies of the valley were scattered in profusion over the ground, and Devorah's garden abounded in multicolored tulips. During her frequent outside wanderings, Melissa gathered fistfuls of beautiful wild flowers and brought them home to her mother, who arranged them in gay displays upon the tables and dressers. The trees were full, green, and leafy; the renewed branches rustled softly in the warm spring breeze. The wild dogwoods were also in bloom, and the entire prairie was fragrant with new life.

The rains had come, bringing life-giving moisture to the ground, and the hardy prairie grass shot up in unchecked growth. The tender shoots of the wheat had also sprouted and were quickly growing taller, stronger day by day. The animals were released from their long winter confinement; the cows and horses were allowed to roam and graze at will, and the chickens clucked noisily in the front yard. Spring had arrived early this year, and the land lay basking, greening, rising from its sleep.

One morning, Ann and Devorah and Melissa all climbed into Ann's refurbished buckboard for their main monthly supply trip into Sutter's Ford. Ann drove the wagon this time and sat proudly, holding the reins securely, letting the passing wind stream the hair back from her face. Devorah glanced over at her and noted the erect posture, the strong hands, the fine lines of her nose and chin. *Oh, I am happy,* Devorah thought serenely, smiling to herself. *I want to tell the whole world of this new love. I want to shout it from the rooftops. I want to hold on to it and never, ever let it go. Dear Lord, I thank You for this love. I feel joined again, and in so joining, I am complete.*

After they arrived in town, they wasted little time in purchasing all the required supplies, and when everything had been neatly stacked in the back of the wagon, they set off jauntily on a little shopping spree. Devorah bought another dress for herself, a new pair of pants and a shirt for Ann, and two more dresses for Melissa.

"This had better be all, Devvie," Ann cautioned her. "We probably don't have much money left in the account."

"There's enough to see us through," she replied confidently. "It's spring; we need to treat ourselves."

"Are we done now?"

"Yes. Oh, wait! I want to buy some more material. I'm going to make new curtains for both bedrooms."

They all trooped into a small shop on the corner of the street. Ann patiently held Melissa's hand while Devorah browsed through the stacks of variously colored materials. She selected a soft blue printed pattern for the child's bedroom and a bright yellow flowered pattern for their own room, and she carried the bolts of cloth up to the clerk at the front counter.

"Excuse me, but do you also have any lace?" asked Devorah. "I couldn't seem to find any."

"Yes, madam. One moment, please," said the woman. She located a small bolt of white lace and set it on top of the counter for Devorah to examine. "I'm afraid there's not much left," she apologized. "Most of it was bought by another woman for a bridal gown, and I don't think you'd have enough here to make a dress out of it. Perhaps you would prefer to wait until we have a chance to order some more."

"Ummm . . . no," Devorah said slowly, fingering the short length of lace. She envisioned the bedroom windows in her mind and thoughtfully calculated their dimensions against the available lace. "I think this will be just right for what I have in mind. Yes, this will do fine," she stated firmly.

It was time to plant the corn. Devorah joined Ann in the fields; they both slung the heavy canvas sacks over their shoulders once again and plodded steadily up and down the long rows. They walked side by side, each carrying a long straight stick of wood that had been cross-barred at the bottom in order to ensure making a hole of proper depth in the rich soil. With almost automatic movements, they poked the sticks into the yielding dirt, tossed a kernel of corn into the resulting hole, stepped forward to close the hole with the tip of a boot, and then moved on.

Devorah's corn crop was twice the size of the wheat crop, for this was where she truly made her money during the fall harvest. The wheat was used primarily for fodder for the animals, but the corn was the sustenance, the lifeblood of her existence. The profit she received in the fall, which was usually a substantial amount, had to be squirreled away and depended upon to provide all the necessities of life for a full year until the following harvest. When Billy had been alive, he had competently managed all of their financial affairs, and after his death, Devorah had to learn very quickly how to efficiently run the farm by herself. The corn crop was of paramount importance, for without it, she could not survive. Each seedling was precious to her, which explained why she so often roamed through the fields as the corn was growing, checking out the tall stalks and closely scrutinizing the developing ears for the slightest signs of insects or disease.

Devorah continued along her row, absently pondering these thoughts of the corn, and when she turned her head to say something to Ann, she suddenly realized that Ann was no longer by her side. She stopped and turned completely around then, and with both hands on her hips, regarded Ann curiously from a distance of about twenty feet. Devorah wiped the sweat from her brow, for the afternoon sun was beating down hotly from a cloudless blue sky, and she waited patiently until Ann had caught up with her.

"What happened?" Devorah inquired. "I thought you were right beside me."

"Some of my tosses went wrong," Ann explained. "I had to stop to pick up the kernels."

"Are you that out of shape?" she teased.

"Well, no, but I just haven't done this for quite a while."

Devorah looked out across the distant fields, shading her brow with one hand. "We've just barely started. We've got a long way to go yet."

Ann followed her gaze. "I know it. You've got a lot of land here."

"Should take us about two weeks, don't you think?"

"At least that, if the weather holds." She noted Devorah's worried frown. "What's the matter, Devvie?"

"Nothing, I guess. Just thinking."

"About what?" Ann probed.

"Ohhh, about the land . . . about the corn. I still have this funny feeling . . ."

"That something's going to go wrong?" Devorah nodded. "Aw, come on, Devvie," Ann sighed. "Nothing's going to happen. I told you once before, you worry too much."

"Maybe so, but still . . ."

"Come on, we've got a lot of work to do." Ann took her by the arm, and they walked on.

They labored long and hard throughout the next two weeks, striving to have all of the acres planted by the middle of the month. The sun blazed down upon them, soaking their clothes with pouring sweat and giving rise to dull pounding headaches. At the end of the day, they were both dusty, dirty, and exhausted from the seemingly ceaseless toil. The laundry also had to be done, and twice a week they scrubbed out their garments in a large round washtub, hanging the things up to dry on a sturdy outside clothesline.

In the evenings after Melissa had been tucked into bed, they took baths together and soaked their aching muscles in the relaxing, soothing water. They took turns soaping each other, washing each other's hair, and toweling each other dry. In the bedroom, lying on top of the cool crisp sheets, they gave each other vigorous backrubs to ease the muscle tension and strain. Devorah always made sure that she applied Ann's favorite perfume to herself after her bath, and this simple act never failed to buoy her inner spirits, for they were never too tired to make love. The newness of their affair had not yet worn off, and they continued to delight in eliciting passionate responses from their bodies.

One night Devorah lay prone upon the mattress, and Ann sat comfortably astride her buttocks, giving her another welcome backrub. Her supple fingers moved easily along the contours of Devorah's back, kneading the tight muscles, forcing them to relax, tracing the outline of the spine. They were both naked, for as they slept together, they needed not the hindrance of clothing to keep them warm.

"Mmmm . . . that feels good," Devorah murmured, smiling into the pillow.

"I never tire of touching you," Ann replied tenderly. "It seems I can't get enough of you." Devorah grunted softly in response and allowed herself to be turned over as Ann finished the rubdown. Ann leaned over her, still kneeling astride her body, and lowered her face so that it was only inches away from Devorah's own. "Dev?" she questioned almost timidly.

"Yes, my love?" Devorah attempted to pull her down and kiss her, but Ann resisted.

"What we have between us is good, isn't it?" she said, like a small child seeking assurance. "I mean, you don't think . . . you don't feel . . . bad about it, do you?"

"Why, of course not. Why should I?"

209

"But the first chapter of Romans says—"

"Don't bother to quote to me," Devorah interrupted, placing her fingers on Ann's lips to silence her. "I know what it says."

"And you don't care?" Ann pressed. "You don't care what other people think?"

"I care, but not enough to let them dictate to me what I should or should not do. Loving you has made me free."

"But they'd say we're damned."

"You'd believe that without listening to your own heart first? No matter what happens, we're all God's children, and if He's supposed to be a God of love, then there's nothing evil or sinful in our love," Devorah lectured her. "How can there be? Why try to make something awful and horrible out of something that is only good and beautiful and kind? I feel as if we have been united in a bond that's just as strong as what's between a man and a woman, and I'll go to my judgment feeling just as confident of my salvation as I was before I ever met you."

Ann shook her head in amazement. "Devvie, I'm impressed. You've really changed."

"No, I've just finally come into my own, that's all. I've taken the happiness that's been waiting for me. Who knows what will happen tomorrow, but there's only one thing I'm sure of right now, and that's how very much I love you and want you and need you by my side. Now give me that kiss," she demanded, pulling Ann down again.

"Oh, Dev, I love you, too . . . so much it hurts."

Ann leaned forward into the kiss, gently easing her weight down on top of Devorah's body. Again, the insistent desire mounted and rose higher as hands traveled gropingly, seeking, finding, caressing. Breast pressed against breast, lips crushed lips and then broke away to suckle and stimulate elsewhere, the wetness melted and flowed between them.

"Ann, my darling," Devorah whispered. Even the words were a caress. "I am yours. Take me . . . love me now . . ."

Ann gave herself up completely to the urgency of Devorah's need, and she moved with her, strained with her, rode the same heights of desire, and rejoiced in the same sobbing cry of release.

Ann hastened to finish the planting of the corn. Only another day or two of sowing remained to be done, and Ann had insisted that Devorah should take a rest, saying that she could handle the tedious task on her own. While Ann worked outside, Devorah passed the days in making the new sets of curtains for both bedrooms. She carefully measured the length and width of the windows and then transferred the measurements to the bolts of cloth, cutting out the material with practiced ease. She expertly ran up the side seams on her push-pedal sewing machine, humming softly to herself as she worked at this new labor of love. The lace curtains, which would hang on a separate rod inside of the outer heavier cloth curtains, had to be hemmed by hand since the material was too fine and fragile for the needle of the machine.

A few days later, when Devorah had completed the job, she called out to Ann to assist her in hanging the new curtains. They went into their own bedroom first and took down the old faded panels. Ann attached a second rod to the upper part of the window frame and hung up the delicate lace curtains. Then she set up the cheery yellow flowered curtains on the other rod. Devorah pulled back the outer panels so that the daylight filtered in through the white lace, and they both stood there admiring the brightened but softened effect of the room's light.

They then went into Melissa's room, and after the lace panels had been installed and the soft blue printed curtains hung, the child pushed her way between them and clung excitedly to her mother's skirts.

"Gee, Mommy, they look so nice," Melissa said eagerly. "Blue's my favorite color."

"I know, sweetheart. I'm glad you like them." Devorah gave her a quick hug, then bent to kiss her cheek.

"Devvie, why don't I go outside and take down the storm windows?" Ann suggested. "They're just hanging open right now to let the light in, and it'd be nice to have the breeze coming through the house again."

"Well, I don't see why not," she agreed. "It's warm enough during the day now. Go ahead, I want to see how the lace moves with the air."

Ann went outside and quickly detached the wooden storm shutters, storing them in their customary place in the tool shed at the rear of the house. By the time she returned to the bedroom, Devorah

211

had already opened the window and the warm spring air was sweeping in through the screen, puffing out the lace curtains and cleansing the stale air inside the room.

Ann breathed deeply of the incoming breeze. "Ahhh, that air smells fresh and clean. Shouldn't take long to get the house aired out." She paused. "I really like the new curtains, Devvie. You did a fine job."

"Thank you, Ann. I thought it was about time we changed the old ones. They'd been up there ever since Billy and I . . . uh . . . for a long time anyway," she corrected herself with a quick shake of her head.

"Sort of like erasing the slate, huh?"

"You might say that," Devorah conceded. "A farewell to the past and everything in it."

"Lissa, honey!" Ann swept the child into her firm embrace. "How would you like me to make you a table and chair set all for your very own?"

"All for me?" the child echoed in disbelief.

"Uh-huh, all for you," Ann confirmed. "So you and your dolly can have tea just like grown-ups."

"Real tea or pretend tea?" she asked suspiciously.

"Why, real tea, of course! And special little tea cakes, too. You can invite Mommy and me to your party, and we'll all come dressed up."

"Careful, Ann!" Devorah cautioned her. "She'll hold you to it."

Melissa's eyes sparkled with enthusiasm. "Mommy, can we have a fancy party? A grown-up party?"

"Of course, dear," Devorah smiled down at her, ruffling her hair.

It didn't take Ann very long to make the child-sized furniture. Since all the planting had been completed, there was nothing left to do except look after the animals and wait patiently for the crops to grow. Ann sorted through the pile of scrap lumber that was kept in the barn, selected several good pieces of wood, and set briskly to work on this new project. She sanded down a long flat plank that would serve as the table and also sanded four other smaller pieces that would make up the two chair seats and backs. She sawed off short lengths of wood for the legs, carved them to fit, and attached them securely with a strong carpenter's glue. She also made support-ive rungs for the legs and inserted them into the proper spaces. After the glue had dried fast and hard, she covered all the wood surfaces with a protective coating of clear varnish. She surveyed her work with pride. Once again, she had created something with her hands.

Ann carried the little table from the barn into Melissa's bedroom and set it in an open area near the window. She went back inside to get the two little chairs and arranged them on opposite sides of the table. Melissa fluttered about her in ecstatic glee, sitting down on each chair to try it out for size as Devorah stood in the open doorway of the room, smiling and nodding approvingly.

"That's a handsome piece of work, Ann," she complimented. "You seem to be getting better at this all the time."

"Thanks, Devvie. It's really not a hard thing to do once you get the hang of it."

"Mommy, can we have our party now?" Melissa bubbled. "Can you make the special cakes?"

"All right, Lissa. Give me some time."

Ann and Devorah went into the kitchen and Ann brewed a pot of herbal tea while Devorah quickly popped a tray of cupcakes into the oven. She had already prepared the batter beforehand, knowing that Ann would be finished with the furniture that afternoon and also knowing that the child would insist upon having the party imme-diately. After the cupcakes had been baked and set upon a metal rack to cool, Melissa came bursting out of her room and dashed up to her mother. She had dressed herself in her Sunday best, and she now wanted Devorah to button up the back of her dress.

"Hurry up!" Melissa urged them both. "You have to dress up. You promised!" She pointed her finger accusingly at Ann.

"Aw, Lissa!" Ann grumbled good-naturedly.

"I warned you, Ann," said Devorah with a wry smile. "You can't make idle promises because she never forgets what you say. You got us into this, so come on, let's go." She pulled Ann up from the chair and led her by the arm down the hallway.

Ann looked back pleadingly over her shoulder. "Lissa, can't we just . . ."

"Nope," the child said adamantly. "You have to wear hats an' gloves, too. This is a formal party!"

"Lissa!" Ann almost shrieked in despair.

Devorah dragged her resolutely on. "Come on, girl."

Devorah changed into one of the dresses that she usually wore to Meeting and Ann also—reluctantly—slipped into her own dress. Devorah donned her fancy hat and put on a pair of white gloves, then rummaged around in the closet for another older hat and pair of gloves for Ann to wear. Ann stood there totally mortified, appearing very dainty and feminine except for her boots, which she flatly refused to remove from her feet.

"Devvie, I can't do this," she protested uncomfortably. The hat was perched primly upon her head, and she kept her gloved hands thrust out of sight behind her.

Devorah giggled in amusement. "Why, of course you can. You look rather sweet."

"I feel silly."

"But you look lovely. Perhaps you should dress like this more often." Ann rolled her eyes upward to the ceiling and groaned. "Oh, come now. It isn't that bad. Just do it for me and next time keep your mouth shut." Devorah stepped up to her and kissed her sweetly on the lips. "Is that better?" Ann glumly shook her head. "No? Well, I'll make it up to you tonight." Devorah laughed again—a low, throaty, chuckling laugh.

They set Melissa's new table with dessert plates, cups and saucers, and silverware. Devorah carried in the pot of tea and the platter of cupcakes while Ann brought along two kitchen chairs for them to sit on. Melissa had already placed her doll in an upright position on one of the small chairs and she was seated directly opposite the doll. Devorah poured out the tea, added sugar to the child's cup, and passed around the cupcakes. The party was in full swing.

"I am so pleased that you could come to my party today," Melissa said in a haughty tone of voice. "Have you traveled far?"

"Uh . . . yes we have, Miss uh . . ." Ann faltered. The hat began to slide down her forehead, and she quickly pushed it back.

"I am *Mrs.* Smith, and this is Mrs. Jones," the child said, gesturing toward the doll.

"We thank you for your kind invitation," Devorah spoke impassively.

"I have not been receiving guests lately. I have been ill, you know."

"Oh. Uh . . . no, we didn't know." Ann's fingers began to itch under the gloves and she suppressed a sudden urge to scratch.

"Perhaps a little nourishment would make you feel better," Devorah continued smoothly.

"Of course. Please join me. And don't forget to hold your pinky out like a lady." Melissa took a noisy slurping sip of her tea, extending her finger outward in a shining example of propriety.

Ann and Devorah both tried very hard to maintain straight faces.

Thirteen

The day had been oddly uncomfortable from the beginning. All morning long, the pale sun had struggled to peek out from behind a gray lowering cloud cover, and by noontime, the occlusion was complete and the sun was gone. As the afternoon wore on, the sky became more threatening, and the gentle breeze that had stirred the leafy branches of the trees gradually petered out and then vanished altogether. The prairie lay hushed and still, the air seemed close and charged with static electricity, and the sky was suffused with a strange greenish light.

Ann and Devorah stood on the front porch, anxiously gazing up at the unsettling sky. Ann was alertly concerned, but Devorah was almost beside herself with nervous agitation. She paced back and forth across the wooden floorboards, clasping her folded arms tightly to her chest, rubbing and squeezing them absently as she scanned the darkening clouds. Her brows knitted together in a worried frown.

"Ann, I don't like that sky," she said fearfully.

"I know, Devvie. I don't, either. Looks like we're in for a good storm."

"What if . . . what if it's a twister?"

"Nothing's happened yet. Maybe it'll all blow over, and we'll just get rain." Ann tried to allay her fears, but Devorah paced on, unheeding.

"I don't think so. I can almost feel it coming."

"Tell you what, Devvie," Ann offered. "I'll walk out to where it's flat and level so I can get a good view of everything, and if I see anything heading this way, I'll come running."

"Well . . . all right, but be careful."

"Don't leave the house. I don't want to have to come looking for you."

Ann walked quickly across the open fields until her line of sight was no longer blocked by the house and barn. She stood upon a

216

slight rise in the ground and turned slowly in all directions, her eyes sweeping the distant horizon. Behind her, the sky was fairly light, but in front of her to the southwest the oncoming clouds were pitch black and bulging ominously downward. The sky rolled in upon itself, the clouds dipped and surged, the vanguard of the approaching storm steadily advanced and bore down upon her. Jagged streaks of white lightning speared through the rolling black mass, and crashing echoes of thunder assaulted her ears. Ann had seen this kind of sky several times before, and she knew instinctively what it meant: terror and sweeping destruction.

The grazing cows lowed uneasily and wandered aimlessly in jerking gallops, unsure of which direction led to safety. The horses were confined to the paddock beside the barn, and they bucked and neighed in mindless fear, running in frantic circles within the small enclosure. *Even they know,* Ann thought.

She turned her gaze from the agitated animals back to the threatening sky and watched in spellbound awe as a whirling finger of cloud detached itself from the swirling mass above it and hung pendulously downward, dipping, rising, stretching inexorably toward the land. The twister hit the ground with a shuddering bang, dirt was immediately sucked up into the greedy maw, making the funnel seem blacker than the accompanying clouds, and nearby trees exploded and were flung violently outward. The earth shook and trembled as the fearsome thing churned and plowed onward relentlessly.

Ann stood where she was for a moment, rooted in disbelieving shock, feeling the intensifying wind blowing her hair, ripping at her clothes. The spell was then broken and she ran madly toward the house, galvanized into action by her swiftly mounting panic. She stumbled once and fell in a headlong tumble, but picked herself up again and careened into the front yard, where she ran straight for the paddock gate. Devorah came out onto the porch, her long skirts whipping about her in the fierce wind, and called out to her. Her voice was almost lost in the shrieking, howling air.

"Ann! Is it—"

"Hit the cellar, Devvie! *Now!*" she screamed.

Devorah rushed back inside and headed for the bathroom while Ann struggled desperately to open the heavy gate. The stubborn latch finally gave way, and the gate was torn from her grasp. Shielding her face against the driving, blinding, stinging particles of dust and

217

dirt, Ann pushed her way inside the paddock and grabbed the horses by their manes, by their tails, by whatever she could reach out and get a hold on, and she shoved them, kicked them, slapped their flanks, urged them toward the opening. The pounding hooves thundered around her, passed perilously close to her, but she ignored the danger. In an instant, they swept past her and were gone. She dashed for the house, running through the flapping, squawking chickens, and she tripped up the porch steps, seized the railing to break her fall, and clambered on. Melissa came out of the open doorway and collided breathlessly with her.

"My kitty's gone! Have to find my kitty!"

Ann snatched the child roughly by her collar. "Damn it, *no*, Lissa! Get inside!" she roared.

Ann gathered her up in a tight embrace and ran down the hallway to the bathroom, where Devorah had already yanked the rug back from the opening to the storm cellar. The trap door had been pushed back on its hinges and the hole yawned dark and waiting like the entrance to a tomb. Devorah went down the steps first, holding the lamp out in front of her so that she could see the stairs. When she reached the bottom she set the lamp on the dirt floor and turned around, arms outstretched, waiting for Ann to hand the child down to her. Ann came down the steps last, pulling the trap door shut behind her and pausing to throw the inner bolt.

They huddled together in a small tight ball up against the dirt wall of the far corner of the cellar, near the burlap-covered packing crates. Ann sat in the middle and wrapped a protective arm around each of the other two. Melissa lay whimpering quietly against her side, but Devorah still trembled uncontrollably. The soft glow of the lamp played over their taut faces and cast their shadows over the walls as the savage storm continued to rage above them. The howling wind had not diminished, and the entire house seemed to shudder and quake on its foundations. They heard the shattering sound of breaking glass. At that moment, Devorah flinched, moved closer to Ann, rested her head upon her shoulder, and closed her frightened eyes.

The storm was over just as quickly as it had come. One minute there was only the ripping, tearing sound of the wind, and then there was nothing but an eerie, ominous silence. They remained where they were for a short while longer, and when nothing further happened they slowly uncoiled their legs and stood up.

"I think it's over," Ann said. "We can go up now."

"Ann, I'm afraid . . . to see . . ."

"Come on, Devvie. We have to know."

They left the safety of the storm cellar and wandered in a daze throughout the house. The front door had been left open in their hurried scramble for shelter, and the powerful force of the wind had swept in unchecked, tumbling some of the lighter pieces of furniture into a jumbled heap against the far wall of the living room. Ashes from the fireplace were scattered in a gray, dusty blanket over everything. Dead leaves and twigs also littered the floor, and most of the small throw rugs were askew. In the kitchen, cabinet doors had popped open, and the wind had capriciously plucked out some of the plates, cups, and glasses and sent them smashing to the hard floor. Devorah walked numbly through her ruined kitchen, the broken shards crunching sharply under her tread. Suddenly there came a piercing cry from the direction of Melissa's bedroom.

"Mommy, Mommy! Come quick!"

They both dashed into the room, seeking the child, and they followed her pointing finger to stare in complete dismay at what was left of the window. A massive, thick tree branch had been hurled through both glass and screen and now lay balanced at a crazy angle, half in and half out of the window frame. The blue curtains were still hanging, but the second rod holding the sheer lace panels had torn away from its place, and the fragile lace had been ripped and shredded beyond repair. Broken glass lay scattered everywhere like a pall. Devorah stooped to pick up a smudged, dirty piece of what had once been beautiful lace, and she held it loosely in her hand, gazing blankly at it, not really seeing.

"Get that out of my room!" Melissa cried in a shrill voice. "I want it out, out!"

"We will, honey, we will!" Ann assured her soothingly. "Don't worry, everything will be all right."

No, it won't be, Devorah thought in rushing, gripping terror. *This is an omen, an* omen, *and it will never be all right again. I knew it, I knew it, but nobody would listen to me.*

"Dev," Ann said, placing a gentle hand upon her shoulder. "Don't you think maybe we should . . . go outside now?"

219

Devorah allowed herself to be led along, and they stood upon the porch, surveying the front yard. Sticks, twigs, and larger branches littered the ground; some of the white picket fencing around the garden had been uprooted. A large hole gaped in the roof of the barn where the underlying shingles had been ripped away. Both barn doors stood open, and the chickens clucked and fluttered together. The missing tomcat slowly sauntered out of the depths of the barn and sat supremely composed in the center of the wide doorway. The air was filled with the squeals and grunts of the pigs as they moved restlessly in their pen. A dreary pouring rain covered all, falling steadily from a leaden sky.

Devorah lifted her saddened eyes and looked far across the fields to where the cows were straggling home one by one. The horses still pranced and ran, unheeding of the rain; they would have to be rounded up and led back. Devorah took this all in, absorbed it through eyes made dim by swimming tears, and then she gazed in sudden sickening horror at the utter devastation that had been wrought by the twister to her fields, her corn, her pulsing lifeblood. She stepped off the porch and ran blindly, splashing through the widening puddles, uncaring that her skirts were being dragged through the mud.

Ann ran swiftly after her. "Devvie, no! Wait!"

The funnel had skipped lightly through the acres of wheat, churning up and spitting out the tender shoots as if it had not particularly cared for them, but it had plowed with slashing fury through the fields of corn, tearing up the ground and scattering the kernels far and wide. All the hard work of plowing and planting, all the labor of sweat and tears had been negated, erased in an instant by the twister's furious passage. The fields lay gashed and open; the drenching rain had turned the rich black soil into cascading rivers of mud.

Devorah stood helplessly at the edge of the fields, staring ahead with opened mouth and disbelieving eyes. Her clenched fists hung impotently down at her sides; her flowing tears mixed and mingled with the rain streaming down her face. "No . . . oh no . . . ," she moaned, shaking her head incomprehendingly from side to side.

Ann stepped up beside her and felt anger at the destruction, grief at Devorah's piercing hurt. She attempted to console Devorah by giving her a tentative hug, but Devorah pulled away from her and refused to be comforted.

"My crops . . . my corn . . ."

"It's not that bad, Devvie," Ann said softly, knowing in her heart that it truly was. "We can replant."

"Dear God . . . what have I done to deserve this?" she whispered dully.

"Devvie, don't . . . don't take on like this."

She was stricken, stunned, defeated. "My corn . . . my fields . . . ruined . . ."

"Devvie, please!"

"Oh, *why?*"

Devorah sank to her knees in the watery mire, bending her head forward upon her chest, letting the soaked strands of her hair fall in disarray about her shoulders. There in the rain and the mud she buried her face in her hands and wept.

Ann was filled with a tender pity for her as she knelt sobbing inconsolably. She got down on her own knees in front of Devorah and reached out to her, pulled her hands away, gathered her into her supportive arms, rocked her gently back and forth.

They walked back to the house, arms around each other, and they both changed into dry clothes. Ann made a pot of hot coffee, searching for two cups that had not been broken. She untangled the jumbled furniture in the living room, swept some of the ashes away from the grate, and built another warming fire. After Devorah drank some of the steaming liquid, she began to feel a little bit better, pulling herself together with the old customary determination of will.

"Well, I suppose we'd better get moving," she said, rising from her chair in front of the fire. "I'll start cleaning up the house."

"And I'll go take care of the animals," Ann volunteered. "Devvie, are you sure you're all right?" Ann was deeply concerned about her.

Devorah tried to smile. "Yes, I'm fine, really. You go on," she urged Ann.

"I'm just glad none of us was hurt."

"I am, too." Devorah sighed heavily and reached for the broom.

Ann put on her rain slicker and went out to the barn. The chickens had already gone inside to roost, and the cows had instinctively found their way into the stalls. Ann took the halters down from their pegs on the wall, closed the barn doors, and trudged across the fields in search of the horses. She approached them cautiously, calling softly to them, and when they slowly paced up to her, she slipped the halters over their heads and led them home, walking between them. She got them in the barn and brushed them down, running her hands soothingly along their flanks, talking to them in a low, easy tone of voice. She fed the pigs, scattered feed for the chickens, and forked out piles of hay for the other animals. She would return after dinner to milk the cows, but first it was most important to make sure that all the animals were sheltered, fed, and dry.

Ann cast her gaze upward to the high rafters where the gray light was coming in through the hole in the barn roof. It was not irreparable, but she would have to wait until the rain stopped and everything dried out before she could climb up onto the roof. The incoming water would not do a great deal of damage to the bales of hay, for none was stored at the spot directly underneath the hole. *We'll have to go into town and buy some more shingles, though,* she told herself.

Ann left the barn and went into the tool shed, where she picked up an axe and a saw; then she stood in front of the huge, heavy tree branch that had rammed itself through Melissa's bedroom window. She hacked and sawed at it, making smaller, more easily manageable pieces out of it, and was at least able to pull the rest of it out of the window frame. More glass broke off and tinkled down inside, but the frame itself was still secure.

Ann stacked the chunks of wood on top of the woodpile and returned to the barn in search of some planks that could be temporarily fastened to the window frame to keep out the rain and the wind until the broken glass could be repaired. With hammer in hand and nails sticking out from between her lips, she quickly boarded up the ragged opening.

When Ann finally entered the house, she found Devorah standing at the kitchen stove making a pot of hearty soup. The furniture had been rearranged, the floor had been swept, the throw rugs were lying flat, and all the broken shards of plates and glasses had been removed from the kitchen. Devorah had just finished going through the cabinets and determining which items were beyond repair and which ones were still useable.

They all sat down to a quiet meal, and after the dishes had been washed, they went into Melissa's bedroom and began to clean up the remaining debris. Ann carefully swept up the broken glass while Devorah picked up the remnants of the lace curtains and straightened the blue ones that were still hanging. Nothing else in the room had been damaged, but the curtains now looked out onto the darkness and finality of the wooden boards.

They had been through a great deal of strain that day. Their weariness of body and soul dictated that they should go to bed early and leave everything else for tomorrow. In bed together with the lamp turned out and the covers drawn up, Ann and Devorah clung to each other with an intense desperation, for they seemed to wordlessly realize how close they had come to losing their lives in the storm. Their desperation quickly changed to desire, and they kissed and touched almost frenetically, brought each other to explosive climax, and were somehow restored and renewed in their love.

The following day dawned bright and clear. The warm sun gradually dried out the sopping ground, causing the standing puddles of water to be absorbed into the air. Ann decided to take the buckboard into town in order to purchase the shingles for the barn roof and several additional sacks of corn for the replanting.

"Might as well get right on it," she told Devorah. "It'll be a lot of work. Sure you don't want to come along?"

"No, Ann, you go ahead. I want to dust the furniture and scrub all the ashes off the floor. When you get back we'll rake up the yard."

"All right, Devvie. I won't be long."

The first stop that Ann made was at the granary, where she loaded up the back of the wagon with sacks of seed corn. Then she picked up the shingles and another small bucket of black pitch. Lastly, she stopped to get new panes of glass for the window. The store clerk informed her that the glass would have to be specially made to order from an outfit in Kansas City, so she left the measurements with him and was told to return in a week.

On her way out of town, she noticed that most of the shopkeepers were still engaged in their spring cleaning and sprucing up of the storefronts. The twister had not struck Sutter's Ford, but it had passed quite closely, causing minor wind damage. The streets were littered with debris, a few storefront signs had been ripped away

223

from their mountings, and some of the shop windows had also been broken and boarded up. *I guess we're not the only ones who need glass,* Ann thought, *but I wonder how many others will have to re-plant.*

Ann hurried home and found Devorah tending the garden and trying to reinsert the picket fencing back into the ground around its borders. After Ann had unhitched the horse and unloaded the wagon, she and Devorah both spent the rest of the afternoon raking up the yard and clearing away the branches that had been left behind in the twister's wake. Later on when the sun was no longer beating down directly overhead, Ann hoisted the heavy wooden ladder up against the side of the barn and set about the task of patching the hole in the roof. She measured the opening, sawed off planks to fit, and nailed them securely to the exposed rafters. She sealed the edges of the new wood with the pitch, and after this had dried sufficiently she attached the replacement shingles. By the time she finished the job, the roof looked as good as new, and the patch was not readily noticeable to the observing eye.

"How's that, Devvie? Pretty good, huh?"

"Ann, you have such incredible talent in your hands," Devorah said admiringly.

"Oh, it's nothing," she demurred. "I've done my share of roofing, too. I've learned how to do a lot of things along the way."

"I don't know what I'd do if I didn't have you here. I'd be lost without you." They looked at each other and smiled, giving each other a quick embrace.

"Now see, Devvie, I told you it wasn't so bad," Ann said, gesturing toward the yard and the barn. "We're getting everything back together again."

"But I can still see my fields lying there all torn up. And a piece of my heart has also been torn up along with them."

"Devvie, please don't worry," she pleaded earnestly. "We'll take each day as it comes, and we'll do it slowly, we'll take care of it all together. Trust me, everything will be all right, I promise you."

The only thing that Devorah really trusted was the small inner voice deep within her brain that whispered to her of unnamed, unspecific calamity yet to come. The passing of the storm had not put her fears at rest, but had only served to increase them and intensify them. She felt as if they were all moving steadily toward some precipitant disaster, but not yet knowing what to look out for, she felt powerless to prevent it.

A few days later, after the ground had completely dried out from the soaking rain, Ann hitched up the plow and moved it through the fields again. Not all of the acres needed to be replowed, but just the places where the roaring funnel had churned deeply into the land. Ann had discovered, to her great relief, that only small portions of the growing wheat had been damaged or destroyed. They would just have to let it go and hope for the best; the replanting of the corn was far more urgent and important. With luck they could have it done by early June, although they would still be about a month behind in harvest. Time was essential and Ann felt that there were not enough working hours in the day.

When the week's waiting period for the new glass window panes had ended, Ann made another trip into town, and this time both Devorah and Melissa accompanied her for the ride. They picked up the glass and carefully placed the pieces into the back of the wagon, which had been thickly lined with old blankets to cushion the panes and prevent breakage. They traveled very slowly because of the fragility of the glass. Devorah spied Delilah Emerson coming down the sidewalk toward them, and she requested that Ann pull over and stop so they could speak to the woman.

"Lilah!" Devorah called out to her and waved at her.

"Wal, I do declare! If it ain't Miz Lee, the ol' eyes're deceivin' me," she replied with a wide grin. She stepped up to the wagon, gave first Devorah, then Ann a firm handshake, and reached out to pat Melissa's cheek. "Haven't seen ya lately. How y'been?"

"Quite well, thank you. And you?" asked Devorah.

"Oh, not bad. Been busy. Been fixin' up the ol' place." She pointed to the saloon across the street.

"Say, that's really nice, Lilah," Ann smiled, observing the new paint on the building and the flagstone walkway around it.

"Yep, we're really movin' aroun' here. Even Parson's givin' the church a good workover. Got 'imself some new shrub'ry an' a new bell, too—sounds louder'n the ol' one. He's got people down there right now paintin' the place." Delilah gestured down the street to where the church stood, a bustle of purposeful activity as groups of volunteer townsfolk entered and exited the foyer, carrying ladders,

225

cans of paint, and brushes. "Say, uh . . . Miz Lee," she said, turning back to Devorah. "That wuz quite a bad storm we had. Hope nothin' happened out yer way."

"Well, we had a little damage to the house and barn," Devorah answered, "but nothing that couldn't be repaired. However, my fields . . ." She broke off with a sigh.

Delilah frowned. "Bad?"

"The wheat's all right, but we have to replant all the corn," Ann informed her. "The twister really ripped it up."

"Wal, I'm right sorry t'hear that. Most folks got some damage, but the only one who came out smellin' like a rose wuz Ace Fairlane."

"Ace?!" Ann jerked her head up at the sound of his name.

Devorah stared in surprise. "What? No damage at all?"

"Nope. His place wuzn't touched. Twister jist hopped right over it."

Devorah closed her eyes and gave a small, tight shake of her head. *There is no justice,* she thought in dismay. *A man like that . . . while we have to sweat and slave . . .*

"Mebbe y'haven't heard 'bout 'im," Delilah continued. "Sez 'e's gone back t'the land, an' 'e's fixed up 'is own place an' planted 'is crops. Sez 'e's quit drinkin', too, an' I ain't seen hide nor hair o' him in m'saloon."

"He actually stopped drinking?" Ann said with disbelief in her voice.

Delilah shrugged. "Guess 'e has. I ain't seen 'im drunk since . . . January, it wuz. Got 'imself stuck in jail fer a month back when we had that big blizzard. Claims 'e's all dried out, but I dunno," she said doubtfully. "I don't really see 'im much these days cuz 'e keeps mostly t'imself."

Devorah leaned forward. "Lilah, give me your honest opinion. Has he really, truly changed?"

"Nope. Ain't no change in *him* 'cept fer gittin' worse," she stated emphatically.

"Then how do you explain . . .?"

"That's jist it, Miz Lee. I can't. But I've known 'im long 'nuff t'know it ain't gonna last. He ain't been botherin' y'none, has 'e?"

"Uh . . . no . . .we haven't seen him, either," Devorah replied, nervously biting her lower lip.

"Wal, count yerself lucky, then. But if I wuz you, I'd keep a loaded shotgun handy cuz one o' these days y'might need it."

"Are you saying . . . that he might show up at our place again?" Devorah asked fearfully.

"Trouble with Ace is, y'don't know what 'e's gonna do. I ain't sayin' nothin' 'cept take care o' yerself, Miz Lee, an' both yer gals here."

Oh, I am afraid, I am afraid, Devorah thought anxiously. *I can still see his face. How can I be free of this fear when it is everywhere, all around me and inside me?*

"Devvie, don't worry," Ann spoke up. "I swear I won't let anything happen to us." She sought Devorah's hand, held it tightly, reached out to touch her face.

Delilah's knowing eyes took in this simple gesture, absorbed it, analyzed it, and arrived at a conclusion. She noted how they looked at each other, how they acted toward one another, and without having to be given any further information, she *knew.* A slow and satisfied smile played over her face, her heart was uplifted and made glad, and she felt a sudden rush of motherly concern for their welfare. *I knew,* she thought, nodding to herself. *I allus knew. An' I'm happy fer 'em. They look fine t'gether an' right. God bless 'em!*

One morning on his way to his office in town, Doc McClintock decided to stop by Devorah's farm to pay them a friendly visit. He was concerned as to how they had fared through the recent storm, and he wanted to make sure that they were getting along well. At the same moment he reined his horse to a halt in the front yard, Ann was just coming out of the barn, carrying full milk pails in each hand, and she stopped and looked up at him in startled, pleasant surprise.

"Why, Doc! How nice to see you."

Doc stepped down from the carriage. "Good morning, Ann," he responded. "Lovely day, isn't it?"

"It certainly is," she agreed. "What brings you out this way?"

"Well, I haven't been out here for so long, I thought it was about time to check up on you, make sure everybody was all right—especially after that bad storm we had. Looks like you managed to get through it all right," he observed, glancing around at the house and the yard.

227

"Oh, we were hit, but not directly. We had some wind damage, and I had to fix a hole in the barn roof and replace the glass in one of the house windows. We also have to replant all the corn, but we're gradually getting back to normal."

"Ah, that is most unfortunate. Have you finished working on the old wagon yet?"

Ann grinned. "I sure have, Doc. It's really great, looks as good as new, and I've been driving it around."

"Well, I'm glad to hear that," he smiled back at her. "Tell me, is Devorah here?"

"Yes, she's in the house. Why don't you go on inside?" she gestured. "I'll be along as soon as I've put this milk up."

Ann went around to the rear of the house. Doc rapped softly on the front door, opened it, and stepped inside. Devorah was washing the breakfast dishes at the kitchen sink, and she turned to see his familiar beloved face. She quickly wiped her hands on a towel and rushed up to greet him, glad that he had stopped by to see her once again.

"Doc! Come in, come in! I'm so happy you're here."

Doc took both her hands in his and leaned to kiss her cheek. "Devorah, my dear, it's been a long time."

"Oh, too long! I've missed you so!" She threw her arms around his neck and embraced him. "Will you stay for a while and have coffee with us?" she questioned eagerly, leading him toward the kitchen table.

"Why, that's most kind of you, Devorah. I shall be happy to join you."

They sat drinking their coffee and Devorah asked him if he had been as occupied throughout the past winter as she had heard tell. Doc related to her various humorous incidents that had happened to him and also informed her of the birth and christening of Cora Anders' twins. Devorah was truly elated to learn of this event, for she had felt deeply for Joseph and Cora in their sorrow and loss. Ann entered the house through the back door, having finished her morning chores, and sat down at the table with them.

"Well, Devorah, I understand that Ann is quite a hard worker," Doc said, winking at Ann. "She told me she fixed up the wagon and the house and barn, too."

"Yes, she did. She's helped me with so many things," Devorah answered with evident pride. "There's always so much to do, and we've been very busy lately."

"I'm sorry to hear that you must replant the corn." Ann and Devorah both nodded grimly. "But I'm sure that everything will turn out right," Doc continued. "I have always wanted only the best for you, Devorah, you know that," he said sincerely.

She smiled at him. "I know, Doc."

"Your happiness and well-being are of utmost concern to me, and your joy is also mine."

Devorah reached across the table to clasp his hand. "You're sweet to say such things. I assure you that I am truly happy. I'm happier than I've ever been in a long, long time. But, Doc, I'm also concerned for you. Please tell me honestly how you're getting along."

"Ohhh, I'm doing fine, quite fine. My practice keeps me very busy, what with all those little old ladies and their spells of arthritis and gout. I've met some new people, too. We've got a couple of new members in the community who've just recently moved into town."

"Oh, really?" she brightened. "Who?"

Doc chuckled softly. "Ah, Devorah, my dear, this is springtime, you know, and they always say that's when a young man's fancy turns to thoughts of love." His eyes twinkled merrily.

Ann and Devorah looked askance at each other, brows knitted together in a curious frown. They pressed him for additional information, but Doc refused to elaborate further on the tantalizing hint.

As Doc rode the rest of the way into town, he paused to reflect upon the upward turn of events that had rescued him from his earlier depression and buoyed his flagging spirits. For a long time, he had keenly felt the ache of Devorah's rejection of his marriage proposal. His heart had been broken, his spirit bowed in pain, but he had resolutely carried on with his medical practice, seeking to bury himself completely in his work in an effort to forget. His grief had faded slowly with the passage of time, and the intense love that he had once felt for Devorah had gradually changed from sweeping passion into a gentle caring and concern for her welfare. Another two months had elapsed since their last strained conversation in the foyer of the church, and he had wanted to see her again today to let her know by his actions that he had forgiven her and that he was desirous of resuming their once friendly relationship.

This change in Doc's attitude had been primarily brought about by the advent of the two new members of the community. He had met them one day last month after the church services—an attractive widow named Laura Munroe and her elderly but still spry mother, Frances Callison. Laura had shoulder-length dark hair which fell in curled ringlets about her face, deep brown eyes, and a winning smile that accentuated her lovely features. At thirty-seven, she was closer to Doc's own age, and she was still slim and breathtakingly beautiful. From the very first moment that Doc had met her, he had been instantly captivated by her quiet charm and easy grace. He had begun to court her, feeling almost as shy and awkward as a young man with his first love, and he had passed many evenings in her delightful company. He had taken both Laura and her mother out on numerous afternoon picnics in the sunny countryside, and he had often been invited to their small farm for dinner.

A romance had begun to blossom between them like the slowly opening petals of a rose, bringing a sweet promise of future happiness. Doc's past problems had seemed to vanish overnight; they no longer held any importance for him as he redirected his energies and refocused his attentions upon Laura. He felt as if he had been made young again and had been granted a new outlook on life. He rode briskly along, smiling to himself and eagerly anticipating their coming meeting that night. *I'm really a lucky man,* he thought. *She's becoming so dear to me. One of these days I shall have to take her into Kansas City on a shopping spree. Perhaps there is still hope after all that I might have a son to carry on my name.*

The following Sunday at Meeting, Ann and Devorah sat amid the pungent smell of fresh paint. The renovation of the church had almost been completed, and they were deeply impressed with the new look of the place. Even new hymnals, their pages crisp and clean, had been bought and placed among the pews, and a new white cloth had been draped over the altar in front of the pulpit.

Devorah sat quietly with her head bent slightly forward, studying the black cover of the Bible that reposed upon her lap. *Dear Lord, I thank You again that none of us was hurt in the storm,* she prayed fervently. *I thank You that we are all still together and whole.*

Please watch over my crops and give us another good harvest this year. And oh, dear God, how much I thank You for Ann! For sending her to me, for her love, for letting me love her in return, for this beautiful happiness of ours. I feel that this is right, so perfectly right. I pray that You will bless us and look down upon us in Your love.

Ann, as always, was more interested in observing the townspeople as they entered the church and selected their seats. She watched Doc McClintock walk down the aisle, ushering along a dark-haired woman and another older white-haired woman. They sat in a center pew on the opposite side, with Doc taking the outer seat closest to the aisle. Ann closely scrutinized the younger woman's face, feeling a certain curiosity and mysterious fascination. *My, but she's beautiful,* she thought admiringly. *Her face is truly lovely, and she looks at him like . . . Oh, my goodness! Could it be . . . is it possible . . . Doc's courting her?! Oh, my golly!* The corners of Ann's mouth turned up in a wide impish grin. She would not mention anything to Devorah about it or urge her to turn around and see.

After the service was over, the townspeople milled about in the front foyer, chatting animatedly. Ann and Devorah politely pushed their way through, and Devorah held on tightly to Melissa's hand. Doc spied them coming toward him; he excused himself from his group and approached them.

"Ah, Devorah . . ."

"Why, Doc!" she beamed at him. "Would you care to come out to the house and join us for lunch? I know it's short notice, but—"

"Devorah, I would like very much for you to meet someone," he said, cutting her short. "Please come this way." He escorted her along with a firm but gentle touch on her elbow, and Ann followed closely behind with a knowing, smirking smile. Doc led her up to Laura and her mother, released Devorah's arm, and stepped over to Laura's side. "Devorah, I should like to introduce you to Laura Munroe and her mother, Frances Callison. Laura, this is Devorah Lee and her friend Ann Johnson, and this is Devorah's little girl, Melissa."

"How do you do, ma'am," Ann said politely, shaking Laura's hand.

Laura smiled charmingly. "Such a pleasure to meet you." She extended her hand toward Devorah; her grasp was firm and self-assured.

231

"How do you do," Devorah replied frostily.

"Doc has told me so much about both of you."

Devorah arched her eyebrows. "Oh . . . has he?"

"Yes, indeed. He spoke very highly of you. You both appear to be very confident, independent young ladies, and I must tell you that I admire you very much."

"Thank you," Devorah said stiffly.

"Won't you and this lovely child come out and join us all for lunch today? We would be honored and pleased to have you there."

"We appreciate your kind invitation, but perhaps another time, thank you." Devorah did not want to go at all.

"Very well, then, Mrs. Lee. We shall look forward to another occasion." Laura was smoothly accepting, her manner elegant and refined.

"Laura, my dear," Doc interrupted, "the hour is getting late, and we must go now if we are to make that early evening concert in Kansas City."

"Of course, darling," she said, patting his hand. "I have not forgotten that. Good day to you, Mrs. Lee and Miss Johnson. I am happy to have made your acquaintance."

"It was our pleasure," Devorah responded, inwardly fuming.

Doc nodded to them both and offered one arm to Laura and one to her mother. As he escorted them out of the church, Devorah stood looking after them with smoldering jealousy clearly imprinted upon her face.

"She seems quite nice, don't you think, Devvie?" said Ann, standing beside her.

"Mmm-hmmm." Devorah's lips were pressed together in a tight, thin line, and her eyes blazed with a cold fury.

"And that was really a nice thing for her to do—to invite us out. When do you think we should go, Devvie?" she inquired innocently and yet deliberately.

"We will not!" Devorah said icily.

Ann was secretly amused at Devorah's reaction and had to bite her lip to keep from laughing aloud.

With the arrival of June, the summer finally came again to the prairie. The tall green grasses rippled gently in the warm breeze; the birds chirped and twittered, made their nests, hatched their young.

232

The asparagus was ready to be picked, and Ann and Devorah enjoyed their first vegetable of the season along with a tender roasted chicken that had been basted with various herbs and spices. The rhubarb was also ripe, and the strawberries quickly followed. Devorah made fruit pies again and shortcakes with freshly whipped cream, upon which, for dessert, Melissa eagerly pounced. Now that the night air was staying warm, the two women slipped back into their old habit of sitting out on the porch after Melissa had gone to bed, drinking coffee while they talked quietly.

One bright morning Ann and Devorah both took a rest from their time-consuming task of replanting the corn so that Ann could take Melissa on a fishing expedition as she had once promised the child. The two of them set off toward the forest, carrying pails and bait and with fishing poles resting against their shoulders. They entered the woods and walked along the winding trails until they came to the rushing brook that meandered through the trees. Ann sought out a spot where the stream was quieter and more still-moving. There, they set their equipment down upon the ground.

Ann baited the hook for Melissa and showed her how to hold the long thin stick at the proper angle above the water. She set her own hook then, and with stick held loosely in hand, she settled back against an old tree stump, observing her surroundings, breathing deeply of the fresh clean air. The sun glinted brightly off the water; the toads and frogs croaked and splashed noisily. Small fish occasionally broke the smooth surface of the water, flipped briefly, and fell back. Birds flitted and sang around them; the forest was alive.

Melissa caught sight of a fat toad nearby and left her pole momentarily unattended as she scrambled to her feet and pursued the hopping creature. She snatched it just before it landed in the water, and she held it up close to her face, eyeing it curiously.

"Hold it gently, Lissa," Ann called out to her. "Don't squeeze."

Melissa moved over to Ann's side so that Ann could see the toad. "They don't bite, do they?"

"No, honey, they don't bite," she assured the child.

Melissa stroked the warty skin. "How come they're all bumpy?" she wondered.

"Well, Lissa, it's just a form of protection," Ann patiently explained. "If other animals try to eat him, they have to let him go because he tastes bad." She looked beyond the child, her attention suddenly caught by the unattended pole which had begun to jerk spasmodically. "Pay attention, Lissa," she pointed. "You've got a bite!"

Melissa dropped the toad and scuttled back to the bobbing pole. Ann stood beside her and helped her land the fish, which was only a rather small one.

"It's too small for us, honey. Let's throw it back and wait for a bigger one."

"But it's my first one," she protested.

"That's all right. There are plenty more, and we've got all day."

Ann released the fish, rebaited the hook, and cast the line back into the water. A short while later, Melissa caught a larger fish and Ann disengaged the hook from its mouth and placed it into the waiting pail.

"How's that one, Ann?" The child's eyes were bright, and she was quite proud of herself.

Ann smiled down at her. "Good, Lissa, very good."

They continued to fish until the noontime sun made the water too hot for any further nibbles on the lines. Then Ann packed up all their gear and they headed home for lunch. Devorah was working in the garden when she saw them coming. She wiped her hands, pushed back her falling hair, and met them in the yard. Melissa left Ann's side and ran up to her mother, dancing excitedly around her skirts.

"Look, Mommy, look what we got!"

Ann held out the pail, and Devorah leaned over, looking into it.

"Oh, six!" she said, counting the fish. "We shall have them for supper tonight. Did you catch them all, sweetheart?"

"No, I just got four," Melissa told her.

"I got the other two. She really had a good time, Devvie," said Ann, laughing. Devorah smiled.

Fourteen

Ann persuaded Devorah to give her a haircut, complaining that her long tresses were lying too hot and heavy upon her neck, even though she had tried to keep them tied back with a ribbon. She wanted to feel free, she said, and the long hair was beginning to make her uncomfortable in the summer heat. In the bathroom, seated upon a small stool, she waited while Devorah clipped away the bothersome locks. When Devorah finished, the hair had been expertly cut into a short bob, and all traces of the concealing hair dye were now completely gone.

"Ann, don't you think you should color your hair again?" Devorah fretted worriedly.

"Nah. What for? It's too much of a bother. Besides, I've always had my hair short like this, and I've never had to worry about dyeing it before."

"Yes, but . . ." Devorah hesitated.

"But what, Devvie?" she insisted impatiently.

"You colored it because Doc and I were afraid that Ace might recognize you. Have you forgotten about that?"

Ann paused to consider this. "Oh. Well . . ."

"What if he sees you again?"

"But we haven't seen him since last year." Ann counted off the time on her fingers. "Seven months, Devvie. That's a long time. He's probably forgotten about me."

"How can you be so sure?"

"Well, all the other times he did see me, I was in a dress. He thinks I'm your niece. Besides, Lilah says he keeps mostly to himself nowadays. *She* hasn't even seen him."

"Lilah also warned us to be careful."

"But of what, Devvie? Do you think after all this time he's going to come out here looking for me?"

Devorah frowned. "I don't know." She began to sweep up the pile of cut hair.

"Have you forgotten that talk Doc supposedly gave him after the harvest dance?" Ann reminded her. "Obviously it must have done some good because he's left us alone ever since."

Devorah sighed. "I hope you're right."

"Of course I'm right," Ann said in firm dismissal.

Devorah did not feel as confident as Ann, but she allowed herself to be reluctantly persuaded that all was well.

By the end of the second week of June, all of the replanting had been completed, and Ann and Devorah hugged each other in relief. The amber wheat was growing tall and strong, the garden would soon be producing, and now the corn had been resowed and could be left to the care of the sun and the rain.

"I'm going out for a ride, Devvie," Ann told her one afternoon.

"Oh? In the wagon?"

"No, I'm taking the horse. After all this hard work, I feel like I just want to relax with a good long ride over the fields."

"Well, all right, but be careful."

"Sure you don't need me for anything?"

"No, go ahead. You've earned it," Devorah said lightly.

Ann took one of the halters from the barn and walked out to the fields where the horses and cows were grazing contentedly. She did not want to use a saddle, but only bridled the horse and swung herself easily up onto its bare back. With her legs firmly clasped around its belly, she turned the horse and cantered off.

Ann reveled in the sense of freedom that riding gave her. She loved the feel of the horse beneath her—the rippling pull of the strong corded muscles, the pounding beat of the flying hooves, the sense of being on top of controlled power. She urged the horse into a fast gallop, the ground was a passing blur under her feet, the wind rushed against her face and clothes. A fence loomed in front of her and she jumped it easily, leaning forward with the horse's straining body, making herself one with its surging movements. She left the boundaries of Devorah's land behind and the miles flew swiftly by as the horse galloped freely on.

She was blissfully unaware of the exact moment when she passed onto Ace's property.

Ace Fairlane had a very good spring. The two passing drifters that he had hired had helped him perform a great deal of backbreaking work. The sagging porch had been repaired, both the house and barn had been repainted, and the fields that had lain fallow for so long had been plowed and planted. After their labors were over, the two drifters had moved on and Ace, being in good spirits, had paid them fairly and well.

Both the wheat and the corn had been sowed early; the crops were now well established and ripening toward the harvest. Ace had considered himself extremely lucky when the twister had skirted his property, and he felt that perhaps the Reverend's God was finally on his side, watching out for him, helping him to make a better man out of himself. He still had not touched a single drop of alcohol and was proud of the fact that he had not the slightest desire to drink. He had made only a very few trips into town for needed supplies. When he did so he studiously avoided both the saloon and the church, arriving during those times of day when the streets were most likely to be more or less deserted. He had not wanted to engage in protracted conversation with any of the townspeople or even with his old buddies, preferring instead to let them think that he had mysteriously dropped out of sight. The demanding sexual desires that were stimulated by his drinking had been somewhat pacified and sublimated as he directed all of his efforts into working with the land.

On this particular afternoon, Ace wandered slowly through the fields, examining the waving wheat and the growing stalks of corn. *Yep, ain't bad,* he thought, nodding to himself. *Ain't bad at all fer a man they said'd never amount t'nothin'. All them bastards oughtta c'm on out here an' see fer themselves what I done wi'this place. They ain't got no call t'be so down on a hard-workin' man, 'spesh'ly that Miz Lilah. Ain't got no faith, that's whassa matter with 'er. I'll pay 'er back in time, not t'worry. Yeah, I'll pay 'em all back when the time's right. Ain't nobody shits on ol' Ace an' gits away with it.* He chuckled softly and rubbed his hand across the rough stubble on his face, his fingers lightly toying with the jagged pink scar that marred one cheek.

Ace reached the end of the corn rows and stood gazing out across the distant grassy meadow. *Yep, they gotta be shown,* he mused, thinking deeply. *They jist gotta learn their place. Why, I*

237

bet'cha—huh? Whozzat? His attention was captured by a swiftly moving horse and rider that suddenly came into his line of sight. He quickly leaped back into the concealing cover of the corn rows, crouching down low on his hands and knees so that he would not be seen. He watched intently as the horse galloped closer, his eyes squinting and straining to identify the rider's face. *Who is that,* he asked himself. *That guy looks awful familiar. Know I've seen 'im b'fore, jist know it, but I can't . . .* And then the horse thundered past him, and he looked up into the smooth hairless face of a young woman, saw the outline of her small breasts pushing through the fabric of her shirt, noted the man's clothing, the short closely cropped hair, the heavy boots. All of this pertinent information crowded upon him within a few split seconds; he looked, he saw, he knew, and his brain suddenly clicked and exploded into triumphant recognition. *That ain't no him,* he realized, open-mouthed. *Goddammit, thassa gal! That's the one I been lookin' fer all this time—the one who's been livin' with Miz Lee. How the hell could I a been so blind? Niece, my fuckin' ass!*

Ace ran for the house, grabbed his gun holster, and quickly saddled his horse.

It was late afternoon by the time Ann finally returned to the farm. She put the horse in his stall in the barn and curried him, brushing out the knotted tangles from the long mane and tail. Her blood was still singing from the exhilarating ride, and she decided to do the evening chores early before her energy left her and weariness set in. An hour later, she entered the house and found Devorah preparing dinner. Two loaves of bread and a freshly made fruit pie stood cooling upon the kitchen table, and the aromas made Ann realize just how hungry she was.

Devorah glanced up at her. "Did you just get back, Ann?"

"No, I've been back for a while, but I did the chores early so I could collapse later." She leaned over the pie, inhaling deeply. "Mmm, boy, that smells good! Is dinner ready yet?"

"Almost. Go wash up. Did you enjoy your ride?"

"Ohhh, loved it!" Ann said. "It's been so long since I've been on a horse."

After supper was over, Devorah excused Melissa from her usual job of assisting with the dishes and the child went into her bedroom to play with her doll and the new furniture. The two women stood at the kitchen sink, one washing, the other drying, and Devorah deliberately kept her voice low so that Melissa would not hear her words.

"Ann, have you heard any rumors about roving packs of wild dogs?"

"Why, no, Devvie," she said with mild surprise. "Why do you ask?"

"Well, the last time we were at Meeting, I overheard some of the men talking about it. Seems they've lost a few chickens to these dogs, and they said it was a moving pack. I wonder if they could be headed this way."

Ann attempted to reassure her. "I haven't heard anything outside lately, if that's what you're worried about. We haven't lost any chickens, either."

"Just the same, I don't want Lissa going outside after dark. And don't you go out without the rifle, do you understand me?" Devorah spoke sternly.

"All right, Devvie. Take it easy."

"And be alert. Listen for them," she added.

"All *right*. I *will*."

"I don't want anything to happen to either of you. You're both too precious to me."

Ann put her arm around Devorah's shoulders, gave her a quick hug, and patted her back. "I know, Devvie. I'll take care of us all."

"I'm going to go take a long relaxing bath now. Don't bother me unless it's an emergency," she quipped.

Ace Fairlane was at the saloon for the first time since New Year's Eve. He had been standing alone at the bar for the past several hours, drinking steadily and spurning all friendly offers of companionship. Many times he had either snapped irritatedly at the other men in the saloon or simply ignored their attempts at sociability. They had eventually moved away to form their own little groups, thus leaving Ace to himself, sullen and morose. He had already finished a full bottle of whiskey and was well on his way through a second one. He had not eaten anything since noontime, and this, along with the fact that his system was unused to receiving such great quantities of

239

alcohol, had made him sink very quickly into the depths of total ine-
briation.

When Ace had no longer been able to remain on his own two
feet at the bar, he had slowly shuffled over to a lone table in the
corner of the room, taking the half empty bottle with him. He had
sat there hunched over, surrounded by occasional, curious glances
from the other men, gulping long swallows of whiskey directly from
the bottle, and mulling over a disjointed plan of revenge. A couple
of the madam's girls, dressed in their low-cut revealing outfits, had
sidled up to him and tried to elicit his interest, but he had roughly
shoved them aside, uttering foul curses at them.

Lessee now, he thought, frowning deeply with half closed eyes.
*I gotta think, I gotta plan this right. That gal deserves t'die, no doubt
'bout that. She's been hidin' away from me fer too long, runnin'
scared, thinkin' I'd never find 'er, thinkin' mebbe I'd fergot all 'bout
'er. Thought she had me fooled there, huh? But ol' Ace never fergits
a face, never fergits what's due. I'm gonna do what I shoulda done
a long time ago—blast 'er damn face in. An' then I'm gonna git that
other bitch, Miz Lee. She's been holdin' me off all this time, tryin'
t'play coy an' hard t'git. Wal, I'm gonna git 'er, too. I'm gonna screw
'er but good an' make 'er beg fer it. But lessee now . . . How'm I
gonna git to 'em? First one, then the other or both of 'em t'gether?
In through the window or jist bust down the door? No, I can't jist
blast in. I gotta do this real slow an' easy, I gotta sneak. Mebbe if I
git the kid first an' then use 'er t'git . . . aha! The kid . . . yeah, the
kid. That'd really set Miz Lee in stitches.* An evil, malicious leer
slowly spread across his features as he seized upon the solution to
his dilemma.

"Hey, barkeep!" Ace yelled drunkenly. "Bring me 'nother
bottle!"

"Ain't'cha had 'nuff yet, Ace?" Sam called back from behind
the bar. "Y'ain't even finished what'cha got."

"I will, soon 'nuff. C'm on, let's have 'nother one!" Ace pounded
on the table with his fist.

Delilah Emerson descended the stairs just then and Sam beckoned silently to her. They engaged in a hurried, whispered conversation. Delilah walked up to Ace's table, regarding him with an
expression of sickened disgust.

"Y'rotten scondrel! What'cha doin' here?" she demanded, placing both hands on her broad hips.

Ace looked up at her through reddened eyes. "Jist havin' a friendly drink izzall. Nothin' wrong wi'that, izzere?"

"Y'don't look too friendly t'me. An' what's wrong is *you*. I thought'cha'd gotten off the sauce."

"Aw, Lilah!" he groaned, casting his eyes upward. "I need it t'think."

"Y'lyin' asshole! I knew y'hadn't changed none. What'cha need's a good swift boot outta here. I want'cha t'leave now afore y'start tearin' up the place."

"I ain't touched nothin'," he said defensively.

Delilah was adamant in her insistence. "An' y'ain't gonna, either. G'wan, scram, 'fore I haul y'out by the seat o' yer pants."

"What's it t'you if I sit here mindin' m'own biznizz? I'm payin' fer it, ain't I?" he grumbled sullenly.

"I don't want yer money, ya rat. Ya've had too damn much already, an' I say no more, y'hear me?" She reached out and grabbed him by the back of his collar.

Ace suddenly jumped up from his seat, wrenching himself away from Delilah's grasp and causing the chair to totter backward and fall with a dull thud to the floor. He wiped his mouth on his dirty sleeve, glaring at her with thinly disguised hatred and fury.

"Damn ya!" he raged at her. "Yer jist like alla rest of 'em. Y'need t'be taught a lesson, too, jist like they do. An' soon's I git done wi'them bitches t'night, I'll be back fer ya, y'wait 'n see, Goddamn if I don't!" He snatched his hat and started for the door.

"Ace! Where y'goin'?" Delilah tried to detain him by holding on to his sleeve. When he had stood up she had seen the heavy holstered gun buckled over his hips.

"Out! Leggo o' me! I'm goin' out t'settle a long overdue score." He pried her fingers away from his arm, cruelly crushing the rings together, and pushed her aside.

Delilah watched him go, massaging her hand to ease the numbing pain in the fingers. She was highly suspicious of Ace's actions, and she had never before seen him come into the saloon with a gun strapped to his hips. *He's out fer blood,* she thought grimly. *He's got a corncob up 'is ass, an' 'e means it. He's fired up t'kill, but* who?

241

Where could 'e be goin' this time o' night? Whadde say t'me—them bitches? Who're they? Who . . . oh, Lord preserve us! It's Miz Lee an' Ann, she panicked. *Got t'be! An' the child . . . he wuz carryin' on the same way right b'fore that other li'l gal got killed. Oh, mercy! If 'e dares t'hurt that sweet li'l gal o' Miz Lee's, I'll never fergive m'self if I don't try t'stop 'im.*

Delilah spun around and dashed up the stairs, taking two steps at a time. With amazing speed, she lumbered down the narrow hallway and burst into Ruby's room.

"Ruby!" she gasped. "Git yer boy Jesse an' send 'im over t'Doc's office t'see if 'e's left a message where 'e kin be reached. Then have 'im git the sheriff an' high-tail it back here t'me."

Ruby glanced up in startled surprise. "What's happened?"

"Nothin' yet, but somethin's gonna. Now move it, gal! Do as I say!"

Delilah nervously paced the floor, wringing her hands in agitation as she waited breathlessly for Jesse to return. Fifteen minutes later, the boy came through the door with the sheriff in tow.

"What's up, Miz Lilah?" Andy Hanks said brightly.

Delilah advanced upon him, shaking her finger at him. "Now y'lissen t'me cuz I know what I'm talkin' 'bout. Ace's been in here drinkin' all night, an' 'e's guzzled two bottles o' whiskey. He's got a gun, an' 'e's fit t'be tied, an' 'e's jist left fer Miz Lee's farm with blood in 'is eye. Ya've got t'git out there right quick cuz there's liable t'be some shootin'."

"What if 'e's jist gone home t'sleep it off?" Hanks suggested.

Delilah refused to be placated. "He ain't gone home, no, sir! Where's the doc?"

"His slate sez 'e's off at Laura Munroe's."

"D'y'know where that is?" she pressed relentlessly.

"Wal, yeah, but I ain't got no call t'go disturbin' 'im."

"Y'got call!" she insisted, the fire blazing in her eyes. "You g'wan out there an' git 'im, an' then both o' ya make a beeline fer Miz Lee's farm."

"But, Lilah . . ."

"*Move,* damn yer hide!" she thundered at him. "Or else I'll see to it yer run outta office, an' I'll rip yer badge off m'self!"

"Awright, awright, I'm goin'!" Hanks quickly backed out the door.

242

Devorah was languishing in the bathtub. Her legs were stretched out in front of her, her back was propped up against the sloping rear of the tub, and she was enjoying the feel of the warm soapy water. Her nerves were being soothed, her taut muscles were relaxing, and all of her cares were dropping away as she leaned back and closed her eyes. *Oh, this feels so good,* she purred contentedly. *After a long hard day, to just lie back here and take it easy and not be bothered by anybody. Such a good quiet place to unwind.* She ducked her head underneath the water, then sat up and began to give her hair a vigorous shampoo.

Ann was reading quietly in the living room, patiently awaiting her turn in the bathtub. No fire was burning in the grate because the night itself was warm. Although the lamp had been turned up so that she could easily read the printed page, Ann felt herself gradually becoming sleepy, and she had caught herself nodding off several times. *Hurry up, Devvie, so I can take my bath, too,* she thought. *Then we can crawl into bed together and hold each other and touch each other and make love. Oh, how I love to go to sleep nestled in your arms, close to your warm softness. I feel complete when I'm with you, as if together we could take on the whole world.*

Melissa had already been put to bed quite some time ago, and she lay soundly asleep, her blonde hair fanned across the pillow and one arm protectively hugging her doll to her small chest. She dreamed of whatever good things children always dream of—all sweetness and light and eager anticipation for the morrow.

None of them had the slightest intimation that a dark net of invisible evil was slowly, inexorably tightening itself around them. Tragedy would soon descend upon them.

Ace Fairlane rode quietly up the lane leading to Devorah's house and brought his horse to a halt in the front yard. He slid down from the saddle, took a few stumbling steps, caught himself before he fell, and stealthily crept up to one of the darkened bedroom windows. He braced himself unsteadily against the sill, pressed his face to the open screen, and peered inside the room. After his eyes adjusted to the dim light within, he was able to make out a small form lying covered up on the bed. His instincts told him that it was the child, and another sardonic grin spread across his features. He began to whisper softly to the sleeping child, scratching his dirty broken fingernails over the mesh of the screen.

"Hey, kid! Wake up, kid. C'm'ere! C'm'ere 'n see what I got fer ya."

Melissa opened her eyes and sat up in the bed, glancing curiously around for the source of the sound that she had just heard. She saw Ace's head and shoulders through the screen, hopped down to the floor, and walked trustingly up to the window.

"C'm'ere, kid. 'Atsa gal," he continued smoothly. "What's yer name?"

"Melissa."

"Wal, Missy, eh? Yer a right purty li'l gal, y'know that?"

Melissa stood rubbing her eyes. "Who're you?"

Ace smiled suavely. "Oh, I'm jist a good friend o' yer mother's. A *very* good friend. Whyn't'cha c'm on outside with me, huh? Y'wanna go fer a ride on m'horsie?"

"I'm supposed to be in bed," Melissa said warily. She was reluctant to incur her mother's wrath if she disobeyed.

"Hey, that's okay. Yer mother won't mind if y'go fer a ride with me. Jist a li'l ride aroun' the yard, huh? Y'kin pet m'horse an' brush 'im an' give 'im a lump o' sugar. Whaddya say, huh, Missy? C'm on, let's have some fun!"

"Well . . ." Melissa was still uncertain, but the man seemed so nice and polite.

"Lookee here. I got somethin' fer ya. Promised ya somethin', didn't I?" Ace rummaged through his pockets, found a wrapped piece of candy, and held it up for the child to see. "How 'bout that, huh? I got some more if y'want it. All y'gotta do is slide the catch back on that screen so's I kin lift up the window."

As soon as Melissa saw the candy, all of her fears instantly departed. The man seemed so kind, and he smiled at her just like her daddy used to smile. She unfastened the catch on the screen.

" 'Atsa gal, Missy. Slide it alla way back," he urged her approvingly. He noiselessly lifted the window, handed her the piece of candy, and reached inside to pick her up, pulling her through the window frame. He set her down gently upon the ground and quickly put a finger to his lips. "Now y'gotta be quiet, y'hear? We don't want yer mother t'know we're out here jist yet."

"Why not?"

"Cuz it's gonna be a s'prise. Y'wanna s'prise 'er, huh?" Melissa nodded eagerly, her eyes bright. "Wal, c'm on, then, come with me."

Ace started to lead her by the hand over toward the barn, also grabbing the horse's dangling reins and pulling him along. He had no trouble finding his way, for the bright white light of the full moon shone down, bathing the land in stark outlines, but he wanted to move the horse into a place of shadow so that it would not be readily visible from the house. Ace drew back the bolt on the heavy barn doors, pulled open one of the doors, and began to drag Melissa into the shielding darkness. Here, the child balked.

"Where are we going? I thought you said we were going to ride the horse."

"Shaddup, kid!" he growled.

He seized her thin arm with one huge hand and held her in a painful viselike grip while the fingers of his other hand hastily fumbled at the buttons of his pants. He realized he would also have to unbuckle his holster, and although he was reluctant to do this, there seemed to be no other easier way. Still holding on to the child, who was now attempting to squirm away from his grasp, he allowed the holster to drop to the ground and unclasped his belt buckle. As he pushed the pants down around his hips, his hardness sprang erect and poked out through the folds of his underwear. He abruptly released Melissa's arm and grabbed her by the hair, yanking her toward him and forcing her to her knees in the dust. He rubbed himself excitedly across her face, thrusting forward with his hips and trying to pry open her clenched mouth.

"Open up, dammit!" he snarled savagely.

Melissa began to whimper softly, but she refused to part her lips. She pounded ineffectively against his stomach and legs with both her hands, and although she struggled mightily, the man was much stronger. She could not understand why he wanted to hurt her after he had been so nice in offering her the candy and a ride on his horse. Hadn't he said they were going to surprise Mommy? Where was the surprise? Why was he doing this to her, holding her this way, forcing her to do what she instinctively knew *had* to be wrong? What was this thing, this awful big hairy thing that he kept poking into her face, kept insisting that she touch and fondle? Why did he want her to open her mouth? All she knew was that the nice man had suddenly turned mean, and she no longer wanted to play with him. He was too rough, and he was hurting her, hurting her hair and her arm and rubbing this hard, ugly, stinky thing all over her face. She tried to twist her head aside, but that only seemed to make him madder, and he yanked harder at her hair, making her cry out in pain. She was frightened now, sorely afraid, and she wanted her mother, wanted her to come outside and make the bad man stop, make him go away and leave her alone.

Inside the barn, the animals grew restless at this unusual disturbance. The chickens began to squawk and cluck; the horses snorted and stamped their hooves uneasily.

Devorah was still in the bathtub. She had finished washing her hair, but she had wanted to lie back in the relaxing water for just a few more minutes. Finally she stood up, reached out for the towel, and began to dry off her body. She wrapped another towel around her wet hair and stepped out of the tub.

Ann was slumped in the chair in the living room. The book lay open and forgotten upon her lap as she dozed fitfully. Suddenly her head snapped back and her eyes flew open as she heard or thought she heard a strange half-muffled sound. She sat up and listened intently, straining to hear the sound again. It was repeated, and she realized that it came from the animals in the barn. *What's going on?* she wondered worriedly. *The dogs? Are they after the chickens? Perhaps I'd better check.* She rose from her chair and picked up the rifle.

Ann opened the front door and slowly pushed back the screen with her one free hand. The inside light spilled out into the yard, but the quality of illumination was poor, and she could not see the barn very clearly. When her eyes grew accustomed to the darkness that had been caused by a large cloud passing across the face of the moon, she was able to discern the gaping barn door and two struggling figures, one larger, one smaller, in front of it. One figure appeared to be bending over the other one, and Ann stared ahead in puzzlement, ready to bring the rifle up to her shoulder if necessary.

Ace heard the gentle creak of the screen door swinging open and became aware of the lamplight that now threatened to expose him. He whipped his head around and saw Ann standing on the threshold.

The concealing cloud cover slowly pulled away from the face of the moon, and the revealing light shone brilliantly down, falling directly upon the two struggling figures in front of the barn. Half of Ace's face was still in shadow, but the other half, the side that was turned toward Ann, clearly showed the ragged scar on the cheek.

Ann saw Melissa vainly trying to break free from his grasp, and then she looked at *him*, saw the pants pushed down around the hips, saw what he was doing to the child, saw the holster lying on the ground. She looked at his face and saw the scar, saw the cruel expression, saw the hate and malice reflected there, noted the precise manner in which he was bending over the child. A bolt of lightning seared through her brain as her lost memory returned and swept over her in instantaneous recognition. *Oh my God*, she screamed in silent fear. *It's him! It's Ace! He's the one who . . .*

"Devvie!" she cried out. "Devvie, come here!" She let go of the screen and stepped out onto the porch.

Devorah had dressed herself in her nightgown and robe and was now drying her hair. She brushed the long tresses away from her face and hummed softly to herself. She did not hear Ann's cry.

Ace had heard her, however, and he grimaced in impotent rage. He suddenly released the child and fumbled to pull up his pants.

Melissa fell away from him and scampered around behind him. She began to run for the safety of the house.

"Mommy!" she shrieked in terror. "Annie! Annie!"

The hem of Melisssa's nightgown became entangled in Ace's spurs. She jerked herself away, ripping the material, and ran on.

Ace was caught off balance as he struggled to button his pants. Still drunk, he lost his footing and came crashing down to the ground.

"Lissa!"

Ann opened her arms to receive the fleeing child. She still held the rifle.

Ace groped for the holster, drew out the gun, and aimed it shakily at Ann. He fired.

The bullet entered Melissa's back, passed through her frantically beating heart, and exited her chest, whistling through the air close to Ann's head.

Melissa's face registered a shocked surprise. She paused in her flight, hung suspended in the air for a brief instant, and toppled face first into the dust at Ann's feet.

Ann's mouth fell open and she looked back at Ace.

Devorah heard the shot and rushed out of the bathroom. She ran down the hallway.

Ace was taken aback. He had not intended to shoot the child.

Ann spurred herself into action. She cocked the rifle and strode toward Ace.

"You filthy bastard!" she screamed at him. "I know who you are now! May you rot in hell!"

A distance of only twenty feet separated them. Ann swept the rifle up to her shoulder and fired.

The bullet tore into Ace's throat, opening up a gaping wound. Blood bubbled from his mouth in a red froth.

Ace squirmed in agony on the ground. He raised his gun in an attempt to protect himself and leveled it at Ann's face.

Ann never gave him a second chance. She rapidly closed the distance between them and stood almost directly above him, made momentarily fearless by her choking rage. She fired again.

The bullet smashed into Ace's brain, exploding his eyeball. He twitched once and then lay still. His limp fingers continued to hold onto the gun.

Ann's legs were trembling with the rush of adrenalin that had sped through her system, and she slowly sank to her knees. She was aware that she had just killed a man, and the sweat began to bead upon her brow.

Devorah flung the screen open with a bang and rushed out onto the porch. She saw Melissa lying on the ground and she ran down the steps. She knelt in the dust and turned the child over.

Melissa's eyes were open, but they were glassy and unseeing. Her chest was still rising and falling, but the movement was gradually slowing down and becoming fainter. Blood spilled out over her back and chest.

Devorah gathered the child into her arms and rocked her gently back and forth, not caring that the blood was staining her hands and clothes.

"Don't worry, honey," she murmured softly. "Doc is coming. He'll be here soon. You'll be all right, you'll be all right."

Melissa jerked, gave a sudden gasp, and her breathing stopped. The eyes clouded over and closed.

"Honey, please speak to me," Devorah pleaded. When she received no response, she realized that the child was dead. "Melissa Jane Lee!" she shouted in a loud voice. "Oh *God!*" She threw her head back and screamed then—a long, wailing, piercing scream. She fell forward over the child's body and sobbed.

Ann had been watching this last scene unfold from her position near Ace's body. She had been afraid to go to Devorah, afraid to find out what had happened to Melissa. When she heard Devorah's scream of despair, she knew. She bent her head forward upon her chest and wept bitterly. Her clenched fists beat the dust again and again.

Doc McClintock had been spending a relatively quiet evening at Laura Munroe's farm. When the sheriff had pounded on the door with the urgent news that he was needed immediately, Doc had bid a hasty farewell to Laura and her mother and had left, grabbing his hat and his medical bag. He drove his carriage, and the sheriff sat astride his own horse. As they rode along, Hanks briefly reported to Doc what the madam had told him. They were not too far away from Devorah's farm when they both heard the sounds of three shots fired in rapid succession.

"Hear that?" said Hanks, turning his head in the direction of the sounds.

"Hurry, man!" Doc urged him. "We may already be too late."

The sheriff galloped on ahead of him, and Doc followed closely behind, careening the carriage into the lane leading up to the house. When they reached the front yard, Hanks leaped off his horse and ran forward, drawing his gun from the holster. Doc snatched his medical bag and ran after him.

They were stunned at the carnage that lay before them. Ace Fairlane was sprawled dead on the ground in front of the open barn door, his bloody destroyed face barely recognizable except for the long scar on his cheek. Ann was huddled weeping next to him, her face buried in her hands. Devorah was sitting in the dust at the foot of the porch steps with Melissa's inert body draped across her lap. She still cradled the child's head in her arms, and the sound of her grief-stricken sobbing was truly heart-wrenching to hear.

Doc was torn between treating Ann or Devorah first. He was closer to Ann, so he stepped up to her, bent over her, and placed his hand tenderly upon her shoulder.

"Ann . . . ," he said quietly.

She looked up at him with tears streaming unchecked down her face. "I'm all right, Doc, I'm all right," she told him. "Go to Devvie," she gestured weakly.

Doc walked over to Devorah and knelt by her side. He reached for Melissa with the intent of examining her, but Devorah resolutely gripped the small form tighter in her arms.

"No! Please don't take her away from me," she gasped brokenly.

"Let me see," Doc said gently.

He opened his bag and applied the stethoscope to Melissa's chest, searching and hoping against hope for some faint sign of life. He found none, smoothed the hair back from the child's forehead, and sighed deeply, sadly.

"Is she . . . will she . . . ," Devorah began hesitantly.

"Let me have her, Devorah."

She reluctantly released her hold on Melissa, and Doc scooped the child up into his arms, carrying her tenderly to his carriage. Devorah stumbled after him, stretching out her arms in silent supplicatory assistance. He spread a blanket over the back seat of the carriage, placed the child's body upon it, and covered her up.

"Come, my dear," he said, turning back to Devorah. "Let's go inside."

Doc put his arm protectively around Devorah's shoulders, and they walked slowly toward the house. She laid her head upon his chest and slipped one arm around his waist. She allowed herself to be led into the bedroom, where she reclined upon the bed, and Doc gave her a strong sedative. He was gravely concerned about her, for she appeared to have withdrawn deeply into a state of shock. He pulled up a chair and sat next to the bed, holding onto Devorah's hand, and he remained at her side until she passed into sleep.

Ann was standing dazedly in the front yard. Her tears had ceased to flow, but her hands still continued to shake uncontrollably, and she folded her arms across her chest in an effort to stop the aimless trembling. She watched passively while the sheriff slung Ace's body over his back, walked up to Ace's waiting horse, and heaved the body face down across the saddle. Hanks beat the dust from his pants, readjusted his hat, and moved to stand beside Ann.

"Uh, ma'am . . . I hope y'don't mind, but I gotta ask ya some questions," he said humbly.

"Go ahead," Ann replied dully.

"Wal, first of all, how'd the kid git outside?"

Ann turned on him suddenly. "She's not a kid! She has a name!"

"Oh, uh . . . beggin' yer pardon, ma'am," Hanks quickly apologized. "Okay, how'd she git outside?"

"She must have . . . crawled through the open window there," she offered, pointing toward the house. "He must have stood outside the screen and . . . called to her."

"But ain't the window locked from the inside?" Ann nodded. "Then how'd she git it open by 'erself?"

"He must have . . . talked to her . . . told her to release the catch . . . lured her out somehow. I don't know!" she gestured in exasperation.

"An' when 'e got 'er out, where'd 'e take 'er?"

"To the barn. He had opened the doors . . . he was going to take her inside . . ." She trailed off, suddenly helpless.

Hanks tried to be kind. "Now I know this is hard fer ya, ma'am, but y'gotta tell me what 'e did."

"He never got her inside the barn. She must have refused, she was trying to get away. He was holding her . . . he was standing over her. She was on her knees in front of him. His pants were down and he was . . . he was forcing her to . . . to . . ." Ann shut her eyes tightly and covered her mouth with one hand as the tears started up again.

"Are y' sayin' 'e wuz molestin' 'er?"

"Yes, damn it!" she snapped. "Isn't that clear?"

"Awright, take it easy, ma'am," Hanks said soothingly. "Then what happened?"

"I heard a noise. It was the animals . . . and I came outside with the rifle. I saw him . . . what he was doing . . . and she broke away from him . . . he fell . . . she ran toward me . . . and he shot her. She never had a chance."

"Deliberately?"

"No. It was meant for me. She just got in the way. I shot him then. I killed him," she said in a monotone.

"Why wuz 'e aimin' t'shoot'cha?"

"He's been after me for a year now. Remember the killing of the little Anders girl? He was trying to pin it on me . . . make me the scapegoat. He's the one who really did it, Sheriff. He's your killer."

Hanks frowned in surprise. "Y'know that fer a fact?"

"I know," Ann spoke firmly. "I was there that night . . . in town. I saw him in the alley . . . bending over the child's body. He's been after me because I was the only witness."

"Wal, whyn't'cha tell me 'bout this a long time ago?"

"Because, Sheriff, I didn't know who it was I saw that night. I mean, my mind knew it, but I just couldn't remember until I saw his face in the moonlight tonight." Ann tried to find the right words to explain her loss of memory. "Doc told me not to worry about it. He said I'd remember when the time was right. I had plenty of nightmares about it, though. By the time I finally did know who he was . . . it was too late," she ended in a soft whisper.

Hanks let the air out of his lungs in a rush and tipped his hat back on his head. "Guess the Anderses oughtta be relieved t'find this out."

"Be sure you tell them that it was a man. Tell them it wasn't a woman," Ann said tonelessly.

Hanks eyed her curiously. "Huh? Whaddya mean by—"

"Nothing. Is that all, Sheriff?"

"Wal, I reckon so. Clear cut case o' self-defense, the way I see it. Y'kin go now, Miz uh . . ."

Ann was already walking away from him. She went into the barn, brought out a rake and shovel, and stood above the blood-soaked spot where Ace's body had lain. She pushed the edge of the shovel into the hard ground, turned the dirt over, and raked it smooth, thus obliterating all traces of the spilled blood. She moved over to the other spot in front of the porch steps and stood for a long moment gazing silently down with bowed head and tear-filled eyes. She straightened up, and the shovel bit into the earth once again.

The sheriff escorted Ann into the house. Doc had just closed the door to Devorah's bedroom, and he met them in the living room, fastening the snaps of his medical bag. Ann advanced upon him, regarding him with a worried frown.

"Doc, how is she?"

"I've given her something to make her sleep," he said. "She'll be out until morning. Are you through here yet, Hanks?"

"Uh, yeah, Doc. I wuz jist wonderin' what'cha want me t'do wi'the uh . . ." The sheriff jerked his thumb over his shoulder in an obvious reference to the bodies outside.

"Well, I suppose we'll have to—"

"Doc, please don't leave just yet," Ann interrupted him, placing her hand upon his arm. She looked down at herself, suddenly aware of her blood-spattered clothes. "I feel . . . I want to take a bath, and if Devvie's asleep . . . I don't want to be alone. Could you . . . maybe make some coffee for us? Won't you stay, please?" she entreated.

"Of course, my dear," he answered, patting her hand. "Go on, then, I'll wait here."

After Ann had left the room, Doc turned to the sheriff and stared at him thoughtfully, shaking his head. Hanks shifted uneasily under the hard gaze.

"Didn't I tell you? Didn't I warn you about that man?" Doc said in a low, sad voice. "And did you believe me, did you believe any of us? No. And now, another child is dead."

"Aw, c'm on, Doc, gimme a break! I couldn't jist . . ."

"Save your breath," he sighed tiredly, waving his hand at Hanks. "What did Ann tell you out there?"

The sheriff related to him what had happened, including Ann's explanation of her loss of memory and her sudden recognition of Ace as having been the murderer of the little Anders girl. Doc listened quietly, nodding his head and occasionally asking a few brief questions.

"So that's 'bout it, I guess," Hanks ended. "I'd say self-defense, don't'cha think?"

"Hmmm, yes, I quite agree. All right, then, I want you to take them both to the mortician's. I'll be staying here tonight, so you'll have to take my carriage along with you—just hitch it in front of my office. First thing in the morning I want you to tell the Reverend and also go see the Anders and tell them, too."

"Wal, okay, but I ain't gonna git much sleep t'night."

"None of us will anyway. I'll see you again in the morning."

Doc showed him out the door and watched while Hanks tied both his own horse and Ace's horse to the back of the carriage, then climbed up to the seat and drove off. Doc quietly shut the door, went into the kitchen, and began making the coffee.

Ann had gingerly stripped off her stained and soiled clothes, dropping them in a heap on the bathroom floor. She now sat in the tub, vigorously scrubbing herself over and over in an anxious attempt to become clean. She had not gotten any of Ace's blood upon her skin, but she still felt as if she had somehow been contaminated with it. *I've killed a man, I've killed a man,* she repeated to herself. *I've got to wash off the blood. I've got to be clean. And I've got to live with this for the rest of my life.* She held her hands up in front of her face and studied them, turned them over. *These hands,* she thought numbly. *With these hands. Oh, dear God . . .*

She swallowed her rising panic and forced herself to remain calm. Knowing that Doc was waiting for her, she quickly finished her bath and dressed herself in her nightgown and robe. As she passed down the hallway she paused in front of the bedroom and softly opened the door, intending to look in on Devorah. Ann saw her quiet form lying on top of the quilt, and she suddenly realized that Devorah was still wearing her blood-stained robe.

"Doc!" she whispered urgently. "Doc, please come here."

He was at her side in an instant, full of tender concern. "What is it? Is she awake?"

"No, no," Ann assured her. "Would you just help me to get her robe off?

"Ah, of course, my dear. I'm sorry, I hadn't thought of that."

They entered the room, and Ann lit the bedside lamp, but kept it turned very low. Doc supported Devorah's limp body in a sitting position while Ann divested her of the robe; then he lifted her up off the bed so that Ann could draw back the covers. He set her down gently, laid her head upon the pillow, and was about to pull up the quilt when Ann stopped him.

"Wait! Please. Let me wash her hands."

Ann left the room for a moment and returned carrying a basin of water and a clean cloth. She set the basin down on the bedside table, dipped the cloth into the water, and sat on the edge of the mattress, sponging Melissa's blood off of Devorah's hands and face. By the time she had finished, the water had turned a deep pink color. She lovingly folded Devorah's arms across her chest, kissed her lightly on the cheek, and stood up, allowing Doc to tuck the quilt about her face.

"Come, Ann, let's leave her now," said Doc, taking her elbow. "I've made coffee for us."

Ann extinguished the lamp, carried out the robe, and emptied the stained water into the bathroom sink. She went into the kitchen then, joining Doc as he sat at the table. He was already drinking his coffee, and he had also poured out a cup for her. They sat quietly, unmoving except for the hands that raised and lowered the cups. Each was lost in his own separate thoughts, and neither one knew quite what to say to the other.

"What about . . . ," Ann began, and halted uncertainly. She took a deep breath and started over. "What about the funeral arrangements? I have to plan . . ."

"Don't worry about that right now, Ann. I'll take care of everything in the morning."

"What about the clothes . . . the coffin? I have to pay . . ." She clasped her hands to her temples and shook her head. "I can't think straight. It's too much . . ."

Doc pulled her hands away and held them in his own. "Ann, please. Don't think about that now. Leave everything to me. Just try to relax and take it easy. Perhaps you should go on to bed and try to get some sleep," he suggested kindly.

"You won't leave, will you? You'll stay?" she asked in a small frightened voice.

"Yes, yes, of course I will," he promised. "I'll sleep on the sofa."

Ann breathed a sigh of relief. "Thank you, Doc. I don't know what I'd do without you."

"Quite all right, my dear. Are you sure you wouldn't like a little something to help you sleep?" he offered.

"No . . . I'll be all right." She stood up from the table and took a step, then turned back to face Doc. "But will Devvie?"

"I hope so . . . but God only knows."

Not wanting to disturb Devorah, Ann went into Melissa's bedroom and softly closed the door behind her. She let her robe fall to the floor and slipped under the covers, lying flat on her back and staring up at the ceiling. The night's stunning events continued to flash brokenly before her mind's eye, and she reviewed the sequences over and over again, searching for some minor thing that might have been omitted on her part, wondering if there could have been some little thing, no matter how small, that she might have done in order to prevent the senseless tragedy. At length, her eyes closed and she drifted off into a restless sleep.

Fifteen

At dawn, the sheriff stopped over to inform Reverend Todd and then together they went to see the Anders couple. Joseph answered the subdued knocking at the door and opened it to admit Hanks and the preacher. They both stepped inside and Hanks immediately took off his hat.

"Why, Sheriff . . . Reverend Todd," Joseph said in surprise.

"Who is it, dear?" Cora called to him from the kitchen. She entered the room, wiping her hands on her apron, saw the two guests, and stopped short, one hand reaching for her throat. "Oh! What is it? What are you doing here? Is something . . . ."

"I've got some good news an' some bad news fer ya, ma'am," Hanks spoke up. "The good news is, we've found out who killed yer li'l gal."

"Who was it?" she asked breathlessly.

"Ace Fairlane, ma'am."

"Did you arrest him?" Joseph demanded.

"Wal, uh . . . . not exactly . . ."

"Well, why not?" Cora said shrilly. "My baby—"

"Fact is, ma'am, 'e's dead. An' the bad news is, so's Miz Lee's li'l gal."

Cora was shocked. "Melissa! Oh my goodness!"

"What happened?" asked Joseph.

"Wal, it seems Ace went out there t'kill Miz Johnson an' shot the kid by mistake. Then Miz Johnson took a rifle to 'im an' killed 'im."

"Oh, Joseph, how awful!" Cora exclaimed, beginning to cry. She reached out to her husband for support, and he moved to stand by her side, placing his arm around her shoulders. "How horrible! Devorah must be beside herself. We must go out there, Joseph. We must pay them a visit."

"Of course, dear. Reverend, would you care to join us for breakfast?"

"Uh, well . . . I wouldn't want to intrude," the preacher said nervously.

"Please stay. I think my wife would appreciate your company. Wouldn't you, honey?" Cora nodded through her tears.

"Wal, then, that's all I got t'say, so I guess I'll git along." Hanks moved toward the door, suddenly remembered something, and turned around again. "Oh, uh, ma'am . . . Miz Johnson tol' me t'be sure an' tell ya somethin'. She said, 'Tell 'em it wuz a man an' not a woman.' Y'have any idea what she meant by it, ma'am?"

Cora merely nodded wordlessly, her cheeks flaming a bright scarlet.

Not having slept very well at all, Ann rose first, dressed herself almost mechanically, and went out into the kitchen to brew some fresh coffee. As soon as Doc smelled the aroma he got up from the sofa, stretched wearily, and straightened out the lines of his rumpled suit. He sat down at the table, and Ann poured a cup for each of them; then for want of something to do to keep herself busy, she began to fry up eggs and bacon.

They were both startled to see Devorah as she slowly approached the table and lowered herself onto a chair. She was wearing another robe over her nightgown, and she clutched the open neck of the robe tightly around her throat. Her hair was in a mild state of disarray, and she absently pushed the fingers of her other hand through her long tresses. She neither acknowledged the presence of Doc and Ann nor spoke to them.

"How are you feeling, Devorah?" Doc inquired solicitously. She did not respond to him.

"Do you want some coffee, Devvie?" Ann offered. She nodded mutely.

Ann set another cup in front of Devorah and also gave her her own portion of bacon and eggs. She made some more for herself and Doc and then sat down at the table to eat. Ann did not feel very hungry, but she forced herself to eat as much as she could, and in between bites both she and Doc glanced worriedly over at Devorah.

Devorah kept her eyes glued upon her plate, still refusing to meet their gaze. She took a few half-hearted bites of the food and then pushed the plate away.

257

"Devvie . . ." Ann broke off and bit her lip. She looked at Doc, silently pleading for assistance.

"Devorah, please, you must eat," Doc urged her.

"Not hungry," she mumbled. "More coffee, please."

They continued to sit in strained silence. Finally, Devorah stood up and shuffled slowly back toward the bedroom. With pain showing on her face, Ann watched her go, and Doc sadly shook his head.

A short while later there came a knock at the front door. Ann opened it and found Reverend Todd standing on the porch.

"Good morning, Ann. I have come to pay my condolences."

"Thank you, Reverend. Won't you come in?"

"Yes, thank you. Hello, Doctor. How is Mrs. Lee?"

"Not well, I'm afraid," said Doc.

"Oh, I am sorry to hear that. Miss Johnson, I can't tell you how shocked we all are to learn of this terrible tragedy." Ann simply nodded in reply. "Would it be ah . . . possible for me to speak with Mrs. Lee?"

"Well . . . she's resting right now," Ann informed him.

"I assure you I will not stay long."

"All right then," she conceded. "Follow me."

They all walked down the hallway to the bedroom. Ann tapped softly on the closed door, opened it slowly, and peeked inside. Devorah was reclining upon the bed with her back propped up against the pillows. Her eyes were open and she was staring blankly out the window.

"Dev . . .?" Ann spoke almost fearfully, hesitant to disturb her. "The Reverend's here to see you. Shall I send him in?" Devorah neither turned her head nor answered.

They filed quietly into the room and the preacher stepped up to the side of the bed and stood stiffly erect, gazing down into Devorah's vacant face.

"Mrs. Lee . . ." Still no response. The preacher cleared his throat and tried again. "Mrs. Lee, I want you to know that we all grieve along with you. Mere words cannot express the depth of our sincere sympathy." Devorah looked up at him. "I am respectfully at your service, and if there is anything I can do for you—"

"Why are you here?" she abruptly blurted out.

"Why, to offer you consolation in your time of bereavement, of course. My dear woman, I only want to—"

"I don't need you. My child is still here," she said harshly. "Lissa! Lissa, come in here!" she called anxiously.

Oh Devvie, no, Ann thought miserably. She covered her mouth with her hand as she felt the tears start up again.

Doc moved swiftly over to the bed and sat down next to Devorah, cupping her chin in his hand and forcing her to look at him.

"Devorah, listen to me," he said sternly. "Melissa is dead."

"No! No, she's not!" She shook her head in denial, her eyes darting wildly.

"Yes, she *is*. It's all over, and you must accept it, you must cope with it."

"Oh Doc . . . oh Doc . . ."

Devorah began to shriek in sudden mindless agony and Doc slapped her smartly across the cheek. Her face crumpled and she dissolved into wracking sobs, falling forward into his open arms and clutching him tightly to her breast. The preacher stood aside in great unease. Ann turned away, leaning weakly against the doorframe, closing her eyes and choking back her own sobs.

After Doc had gotten Devorah calmed down again, he remained at her side while she sipped a cup of hot, soothing herbal tea. He had at first been tempted to give her another sedative, but had quickly decided against it because he wanted her to hopefully recover herself quickly. He had, however, given her some powdered willow bark to take along with the tea in order to alleviate the throbbing headache that she had acquired from crying to excess. When she finally closed her eyes and seemed to be resting quietly, Doc left her alone and joined Ann and Reverend Todd, who had both gone back into the living room.

Ann rose from the sofa. "How is she, Doc?"

Doc mopped his brow with a handkerchief. "She's resting," he replied tersely.

"I'm terribly sorry if I've upset her," said the preacher. "Please forgive my intrusion."

"It wasn't your fault, Reverend," Doc assuaged him.

"Doc, what am I gonna do with her?" Ann said desperately.

"Just keep her in bed, keep her quiet, give her tea, not too much coffee. Try to get her to eat something later on, if you can. And give her some of this if she complains of a severe headache," he added, handing her a small vial of powder. "Just stir a little pinch of it in with her tea."

"Will she snap out of this?"

"Well, Ann, I hope so. This is understandably a very difficult time for her, and you've got to be with her and help her and be strong for her, too."

Ann sighed, briefly closing her eyes. "But I'm almost at the end of my own rope, Doc."

"I know. Aren't we all?" He smiled kindly, placing his hand upon her shoulder. "Now, Ann, I've got to get back into town. Reverend, would you be so kind as to let me ride along with you?"

"But of course, Doctor."

"All right, then." He turned back to Ann. "There are many things that I must take care of—for you as well as for myself. I will try to get back here as soon as I can."

"All right, Doc," she nodded.

"Oh . . . Ann? Would you please give me some clothes before we go?"

She frowned blankly. "Clothes? Oh . . . uh . . . for Lissa. Of course."

Ann went into Melissa's room, opened the closet door, and stood for a long moment staring at the little dresses that hung so neatly upon the rack. There were plain ones, fancy ones, lacy ones, rainbow colored ones. *Which one do I pick?* she wondered uncertainly. *What would Lissa want? What would Devvie want? Why does it have to be up to me?*

After some hesitation, she chose a pale blue dress with white lace down the front that had been one of Melissa's special favorites. She also selected some underthings and took the shiny black shoes that the child had always worn to Meeting. She folded the items neatly on top of one another; then she carried all the clothes out and wordlessly handed them to Doc.

When they arrived in Sutter's Ford, Reverend Todd dropped Doc off in front of the mortician's and continued on to the church. Doc went inside and spoke with Quentin Thurgood, a short round man in his late forties with spectacles and a balding head.

"You have received the bodies, I presume," Doc said brusquely.

"Yes, Doctor. I'm attending to them now," Quentin responded obsequiously.

"Any problems?"

"No, no, none at all."

"Very well, then, when you finish with them, send them on over to the church." Doc set the pile of clothes on top of the counter. "I've brought you some things for the child."

"Ah, thank you, but . . . but what about . . . the clothes for the other body?" Quentin stammered.

"Thurgood, I don't care what you do with that son of a—!" he exploded, suddenly furious. He caught himself and struggled to regain control of his temper, pressing the fingers of one hand against his temple. "Just leave him as he is and nail the lid shut," he said tightly.

"But . . . but perhaps the relatives would want—"

"There are none!" Doc cut him off abruptly and stalked out the door.

Doc strode down the sidewalk and entered his office, noting with indifference that the sheriff had indeed tethered his horse and carriage to a wooden post just outside. Doc stripped off his outer jacket and sat wearily down behind his desk, leaning forward on his elbows and covering his face with his hands. He had not been there very long when the door suddenly flew open and Delilah Emerson burst in.

"Doc! I've been lookin' fer ya all mornin'!" she cried. "I saw yer horse outside an' came over here earlier, but'cha wuzn't here."

"I only just got here. I've been out at Devorah's farm all night."

"What happened? Ya've got t'tell me! I've been worried sick all night."

Doc rubbed his tired eyes. "What is there to tell? It's all over. Ace went out there to kill Ann and shot Melissa by mistake. Ann killed him."

"Thank God fer that! But the child . . . how . . . ?"

"She's dead, too," Doc intoned sadly.

Delilah's hand went to her breast. "Oh, mercy! Oh no! Dammit, I knew it! I knew 'e wuz gonna pull somethin'!" She pounded her fist forcefully upon the desk, her face a mask of anguished rage. "I tried t'stop 'im, but 'e ran outta m'place. I saw that gun on 'is hips an' I sent the sheriff after ya."

"We were too late. By the time we got there . . ." Doc trailed off helplessly and shook his head.

"Dammit!" she raged on, angry at herself. "I shoulda gone after 'im m'self. I shoulda taken a gun to 'im an' shot 'im right b'tween the eyes. They mighta hung me, but I'da done us all a favor."

"It wasn't your fault, Lilah. You did what you could."

"But I shoulda done more," she insisted. "I'll never fergive m'self."

"No . . . ," he said slowly, "I'll never forgive *my*self because I wasn't there when they needed me. If only I had stopped by . . . checked on them . . . I might have been able to prevent it."

"P'rhaps we're all t'blame," she said softly.

By noontime, the mortician had completed his work with the bodies and he had delivered both pine coffins, one small and one large, to the church. Quentin Thurgood now stood outside the closed door leading to the preacher's study and rapped quietly upon the thick wood. Reverend Todd, who had been kneeling in silent meditation, rose to his feet and opened the door.

"I've finished the job, Reverend," Quentin told him. "Where do you want me to put the boxes?"

"Where are they right now?"

"Just outside. Do you want me to bring them on in?"

"You may set the smaller coffin in front of the altar, but don't you dare bring that murderer's body in here. This is a sanctified place, and I will not have it desecrated. Take him around to the back and leave him outside the fence," he said, stressing the word *outside*.

"Outside the fence?" Quentin repeated. "You mean . . . ?"

"He will not be buried on the church's property. Our cemetery is only intended for those good people who have been saved."

"You mean he doesn't even get a funeral?" Quentin asked in surprise.

"Most certainly not," the preacher stated firmly. "He deserves only to be buried like the carrion he is."

Later on that afternoon, Doc went over to the church in search of Reverend Todd. Not immediately finding him in the study, Doc passed through the church and exited the rear doors. He spied the

262

preacher standing on the grass at the very edge of the church's property line. Beyond the fence, two gravediggers were busily scooping the dirt out of a long, deep hole in the ground. Ace's coffin stood forlorn and waiting beside the yawning hole.

Doc placed his hand upon the preacher's shoulder. "Reverend?"

"Hello, Doctor," he responded quietly.

"Ah . . . I have come to discuss the funeral arrangements with you."

"Of course," the preacher agreed readily, "but shouldn't we also consult with Mrs. Lee?"

"I would prefer that she be disturbed as little as possible over this. Therefore, you and I shall make the arrangements, and I will inform Miss Johnson."

"Very well, then, Doctor. Shall we say tomorrow afternoon?"

"Yes, tomorrow. At what time?"

"One o'clock? Two o'clock? Whichever you prefer."

"Two o'clock, then," Doc said with finality.

They watched impassively as the two gravediggers looped a set of ropes under and around Ace's coffin and slowly lowered it down into the hole. When it reached the bottom, the ropes were detached and recoiled, and the men stood looking expectantly at both Doc and Reverend Todd.

"Wal, ain't'cha gonna say nothin' over the body, Rev'rund?" asked one of the men.

"There is nothing to be said," the preacher told him solemnly.

The other man gestured toward the coffin. "Ain't'cha even gonna bless it?"

"No, no blessing," said Doc. "Only a curse. *Damn his soul!*" he muttered vehemently.

"Cover it up," the preacher directed.

They stayed until the grave had been completely filled in, and then they turned away.

Devorah had remained in bed all day. At lunchtime, Ann had brought her something to eat, but she had stubbornly refused it and ignored Ann's pleadings. She continued to drink more tea with the willow bark powder stirred into it, and her eyes were still puffy and swollen from weeping. Ann had attempted to take her into her arms

263

and comfort her, but she only pushed Ann away and turned to face the open window.

Ann had gone ahead and performed the morning chores for want of something to keep herself occupied. She had eaten a small lunch, and she now sat out on the porch steps with her legs bent at the knees and her arms folded there. Her thoughts were centered upon Devorah's semi-catatonic state, and she felt at a loss to help Devorah deal with her grief.

She glanced up at the sound of approaching hoofbeats and saw a carriage pulling into the yard. Joseph Anders stepped down to the ground first, then went around to the other side to assist his wife. He took the covered plate that she had been carrying, and they both walked up to Ann, who rose and moved out to meet them.

"Oh, my dear! We are so sorry, *so sorry*!" Cora spoke first, opening her arms and sweeping Ann into a firm embrace.

"Thank you, ma'am," Ann replied politely, "but, uh . . ." She was momentarily confused.

"Don't you know us, dear? I'm Cora Anders, and this is my husband Joseph."

"Oh . . . uh . . . how kind of you to come." Ann felt slightly uncomfortable in the presence of the woman who had once been so quick to judge. She had heard the rumors, yet had kept silent, not knowing the source.

Joseph took Ann's hand and patted it gently. "We are here to offer our assistance. If there's anything at all that we can help you with . . . the chores, the cooking . . . please don't hesitate to ask."

"Thank you. We do appreciate it."

"Ann, my dear child," Cora began, "there is something I must tell you." Ann turned to her and waited expectantly. "The sheriff . . . gave me your message." Ann looked down at the ground, made even more uncomfortable now by this revelation. "I know now it wasn't you who . . . I cannot imagine how I could have thought such a terrible thing about a girl as lovely as you. I want to apologize to you. I feel so . . . so ashamed," she faltered helplessly, blinking back the tears. "Won't you please . . . forgive me?" she choked.

"Oh, Mrs. Anders . . ." Ann gathered Cora into her arms and patted her back. "Of course, of course," she murmured reassuringly. A new bond had been formed between them, forged by their mutual pain.

"How is Devorah?" Cora said at last, wiping her eyes.

Ann sadly shook her head. "Not well. She stays in her room, won't come out, won't eat, won't talk. I just don't know."

"Perhaps . . . could we see her?" Cora requested.

"I wish you would. Maybe you can help her, get through to her. I haven't been able to."

"I can only try," she sighed. "Oh, please forgive me—these are for you." She took the covered plate from Joseph and held it out to Ann. "They're muffins. I made them this morning."

Ann smiled. "Thank you, Mrs. Anders. You're very kind. Why don't we go inside now?"

Ann set the plate of muffins on top of the kitchen table, and then she led them down the hallway to Devorah's bedroom. She rapped softly upon the closed door, opened it, and looked inside. Devorah was still reclining upon the bed and her eyes were half closed.

"Dev . . . ? Mr. and Mrs. Anders are here to see you." Ann did not wait for a response, but turned back to the Anders and ushered them inside. She closed the door again and went into the kitchen, thus leaving them alone with Devorah.

"Oh, Cora . . . Joseph . . . I'm so glad to see you," said Devorah, sitting up. She opened her arms to receive Cora, and Cora moved into the embrace, holding her closely, comfortingly.

"How are you, my dear?" Cora asked, her eyes searching Devorah's pallid face.

"I'm all right," she nodded, sniffling. She attempted to manage a ghost of a smile.

"Is there anything we can do for you? Can I get you a cup of soup?"

She shook her head tightly. "No . . . no . . ."

"Devorah, you must know that we, of all people, truly understand what you're going through. We do know how you feel," Cora said sincerely, thinking of her own daughter's death.

"Oh Cora . . ." Devorah regarded her for a long, silent moment; then the tears began to overflow her eyes and trickle slowly down her cheeks. "First my husband, now my child! I have no one left! What am I to do?" she wailed, dissolving once again into great tearing sobs.

Cora pulled her forward into her arms and held her tenderly, smoothing her hair and rocking her gently back and forth. For an endless moment, they stayed like this, mother and mother. After Devorah had calmed down somewhat, Cora released her and pushed her back down against the pillows so that she was resting in a sitting position.

"Stay with her, Joseph. I'm going out to make her some soup."

He placed a chair by the side of the bed and sat holding Devorah's hand while Cora left the room and went into the kitchen. Ann was standing at the sink and turned at her approach.

Cora searched through the cabinets for a small pot. "I'm going to make her some soup," she informed Ann.

"But I told you she won't—"

"Yes, she will. She'll eat for me," Cora said with firm determination.

Ann smiled in admiration. "You're something else, Mrs. Anders."

Cora quickly made up a weak broth and added to it bits of already cooked chicken and a handful of rice. She allowed the soup to simmer slowly for a while; then she ladled it out into a deep mug and brought it in to Devorah. Joseph stood up to let his wife have the seat by the bed.

"Oh, Cora, you shouldn't have," Devorah protested. "I really don't want—"

"Please. Try to eat something," she urged, pressing Devorah's hands around the mug. "It'll help you feel better. We'll stay right here with you."

Ann brought in another cup of tea while Devorah was eating the soup, and when she had finished everything, she lay back against the pillows and closed her eyes. Joseph and Cora remained with her until she had fallen into a light slumber, and then they quietly left the room.

After Doc had finished seeing the day's load of patients in his office, he returned to Devorah's farm on his way home shortly before dinner. Ann met him at the door, took his hat and medical bag, and placed them upon a nearby chair.

"I have taken care of everything," Doc told her. "The funeral is scheduled for tomorrow at two o'clock."

"Oh. Thank you, Doc."

"Both of you will ride with me," he continued. "I will come by and pick you up at one."

"Doc, I can't tell you how much I appreciate all you've done for us," Ann said gratefully. "Without you, I wouldn't have known where to begin."

Doc placed an arm around her shoulders and gave her a quick hug. "No thanks are needed, my dear," he smiled kindly. "Tell me, how is Devorah doing?"

"A little better, I think. She's been in her room all day, but Mr. and Mrs. Anders stopped by this afternoon, and Mrs. Anders finally got her to eat something."

"Well, I'm relieved to hear that. Did you give her some more of the powder?"

"Yes, but she's still crying off and on. When I hear her, I go in the room to check on her, but she just pushes me away."

"Mmmm," Doc nodded, frowning with concern.

"Would you care to stay for dinner?" Ann offered. "It's almost ready."

"Why, thank you, I believe I will. I'm quite tired, but I hadn't realized how hungry I was."

"Why don't you go look in on Devvie and see if you can get her to join us?" she suggested.

"All right." Doc moved down the hall and entered the bedroom, walking up to Devorah and sitting beside her on the mattress. "Devorah, how are you feeling?" he inquired, reaching for her hands and taking them into his own.

"Better," she answered in a small weak voice.

"Have you been eating?"

"A little."

"Ann tells me that dinner is almost ready. Won't you come out and join us at the table?"

"Well . . . ," she said hesitantly.

"Please, Devorah. You should be moving about. I want to make sure you get some nourishment into your system. You cannot continue to lie here and waste away like this."

Devorah got out of the bed, put on her robe and slippers, and allowed Doc to escort her into the kitchen. Ann had prepared a beef roast along with roast potatoes and fresh early peas. As they ate,

267

Doc and Ann talked briefly about the weather and the developing crops, but Devorah remained silent, unwilling to enter into the conversation. She had not eaten much, but she had dutifully consumed everything on her plate. After she finished her coffee she excused herself and headed back to the bedroom.

Ann sighed heavily. "Well, at least she's eating again."

"She'll need all the strength she can get for tomorrow," Doc said. "It'll be a long, hard day for her."

"Everybody'll be coming over here after the funeral, won't they?"

He nodded. "Yes, you can count on that."

"How are we going to get her through it all? I don't know if she can take it."

"One step at a time, Ann, just one small step at a time. Now, if you'll excuse me, too, I think I'll go home. I'm very tired." Doc rose from the table, bid her good night, and left.

Ann quietly cleared the table, washed the dishes, and put them away. After she had performed the evening chores, she went into the other bedroom and wearily flopped across the mattress, not even bothering to take off her clothes.

Sixteen

Sometime during the night, it had started to rain. The morning dawned wet and warm, and the rain changed into a steady, misty drizzle that sifted down from a gray, overcast sky. Ann assisted Devorah in taking a bath, helped her to dress, then took her own bath and also put on a dress. Too agitated to eat lunch, they both waited nervously until Doc McClintock arrived. He took Devorah by the elbow, holding his umbrella between them, and led her out to his carriage. Ann followed along behind them, carrying her own umbrella, and she sat in the back seat while Devorah took the front seat. Ann glanced down beside herself, suddenly remembering that Melissa's body had recently lain where she was now sitting. She briefly closed her eyes, swallowed hard, and then turned her head to stare out at the passing countryside.

When they pulled up in front of the church, Ann noted that both sides of the street were lined for a distance of several blocks with parked carriages. *Why, the whole town's turned out!* she thought in amazement. They went up the steps and entered into the foyer.

Indeed the news had quickly spread like wildfire throughout the small town. Word of Ace's and Melissa's deaths had traveled fast, and the townspeople were shocked, stunned at the tragedy. They came in droves, all of them, to pay their last respects to the child. They gathered around Doc and Devorah and Ann as they attempted to push their way through, offering assistance, consolation, kind words of regret. They reached out to touch Ann and Devorah, to embrace them, to pat their hands, to kiss their cheeks. Devorah smiled at them through her tears, accepted their warmth and caring. Ann thanked them softly, passed from one face to another.

Dazed by the attentions of the crowd, they somehow managed to get through, and Doc escorted them down the aisle, leading them right up to the front pew. He sat with them. Laura Munroe and her mother sat in the pew directly behind them. Melissa's coffin reposed upon a cloth-draped bier in front of the altar. As soon as Devorah saw it, she caught her breath and Ann reached out for her hand, lacing her fingers through Devorah's and gripping the hand tightly.

The funeral service began promptly at the hour of two. Reverend Todd came out from his study, stepped up to the pulpit, and opened the heavy Bible. He solemnly surveyed the faces of the people below him and noted grimly that for once the church was packed.

"Christian brothers and sisters," he began in a clear strong voice, "we are gathered here to pay our last respects to a bright, beautiful child who has suddenly been taken from among us. In the midst of life, we are in death. The Lord giveth, and the Lord taketh away. He gave us this child that we might know her and love her and be enriched by her . . ."

And I have been enriched, Ann thought. *I taught her and loved her as if she were my own.*

". . . and now He has called her so that she may be with Him in eternity. Her work upon this earth was finished, and she has met her just reward."

To be shot was her just reward? Ann wondered. *She was innocent!*

"Precious in the sight of the Lord is the death of one of His saints. His eye is on the sparrow, and He has not forgotten this child. And neither has He forgotten the mother who bore her, who gave her life, who raised her and trained her to follow in the ways of the Lord. He will wrap His loving arms around her and comfort her, bring her solace from her grief . . ."

No, He won't, Devorah thought. *No one can console me. My child is dead, and my heart has been torn from me.*

"What man can live and never see death? For as by a man came death, by a man has come also the resurrection of the dead. For as in Adam all die, so also in Christ shall all be made alive. For the wages of sin is death . . ."

And I have sinned, Devorah realized. *I have sinned against my God, and I am paying for it. He has taken my child, and I have been warned.*

". . . but the free gift of God is eternal life in Christ Jesus our Lord. Job once asked, 'If a man die, shall he live again?' And Christ answered, 'I am the resurrection and the life; he who believeth in Me, though he die, yet shall he live, and whoever liveth and believeth in Me shall never die.' And again He said, 'I am the light of the world; he who followeth Me will not walk in darkness, but will have the light of life.' "

And I have not followed Him, Devorah acknowledged. *And I walk in darkness now.*

"And yet again He said, 'I am the way, and the truth, and the life; no man cometh unto the Father, but by Me.' For God so loved the world that He gave His only begotten Son, that whoever believeth in Him should not perish but have eternal life. He begs us, He entreats us, He pleads with us that we should come to Him and lay all of our sins and our griefs at His feet. He promises us forgiveness . . ."

I cannot be forgiven for what I have done, Devorah thought. *I sought my own pleasure. I have done something so awful, so unspeakable . . .*

". . . and He urges us to be faithful unto death, and He will give us the crown of life."

I have not been faithful, Ann realized. *I was not awake, I was not watching, and he came like a thief in the night.*

"He tells us, 'He who hears My word and believes Him who sent Me, has eternal life; he does not come into judgment, but has passed from death to life.' "

I have ignored His word, Devorah thought, *and I have come into judgment.*

"And He says, 'If anyone keeps My word, he will not see death.' "

I have ignored His word, Devorah repeated in shame. *I have seen death, and I am condemned.*

"The hour is coming when the dead will hear the voice of the Son of God, and those who hear will live. Yes, the hour is coming when all who are in the tombs will hear His voice and come forth, those who have done good, to the resurrection of life. For God has promised us that He will swallow up death forever, and He will wipe away every tear from our eyes, and death shall be no more, neither shall there be mourning nor crying nor pain any more, for the former things have passed away. O grave, where is thy victory? O death, where is thy sting? For me to live is Christ, and for me to die is gain . . ."

I wish I had died instead, Ann grieved. *Oh, Lissa! If I could have only given my life in exchange for yours . . .*

271

". . . for blessed are the dead who die in the Lord. Blessed indeed, that they may rest from their labors, for their deeds follow them."

I will never rest, Ann thought, *for I allowed a child to die.*

"And at the end of the world, when the Lord Himself descends from Heaven with a cry of command, with a shout of triumph, when He finally comes to take us all together with Him in the clouds to meet Him in the air so that we might dwell with Him throughout all eternity, then I say to you, I swear to you, the graves shall be opened, and this lovely, beautiful child named Melissa Jane Lee will live again, and she will take her mother by the hand and lead her into Heaven!"

Reverend Todd had worked himself into a passionate frenzy, and he stood erect with one hand firmly grasping the edge of the pulpit and the other hand impressively pointing skyward. *This is really all so unnecessary,* Ann thought wryly. In any other instance, she might have giggled or suppressed an outright laugh at his antics, but for this particular occasion she did not feel like laughing. She glanced over at Devorah, saw that she was on the verge of tears, and pressed her hand again in silent comfort. Reverend Todd took out his handkerchief, mopped his sweating brow, adjusted the lapels of his black suit, and continued in a softer tone of voice.

"The good Book does speak of 'an eye for an eye, and a tooth for a tooth.' We must not forget that there is one brave young woman among us who tried to follow the law of God. His will was done, and justice was served, and to her we owe a debt of eternal gratitude. She has indeed earned her rightful place in this community of ours as a fine, honest, intelligent, morally upright individual. We welcome her with open arms and with love in our hearts."

But I've killed a man, Ann thought remorsefully. *I've got his blood on my hands. I didn't stop to think; I blew his face off in an uncontrollable rage.*

"And now if you will turn to page twenty-four of your hymnals, we will stand up and sing."

The old pipe organ boomed forth its quavering tones, and the strong voices of a hundred people echoed and re-echoed around the walls of the church.

Blest be the tie that binds

Our hearts in brotherly love.
The fellowship of kindred minds
Is like to that above.

When the hymn was ended, the organ music slowly died away and everyone sat down again.

"Christian brothers and sisters, go in peace. And may the Lord bless you and keep you and guide your steps aright until we meet again. Will the close friends and members of the immediate family please remain in their seats until after everyone else has left."

The townspeople rose and quietly filed out of the church, leaving only Doc and Devorah and Ann, Joseph and Cora Anders, Laura Munroe and her mother, and Sheriff Andy Hanks. Doc, Joseph, and Hanks stepped up to the coffin, acting as pallbearers, and they lifted it, carrying it through the back doors of the church with Reverend Todd leading the way and the other women following along behind.

The coffin was gently lowered down onto another waist-high bier that had been set up adjacent to the gravesite. The two gravediggers stood next to it, waiting with their coiled ropes and shovels. Umbrellas were unfurled against the drizzling rain, and everyone gathered in a half circle around the open hole in the ground. Each person looked beyond the fence at the long mound of dirt that marked Ace's grave, uncomfortably aware of it, knowing it was there almost as a silent sentinel. The rain had puddled on the tamped earth of the mound, causing it to turn into a running sea of black mire.

In front of the church, Delilah Emerson and Ruby sat quietly in their carriage. Delilah was dressed in somber black, and Ruby also wore a subdued color. Delilah had pulled up in the middle of the funeral service, and not wanting to disrupt the church as she had done at Easter, she had chosen to remain outside until it was over. When she saw the line of people emerging from the rear of the church into the cemetery, she reached for her umbrella and started to get out of the carriage.

"Where y'think yer goin'?" Ruby hissed at her. She snatched at Delilah's wrist, but Delilah shook her hand away.

"Y'got eyeballs. Where y'think I'm goin'?" she responded gruffly. "I'm goin' over there t'pay m'last respecks, what's it look like?"

273

"But'cha didn't wanna go inside b'fore."

" 'At's diff'runt."

"Why's it diff'runt?" Ruby wanted to know. "Y'know what them people think o' ya."

"Not these people," Delilah said, pointing toward the small group standing in the cemetery. "They know me. They know I ain't got some kinda silly disease. 'Sides, I got friends, too, y'know," she stated huffily. "Doc an' Miz Lee an' Ann. An' that child o' Miz Lee's . . . I jist feel fer 'er, that's all. I got t'go." Delilah stepped down to the ground and opened her umbrella.

"Don't'cha go makin' no waves now," Ruby admonished her.

She gave Ruby a short gesture of dismisal. "Don't worry yer purty li'l face 'bout it."

Delilah walked straight across the rain-soaked lawn to the cemetery and moved to stand quietly next to Devorah's side. Devorah sensed the movement beside her and turned to look up into the face of another friend.

"Oh, Lilah . . . ," she said brokenly, the tears instantly springing to her eyes. She could say no more, and Delilah put one arm around her shoulders, holding her protectively.

Reverend Todd opened his Bible. "Let us begin," he solemnly intoned. "The Lord is my shepherd, I shall not want . . ."

Oh, I want, Devorah thought in anguish. *I want my child!*

". . . He maketh me lie down in green pastures. He leadeth me beside still waters; He restoreth my soul."

Will we ever be restored? Ann wondered sadly. *Will there ever be comfort for us? Our lives are empty . . . destroyed . . .*

"He leadeth me in paths of righteousness for His name's sake. Even though I walk through the valley of the shadow of death, I fear no evil, for Thou art with me; Thy rod and Thy staff, they comfort me."

No comfort, no comfort, Devorah thought, slowly shaking her head. *My agony . . . my pain . . .* She closed her eyes, and a sob escaped her lips. Delilah held her tighter.

"Thou preparest a table before me in the presence of my enemies; Thou anointest my head with oil, my cup overfloweth."

With guilt, Ann admitted, *and more guilt, and tears.*

"Surely goodness and mercy shall follow me . . ."

No goodness, no mercy, Devorah thought. *How could this have happened?*

". . . all the days of my life; and I shall dwell in the house of the Lord forever."

How can we now? Devorah asked herself. *We are outcast because of what we have done.*

"Our Father, who art in Heaven . . ."

". . . hallowed be Thy name. Thy kingdom come, Thy will be done . . . ," the others chanted in unison.

When the prayer was finished, Reverend Todd motioned to the two gravediggers. They stepped up to the coffin and slowly drew back the lid, which had not yet been nailed shut. Each mourner filed past, glanced briefly inside, and moved on. Joseph and Cora clung to each other, silently remembering their own child. Doc and Laura stood together and Laura groped for his hand. Delilah considered her own past and wondered if it would help Devorah to know what she herself had experienced. Then it was Ann's turn and she stood for a long moment in front of the coffin.

Lissa, honey, she thought, sniffling. *Oh, Lissa! I'm so sorry I wasn't there . . . to help you . . . to save you . . . I was too late . . . too late . . . It was my fault . . . oh God!* Ann bit her lip and turned away.

Finally Devorah came and gazed lovingly down at the child's serene face. Her eyes traveled over the curled blonde ringlets of hair, the pert little nose, the softly rounded jawline, moved down to take in the small folded hands, the pretty blue dress, the white frilly lace, the shiny black shoes, then moved back up to look upon the face again. Past scenes flashed quickly through Devorah's mind and she saw herself running across the sun-warmed prairie with Melissa's hand held tightly in her own, smiling, laughing, scampering through the tall grasses, the wind blowing freely at their hair, stopping to pick a wild flower or to examine a bird's nest containing tiny blue eggs. And then Billy was there with his handsome suntanned face, his sky-blue eyes, his strong capable hands, and he called to Melissa, she ran to him, was swept up into his firm embrace, wrapped her arms around his broad back, and they both waved, laughing, at Devorah and urged her to join them.

Lissa, my darling child, Devorah thought, smiling feebly through her brimming tears. *Flesh of my flesh and blood of my blood.* She reached out to caress the face, smoothed back the golden hair. *Go with God, my sweetheart, and laugh and run and play with Him where the sun will never set and where you will never hurt or cry again.* She bent down to kiss the lifeless forehead, straightened up, and took a deep breath.

"I love you, honey," she whispered, and choked on the words.

Devorah stepped back from the coffin, and Reverend Todd directed the gravediggers to nail the lid shut. The hammering sounds echoed ominously through the quiet air. They slung the ropes around the coffin and began to lower it into the ground.

"Father, into Thy hands we commit the spirit of Melissa Jane Lee," said Reverend Todd. "For as it is written, 'earth to earth, and dust to dust.' In the name of Christ our Lord, amen."

Devorah suddenly felt very lightheaded. The ground spun around her in a dizzy whirl; she closed her eyes and pitched backward in a faint.

"Oh, m'goo'ness!" Delilah shouted in alarm. "Here! Catch 'er!"

Doc and Joseph rushed to her side and caught her before she fell. Doc carried her back into the deserted church, where Delilah produced a vial of smelling salts and held it to Devorah's nose. Everyone gathered around her in concern, and Reverend Todd brought her a glass of water. When Devorah recovered from her collapse, she moved into Delilah's massive arms and sobbed bitterly against her breast.

Doc drove Ann and Devorah back to the farm, where they steeled themselves to receive the hordes of sympathizing townspeople who would soon descend upon them. Ann made a pot of fresh coffee while Doc and Devorah sat quietly in the living room. Scarcely half an hour had passed before the first few groups of people began to arrive. Doc was the one who greeted them at the door and bade them enter. Within an hour, the house was filled with the crowd and although some of them left early, others still continued to take their places.

They were all kind and well-meaning people, for each couple brought along a covered dish of some sort. The kitchen table was piled high with food, and much of it spilled over onto the countertop and other nearby tables and chairs. There were hams and beef roasts, chickens and pork roasts, various casseroles and other side dishes, loaves of freshly baked bread, fruit pies, muffins, and cakes. Ann was stunned at their generosity; she had never seen so much food since her childhood days when her parents would host gala parties and barbeques in the backyard of their affluent mansion in Texas.

Reverend Todd was there, and the Anders couple, and also Laura Munroe and her mother. The only ones who did not come out to the farm were Sheriff Hanks and Delilah, but Ann could easily understand the madam's reluctance to appear among those who still looked down upon her for the type of business she operated.

Ann moved among the milling people, attending to their needs, making sure they had enough to eat, brewing pot after pot of coffee, barely stopping long enough to grab a quick bite for herself. Devorah stood beside her rocking chair, one hand grasping its curved back for support, and she received each person in turn, embracing them all warmly, thanking them for their expressions of condolence. Doc hovered anxiously near her, afraid that she might tire herself out and possibly collapse again.

It was well past seven o'clock before the last of the couples departed. Only Joseph and Cora still remained, and both Doc and Ann looked at each other and breathed a sigh of relief. Devorah approached Doc and embraced him, holding him tightly.

"Oh Doc, I thank you for all you've done," she murmured, kissing his cheek.

"Of course, my dear," he responded. "It's been a long day for you. Perhaps you should lie down for a while."

"Yes," she agreed, "I'm exhausted. Good night, then, everybody. I'll see you in the morning, Ann."

"Do you want me to help you to bed, Devvie?" Ann offered.

"No. Cora, would you please come with me?"

Cora followed her down the hallway while Ann regarded Doc with an expression of pained rejection, but he merely shrugged helplessly and shook his head. Ann began to wrap up all the leftover food and to clear away the dirty dishes. Cora soon returned to help her clean up the entire kitchen, and before she and her husband left, Ann thanked her profusely for her welcome assistance. Finally Doc was the only other person in the room. He sat down at the kitchen table and Ann poured out more coffee for both of them.

"Well, I appreciated them all," Ann sighed, "but I thought they'd never leave."

Doc rubbed his tired eyes. "I know. The day is finally over."

"No, not quite. I still have to do the chores."

"Oh. Do you want some help?"

"No, Doc, that's all right. You've done enough."

"No, damn it, I didn't do enough!" he exclaimed angrily, hitting the top of the table with his fist. "If I had only been here that night! But no, I wanted to be with Laura. I could have been here . . . to prevent it . . . to stop it somehow . . . to kill him myself! Devorah needed me, her child needed me . . . and I came too late."

"Well, how do you think *I* feel?" Ann cried. "I *was* here, and I was asleep in that chair over there! All the time I was sitting there, he was outside doing that to her, and I didn't even know! How do you think that makes *me* feel, knowing that she was being . . . being . . . If anyone was too late, it was I!"

"We both blame ourselves, then," Doc said quietly.

"No! I blame *my*self!"

Doc took her hands into his own and searched her face with his soft dark eyes. "Ann, my dear," he began, "can you imagine what would have happened if you had not gone out there and stopped it when you did? He would have taken her into the barn, forced himself upon her, ripped her open, and then strangled her just like he did to Bonnie Anders." Ann tore her eyes away from his and looked down at her hands. "Yes, yes, he would have," Doc insisted. "She would have died a far more horrible death that way instead of a quick, almost painless one from a bullet. You have that much to be thankful for—that he chose a bullet instead of his own hands." Ann was silent, the tears streaming down her face, and then Doc continued in a more gentle, reminiscent tone of voice. "You know, I remember when Devorah's husband was still alive . . ."

"What was he like, Doc?" she asked curiously. "Devvie never told me much about him."

"Ohhh, he was tall . . . blonde . . . blue-eyed. A hard worker, a good provider, a fine man. We all liked him. Devorah adored him, and he worshipped her in turn. They stole the show at the harvest dance one year. He loved Melissa . . . she was his world. Then after he died . . . an accident, you know—the mule kicked him in the head . . . why, Devorah just wasn't the same any more. Sure, she tackled this farm all by herself, and she managed quite well at it, too, but she just didn't have any more happiness. It was almost as if a spark went out of her. Like something died inside of her, and she kept on mourning him. You know, I loved that little girl myself, just as if she had been my very own. She needed a father, and I wanted to be that father for her. I kept my distance from Devorah, wanting to be respectful and all, but the more I looked at her . . ." He trailed off wistfully, sighed, and shook his head.

"You were in love with her, weren't you, Doc?"

"Ah, yes, that I was," he admitted sadly. "I'd asked her to marry me, and she told me she had to think about it. Then when I pressed her for an answer, she . . . she turned me down."

"What did she tell you?" Ann probed, wanting to know.

"She said it wouldn't have been fair to me . . . wouldn't have been right. She told me she loved me only as a friend and no more. Perhaps if I had been more patient with her, more understanding . . . maybe then she might have learned to love me. Perhaps it was my fault that I pressured her too much."

"I really don't think that was the reason at all," Ann said, trying to shift the focus away from Doc's own actions, trying to tell him not to blame himself for Devorah's refusal.

Doc stared hard at Ann, frowning suspiciously, and she felt herself wilting under his gaze. "No . . . no, I don't think it *was* the reason," he said sharply. "Hmmm, I should have realized . . . You love her, too, don't you?" he asked. The question was almost an accusation.

Ann's face flamed hotly. "Uh . . . yes . . . yes, I do," she confessed bravely.

Doc smiled kindly at her. "Well, Ann, my goodness! There's nothing to be ashamed of, dear girl. I told Devorah that I only wanted what was best for her, and if this is how she found her happiness, then who am I to judge either of you? No . . . no, I bless you both!"

Ann was overwhelmed. "Oh, Doc!" They both rose from the table at the same time and moved into each other's arms. Their friendship was cemented from this day forth. "What . . . what about Laura?" she wondered timidly.

"Ah, yes, Laura," he replied, a bright twinkle returning to his eyes. "I believe I shall ask her to marry me before the summer is over. Perhaps a fall wedding before the harvest dance."

"I'm really very happy for you, Doc," she smiled at him.

"Thank you, my dear. And now I really should be going home. You still have your chores to do, and you must be tired, too. I'll come back in a few days to check on Devorah."

"All right. Thank you, Doc." Ann saw him to the door and handed him his hat; then on impulse she leaned to kiss his cheek. "I love you too, for all the kindnesses you've ever shown me," she said, and rejoiced in his wordless answering embrace.

Seventeen

For the past three nights, Ann had considerable difficulty in sleeping in Melissa's room. For one thing, Devorah no longer lay beside her and she was deprived of the warmth and nearness of her body. For another thing, she was still surrounded by all the toys, books, and clothes that had once belonged to the child. Ann felt that the best thing to do would be to pack up all the items or to give them away to others who would be able to make use of them, and so the following morning she attempted to gently broach the subject to Devorah.

"Uh, Dev . . . don't you think maybe we should have another spring housecleaning?" she suggested.

"Why? This is summer. We already cleaned up after the twister."

"I know, but I thought perhaps we could clean out the closets, go through all our clothes, decide what to keep and what to throw out. Don't you have anything that you just don't wear any more, that you'd like to get rid of?" Ann tried to sound casual about it.

"No, not really," said Devorah.

"Well, then, how about . . . how about Lissa's bedroom?"

"That is *your* bedroom," she said stiffly.

"But Devvie, I can't sleep in there with all her things around me. We've got to pack them up, put them away."

"Those are Lissa's things. I will not have them touched."

"Well, what are you going to keep them for, anyway?" Ann said in exasperation. "She's not coming back."

"You're not very tactful, are you?" Devorah responded curtly.

"Devvie . . . Devvie, please! It's got to be done," she pleaded.

"I'm not ready to go in there yet."

"Well then, I'll do it for you. I'll—"

Devorah instantly flared up. "No! I said no! Do you understand me? Leave her things alone!"

"You're not coping with this very well," Ann accused.

281

"I'm doing the best I can!" she shouted angrily.

"No, you're not!" Ann shouted back. "You're lounging around here in your robe all day, and you're not doing a damn thing! I'm doing the cooking and the cleaning and all the chores too! I've been pulling more than my share of the weight around here while you've been lying around like some sanctimonious martyr!"

"Well, I'm sorry! I'm really sorry! I don't feel like doing anything! Maybe if you'd get down off of your high horse and quit patting yourself on the back, you could start to have a little sympathy, a little consideration for me, too!"

Ann was incredulous. "Me?! *My* high horse? What about the one you're on?"

"I have just lost my child!" Devorah raged at her. "I ache, I hurt, I feel pain!"

"You don't think I do, as well? I loved her, too!"

"How could you? You were never a mother! How could you possibly know what it's like?"

"Just because I've never had a child of my own doesn't mean I can't learn to love somebody else's!"

"Oh, love!" Devorah said disgustedly. "Don't you speak to me about love! You don't even know what it's like to have a man!"

"No . . . can't say as I do," Ann conceded softly. "I only know what it's like to love a woman. It's times like these that should bring us closer together instead of pushing us farther apart."

"I *cannot* be close to you any more!"

"Why not? I love you, Devvie," she said gently, "but you won't take my comfort. You don't even want me near you at night any more. Why? Have you changed your thinking? Do you feel it's wrong?"

"*Yes*! Yes, Ann, I do! We shouldn't have done it!" she stated bitterly.

"But how can you say that after what you said before? Hey, I have to live here, too, you know. I have needs, too. I need to be held and comforted and—"

"Perhaps you should take your needs elsewhere," Devorah said coldly. "You don't have to stay here."

Ann was stunned. "Devvie! Do you *want* me to leave?"

"It's up to you. I don't care," she answered dispassionately.

"Don't you . . . don't you love me any more?" Devorah did not reply, but turned her back to Ann. Ann stood there, suddenly alone, hit by a sinking despair; her clenched fists hung down at her sides. "Do you have any idea how much that hurts . . . to be told that someone doesn't care?" Devorah still did not respond. "Devvie . . . Oh, *hell*!" Ann spun on her heel, stalked toward the door, wrenched it open, and slammed it violently behind her.

Late that evening when she returned from the day's work in the fields, she found a small folded note from Devorah propped up on the kitchen table. She opened it hesitantly, almost afraid to read what Devorah had written:

> I have already had my dinner and I have gone to bed early. I do not want to be disturbed. Eat some of this food before it spoils!

The note had not even been signed. Ann let it slip from her hand and it fluttered silently to the floor. She ate alone and later she threw herself across the bed and wept.

The next day was no better. They were very tense around each other, and the most minor, inconsequential things gave rise to flaring tempers. Conversations were strained and often swiftly degenerated into bitter arguments. They tried to avoid each other as much as possible.

"Why are you always on me?" Ann complained. "Why can't you be civil?"

"Why can't you?" Devorah retorted.

"Maybe it's because you're not!" she snapped.

"You can be very insulting at times."

"Oh, I see. *I'm* insulting. And you're the perfect, cultured lady, huh?" Ann said sarcastically.

"Don't you take that tone of voice with me!" Devorah warned her, shaking a finger threateningly at her. "I'll not tolerate your impudence!"

Ann smiled humorlessly. "Ohhh, that struck a nerve, huh? What's the matter, Devvie? Finally found someone who's brave enough to stand up to you?"

"You . . . you infuriate me!" Devorah sputtered.

283

"Really? Well, you kind of irritate me, too, you know. All we've done for the past two days is fight like tigers. Why?" she demanded. "Are you blaming me for Lissa's death, and you think you want to get back at me somehow?"

"No punishment could be harsh enough!" Devorah muttered vehemently under her breath.

Ann seized upon it. "Aha! You do! You do blame me!"

"Wrong! I blame both of us!" she cried. "You were asleep in that chair and I was in the bathtub. Both of us, do you hear me? Lissa's passing was all our fault!"

"Devvie—"

"I should have nailed that window shut!"

"Devvie—"

"*And you should have remembered!*" she shrieked, bringing her fist down hard on top of the table.

"Well, I'm sorry!" Ann shouted angrily. "I did remember, but not soon enough to do any of us any good! Both you and Doc kept telling me, 'Don't worry about it, don't worry about it.' Don't you think I feel guilty? *I'm tormented by guilt!*"

"You swore to me you'd protect us!" Devorah accused bitterly. "You swore you'd never let anything happen to us!"

"I killed him, didn't I? I killed him to protect you and myself as well as to avenge Lissa! Do you want to know what he would have done to her? Shall I tell you?"

Devorah clapped both hands over her ears. "No! I refuse to hear it!"

Ann strode up to her and roughly pulled her hands away. "Well, then, listen to this! It's over, damn it! It's over and done with, and there's not a thing that either one of us can do about it now! You have to accept it and let it go! *You have to go on!*"

Devorah twisted herself out of Ann's grasp. "I accept nothing! This was something that never should have happened!"

"It was an *accident*! The shot was meant for me, not Lissa! Your husband was killed in an accident, too!"

"God may have taken my husband, but fate has taken my child! This never would have happened if we had not . . . not . . ."

"Not what? Loved?"

"Yes! We have broken God's law! We have sinned! We have done something unnatural!"

Ann sighed, sinking wearily down onto a chair. "Oh, Devvie! Don't tell me you believe that miserable lie?"

"It isn't a lie! It's God's holy scripture! He has warned us!"

"How? By taking Lissa? Oh Devvie, for Heaven's sake!" Ann shook her head sadly, not knowing how to fight the word of God. "Nothing is unclean in itself except for those who think it so."

"You're looking at one of them," she said quietly.

"Well, I don't! Devvie, for the love of everything that's happened between us, if you have any shred of feeling for me, don't reject me like this! *Please!*" Ann begged earnestly. She rose from the chair, stepped up to Devorah, and attempted to embrace her, but Devorah evaded the open arms and walked away from her, turning her back once again. "Devvie . . . don't do this to me!"

"Go away, Ann," she said in a dull, flat voice. "Get out. Leave me alone."

Ann could not trust herself to speak further, and she stood there, her fist pressed against her mouth, struggling to hold back the piercing agony that threatened to break through her defenses. Finally, she wheeled and fled out the door, not bothering to slam it this time as she had so often done before.

Ann ran straight for the haven of the forest. Many times its quiet restful beauty had helped to ease her troubled soul and to uplift her flagging spirits, but this time she stumbled down the trails with no thought of its primeval solitude. She angrily slammed her clenched fist into the broad base of a tree and cried out in pain as the rough bark bruised her hand. She looked down at the knuckles, which had now begun to bleed, and cradled the hand against her chest, wincing at the sharply throbbing ache that traveled up her arm. Overcome by anguish and despair, she slowly sank to her knees and bowed her head.

Oh God, oh God, oh God, she prayed in silent misery. *What have I done to deserve such pain? What crime have I committed, what error, what sin, in that I chose to love another with all my heart and soul? Now who will come for me, who will take my hand and lead me? Who will want me, who will need me, who will hold me through the night? I have lost her. I have lost her. I am alone.*

How can she not think I hurt, too? How can she not know I feel? My guilt . . . my grief . . . my pain . . . oh Lissa! Dear God, please help us! Please . . . before we end up destroying each other . . . and hating each other, too.

Perhaps I should leave and go somewhere else and start over, put it all behind me. But what kind of a life would it be without Devvie? A very lonely one . . . an empty one. No matter who else I loved, it would never be the same. No one else has ever come near to what I feel for her. No one else has ever had a child that I could love as much as if she were my own. No one else has ever . . . but it's over now. It's over. God, how much I loved her and still do! How much I adored her! But she doesn't feel anything for me now . . . nothing. She's become cold and bitter. Perhaps I should go home and pack. Home? Hah! I have no home. I've been a wanderer for many years now. Yes, perhaps it's best.

Meanwhile back at the house, Devorah paced agitatedly up and down the floorboards of the living room. She knew she had been exceedingly mean, almost brutal, to Ann, but she was lost in the depths of her own despair and all she could do was lash out in anger at the one person who had been closest to her. She had fallen back upon the Bible's ominous words of condemnation, and she had taken Melissa's death, however accidental, as incontrovertible proof of God's punishment upon her for daring to love another woman.

I have sinned, she thought guiltily, *and I have lost my child because of it. I have shamed myself before God, and He has spoken. His answer could not have been clearer if I had been struck by a bolt of lightning. I have paid in the ultimate way for my impulsive self-indulgence. I sought my own gratification without considering the possible consequences, and now I have paid . . . oh how I have paid!*

Lissa, honey, can you ever forgive me for what I have done? Oh, what I would give if only I could have you back here with me again! If only I could go back and erase it all, I would never have gotten involved this way. I should have married Doc . . . yes, I should have. It would have been right and natural and blessed before God, not this . . . this awful thing that has no . . . no sanctification. Yet what can I do about it now? I can't even go back to Doc and beg his forgiveness, beg him to take me, because he . . . he has someone else. He doesn't want me any more, he has no need for me any more. Oh, what am I to do? I am alone . . . alone . . .

Devorah's thoughts were interrupted by a sudden knocking at the front door. She opened it and was quite surprised to find Delilah Emerson standing there in conservative dress and plumed hat.

"Why, Lilah!" she exclaimed. "Won't you please come in? Forgive me, I'm not . . . dressed," she said in embarrassment, indicating her robe.

"'T'ain't nothin', Miz Lee," Delilah responded, breezing in. "No reason t'git yerself all decked out jist fer me. I've come by t'see *you,* not what'cher wearin'." She took off her hat and placed it carefully upon a nearby chair. "How're y'feelin'?"

"Much better now, thank you."

"C'm on, now, tell ol' Lilah the truth. I don't wanna hear what y'been tellin' ever'body else. You 'fess up with me!"

"Oh, Lilah . . . ," she choked, the easy tears starting up again. "I feel . . . miserable!"

"C'm'ere, gal," Delilah said softly. She opened up her arms to Devorah, and Devorah moved into them, accepting their tender comfort. "C'm on, let's siddown here," she suggested, leading Devorah over to the sofa and seating herself beside her. "So y'feel mizzerble, huh?" Devorah nodded, pulling out her handkerchief and wiping her eyes. "Wal, that's t'be expected. Ya've been through an awful lot lately, an' y'have a right t'feel. Yer gonna feel pain an' hurt an' anger, an' yer gonna cry yer eyes out 'til ya've got it all outta yer system. Bet'cha've even been fightin' like cats 'n dogs wi'that gal o' yers," she stated intuitively.

Devorah blinked in astonishment. "How . . . how did you know that?"

"Honey," she began, taking Devorah's hand, "I don't have t'be tol' these things. I kin see this grief written all over both o' yer faces, an' I know yer too close t'each other t'be able t'see the forest fer the trees. So y'strike out at each other, an' y'circle each other like spittin' cats, an' y'reach out an' give each other a good swipe wi'the claws. Ain't I right?"

"Oh, Lilah, it's been . . . awful! We're getting on each other's nerves. Everything we do . . . everything we say . . ." Devorah trailed off, gesturing weakly with her hand. "We can't even be polite to each other any more. We can't even eat together. I don't know how many times Ann has stormed out of here, slamming that door behind her and leaving me here in tears. I don't even know where she is

287

right now. I've said some terrible things to her, and I'm afraid she must hate me now."

"Naw, she don't hate'cha. She's jist tryin' t'cope wi'this thing same as you are. An' yer both not givin' each other any space t'move in."

"But Lilah, if you could have heard some of the things I said to her." Devorah sighed and closed her eyes, shaking her head in deep regret. "She told me she needed to be held and comforted, too, and I told her to take her needs elsewhere. I told her I didn't care if she left. She begged me not to reject her, and I turned my back on her and walked away. I *turned my back* on someone I loved!" she repeated with guilt-ridden emphasis. "How could I have done that, Lilah? What's happened to me?"

"Yer becomin' bitter, Miz Lee, an' yer lettin' it destroy what you 'n Ann've built up t'gether. D'y'really want 'er t'leave?"

"Yes. No. I don't know! I'm confused!"

"D'y'still love 'er?" Delilah asked quietly.

"I don't even know that any more, either!" Devorah answered in despair. "I keep thinking we shouldn't have done it. I can't help but feel that this is God's punishment."

"What is? Yer child's passin'?" Devorah nodded, gazing down at her lap. "Oh, Miz Lee, no . . . no . . ." Delilah touched Devorah underneath the chin and gently forced her to look up. "Look at me. Lissen t'me. What happened wuz *an accident*. It couldn't've been foreseen or prepared for or prevented. It jist *happened*. It had nothin' t'do with God's will . . . or His punishment, either. He'd want'cha t'be happy, t'smile, t'laugh. He didn't take yer child away from ya cuz 'e wuz angry at'cha fer what y'done. He gave ya happiness in Ann, an' He don't judge ya fer it. Yer judgin' yerself."

"But it's wrong," Devorah insisted.

"Y'must not've thought so b'fore, else y'wouldn't've done it t'begin with. Y'jist follered yer heart an' did what'cha felt wuz right. Ain't nobody gonna fault'cha fer that."

"Do *you* think it's wrong, Lilah?"

"Hmmph!" she snorted. "Yer talkin' t'someone who's seen an awful lotta love. All diff'runt kinds, too. Nah, it ain't wrong if it's what'cha really feel, if it's done wi'the right spirit."

"But then what do I do with all this guilt that's pressing on me, weighing me down, crushing me?"

"Why, y'jist have t'let it go. That's all y'kin do with it. It ain't gonna do either o' ya any good t'be carryin' it aroun' like this. Life does go on, Miz Lee, with or without'cha. The sun keeps risin' every mornin' even if it's b'hind a bunch o' clouds. An' there's nothin' wrong with feelin' yer grief, but there's gotta come a time when ya've got t'say 'Enough!' Ya've gotta pick yerself up again an' start puttin' all the pieces back t'gether."

"It's hard . . . oh, it's so hard!" Devorah whispered.

" 'Course it is!" Delilah agreed. "Nobody said it'd be easy. But you 'n Ann jist can't go blamin' yerselves ferever. Look what it's doin' t'ya right now—it's rippin' y'apart. If y'keep on this way, ya'll both wind up alone at a time when y'need each other most. An' y'know . . . y'oughtta be right proud o' that gal o' yers. She's done so much fer ya 'round here. She's helped y'with all the plowin' an' plantin', chopped wood fer the fire, patched up the barn roof, fixed the window. Why, she's even fixed up that ol' wagon an' made it shine like new. Doc tol' me all 'bout that, said 'e wuz proud o' her 'imself. She's worth more'n 'er weight in gold, an' she loves ya dearly. Ya've got a fine, wunnerful gal there, Miz Lee. Don't let 'er go. Don't lose 'er!" she entreated. When Devorah did not reply, Delilah seized her chance and decided to open herself up even more. "Miz Lee . . . I'm gonna tell ya a li'l story 'bout m'self. It's somethin' that only Doc knows, so I'd 'preciate it if y'wouldn't let on t'anybody else 'bout it."

Devorah frowned, her curiosity captured. "A story? But if you'd really rather not tell . . ."

"I think it's time fer ya t'know, too. I think it jist might help ya." She took a deep breath and exhaled it audibly. "When I wuz thirteen, m'father died. M'mother didn't live too long after that, an' a year later, I found m'self out on m'own. Some guy came along, nice 'n suave-like, an' 'e tol' me 'e could git me a job where I could make lotsa money an' have lotsa nice clothes alla time. Wal, it sure sounded good, an' I went along with 'im. I didn't know it then, but I wuz bein' sold inta white slavery. Y'know what that is, don't'cha?" Devorah nodded mutely. "Had me takin' care o' these johns every night in some grimy saloon up in Nebraska. No way o' gittin' outta it, no place t'run away to. Jist stayed an' got used to it, I guess.

289

"Anyways, I got pregnant when I wuz fifteen, an' I had the kid—it wuz a gal—but the midwife tol' me it wuz dead. I must've passed out while birthin' it, an' when I came to, that's what she tol' me. I didn't hear no cryin' or nothin', so I jist took 'er word fer it, bein' so young an' inexperienced. Didn't even git t'see the body. But I do remember there wuz a terrific thunderstorm goin' on outside—it wuz an awful hot summer night back in . . . ohhh, what wuz it . . . July o' '65, I think. Wal, so I felt bad 'bout it cuz I 'spected t'keep it an' make m'way somehow, bring it up 'gainst all odds.

"Went back t'work an' carried on. But then I saw the same thing happenin' t'some o' the other young gals who got pregnant—they'd have their babies an' be tol' they wuz dead. So I started wisin' up t'what wuz goin' on—they wuz takin' our babies an' sellin' 'em downstate somewheres. Finally had me a confrontation wi'the guy who ran the place, an' 'e admitted it. Fact, 'e threw it in m'face. Said m'child wuz gonna grow up t'be jist like 'er mother, an' 'e laughed at me fer bein' a stupid broad who wuz only good fer one thing.

"Wal, I high-tailed it outta that place, jist packed up m'clothes an' ran. I went to a coupla big cities an' worked 'em fer a while, an' then I came here, where I met Doc. Took over at the saloon here from Ace's mother, who ran it b'fore me, an' when I finally got up 'nuff money, I bought the place fer m'self. An' Doc's been kind t'me; 'e's helped me git through some really bad times.

"I ain't done no other kinda work cuz this is the only kinda life I've ever known. I ain't ashamed o' it, though, but there ain't a day goes by that I don't think o' m'child—the daughter I never had. Never saw 'er, never held 'er . . . don't know what she looks like, what 'er name is, or even where she is. Don't know if she's got someone t'love 'er an' take care o' her an' hold 'er at night. Don't even know . . . if she's still alive . . . but no matter where she is or what's happened to 'er, I love 'er cuz she's mine . . . an' I'll allus love 'er . . . even though I know I'll never lay eyes on 'er . . . never be able t'tell 'er I'm 'er mother or how much . . . *how much* I love 'er." Delilah could not continue; the tears welled up and trickled down her cheeks, and she fumbled for her own handkerchief.

"Oh, Lilah! Oh, I am so sorry!" Devorah embraced her and held her closely, forgetting her own pain and absorbing Delilah's.

"That's why I say, Miz Lee, at least *you've* known the love of a child. Ya've known what it wuz like t'pick 'er up an' hold 'er an'

290

kiss 'er an' read to 'er an' tuck 'er in bed at night. Ya've got all these happy mem'ries o' her, an' y'know that she knew who y'wuz an' she loved y'back. An' lovin' back is so important! That's why ya've got t'still love Ann. Y'both need each other now, so much, so very much! Ya've got yer whole lives ahead o' ya. Don't become bitter an' throw it all away."

Devorah nodded wordlessly, knowing in her heart that Delilah was right. She had not had the faintest idea that the madam's past had also been full of anguish and pain. To have had a child and never to have seen her face or called her by name! How much soul-searching Delilah must have done before she chose to unburden herself to Devorah. Devorah felt closer to her now because of this intimate revelation, and she was glad that Delilah had come to see her, glad that they were friends.

They talked on as the hours grew later. Finally Devorah invited her to stay for dinner, and Delilah accepted only on the condition that she should be allowed to assist in the kitchen. Devorah excused herself in order to get dressed for the first time in two days, and when she returned to the kitchen, Delilah had already gotten out the pots and pans and had begun without her. They cooked together, side by side, and continued to talk, more animatedly this time and more at ease with each other's company.

"Y'know, Miz Lee, mebbe y'oughttta consider sellin' this farm here."

"Sell the farm?" Devorah echoed doubtfully.

"Why, shore! Ain't nothin holdin' y'here anymore. 'Course, y'don't have t'sell it right off, but someday y'might wanna think 'bout it."

"But I've lived here for so long. All my friends . . ."

"We'll still be yer friends, but'cha kin make some new ones, too. Y'kin both pack up 'n leave an' start all over again somewhere else. Why, I've even been thinkin' on goin' out t'San Francisco m'self one o' these days."

"Really? All the way out there?"

"Shore! I like the excitement o' the big city. There's lotsa things out there—warm sun, blue ocean, green grass, oranges an' grapefruit aplenty. An' it'd be nice not t'have t'go through them blizzards we git out here. Yep, one o' these days I jist might say g'bye t'ol' Kansas."

"Well, Lilah, that's really something to think about. I mean, selling the farm and all. I suppose we could do it, but at this point I don't even know if Ann would still want to come with me."

"Then ya've got t'talk to 'er. Y'both've got some real talkin' t'do, y'know."

"Oh, I know! But I'm afraid . . . I don't know what to say . . . how to start . . ."

"Y'jist say whatever's in yer heart." Just then the front door opened and Ann walked in, saw them both in the kitchen, and stopped short. "An' y'start right now," she whispered to Devorah.

Ann did not know what to make of this conspiratorial gathering, and she stood glancing uneasily from one woman to the other. She was afraid to speak first, lest Devorah should snap at her.

"Um, Ann . . . Lilah's staying for supper."

"That's nice. You're dressed," she observed curtly.

"Well, yes . . . I thought . . . since we have company . . ."

"*You* have company," Ann corrected her. "I'll not disturb you."

"Won't you join us?" Devorah requested timidly.

"No. I'll eat later."

"Please, Ann. We'd like you to stay." It was then that Devorah noticed the dark crusted blood on Ann's hand. "Oh! You've hurt yourself!"

"It's nothing. I'm going back outside," she said, heading toward the door.

Devorah watched her leave with a sinking feeling of dismay. *Oh Ann,* she thought, *how can I reach you? Have you shut me out because I've done the same to you?*

"Wal, don't jist stand there, gal! G'wan after 'er!" Delilah ordered her.

Devorah ran after Ann and caught up with her in front of the barn doors, grabbing her by the arm and forcing her to turn around.

"Ann, please! Don't be like this."

"Why not, Devvie? I'm only giving you back what you've been giving me."

"I know . . ."

"Besides, you're only being nice because Lilah's here."

"That's not true."

"Oh? Change of heart?" Ann said sarcastically.

"Please don't make a scene. Please come on inside and eat with us," Devorah begged. "For me?"

Ann reluctantly allowed herself to be persuaded, and she followed Devorah back to the house. While Delilah set the table, Ann went into the bathroom to wash up and to bandage her hand. She returned to the kitchen and sat down warily. They began to pass around the platters of food.

"Wal, this looks mighty good," Delilah said enthusiastically. "I ain't a bad cook if I say so m'self!"

Devorah took a bite. "Yes, very good, Lilah," she complimented. "Don't you think so, Ann?"

"Yeah."

"Ann does very well at it herself, too. She can make a fantastic trail stew."

"Izzat so, honey?"

"I do all right."

"Wal, Miz Lee, how're yer crops comin'? I see ya've got some fine lookin' vegetables out there."

"Oh, yes. I've already picked a few. The beans should be ready shortly; you're welcome to help yourself to them."

"Why, thank ya kindly. How's the wheat, the corn?"

"Fine, growing strong. We had so much to do with that corn, you know. But I think the wheat's almost ready to be taken in. Isn't it, Ann?"

"What?"

"Isn't it?"

"Isn't it what?"

"Almost ready. The wheat."

"Oh. Yeah."

"We've had a good bit o' rain. But y'know, I hear them crickets chirpin' awful loud at night. Wonder if that means we're in fer a long hot summer."

"I hope not. Last summer it was terrible. I could hardly get to sleep at night. Ann, would you care for some more meat?"

"No. Thanks."

"You haven't eaten very much."

"Sure I have. You two have been chattering so much, you haven't been watching me."

293

A brief moment of silence passed while they all looked at each other, and then they broke out into easing, reassuring laughter. This was the first time in almost a week that Ann had heard Devorah laugh, and she now eyed her curiously, wonderingly. For the remainder of the meal, they made small casual talk and Ann permitted herself to be drawn more and more into the conversation. By the time they got to the coffee and dessert, both Ann and Devorah were giving each other long and lingering looks when each one thought the other was unaware. Sometimes their eyes would meet and hold for a short while before glancing away in embarrassment.

Delilah observed their actions toward one another and sat back and sipped her coffee, smiling approvingly to herself. *Yep, they'll git back t'gether,* she nodded knowingly. *They'll patch things up b'tween 'em, an' ever'thing'll be all right. It'll work out fer 'em, I know it. I ain't never seen a bond this strong b'fore. They're drawn t'each other like moths to a flame.*

After dinner was over, Ann excused herself to do the evening chores while Devorah and Delilah cleaned up the kitchen. When the dishes had all been put away, the two women sat down again for one last cup of coffee before Delilah prepared to leave.

"You've been here practically all day," said Devorah. "Won't they miss you back at the saloon?"

"Naw. The place'll still be standin' by the time I git back there. I tol' Ruby I wuz comin' out here an' not t'expect me back in no hurry. I left 'er in charge, an' she kin handle 'erself."

"Ruby is . . . ?"

"She's m'gal. We've been t'gether fer . . . ohhh, six, seven years now."

"Have you ever had any . . . problems?" Devorah wanted to know.

"Why, shore's a dog has fleas! But we've allus worked 'em out."

"Doesn't anybody ever . . . say anything?"

"Not 'less they want a piece o' m'mind," Delilah huffed, swelling out her formidable bosom. "We live an' let live, an' we 'spect other folks t'do the same. It'd be a lot better world out there if all them Christians'd practice what they preach. We never hurt nobody, an' we b'lieve in the word o' God, too."

"Can there be love without condemnation?" Devorah asked softly.

" 'Course there can, Miz Lee. It's what'cha feel in yer heart, an' y'can't deny what'cha feel jist cuz a few misguided souls say it's wrong or it ain't what *they* think is right. God made ya t'love, Himself as well as others, an' ya've gotta go where yer heart leads ya. Y'can't be true t'others an' be false t'yerself. Y'can't give 'em what *they* want an' sacrifice yer own happiness. Love is there fer ya t'take, but'cha have t'hold it gently like a bird in the palm o' yer hand. If y'let it fly away an' it don't come back t'ya, then y'never had it t'begin with. But if it does come back t'ya, then it'll allus be yers." Devorah was quite absorbed in her own thoughts. "I got t'be gittin' along now, Miz Lee, but b'fore I do, is there anythin' I kin do fer ya?"

"Yes, Lilah, there is," she stated firmly. "Follow me."

Devorah led her into the bathroom, where she carefully rolled the rug away from the trap door leading down into the storm cellar. Delilah helped her lift the heavy door back on its hinges, and then together they descended the stairs with Devorah going first and holding the lamp out in front of her. She went straight to the two packing crates and set the lamp down on one of them while she pulled the protective cloth off of the other one and opened its lid. Delilah stood beside her and watched, intrigued.

"Sayyy, from France!" she said, truly impressed. "Must be some mighty fancy stuff y'got here."

"A complete place setting for eight people plus twelve hand-blown glass goblets. It was a wedding present for Billy and me from my parents."

"Wal, whyn't'cha use all this stuff?"

"I'll tell you the same thing I told Ann when I showed it to her last fall. If we ever had a fire here or a twister, and I lost everything else, these would still be safe, they'd still belong to me."

"Shame t'keep 'em down here where nobody kin see 'em or 'preciate 'em."

"But at least I know they're safe. When the twister hit us last month, we had a lot of broken plates and cups and saucers in the kitchen. We survived down here along with these," she said, gesturing toward the crates.

"Mebbe some day if y'move away from here to a place where they don't have no twisters, then y'kin bring 'em out an' use 'em," Delilah suggested hopefully.

"Yes, maybe." Devorah dug down to the bottom of the crate and withdrew the two small drawstring leather pouches. "This is gold dust and nuggets. Almost two pounds. It's my emergency fund. Take one of these bags and take it to the assay office and then use what they give you to pay for . . . for Lissa's funeral."

"Are y'sure, Miz Lee? Can't'cha use anythin' else? I don't wanna take this if it's somethin' speshul."

"I'm sure. There's not enough money left in the bank account to cover it, so I have to do this. I've only had to dip into it once before to pay for Billy's funeral and now I have to do it again for my child. All this gold is turning out to be is blood money," she sighed sadly, shaking her head. "One should be enough," she said, pressing the bag into Delilah's hand. "Please take care of this for me, Lilah. It would be a load off my mind."

"Why, o' 'course I will! I'll even bring y'back a satchel full o' greenbacks in change if it's due ya. Y'kin trust ol' Lilah here with yer life's savin's."

"Indeed, I trust you with my life itself. You may have saved it again."

"Aw, shucks, Miz Lee! There y'go again! Now yer gonna make me bawl!"

Devorah smiled and patted Delilah on the back. She closed the crate and covered it up. They went back upstairs, shutting the trap door behind them. Delilah entered the living room and put on her hat. She tucked the bag of gold dust securely into the cleft between her bosom and patted it with a flourish.

Devorah chuckled. "Oh, Lilah!"

"Safest place on me. Nobody'll dare stick a hand down there!"

"Good night, Lilah. Thank you so much for coming," Devorah said gratefully.

"G'night, Miz Lee. Take care o' yerself, y'hear?"

"I will. And Lilah . . . I want you to know that I deeply appreciate everything you've said to me tonight. You've made a lot more sense to me than I've made to myself in a long time."

"Y'think on it good, y'hear me? Otherwise I'll come back an' pound some more sense inta ya," she warned, shaking her finger at Devorah.

"I will, I promise. Thank you for sharing and caring . . . and understanding, too." Devorah stepped up to her and kissed her cheek, then embraced her and clung to her tightly. After she left, Devorah decided to take a bath.

On her way out to the carriage, Delilah stopped by the barn to speak with Ann, who was just finishing up the chores. Ann was just picking up two full milk pails, but she quickly set them down again when Delilah came inside.

"Jist wanted t'tell ya, Ann, how much I enjoyed yer company t'night."

Ann smiled at her. "Well, thanks for coming by, Lilah. Did you uh . . . have a talk with Devvie? She seems . . . a little better now."

"Oh, land sakes, did we talk!" Delilah said, rolling her eyes. "Chattered away most o' the afternoon."

"Did it even do any good?" Ann wondered dispiritedly.

" 'Course it did! Y'gotta be optimistic 'bout it."

"How can I be when she's practically come right out and ordered me to leave?"

"Naw, she don't want'cha t'leave."

"But she said—"

"That wuz then, honey, this is now."

"I was thinking on leaving anyway. Maybe it'd be for the best."

"Don't'cha do that, gal!" Delilah stressed emphatically. "Don't go walkin' out on 'er at a time like this. She needs ya as much as y'need her. I know she's said some purty rotten things t'ya, but she didn't mean it."

"Oh, she meant it, all right! She was downright vicious."

"An' you ain't been no saint yerself."

Ann shrugged. "Well . . ."

"She's hurtin' bad right now. She's got a broken heart. It'll take time fer it t'heal."

"What about me?" Ann said defensively. "I hurt, too, you know, only she doesn't seem to realize that."

"She knows. It'll take time fer both o' ya. Rome wuzn't built in a day. Look how long it takes fer the corn t'grow—y'don't plant it 'n pick it the next week. Give 'er time, gal. She's only human. Be nice to 'er an' she'll be nice t'you. She'll be all right," Delilah said with self-assured confidence.

"Are you that sure?" Ann asked doubtfully.

"Yep. I'm sure. I know a coupla winners when I see 'em. G'night, Ann."

"Good night, Lilah." Ann watched her leave and then stood leaning against the open barn door, staring thoughtfully at Devorah's bedroom window. After a while the light winked out, and the room was dark.

The following morning Devorah rose before Ann, dressed herself quickly, and went out into the kitchen to begin preparing breakfast. She brewed a pot of coffee, fried some sausage, and mixed up a batter for flapjacks. She set the table for two.

Ann awoke and instantly smelled the delicious aroma that wafted through the air. *Cooking!* she thought in amazement. *Devvie's cooking? What on earth?* She washed and dressed and walked into the kitchen, placing both hands on her hips in dumbfounded consternation.

"Devvie . . . *what* is going on?"

"I'm making breakfast for us," she smiled shyly. "Sit down, Ann. Coffee's ready; I'll get you some."

"Why are you . . .?" Ann gestured weakly, not knowing what to say.

"Because I should," Devorah responded firmly.

"Oh. Well . . ."

"Sit down. Please."

Ann sat, still uncertain as to how to regard this sudden turnabout in Devorah's attitude. Devorah poured out the coffee and brought the sausages, flapjacks, and syrup to the table. They ate in uneasy silence, each one highly aware of the other's presence and both unsure of what to say.

"How is the garden?" Devorah inquired.

"Fine. Needs to be weeded."

"Perhaps I could help," she offered.

"If you want."

Silence.

"Maybe it will rain today. It's cloudy," Devorah said.

"Don't think so."

"We could use it."

"Probably."

Another silence.

"Ann . . ."

"Yes, Devvie?"

298

"I'm . . . I'm sorry . . ."

"About what?"

"The things I said."

"Oh."

"I didn't mean . . . I didn't know what I was saying. I feel very badly about it. Please forgive me."

"I'm sorry, too," Ann said contritely.

"Can we be friends again?"

"I hope so. We can try."

"We've got to."

Three nights later, Ann was walking down the hallway to the bathroom when she overheard the muffled sounds of sobbing coming from behind the door to Devorah's bedroom. Previously, Ann had always respected the privacy of that closed door, and she had never disturbed Devorah after she had retired for the night, but this time, knowing that Devorah was awake and crying, Ann was filled with a rush of concern and tender pity for her. She rapped softly upon the door, not really expecting an answer, and was surprised when Devorah called out for her to enter. She stepped inside the room and saw that the bedside lamp had been lit. Devorah was sitting up in the bed with her legs drawn up to her chest; her arms were wrapped around her knees, and her head was bent forward and down.

"Devvie, are you all right? I heard you. Why are you crying?"

"Lissa. I . . . I miss her so!" she stammered brokenly.

"It was a week ago tonight, wasn't it?" Ann said quietly. Devorah nodded.

Ann stood there in the open doorway, helpless, hesitant to move, her own eyes beginning to brim with tears as she also remembered. Suddenly Devorah, still neither changing her position nor looking up, stretched out her hand, palm upward, toward Ann in a gesture of desperation. Ann reached out to clasp the hand and held it tightly. She was further surprised when Devorah tugged her closer to her side. Ann sat down on the edge of the mattress and placed one arm around Devorah's trembling shoulders, giving her a tentative, comforting hug.

"Can I get you something, Devvie? A cup of tea?"

"No . . . no. Just hold me, please hold me!"

"Oh, Dev . . . Dev . . ."

Ann gathered her into her arms and held her tightly, rocking her gently back and forth, smoothing the limp strands of hair away from her face, murmuring comforting words into her ear. After a while, they both lay back on the pillows up against the headboard, and Ann continued to cradle Devorah close to her breast as she would a small frightened child. When the tears had ceased to flow and Devorah had finally fallen asleep in her arms, Ann slowly released her, covered her with the quilt, bent to kiss her forehead, extinguished the lamp, and left the room.

Eighteen

Once again Reverend Todd had selected a group of volunteers from among the members of his congregation to go out to Ace Fairlane's farm on a daily basis in order to clean up the house, watch over the crops, and tend to the animals. The preacher tried to tell himself that this was only a temporary situation, but as the days continued to pass by, he soon came to regard the task as a depressing burden, for he realized that his parishoners had their own farms and families and their own chores and duties to perform. *They're all hard workers,* he thought, *but they shouldn't have to shoulder the responsibilities of a dead man. I wonder if the farm could be sold intact to some couple who would treat it well and take care of it properly. Some nice young couple who have never owned land before and who really need a home of their own. Hmmm . . . who? The Anders?*

The preacher abruptly left his study and strode along the sidewalks of Sutter's Ford, heading toward Doc McClintock's office. He knocked briskly upon the door, eased it open, and stepped inside the small cramped space. Doc was seated at his desk, surrounded by a mountainous clutter of papers and stacks of patient files.

"Hello, Reverend. Come on in. I've decided to put this place in order again, but perhaps I should have left well enough alone." Doc sighed in mild exasperation.

"Well, Doctor, you know what they say about Satan finding some mischief for idle hands to do," he chuckled, then paused. "I wanted to inquire . . . how is Mrs. Lee?"

"She's doing better, I think. Lilah stopped by the other day and told me she had a good long heart-to-heart talk with her. I feel a bit guilty that I haven't been able to get back out there and see her myself, but I've been simply inundated with all this paperwork."

"Uh, Doctor . . . you are aware of course that I have delegated the duties of maintaining Mr. Fairlane's property to a number of my kind-hearted parishoners, but even they cannot remain on the land for long without experiencing a certain degree of . . . unease. In fact, they are deeming it spooked. But regardless of their personal opinions concerning this . . . enigma . . . would it be possible to sell the farm to an upstanding young couple who might have a sore need for a place of their own?"

"Why, yes, I suppose so. It should be sold quickly before it acquires a bad reputation. Did you have anyone directly in mind?" Doc asked out of curiosity.

"As a matter of fact, yes, I did. May I suggest the Anders couple?"

"Ahhh, Joseph and Cora," Doc said slowly, leaning back in his chair. A satisfied smile played across his face as he considered the idea. "Yes . . . yes . . . they've never had a place of their own, and they need the room for two growing children. He's nephew to the bank president, so he shouldn't have too much trouble securing a loan. They could put their shop up as collateral and still hang onto it as another source of income. Yes . . . ah, yes . . . it could work."

"You approve of my suggestion then, Doctor?" the preacher said, also beginning to smile.

"Approve of it?" *I love it!*" he boomed. "That's one of the best ideas you've had in a long time. Why, I'll go over there right now and speak with Joseph about it." Doc leaped up from his chair, snatched his hat, and headed toward the door.

"Uh, Doctor . . . the land will have to be blessed first."

"Of course, of course! We'll exorcise everything!" He left the preacher standing there in the middle of all the disorganized paperwork.

Doc passed the next several days in consulting with Joseph and Cora about the possibility of their purchasing the farm. They discussed every angle, every contingency. Joseph admitted that the idea was a highly interesting one, and after Cora overcame her initial revulsion about taking land that had recently belonged to a murderer, even she was seized by excitement and began to anticipate the move. Doc accompanied Joseph to the bank to speak with his uncle, and the man was also keenly interested in the proposition. He swiftly paved the way for Joseph to receive the loan, the arrangement was made and finalized, all the necessary papers were signed and sealed, and Joseph returned home in elation to give his wife the good news. They immediately set about packing up all their belongings.

One afternoon Doc decided to make a point of visiting Ann and Devorah in order to ascertain for himself how they were getting along. He had been deeply concerned about Devorah's state of mind after Melissa had died, and he was anxious that she should accept the child's death and come to terms with her own grief. He was also concerned for Ann, but he knew that she was a strong resilient young woman. Devorah, on the other hand, had lost both members of her immediate family within the short space of three years, and her abilities to cope with and adjust to the inevitable continuance of life had been sorely tested, especially, he knew, since the passing of her only child.

Doc drew his horse to a halt in front of the house and stepped lightly down from the carriage. Both Ann and Devorah were busily involved in weeding and hoeing the vegetable garden. When they glanced up and saw him coming they ceased their work, wiped their hands, and moved out to greet him.

"Hello, Devorah . . . Ann," he nodded to them. "How are you doing?"

"Pretty well, Doc," Ann replied easily.

"And you, Devorah? How are you?" he asked kindly, taking her hand into his own.

"I'm all right. I'm doing well," she answered in a small voice.

"Been busy?"

"Yes. We've been trying to get caught up with everything out here."

"Good," Doc smiled, patting her hand.

"Devvie says I'm working her too hard," Ann volunteered. "She says I won't let her rest for a minute."

"Yes," she admitted, "but there's nothing like good hard labor to occupy the mind and strengthen the body."

"Good, good." Doc continued to pat the hand, and then he raised it to his lips and kissed the fingers. "Be happy, Devorah. Both of you."

What does he mean? Devorah thought wonderingly. *Does he know about . . . ?* She looked over at Ann, frowning quizzically, but Ann only smiled back at her, raising her eyebrows in noncommittal reply.

"Devorah, I have some news for you," Doc continued, smoothly changing the subject.

"Oh?" She waited expectantly.

"Yes. Laura and I . . . are going to be married. I've asked her, and she's accepted."

"Oh, Doc! How wonderful!" Devorah said in sincere pleasure. She was genuinely happy for him even if she could no longer have him for herself. She loved him, but she had let him go. By allowing the bird to fly out of her open hand, it had circled and returned to her.

Ann grinned. "Great, Doc!"

"We thought you two should be the first to know. The wedding will be in September. We would be delighted if you would accept our invitation to join us."

"How considerate of you! It will be a great honor for us," Devorah told him.

"Migosh, Devvie, I'm gonna need a new dress!" Ann said excitedly. "A really fancy one!"

"What?!" she gasped, placing a hand over her breast. "Did I hear you right? You actually *want* to wear a dress?"

Ann shrugged. "Well . . . for a special occasion like this . . ."

"There's still hope for you, then. I'll make a lady out of you yet!" Devorah said with firm determination. They all laughed.

"Ah, Devorah . . . ," Doc began hesitantly. "There is something else I have to tell you, too. Joseph and Cora have bought Ace's farm. They will be moving out there shortly."

There was a brief silence as both Doc and Ann eyed her warily, waiting for her response. Devorah turned her head and looked far out across the fields, considering the importance of Doc's words, then sighed heavily and turned back to him again.

"Well, I hope it will be good for them," she stated. "After all this time, they deserve a place of their own. There is a great deal to be said for the satisfaction that comes from loving the land."

"They really need the space for their family," Ann added.

"Yes . . . the children . . . ," Devorah said quietly, a soft tender look coming into her eyes. "How fitting that children should live and run and play on that land. It has come full circle, and justice has been done."

"Yes . . . finally," Ann agreed. Doc nodded wordlessly.

Delilah Emerson was standing at the bar of her saloon, drinking a thirst-quenching beer and bantering good-naturedly with her customers. She was in high spirts and felt as if she were on top of the world. She had come a long way, and her strength of character was invincible.

Andy Hanks entered the saloon and sauntered up to her, doffing his hat and wiping his sweating brow on the sleeve of his shirt. He eased himself down onto one of the bar stools, blowing out his cheeks as he exhaled in a rush.

"Howdy, Miz Lilah. Gettin' purty hot out there."

"Yeah, ain't it, though? 'Nother mizzerble summer," she grimaced. "Whaddya say y'have a beer on me, eh? Y'look like y'could use one."

"Why, thank ya. Much obliged."

"Sam! Bring 'im one!" she called out. She took the bottle that the bartender offered her, opened it, and held it out to the sheriff, who accepted it gratefully and tipped his head back for a long swallow.

"Ahhh!" Hanks breathed, licking the foam from his lips. " 'At's sure good fer a hard-workin' man."

"Hmmph!" Delilah snorted in disdain. "What hard work? All y'do is sit on yer butt day in an' day out, smokin' them stinkin' cigars."

"I do m'fair share, same as you," he protested in mock indignation. "All y'gotta do is keep them rabble-rousers outta here, an' I won't bother y'none."

"Only troublemaker I ever had 'round here is dead 'n buried. An' I say amen, brother!" she declared firmly.

Hanks grinned. "An' I'll drink t'that!" He tipped his bottle toward her in salute, cocked his head, and winked.

Delilah clapped him on the back, turned her massive frame around, and headed for the kitchen, which was located at the rear of the saloon, just off of the bar area. She was extremely particular about the preparation of the customers' food and about how the kitchen itself was run, and she often popped in unannounced for surprise inspections. She passed through the swinging doors, glanced quickly around, and glowered balefully at the cook, who was engaged in playing a hand of poker with a buddy at a small table in the far corner of the room.

"What's goin' on here?" Delilah shouted, standing with both hands on her hips. The cook jumped at the sound of her voice, hit the table with his leg, and scattered the cards and chips in all directions. "I ain't payin' ya t'sit on yer can an' lose yer ass over them cards! An' lookit this place!" She ran her finger along the top of the counter and held it out for the cook to see. "See that? Grease! Prob'ly layin' like scum all over the place!" She pointed to a dusty pile of flour that lay on the floor. "Don't'cha know how t'clean up after yerself? The rats prob'ly c'm in here an' have a tea party!" She picked up a cast-iron pot, inspected it, and tossed it with a loud clatter into the sink. "An' lookit them filthy pots! Blacker'n the bottom of a coal mine! Looks like they ain't never been washed!"

Ruby had heard all the commotion, and she now burst into the kitchen to find out what it was that had Delilah in such a fit of temper.

"What's alla ruckus?" Ruby demanded. "What're y'hollerin' fer?"

"You hush up, gal! I'm layin' down the law!" Delilah turned back to glare at the cook. His buddy had long since fled out the back door. "What the hell kinda place d'y'think I'm runnin' here anyways—a pig sty? This here's a high-class establishment, I'll have y'know! I want this place scrubbed from top t'bottom, an' I want'cha t'git yer tail movin' right now! S'help me, I oughtta git m'self one o' them Chinamen 'steada you an' toss yer worthless hide outta here! Spotless, y'hear me? *Spotless!*" With her fat sausage curls bouncing from side to side, she spun on her heel and stalked out of the kitchen without so much as a backward glance.

Ruby stepped aside and let her pass, staring after her in open-mouthed astonishment. She began to giggle, and then she broke out into gales of raucous laughter.

Reverend Todd's group of parishoners had gathered up every item of furniture that had once belonged to Ace Fairlane and had burned everything in a huge blazing bonfire. Their decisive actions constituted an erasure, a final obliteration of Ace's memory. They had also wanted to torch the house and barn and thus leave nothing standing, but the preacher had persuaded them that the land would be blessed and freed from its evil influence and that the Anders couple would be fitting inheritors of the property.

Joseph had gone out there every day for about two weeks in order to repaint all the rooms and to make minor plumbing and carpentry repairs to the inside of the house. Cora had also gone with him on several occasions, and she had hung new curtains on the windows and planted bright cheery flowers all around the front yard. By the third week, which brought them to the middle of July, and after everyone's wheat crops had been harvested, they at last completed the process of moving out of the old place and moving into the new. Both Doc McClintock and Reverend Todd were on hand for the happy occasion, and all of them stood outside in the yard with the orange glow of the setting sun casting its fading light upon the frames of the house and barn.

"Well, Joseph," Doc beamed, "you've finally gotten yourselves all settled in."

He sighed wearily. "It was quite a job."

"But we loved every minute of it," Cora said, smiling up at her husband. Joseph lifted his arm, placed it around her shoulders, and hugged her closely to his side.

"Now you have plenty of room for all your leatherworking equipment, eh, Joseph?"

"Oh, yes, Doc. I've already set up a bench for it out in the barn."

"Well, I shall have to order a new belt from you soon. By the way," Doc added, "I understand the water isn't too good around these parts."

"We're planning to dig a new well next week," Joseph informed him.

"Honey, sometimes I just can't believe our good fortune," Cora said, shaking her head in bewilderment. "God has been so good to us."

"Well, I just hope I can do justice to this land," he responded, glancing around.

"Justice has already been done, Joseph," Doc told him. "What you need to say is that you'll do right by the land. Come, the Reverend's ready to perform the blessing."

They stood together in a rough circle. The preacher opened his Bible, cleared his throat, and bowed his head.

"O Lord, we stand before You in humble adoration to ask Your blessing upon this land. Remove all traces of the evil and malice that have been here and cast them far away beyond recall, into the depths

307

of the sea. Let Your spirit move across the face of the earth and look down in blessing upon this land. Reach out and touch the fields, the crops, the flowers, that they might thrive under Your care and yield their abundant riches. And look down in tender mercy and love upon this man and this woman who have sought to reclaim the land in the spirit of righteousness. Bless them and their children, that they might grow tall and strong and inherit the earth from their forefathers. Grant them rest from their labors and comfort in Your holy name."

Reverend Todd turned to face Joseph and Cora, and he smiled at them in gentle benevolence. "Hear these words of the Lord and take them to heart: 'Judge not, and you will not be judged; condemn not, and you will not be condemned; forgive, and you will be forgiven; give, and it will be given to you; good measure, pressed down, shaken together, running over, will be put into your lap. For the measure you give will be the measure you receive.' Go in peace, and love and be loved. In the name of Christ our Lord. Amen."

The night stole softly upon them, and the evening star shone brilliantly down from the dark vault of the heavens.

That same evening Ann and Devorah stood next to each other at the kitchen sink, washing the dinner dishes. Over the past few weeks they had labored together in doing the chores, taking care of the animals, tending the garden and the fields, and gathering in the wheat. They had passed many hours in quiet talk, and they had slowly, almost shyly, gotten to know one another again. The hot anger and uneasy tension that had marred their relationship had vanished since the morning after Delilah Emerson's visit, and they were hesitantly, carefully attempting to find their way back to each other once again. Many nights they had lain awake in their separate beds and wondered, simply wondered, what the future might hold for them.

Ann reached for a dish towel and began to dry off the plates as Devorah stacked them neatly beside the sink. Devorah dipped a pot into the soapy water and began to scrub it vigorously.

"Um, Devvie . . . didn't you ever want to . . . maybe do something different?"

"Different?" she repeated. "What do you mean?"

"Well, like when you were growing up. Didn't you have a special dream of something you really wanted to do?"

Devorah smiled wistfully. "Ohhh, don't all little girls? Yes, I had a dream. I wanted to be a seamstress just like my mother. She made some beautiful costumes for the Centennial when I was twelve years old. I used to stand there and watch her while she sewed for hours, and she taught me how to make so many things. I wanted to go to a big city like Chicago or even New York where they have all those fancy operas and plays."

Ann smiled widely, captivated by the idea. "Really? I've never been that far east before."

"I wanted to make all those splendid costumes for the actors and actresses who do Shakespeare. I thought it would be lovely to join in with a troupe and do that. But then I met Billy and married him, and we moved out here and bought this farm. I've never forgotten my childhood dream, though, and I still hope that maybe some day . . . Oh, well," she sighed. "What about you, Ann? Did you have a dream, too?"

"Well . . . just of being a schoolmarm. And I *was* one for a while. I've always loved children, and I enjoy teaching them things, watching them learn, listening to them read out loud. I wanted to have a little red schoolhouse where I could ring the bell every morning and watch them come running."

"Where did you teach before?" Devorah asked.

"Just at home in the parlor. There weren't enough children in the neighborhood to build a school for, and we lived too far away from the closest town. I guess I'd still be there today if I hadn't . . ." She trailed off and shrugged. "Devvie, do you still think there's any chance of both of us realizing our dreams?"

"Oh, I don't know. Maybe. Lilah told me we ought to consider selling the farm some day. She's even thinking of moving out to San Francisco, or so she said."

"We're still young. We *could* move away from here," Ann suggested hopefully. "Maybe . . . together . . . if you wanted . . ."

"It would have to be together. I'd be afraid to move into a big city alone."

"Devvie . . . I know we haven't talked about this . . . and I haven't pushed you about it, either . . . but . . . what about us? Can you . . . talk about it now?"

Devorah was silent. Her hands stopped moving in the soapy water, and she looked down at them, at the hands that had touched and caressed and loved another woman. Ann set the dish towel on the counter and reached out to take her gently by the shoulders, turning her around so that they were both face to face.

"Devvie, look at me. Tell me," Ann pleaded earnestly. "Can it ever be like it was?"

Devorah gazed deeply into the dark eyes that boldly met her own, intently scrutinizing the beautiful, familiar face that hung poised so closely to hers. "No . . . ," she said softly, slowly. "It can be . . . *even better!*"

"Dev . . . ," Ann gasped, suddenly intaking her breath as the full meaning of the words began to dawn upon her.

Devorah placed one hastily wiped hand tenderly upon Ann's cheek. "Ann, I love you. I've never stopped loving you," she told her, and meant it. "With all my heart . . . oh my darling!"

As if from a great distance they bent toward one another, eyes closing, lips parting, arms reaching out to clasp and hold tightly, and then they were swept away into the breathlessness of this first embrace. The bond between them had been re-established and strengthened by mutual pain and grief, and the love that had always been there, yet lying just beneath the surface, had finally broken free to fly again, healed and whole.

"The dishes . . . ," Devorah said, trying to hold back her rising passion.

"Leave them," Ann urged, nuzzling at her neck.

"No. Come on, now. Finish what you started."

"Oh, believe me, I will!"

"Ann! I insist!" Devorah began to chuckle in her vain attempt to free herself from the strong hold.

"So do I."

"Ann!"

"What?"

"Let me go!"

"Never. Ever. You're mine, Devvie. I love you." They kissed again and Ann reluctantly released her.

The dishes were finished with lightning speed, and afterward nothing else remained to be done except that which they now wanted to do for themselves. They prolonged the suspense by first taking a bath together; then Devorah took Ann's hand and led her down the hallway into the bedroom that had once again become theirs.

Their lovemaking was neither rushed nor frenetic. They were shy and reserved toward one another, almost as if they had to rediscover each other's body. Eyes traveled along the gentle contour of breast, hands passed over the sloping curve of hip, fingers pressed the sensitive flesh of thigh, lips kissed, broke away, kissed elsewhere. Breath came faster, desire mounted and grew more urgent, more demanding, arms and legs were locked together, faces were buried deep in wet curling softness. And the panting cries of release that issued from their throats as the passion rolled over them in cresting waves served to unite them, join them, make them as one again.

When it was over and their satisfaction had made them soporific, they lay nestled snugly in each other's arms. Just as Devorah was about to drift off to sleep, Ann raised herself up on one elbow and whispered quietly to her.

"Dev?"

"Hmmm?"

"Do you still think it's a sin?" No answer; Devorah was very swiftly fading out. "Dev?" Ann prodded her.

"No," she mumbled. "No." And then she was gone. Ann smiled.

Devorah rose just before dawn. She draped her robe loosely about her shoulders and moved to stand in front of the window, where she pulled back the curtains and looked out at the lightening sky. The sun was beginning to rise over the distant low-flung hills, and its rays stretched over the land, through the trees, down into the hollows. The sky was an azure cloudless blue; the day promised to be hot and bright.

Devorah leaned against the window frame, allowing the warm morning breeze to gently ruffle her hair. She heard the call of a bird—an abrupt musical note that shattered the quiet air. Then Ann was at her side, softly kissing her cheek, slipping an arm around her waist. Together, silently, they watched the dawn, their faces bathed in the glow of the rising sun.

"This is a new beginning for us," Devorah spoke at last. "A new day, a new life."

"A new love," Ann added.

"Oh, Ann! Never be afraid to take your happiness! Never be afraid to dare!" she said fiercely.

"With you, I am not afraid, come what may."

Ann did the basic chores while Devorah prepared breakfast. After the meal was over, as they sat at the table drinking their coffee, they tried to decide what to do with this new day that had been given to them.

"I have an idea," Devorah said firmly. "Let's get in there and clean out that bedroom."

Ann was surprised at her determination. "You mean . . .? Really?"

"Yes. I've got to face it. We'll pack up all of Lissa's things and we'll . . . Why, we'll give them to Joseph and Cora! Yes, that's exactly what we'll do! We'll even pay them a visit this very morning."

"What a lovely idea! And generous. Devvie?"

"Yes, Ann?"

"You're beautiful. Your soul is beautiful."

They set about the task with a will, dragging out crates, emptying drawers, folding up clothes. Soon everything had been packed away and Ann carried out all of the crates and stacked them neatly in the back of the buckboard wagon. She also took out the child-sized table and chairs that she had made and put them in the wagon, too. The cat scampered out of the way and went to hunt in the tall prairie grass. When they were ready to leave, Devorah climbed up onto the seat, and Ann took the reins, calling softly to the horse. They passed down the narrow lane and swung out onto the road, heading in the direction of Sutter's Ford.

"You know, Ann, Lilah was so right," Devorah observed, musing thoughtfully.

"About what?"

"About everything. She is one incredible woman!"

"That she is, Devvie," Ann agreed wholeheartedly.

"And you know something else? One of these days we *will* move. We can go to New York. Think of it! Concerts . . . operas . . . plays . . . Shakespeare . . ."

" 'O Romeo, Romeo! Wherefore art thou, Romeo?' " Ann intoned in mock seriousness. " 'Deny thy father and refuse thy name.' "

Devorah completed the famous line. " 'Or, if thou wilt not, be but sworn my love, and I'll no longer be a Capulet.' " They both threw back their heads and laughed.

312

And they loved. Nights gave way to days, and seasons changed to years, and still the fairies danced for them. They were young, and the world was theirs to own. They were blessed, and they knew in the soft light of the eyes, in the gentle touch of the hands, in the lingering sweetness of the lips, the wonderment and awe of the love of God.